UPON THE
Broken Range

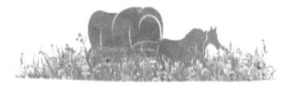

OREGON PROMISE SERIES

by Lynnette Bonner

OTHER HISTORICAL BOOKS
by Lynnette Bonner

<u>THE SHEPHERD'S HEART SERIES</u>

Rocky Mountain Oasis – BOOK ONE
High Desert Haven – BOOK TWO
Fair Valley Refuge – BOOK THREE
Spring Meadow Sanctuary – BOOK FOUR

<u>SONNETS OF THE SPICE ISLE SERIES</u>

On the Wings of a Whisper – BOOK ONE

<u>THE WYLDHAVEN SERIES</u>

Not a Sparrow Falls – BOOK ONE
On Eagles' Wings – BOOK TWO
Beauty from Ashes – BOOK THREE
Consider the Lilies – BOOK FOUR
A Wyldhaven Christmas – BOOK FIVE
Songs in the Night – BOOK SIX
Honey from the Rock – BOOK SEVEN
Beside Still Waters – BOOK EIGHT

Find all other books by Lynnette Bonner at:
www.lynnettebonner.com

UPON THE
Broken Range

OREGON PROMISE – BOOK 4

Lynnette BONNER
USA Today Bestselling Author

Pacific Lights

Upon the Broken Range
Oregon Promise, Book 4

Published by Pacific Lights Publishing
Copyright © 2025 by Lynnette Bonner. All rights reserved.

Editing by Lesley Ann McDaniel Editing – https://www.lesleyannmcdanielediting.com
Proofreading by Sheri Mast – https://faithfulediting.com
Book interior design by Jon Stewart – http://stewartdesign.studio

Cover design by Lynnette Bonner of Indie Cover Design, images ©
Generated by AI using MidJourney

Floral spray by Veris Studio from the Wildflower Forest Floral Flower Set on
CreativeMarket.com.

Scripture taken from the New King James Version®. Copyright © 1982 by Thomas Nelson.
Used by permission. All rights reserved.

Paperback ISBN: 978-1-942982-56-2

Psalm 73:26

My flesh and my heart fail,
but God is the strength
of my heart and my portion forever.

Chapter 1

J eremiah stared at the beautiful woman who had somehow appeared in the sunken compartment in the floorboards of the Slade wagon. Outside, thunder crashed, and a flash of lightning lit the sky so brightly that for one brief moment, he could see the fading bruise on her face that the lights from the lanterns hadn't revealed.

He released the floorboard door to rest against a crate and stretched a hand down to her. "Setting to blow a fierce one tonight. Don't think you'll get much sleep down there. You gonna tell me how you came to be in this here wagon, you better come on up outta there."

Her hand was delicate in his—no bigger than that of a teenage child. And when he hauled her to her feet and helped her balance in the aisle of the wagon on the other side of the trap door, he realized she wasn't much taller than a child, either. How old was she, this delicate, tiny, trembling package of uncertainty?

Her large eyes studied him above the curled arms and fisted hands she tucked beneath her chin as she shivered before him. She looked like a wary boxer about to throw the first punch.

Jeremiah handed her a lap robe and then stepped back and folded his arms so she'd hopefully understand he meant her no harm. "How'd you get in here?"

She made no response other than her eyes growing a bit rounder and her lower lip trembling slightly.

Right. He was frightening her. He relaxed his arms and lowered the trap door into place. He angled his body and stepped to one side as best he could in the cramped aisle of the wagon, before he swung a gesture to the tick stretched across a bed of crates at the back of the space. "Please, take a seat."

She continued to look at him for a long moment before finally easing past him to sit on the pallet.

Good. "Let me get you something warm to drink." Would she still be here when he returned?

He paused at the tailgate to peer out. He dreaded going back into the weather he'd just escaped. His dry clothes would almost immediately be as wet as the set that still lay in a heap on the floor, and he had no others to change into, but there was naught for it.

He reached to swipe the canvas aside.

"Please," she said, the word barely audible above the storm pounding the canvas.

He paused and turned to look at her.

"Please don't go out into that caterwaul on my account. I ate not long ago and need nothing."

Relief eased through him.

There was a slight touch of the South in her words. The sound of it took him straight back to the shanty where he'd grown up behind the plantation home owned by Striker's parents.

He tilted her a nod and bent to retrieve his wet clothes. He wrung them out at the back opening of the canvas and took the opportunity to check the area, but thankfully, no one appeared to be headed his way. One good thing about this storm was that most folks would be tucked away under cover, trying to stay dry. A break in the clouds to the west showed the storm should ease within the hour.

Lantern light still shone from Miss Acheson's wagon. Likely, she continued her work on the parson. Other than hers, most wagons around the circle lay dark and silent.

Another crack of thunder rolled, followed more distantly by a lesser flash of lightning this time.

He turned back into the wagon, gave his wet pants a flick, and draped them atop a stack of crates. He did the same with his discarded shirt.

Then he settled into his heels, folded his arms, and looked down at the bit of a woman who was now at the farthest edge of the tick with her arms wrapped around her knees. She had draped the lap robe over her knees, and behind it she huddled into her blue cape like it was a shield that could protect her. The whole package of her didn't take up more room than a sack of flour. His mama would have said she looked no more substantial than a "cob o' corn the chickens done picked clean."

She was of mixed blood, like him—that much was clear. But he knew all too well that it made no difference to many a man who held power. One drop of black blood was enough to mark a person as lesser in their eyes—enough to justify chains, cruelty, and stolen lives.

Chains which she had only recently escaped, judging by her raw wrists. He eyed her abrasions and felt his fists tighten, ready for war.

He didn't want her to think he was upset with her, however, so he purposely drew in a long inhale and forced himself to ease. He leaned his shoulder against a stack of crates. There had been many times in his life when he'd been ready to go to war, but if there was one thing he'd learned, it was that some battles would drag a man down into the mire of inhumanity, and he never wanted to be that kind of man.

He would need to wrap her wrists, and maybe her ankles too. But he'd give her a minute. Judging by her dry hair and clothes, she'd come this way before the rain.

"What's your name?"

She rolled her lips in and pressed them into a tight line. "Maybe it's best you don't learn my name. I won't be here long. I promise."

He frowned. They could deal with that later. "You want my help, you're gonna have to trust me. You ended up in my wagon. I presume that's because you knew I was a man of color like yourself?"

She shook her head. "Only on account of Betsy telling me. The mercantile owner—she's the one who helped me escape and told me to come here."

Ah. That would explain why the woman had been watching him so carefully the other day. She'd wanted to see which wagon was his. But her sending this girl to him could get them both killed. He bit back a sigh before he made the girl feel like she was putting him out.

"My name's Jeremiah Jackson." He waited. The silence stretched long.

Finally, she said, "My master calls me Delilah."

Something curled in Jeremiah's stomach. A reference to the woman who had been Sampson's weakness? Such a man would want his prize back.

"Don't want the name your master gave you."

Her brow slumped, and she worked her teeth over her lower lip. The silence lingered as she searched his face.

His hands clenched tight again. Some fool who would one day stand before God had her afraid to even speak her own name.

He softened his voice. "You can trust me. What's your real name? The one your mama gave you."

She frowned and swept a glance around the inside of the wagon as though trying to decide. Finally, she settled her gaze on his. "My mama named me Deliverance. You can call me Del. Never had no second name."

Deliverance. He smiled at the woman, pleased that she'd decided to trust him. "Deliverance is a good name. Right glad to meet you."

Now to figure out who she was running from.

Even as the thought registered, weariness washed through him. He pressed his fingers and thumb against his eyes. Wished he wasn't so tired. Last night had been his watch, and he'd only gotten about three hours of sleep. With the long day of rescuing Mrs. Houston from the no-good Brad Baxter, the brother of the fort's colonel, and Brad's subsequent arrest, exhaustion had Jeremiah about dead on his feet.

He eased to his haunches in the aisle. Maybe if he weren't towering over her, this conversation would go better.

"Who you running from?" For some reason, that question set him on edge. Evil was about to be named, and evil did not like to be dragged into the light.

She swallowed. Licked her lips. "My master. C-colonel Boone Baxter."

Jeremiah jolted his head back as the name hit him square in the chest. The man with the most power for hundreds of miles. That was the man she was running from. The man whose brother had kidnapped the parson's wife and those two kids. The man who now held the kidnapper in his jail down in the fort.

Thank God the wagon train was pulling out first thing, and yet a man like that one wouldn't tolerate the loss of a woman such as this. The loss of his Delilah.

If she were caught—

Jeremiah didn't want to think about what would happen to either of them if she were found and he were discovered helping her.

And now it would be up to him to make sure that didn't happen.

Lord, You gonna have to show me how to help this one. I know it's not Your will for either of us to end up at the end of a scourge and then a rope simply because we have different colored skin.

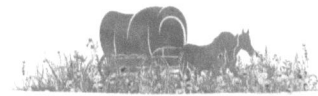

Deliverance wrapped her arms more tightly about her knees as she studied the man squatting in the aisle before her. She'd shocked him, that was certain.

Also certain was the fact that Master Boone was going to tear this wagon train apart as soon as he discovered she was missing! Would he even go down to the basement where she ought to be tonight? Sometimes when he was tired or overworked, he didn't take her to his room. On those occasions, he left her in the basement overnight and only let her out early in the morning to use the necessary before returning her to the basement for another day.

Her arms ached just thinking about it.

She'd planned to simply rest in this wagon's hidden compartment until dark and then make her escape, but the storm had come, and she'd known there would be no shelter for miles in any direction. With a child on the way, no matter how unwelcome—guilt pierced her for the thought—she'd needed to stay dry.

And then this man had found her.

Now, as she waited for him to speak, she studied him. What had she expected to find in a "free man of color" as Betsy had described him? Certainly not this young, strapping man with the broad shoulders stretching his shirt to near capacity, and certainly not those gray eyes studying her in the lantern light. She'd expected an elderly man perhaps, set free after years of service to a master. Or maybe one bent with the weight of servitude. The strength revealed by the taut stretch of his sleeve across his upper arms made her tremble. And yet, he seemed . . . kind. Thoughtful. Generous. Just as Betsy had said he was.

He hung his head and studied the boards between his feet. Ran one broad hand around the back of his neck.

"You really free?" The words blurted out before she could think better of them.

He lifted that gray gaze to her. "Yes'm. Grew up on a plantation in South Carolina, not far outside of Charleston. My master's son took a liking to me, charming sort that I am." He offered her a scallywag's grin.

She tucked away a smile, lowering her mouth behind her knees.

"Striker talked his daddy into giving me to him, and afterward he gave me my manumission papers."

"Striker?" She felt her eyes go a little round. That name sounded rather lethal, like a bounty hunter or a marksman. A tremor slithered down her spine.

But Jeremiah only grinned. "He earned that nickname working at the forge on his daddy's plantation. That fella could shoe a horse faster than anyone in five counties. Can you keep a secret?"

The twinkle in his eyes raised her curiosity. She nodded.

"Striker's real name is Sebastian Jebediah Moss." He grinned. "I like to remind him of it every once in a while so's to bring his feet back to earth, if you catch my meaning."

Deliverance wanted to smile. She liked this kind man who made her feel at ease even though she'd inserted herself into his life without permission. But the most she could summon was a crinkle of her eyes. She felt weary. Exhausted clean through.

Only when she heard him stand did she realize her eyes had fallen closed. She opened them to find him looming above, reaching for her.

She gasped and cowered back.

He stilled and raised his palms. "Easy. I was reaching for the extra quilt there." He pointed past her to a folded blanket on a shelf that extended beneath the driver's seat.

Feeling foolish, she tugged the blanket from the cubby and handed it to him, if only to get him to retreat. "Sorry."

Despite his kind eyes and nod of thanks, she couldn't shake her tension.

He clutched the quilt in one hand, but didn't step back. He hung his head instead for a moment. "You can trust me. Understand?" He lifted those gray eyes to her, brows raised.

It was his hopeful expression that finally helped her relax. She nodded.

"Good." He retreated down the aisle and, with a quick flip, unfurled the quilt in the narrow space between stacks of crates. "I'm gonna need a couple hours of shut-eye before we decide where to hide you."

Del frowned. "I can't hide here?"

"Not if you want to live." The man said the words wearily as he sank onto the blanket on the hard wood floor and pulled the covering over himself. He was breathing deeply before she had the presence of mind to realize she'd stolen his bed.

But with him asleep, maybe this was her time to skedaddle? She rose to her knees and parted the cinched canvas above the bed enough to see out through the slats of the driver's bench.

The rain was naught more than a drizzle at the moment. She glanced back at the man. *Not if you want to live.* He was right about that. Boone would search this wagon train, top to bottom, as soon as he discovered she was missing. And if he found her here in the company of this man . . . Fear pumped a breath past her lips. She didn't want to bring trouble.

Another quick peek at the sky outside revealed that the clouds didn't seem as dark and ominous against the blackness of the heavens now. Maybe she could make it to the trees by the river and find shelter before the storm grew heavier?

It would be better for these folk, if not for her.

She shivered at the thought of wandering through those woods in the dark. Were there wolves? Mountain lions? Snakes? Spiders? She clenched her eyes tight. But facing all of those would be better than getting innocent folk killed.

She turned back to look at the man sprawled in the aisle. He took up most of it with his big frame. She would have to scoot past him to get out because climbing over the wagon bench would likely raise a squeaky ruckus that would wake him.

She stood and scooped up the rucksack Betsy had packed for her, ignoring the pain that flared to life in her wrist when she hefted it. With the pack on one shoulder, she assessed the best path forward. Moving past his legs wouldn't be a problem—she had plenty of room to tiptoe past them. It was his shoulders that would be an issue. Each one nearly touched the crates on either side, and there was no room for her foot. She would have to jump over him, then.

She took a couple of steps back and hefted her skirt enough so it wouldn't encumber her feet.

The man surged upright, rubbing his fingers and thumb into his eyes.

She gasped and plunked backward onto the pallet, feeling the blood drain from her face.

He looked at her, weariness drooping his shoulders. "Listen now. You go out there and you finished for sure. I spent the evening with the colonel today, and he's got a good tracker."

She felt a swirl of lightheadedness. Of course he did. She'd heard Boone mention him more than once in a purposeful way meant to get her attention. She pressed one hand to the base of her throat.

Jeremiah rested his arms against his knees and clasped one wrist with his other hand. "You believe in the Lord?"

Tears blurred her vision. Oh, how she did. She nodded.

"Good. Then I'm asking you to believe that the Lord brought you here to me. And I'm asking you to trust me, weary man that I am at the moment." He pointed to the bed. "Please sleep for just a little while. And let me do the same."

She moistened her lips. "I thought you already was asleep."

His lips nudged upward almost imperceptibly. "You thought right."

For a long moment, they looked at one another. His weariness was evident in the sleepy squint of his eyes. But there was determination, too. He would out-wait her if he had to.

He tilted his head. "You gonna let me sleep and get some for yourself?"

She frowned. "Don't want to bring trouble on you. It's dark now. Best time for me to slip away."

"You won't be able to run fast enough or far enough to outrun Colonel Baxter's tracker and mounted men." His expression was sternly fierce as he continued. "Come morning, that man will be on your trail. The rain will help. But if you run out there . . ." He thrust a blunt finger toward the outside. ". . . they will find you." He pinned her with a stern look. "I'm thinking on a plan. But first, you got to let me rest a bit."

She frowned, but nodded. "All right."

"Reckon your word will do." He flopped back down and tugged the quilt over himself once more.

Almost immediately, his breaths filled the space, deep and steady.

Deliverance eased the pack to the floor and settled herself against the soft tick on the pallet. Weariness washed over her. How long since she'd slept in a bed this soft?

The thought sent a shudder through her. She'd slept in Boone's bed plenty of times—if one could call such subconscious, tense alertness "sleeping." But alone? It had been a very long time ago.

She pulled her blue cape, the lap robe, and the coverlet on the tick over herself like a shield and relished the warmth of it. Closed her eyes. Allowed her weariness to pull her under.

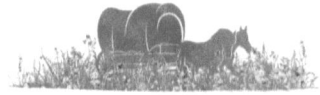

Boone arrived back at the fort, weary and heartbroken over Brad. He wanted to fetch Delilah. To relish the warmth of her in his arms as he slept. But there were too many men still wandering about tonight. She would want to go out to the necessary and might be seen.

He couldn't have word getting about that he had a weakness for a woman. Especially not a woman like her. A man in his position had to maintain authority. And respect.

She'd be fine until morning. It wouldn't be the first time she'd been left for such long hours. But this time his conscience did prick him because there was a child to consider.

But Delilah was a tough little she-wolf. She'd be fine.

And he was too tired to wait for all the hubbub to settle.

Tugging off his gloves, he tromped the stairs to his rooms above the store.

Brad. Stupid fool. He was going to die, and Boone wouldn't be able to do a thing about it. He couldn't risk his career on his no-account brother.

He shuffled into his room and sank slowly onto the edge of the bed to tug off his boots.

Ah. Much better. He massaged his aching feet, then slipped off his uniform and took time to hang each piece carefully in the wardrobe.

After a quick rinse of his face and arms in the washbasin, he toweled dry and then sank against his pillows. Closed his eyes.

Tomorrow, he would shore up his strength. For tonight, he allowed himself to weep for the brother he would lose. Not the adult brother who had caused him so much angst and anger, but the boy he had been. The boy Boone had once loved.

As the thought registered, it eased through him. It was true. He no longer loved Brad. He was simply a burden Boone couldn't disassociate himself from because they shared a last name. Soon, he'd no longer have that burden.

He would cling to that truth. It would help him get through the next few days.

The truth and Delilah. He always found comfort while with her.

Chapter 2

Deliverance woke with a start. The voices of two men speaking quietly at the far end of the wagon sent a surge of fear along the back of her neck. She sprang upright, clutching her blue cloak around herself. Was it Boone? Had he discovered her missing and come looking already?

It was still dark outside. Two silhouettes stood at the tailgate, one inside and one outside, speaking in tones too quiet for her to make out. Was Jeremiah still asleep in the dark shadows between the crates? Or was he one of the men in the conversation? She wished she could see. But it was so dark that the moon must be hidden now by either clouds or trees. Only because another wagon's canvas was a lighter spot behind the speakers could she see the two shadows in conversation.

Terror beat her breaths against her teeth as she waited. One of her hands clutched tightly into the material of the cloak at her throat.

But then the man inside clapped a hand onto the shoulder of the man outside, and that man turned and walked away.

She blew out a slow exhale and scrutinized the shadow turning toward her. He strolled the length of the aisle without tripping over a sleeping man, so he must be . . . "Jeremiah?"

"Yeah. Sorry if we frightened you." He sank to a squat.

She couldn't see his face in the darkness. "What is it?"

A brief flash of white must be him smiling. "The good Lord sent you a baby."

She snatched a silent inhale. How did he know? She wasn't far enough along to even be showing yet. Only two months of missed cycles, with the third nearly upon her. And she could hardly feel this child had been sent from God.

"Not all children are hoped for." The bitter words were out before she thought better of them.

The sound of his boots shifting against the ground made her feel ashamed of her sentiment. "Mrs. Hawthorne—she's the one expecting—sure seems to be of a different mind. This child will be number eight. Maybe eight and nine since she already has a passel of twins." He chuckled. "Imagine that, if you will."

Relief rushed through her. He'd meant another baby, not hers. How would the impending arrival of a child help her? A headache pinched, wrinkling her brow. She had too many questions and not enough answers. Too many looming threats and only the slimmest hope of escape.

"What time is it?" she asked, wanting to move on from the talk of babies.

"Almost dawn. That was my friend Striker. He'll be back in a moment. Got your pack?"

"It's here." She fumbled for it in the darkness.

"I'll take it. You'll get it back, don't worry, none." Jeremiah stood, and she heard him swing the pack onto one shoulder.

At the back of the wagon, someone whisper-whistled. "Jer? We're ready."

"Follow me." Jeremiah turned and scrambled out into the darkness.

Swallowing down her trepidation, Del eased off the pallet and padded after him. *Lord? You still watching me?* At the tailgate, she found Jeremiah holding a burlap sack. He had handed her pack to the other man, based on the shadowy lump on one of his shoulders.

"Don't get down yet. You need to put your feet in here."

Del's heart hammered. What was going on here?

Jeremiah must have sensed her uncertainty because he hurried to add, "It's so the tracker doesn't have as easy a time with your trail. This will keep you from leaving an inadvertent footprint in the dark. Hopefully, we'll get more rain after we move you across, but we can't take that chance. Here." He thrust one hand up for her to take. "Sit yourself down."

She didn't have much choice in the matter, so she allowed his grip to lend her strength. After he helped her sit on the tailgate, he held the sack until she worked both her feet inside. She was thankful for the darkness that gave her some privacy for the task.

Across? Across where? But she didn't voice the questions hammering through her.

"Good. Now, work your toes into both corners there at the end. We'll take the walk slow, so no need to worry about rushing."

"How far are we going? Can't you just carry me?" She felt heat blast into her face at the blurted comment.

But he didn't seem to mind her question. He was already shaking his head. "A good tracker can assess the depth of a man's footprints. If one of us carries you, our prints will be deeper and raise questions. The sack will leave an odd mark in the grass, but we'll be able to rough those out after we get you to safety."

Safety? Where was that, exactly?

She could hardly believe she was here, striving to keep Boone from finding her. Did she really want to leave him and bring such harshness on these folk? He obviously hadn't checked the basement, or all manner of chaos would be brewing. And while that realization shot her through with a mixture of anger and sadness, it also made her realize this hadn't gone too far. She could go back right now, and he'd never know she'd ever been gone.

When Jeremiah took her hand again and helped her down from the tailgate, she clutched the sack covering her feet with one hand and looked toward the fort. He released her and stepped back.

Starlight stroked enough highlights on wood and rooftops that she could even discern Boone's window on the top floor of the mercantile. The moon was not behind the clouds, then. She looked for it and found the half-moon in the distance, hovering above the western horizon, most of the light obscured by dark clouds. Yet here above them, the skies were clear and the fort lay quiet.

Not too late. Yet, if she went back, how would she get in? Surely Betsy would have locked the back door of the store. Besides, there would be any number of guards roaming about now that all the soldiers had returned to the fort.

"You thinking of going back, you're a fool." Jeremiah's voice was quiet but firm. His boots rustled through the grass.

She turned to search him out in the darkness.

He shook his head. "Don't mean to speak so harshly. But it angers me to think what you must be running from."

"Jer, we gotta go." The other man whispered.

Jeremiah spread a firm hand against her back, turning her away from the fort as he swung his hat to the shadow man. "This here is my friend Striker Moss."

Del shuffled a couple of steps away from Jeremiah's touch. Her fears were foolish since he didn't seem the type to harm a woman, and she'd been considering going back to one who was. There were other considerations, too, of course, but he wouldn't be able to tell she was expecting by touching her back. Still, she didn't want any of these folk to know about this child growing inside her. She still hoped she might resume her cycle any day.

Guilt slammed through her at the thought.

She glanced toward the stars above. *Lord, forgive me, but You know I've got no life to offer this child.* A weary dread of the future filled her. She'd made her escape for this very child she didn't want. Her emotions were at the confusing juxtaposition of wanting to do right by a child she feared she might hate. Yet, how could she hate a mere child? Or live with herself if she did? It wasn't the child's fault that Boone was a cruel master.

"Pleased to meet you, ma'am." Jeremiah's friend's words drew her thoughts from her problems as he touched the brim of his hat and lifted it.

She almost laughed. Only this morning she'd been chained to a wall, and now men were doffing their caps to her? Was she still chained and only dreaming? "Pleased to meet you, Mr. Moss, sir."

"This way." Jeremiah strode out in the wake of the man who still carried her pack on his shoulder.

All around, the camp lay silent. Not even the birds twittered the announcement of dawn yet.

Thankful to see that the men were true to their word and took the way slowly, Del followed them across the middle of the circled wagons to one across the way, where the dim glow of a lantern shone from inside.

Behind the wagon, a woman paced the ground. She was too slender to be the one expecting, though taller than Del by a good several inches. Otherwise, it was too dark to make out other features.

Mr. Moss stepped close to her, and they spoke in low voices.

Del was too tired to strain to hear their conversation, so she glanced back toward the fort. All remained silent and dark.

He didn't look for you. He doesn't care.

She'd known that all along, so why this disappointment pumping in her chest? Was she surprised that Boone had, to his way of thinking, left the mother of his child chained up in the dark? That he hadn't even considered she might need the necessary?

A shadow loomed between her and the fort, bringing her focus back to the here and now.

Jeremiah's gray gaze seemed even more piercing in the dim light of the dawn stars. "You going back? Or going forward?" He swept his hat through his fingers repeatedly.

Back to familiar chains and abuse? Or forward into an unknown future that might bring pain and misery on those trying to help her? *Lord, this seems an impossible feat, this escaping from such a monster. But I got to try for the sake of this child. Please help me not to hate it.*

Tears stung her eyes. Why had God allowed life to form out of so much misery?

She drew in a bolstering breath and looked at Jeremiah. "Forward."

Jeremiah nodded. "Good. I knew I liked your gumption." He swung his hat toward the wagon. "This here is the Hawthorne wagon. Mrs. Evelyn Hawthorne is laboring to bring her eighth child into this world, and Tamsyn thinks it will be a good long while yet. God's timing is always perfect."

He stepped toward her as though to indicate her decision had been made and she ought to move.

Del turned toward the wagon, confusion still pinching her brow. How did a woman giving birth offer help to her?

When she reached the tailgate, Jeremiah's hands swept about her waist and hoisted her up onto the wood that extended behind the canvas cover. He reached a hand up. "I'll take the gunnysack."

As Del clutched the overhead stay and worked to keep her balance and remove her legs from the bag, Mr. Moss helped the other woman climb up onto the tailgate as well.

Once Del was free of the bag and had handed it to Mr. Jackson, the woman held her hand toward her. "My name is Tamsyn. Pleased to meet you. Deliverance, correct?" She didn't wait for Del to confirm before waving her into the interior of the wagon. "Come on, let's get you hidden inside. Mrs. Hawthorne is standing until we get you settled." Though she didn't tell her to hurry, Del could hear the urgency in the woman's tone.

Del took one more look at the men. They were already almost all the way across the field. Mr. Moss mounted a horse and set off at a trot with her bag still on his shoulder. Mr. Jackson tossed the gunnysack into the campfire near his wagon, took up a bucket, and began scrubbing the tailgate where she had sat a moment ago.

That sight set her heart to thrashing even harder than it had all day.

Was he worried the fort might have dogs? *Did* Boone have dogs? She wasn't sure. She'd never heard any baying sounds, but locked up in the basement during the day as she'd always been, would she have heard them?

Dear Lord!

Yesterday, she'd feared what might happen to anyone who helped her, but now that she had faces to go with those people, she knew she would never be able to live with herself if any tragedy befell these good folk simply because they'd tried to help her escape evil.

"This way." The woman named Tamsyn urged her inside by placing a hand on her back.

Taking a fortifying breath, Del cast one more glance at the long stretch of open fields that led into the distance. She could leap down and set to running—running until her legs ached, and her lungs burned, and the sun beat down hard upon her shoulders and filled her with a powerful thirst. Or she could go into the wagon and hide in the darkness. Either way, Boone and his soldiers would likely find her.

Across the field, Jeremiah stopped his scrubbing and turned to look at her. He shook his head. His gaze begged her to trust them.

With a sigh, she stepped into the dim light cast by the lone lamp in the wagon. She was used to darkness. She supposed she could handle it for a few hours more. She only hoped she wasn't about to bring Boone's wrath down on these folk.

An unknown future lay ahead, but she knew the One who had known that future from the beginning of time. She would have to rest in Him.

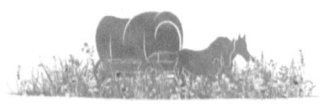

Tamsyn caught sight of the raw skin on Deliverance's wrists as the light of the lantern in the Hawthorne wagon illuminated her. Her stomach turned. A flash of memory froze her in place, seared by the recollection of splintering pain as Samuel had wrapped a hand around her wrist. Why was she thinking of him now? She'd been conquering constant thoughts of him lately. And yet here he was right back at the forefront of her mind. She shook the thoughts away.

Evelyn Hawthorne had sunk back down on her tick, both hands curled around the roundness of her belly. Her face was stretched taut in a grimace.

Tamsyn's heart pounded against her sternum. Was this normal?

The woman's husband had joined his children in their tent for the night, and Tamsyn hoped she wouldn't need to fetch him. She didn't like the way Mrs. Hawthorne's labor was progressing, though she was thankful that one less person would know about the girl. It didn't feel right, hiding an escaped slave in the man's wagon without his knowledge, but Evelyn had assured them it was okay.

Evelyn eased out a low moan and a whimper. "I tell you, this child is a stubborn mite, all elbows and knees gouging my insides."

One child? Or two? The Hawthorne children—three sets of twins among them—all seemed to think their ma would be delivered of another set of twins. The woman was rather large. And her labor had started sooner than expected. Tamsyn only hoped the babe, or babes, would be strong enough to make the rest of the journey to Oregon. Her hands trembled at the thought of the monumental task before her.

One thing at a time. She couldn't help Mrs. Hawthorne until she got Deliverance hidden. But first . . . "Here, please sit, Deliverance. I need to wrap your wrists."

The woman complied, but she searched the interior of the wagon as though halfway expecting a monster to leap from the shadows. "You can call me Del. And my wrists are fine. I don't want to cause no trouble."

There was more connotation to those last words than simply the trouble of wrapping her wrists. Tamsyn longed to reassure her, but the truth was if the soldiers did come looking, they might make Mrs. Hawthorne move.

Striker seemed to think no man worth his salt would want to hang around while a woman was birthing a baby, but Tamsyn feared what might happen if he were mistaken.

She drew in a long inhale. "It's no trouble. Honestly. We're happy to help you."

She dipped her cloth into the basin of warm water she'd prepared and reached for Del's hand. She drew her arm into the light and studied the abraded skin on her wrists. Several places were rubbed raw, the sores a bright red against her dark skin. Tamsyn tucked her lower lip between her teeth. She would need ointment so the wounds wouldn't stick to the wrappings. Thankfully, she still had plenty of the dead nettle and beeswax balm she'd made before the start of the journey in her bag. It only took her a moment to pat the sores clean with her cloth, apply the ointment, and wrap the woman's wrists with clean bandages.

Beside them, Mrs. Hawthorne puffed and gritted her teeth in silent anguish.

"There, that should help those heal up quickly. Now . . ." Tamsyn rose, thankful to see Del rise with her. "We just need to get you hidden." She turned to look at Mrs. Hawthorne.

The woman raised one hand, palm out, as though requesting a moment as she breathed through another contraction.

"It's okay. Take your time." Tamsyn went to work putting her supplies away. It wouldn't do for the soldiers to find her bandages and ointment here in the Hawthorne wagon. Her heart pounded in fear of the feat they hoped to accomplish. What if they got Deliverance killed?

She would simply have to make sure that didn't happen. Surely the Lord had sent Mrs. Hawthorne into labor early to provide just the cover they needed to keep Del safe?

When Mrs. Hawthorne was again able to stand, Tamsyn nudged Del forward and lifted the tick to show her the wooden boxes they'd emptied for her at the far side of the space. "It will be cramped, but at least there's room for your legs to stretch out."

Striker and Jeremiah had emptied two crates of the beans that had been stored inside and cut away the end of each of the crates so the hollow stretched the length of two. The lids could still be wedged onto the frames, so the space could be covered. As long as a soldier didn't crawl onto the tick and open every crate, Deliverance should be fine.

They hoped a woman giving birth on the tick above the crates would be a deterrent.

Once Del had lain down in the compartment, Tamsyn placed the box top over her feet and looked down at her as she held the next lid ready. "We'll get you out as soon as it's safe."

Del nodded. "Thank you, kindly, ma'am."

"Please, just Tamsyn will do." She smiled. "We are happy to help. Try to rest."

With that, she covered the woman, and only once the tick was back in place did she allow herself to shake the tension from her arms.

Mrs. Hawthorne plopped back onto the edge of the pallet, both hands clutching her belly. "Something's not right with this birthing. It's different than my others."

"Here. Lay back and let me feel for a moment." Tamsyn placed her hands on the woman's stomach, not sure she would know a knee from an elbow. But as she pressed and prodded, trying to assess the babe's position, she found a large, round bump up high under the woman's ribs.

Her heart caught in her throat. Was it the baby's head? Shouldn't it be down? Maybe it wasn't the head? Could it be a little rump? If only she knew for certain.

She felt Mrs. Hawthorne's eyes on her and realized the woman didn't need to read her fears. She stepped back with a smile of encouragement. "Feels like a healthy little one vying for exit."

Tamsyn turned on the pretense of reaching for a tiny quilt Evelyn had been working on during the evenings. She tucked her lower lip between her teeth as she folded the small blanket and set it within reach. She didn't like being the woman's only help. And she certainly didn't like the fact that the woman who had already birthed seven babes was saying this birthing was different!

"How about I fetch you a cup of tea? Would that help?" Hopefully, the woman wouldn't see through her excuse, but she needed to escape so she could gather herself for a moment. She didn't want Evelyn to sense her anxiety! "I have some honey and lemon in my wagon. I'll be back in the flicker of a lamb's tail."

She clambered out of the wagon without giving Evelyn time to protest. Truth be told, the woman had her eyes closed and seemed so concentrated on her own pain that she might not even notice Tamsyn was gone!

Chapter 3

Striker had ridden the ten minutes ahead to hide Deliverance's bag, and now, upon his return, found Tamsyn pacing the space outside her wagon like a woman intent on digging a trench. He dismounted, tied his horse to the back of her wagon, and relaxed one shoulder into the wood, enjoying the sight before him.

The rising sun had lightened the eastern sky, and in the distance, the roofs of the fort were beginning to turn a light pink. Strands of Tamsyn's dark hair had slipped loose from her bun, and the morning dew had darkened the bottom six inches of her skirt.

It seemed they had gotten Deliverance hidden in the nick of time. The whole wagon train would be coming awake soon. Was that what had Tamsyn so on edge?

She talked to herself as she paced, flapping her hands as though they might have gone to sleep. "You can do this. You simply have to remain calm and not let her see your fears." She pivoted at the other end of the wagon and returned toward him. The pink light of dawn stroked color against her face and the curls that rested against her cheeks. She had almost reached him before she noticed him and gasped.

His conscience pricked him, and he lowered his gaze to the toe he prodded into the dirt so she wouldn't think he'd been staring like a man possessed. He ought to have let her know he was here, but she always held herself at a distance when he was around. He wished she would relax and let him get to know her better. He remained where he was but lifted his gaze once more. "Something amiss?"

She pivoted and paced three steps in the other direction, turned and retraced her way toward him, then paused. For a long moment, she stared off toward the fort.

Even though he would have loved to sweep that curl off her cheek with the stroke of his fingers, Striker didn't dare move. This was the first time she'd paused long enough for him to feel like she was giving him the time of day. He liked it. Maybe too much. But he didn't like the stiff line of tension in her shoulders. "What is it?"

She hung her head, swiped at a piece of grass that had stuck to her skirt, then lifted her gaze to his. "It's Mrs. Hawthorne. She says this birthing isn't like her others, and it makes me nervous. I think the babe might be turned the wrong way." Her focus fell to her clasped hands, where they fidgeted and twisted into a tight knot. "I don't know why I'm the one they asked for help. I'm n-not sure I can d-do this. And then there's the girl." Her voice fell to a whisper. "What if I accidentally say something that gives away her presence? Or what if she makes a noise? Or what if the soldiers—"

Striker took her hands in his. He hadn't meant to, but now he might as well make the most of it. He slipped his fingers between hers and gave each hand a gentle squeeze.

Her gaze flashed to his, large and terrified in the burgeoning light.

He swallowed and rubbed his thumbs over her knuckles. Drew a step closer to her. What was it about this woman that raised such a protective spirit inside him? He felt her fingers tremble between his own. Heard each shallow breath that puffed rapidly past her lips. Lips that were full and soft in the warm wash of dawn. Lips that he should not be leaning toward.

"M-Mr. Moss, p-please." Though she said the words, she didn't tug for the release of her hands.

He stilled with his face only inches from hers and lifted his gaze. The terror in her eyes made him ease back. But he did draw her hands behind him and settle their clasped hands at the small of his back. He needed to take these next steps slowly, and he knew where he wanted to start.

"Say my name." The request emerged with a husky undertone. "Please?" He swallowed.

The woman undid him.

She peered up at him, and a small smile touched those tempting lips. "Mr. Moss isn't your name?"

He grinned, liking her teasing a little too much. He waited patiently, content to simply stand here with her arms around him.

She tilted her head. "I'm quite certain I've never heard your proper name."

That was true enough. "Name's Sebastian Jebediah Moss. But Striker is the only name I want to hear on your pretty pink lips."

She opened her mouth, but down at the fort a bugle blasted through the morning air. They both released each other and turned toward the sound.

Soldiers boiled from their quarters and rushed to stand at attention in the square. One man was still hopping into his boots as he hurried into position.

This was it then. Striker gripped Tamsyn's forearm, never taking his eyes off the fort. "Is she settled?"

"Y-yes."

He didn't like that the stammer was back in her words, but there was no time for more than curt assurances now because Colonel Boone Baxter stalked up and down in front of his men, no doubt spewing orders about the girl who'd slipped from his grasp.

Striker turned to Tamsyn, lamenting the intrusion into their flirting. "You can do this. If that babe is facing the wrong way, you can turn it. I heard the midwife on our plantation speak of it one time."

"Turn it? H-how?"

"Use your hands on her stomach. Be firm." He shook his head, touched her cheek. "That's all I know." He nudged her back in the direction of the Hawthorne wagon. I'll take care of Edi this morning."

She took a couple of steps but then froze and pivoted toward her wagon as she gave him a self-deprecating smile. "I said I was coming to fetch tea." She rummaged through a basket, and a stoppered glass vial tumbled out and fell to the grass near her feet.

Striker stepped forward and picked it up as she continued to rummage.

When she straightened with a packet of tea and a jar of honey in her hand, he held the vial out to her. "You need this too?"

"Oh." She took it and dropped it back into the basket. "No. Those are sleeping powders. I keep them for the nights when Edi has trouble sleeping." She started away but paused once again and turned back to him. "Thank you. Please say a prayer."

He nodded. "And I'll be nearby if you need anything."

Though she hurried off without comment, for the first time since he'd known her, she didn't tell him to back off and mind his own business, and that gave a man a powerful hope.

A powerful hope, indeed.

Deliverance lay in the darkness of the cramped space, listening to the moaning of the woman on the tick above her. She felt a cramp in her leg, but there was no way to stretch it out. She clamped her teeth against the pain and rested one hand on the flat of her belly. Would her own labor and birthing be so difficult?

She had helped Mama with the birthings on the plantation a number of times and knew some women breezed through the process with only a few hours of labor, while others took much longer.

If this woman had birthed seven babes previously, as Jeremiah had said, her labor should be easier, shouldn't it?

The sound of a bugle sent her pulse skittering.

Deliverance closed her eyes and settled her mind on praying for the woman who had seemed kind and smiled at her despite the pain she must have been in. She pressed one hand over her heart and willed herself to breathe calmly. She would do herself no good by going into a panic in this tiny box that already made her feel closed in and tense.

She prayed for Mrs. Hawthorne and her baby. She prayed for the people of the wagon train. She prayed for Miss Tamsyn and finally for Mr. Jackson. *Thank You, Lord, for sending me to a kind man who was willing to help me.*

She heard smart footsteps and felt the vibrations through the crates.

"Right, I've got your tea here. How are you doing?"

Mrs. Hawthorne groaned softly, and the boards above squeaked as she shifted. Deliverance didn't hear her make any reply, however.

Tamsyn's footsteps drew nearer. "Soldiers will be here at any minute."

Del's heart pounded so hard she could feel it pulsing against her breastbone. She felt certain the woman had said the words for her benefit. But she continued as though she'd been speaking to Mrs. Hawthorne all along.

"I think your babe is turned the wrong way, Mrs. Hawthorne. Have any of your other babes been breech?"

"No. They . . . all came . . . into the world . . . proper-like." Her words were breathy and laced with pain.

"Well . . . Some children are born troublemakers, I suppose." Tamsyn chuckled, and Del wondered if Mrs. Hawthorne could hear the nervousness in it.

If only she'd had time to palpate the woman's stomach, she would know how to help, but she wouldn't be able to call out instructions without giving herself away.

Even as she thought it, a fist pounded the side of the wagon. "Your pardon, ma'am, but we've been instructed to search the interior of every wagon."

Del held her breath. Closed her eyes. Willed herself not to come apart at the seams.

Mrs. Hawthorne moaned loudly—much more loudly than she had been moaning up to this point.

"Search the wagon? Whatever for?" Tamsyn's voice had a slight hitch in it.

Del's lungs burned, but she didn't dare let herself breathe yet. Would the soldiers attribute Tamsyn's nervousness to their presence? Or would it raise suspicions of another sort?

Mrs. Hawthorne cried out again. "Oh, Lord, this child is set to tear me apart from the inside!" While Tamsyn was nervous, Mrs. Hawthorne could have been a thespian straight from one of those fancy theatres Master McNeilly used to visit in Georgia.

Lord bless that woman, and bless her good!

"As you can see, gentlemen, there is a woman giving birth in here." Tamsyn's footsteps clipped smartly along the length of the aisle, and her voice was steady this time.

"Ah, y-yes ma'am. We c-can see that. We won't be but a moment. You haven't seen a strange woman, have you? A, ah, *black* woman?"

"I've been helping Mrs. Hawthorne give birth since last night. Her husband is there by that tent. See him? He'll tell you she went into labor last night. The only time I stepped out was to fetch her some tea. Do you see a black woman in here?"

Del's burning lungs betrayed her, and she sucked in a gulp of air, then hoped the gasp hadn't been heard in the wagon above.

Tamsyn sighed, sharp and short. "Best you come in and look for yourselves. Only don't disturb my patient, please."

The sound and feel of the soldiers' boots tromping the aisle reverberated through the wooden crates. Del forced herself to close her eyes and hold herself together. She would only get these folk into more trouble if she emerged, screaming, from this compartment.

Mrs. Hawthorne cried out again. And the boards above Del squeaked as the woman presumably writhed on the tick. "Tamsyn, you better . . . come take a look, I think . . . this babe is coming now!"

"This woman is having a child, gentlemen. If you're quite done?" Tamsyn's voice rang loudly enough to be heard through the encampment.

"Blazes, Gerald, there's nowhere for a body to hide in any of these wagons. What is the colonel thinking? Did you even know he had a pretty little bedwarmer locked up in his basement?"

"Muzzle it, Bert." The second man's voice was low and gruff. He cleared his throat. "Your pardon, ma'am. We'll get out and let you continue with, ah, what you are doing here."

"Thank you, gentlemen," Tamsyn said. "If we come across anyone we think the colonel should know about, we'll be sure to send word back to the fort." Her words accompanied the retreat of the soldiers' boots on the floorboards.

Del released a breath and relaxed into the hard wood of the crates beneath her. For now, she had escaped detection.

Thank You, Jesus!

She closed her eyes and took the first easy breath she'd taken since leaving the basement with Mrs. Baxter.

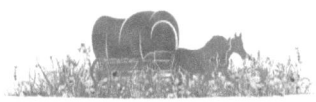

Jeremiah did his best not to appear like an antsy hound stuck in a cage as the soldiers crawled through all the wagons and Boone Baxter paced the center of the field in the middle, waiting for news from his soldiers. Eden had noticed his nerves a moment ago, so he'd plunked himself down on one of the crates near their fire, but all this anxiety thrumming inside had him ready to leap to his feet and holler a challenge to every soldier in the encampment. He forced himself to keep his focus on the grass beneath his boots instead, but that didn't mean all his attention wasn't tuned to the soldiers who had disappeared into the Hawthorne wagon.

Little Afton Slade approached with a bowl of oats that looked too large in one tiny hand and a cup of milk in the other. She smiled up at him and held the oats toward him. "Want some?"

Jeremiah settled his hand on her hair, noting how large and dark it was resting there on her small blonde head. "That's right kind of you, Miss Afton. But you go on and enjoy your breakfast on your own. Here, let me help you." As she squirmed to a seat on a crate beside him, he rescued the tin cup of milk before she could knock it galley-west from Sunday. Once she was settled, he placed the mug beside her. "Careful now. You don't want to spill."

She nodded and worked the spoon into her little mouth with enough gusto to leave honey trailing down her chin.

Jeremiah couldn't help but grin. He was glad he wouldn't be responsible for removing the stickiness from her when she finished. When he raised his head, it was to find Colonel Baxter looking right at him.

Easy. He maintained the man's gaze. He'd already greeted him earlier and didn't want to seem ill at ease.

Finally, the man turned away.

Ahead, at the wagon he'd been driving for the Slade children for the past several days, the soldiers were doing their best to seemingly tear the interior board from board. Crates had been handed out and now lay strewn on the prairie. One soldier had even crawled beneath it to study the undercarriage—and that was after they'd discovered and searched the small compartment where Del had been hiding when he found her. Jeremiah had never been more thankful that he'd listened to his instincts and didn't let Del remain in that wagon.

Finally, the soldiers gave up and emerged, shaking their heads at the colonel. Across the way, the two who had entered the Hawthorne wagon did the same.

Jeremiah couldn't have been more relieved than when the colonel's shoulders slumped in defeat, and he waved a motion for his men to wrap things up and return to the fort.

He was even happier a few minutes later when everyone in the wagon train voted to ride out immediately instead of staying to watch the hanging.

As the wagon folk headed back to their respective wagons, Jeremiah remained with the other scouts and Cranston.

"Think he'll actually follow through on hanging his own brother? Sure would hate for the sorry cuss to catch up to Mrs. Houston again out of some sort of revenge." Cody dusted at the leather of his buckskin breeches as he spoke the words Jeremiah knew had lingered in his own thoughts as well.

Cranston stroked his beard. "I considered the same. Would ease all our minds, I think, to know the man's sentence is carried out." He glanced at Cody. "What say you and I remain behind until the trial is over? I know you stood watch with Striker last night, but they claim the proceedings will be quick. We should easily be able to catch up to the wagons afterward."

Cody lifted one leather-fringed shoulder. "Fine by me."

Cranston gave a definitive dip of his chin. "Good. You two, if we don't reach you by evening, camp at the flats near Plum Creek. It will make for a long day, but the weather seems good for it, and this part of the trail is flat and easy."

Striker nodded. "Sounds fine. You think Evelyn Hawthorne will be okay to travel that far?"

Cranston sighed. "I told Hawthorne when they joined up, that if they needed to stop, they'd be on their own."

Striker met Jeremiah's gaze with a grim one of his own, and Jeremiah wondered if he knew something that he didn't.

"Right, then." Cranston stroked one hand down his beard. "Cody and I will stay long enough to make sure that no-good dangles, and we'll see the rest of you tonight. Strike, you're in charge till we get back."

"Yes, sir."

Jeremiah longed to rush to the Hawthorne wagon and help Del from hiding, but knew he couldn't do that yet. Danger still lurked too close for her.

With a clench of his jaw, he turned to the Slade wagon. Wyatt and his little brother Ash were already beside it, trying to make things right.

"Ash, you have to lift!" Wyatt snapped.

"I'm trying. But Pa's tools are heavy!"

The boys struggled with a large crate as they attempted to hoist it into the wagon. Wyatt's end was significantly higher than Asher's, which had barely risen off the prairie grass where the soldiers must have tossed it earlier. Ash stumbled back a couple of steps, and Jeremiah rushed forward before the seven-year-old could be flattened beneath the weight of the crate.

"Here. Let me help you." Jeremiah took Asher's end of the box.

Wyatt glowered at his brother before lifting his gaze to Jeremiah. "Thanks for the help."

"Happy to. Those soldiers sure did make a mess, didn't they?"

"Yes, sir."

Jeremiah shoved the crate into its proper place at the base of one sidewall.

Noting Asher's head hanging, he ruffled one hand across the boy's head. "A man never lets himself be defined by his weakness. Everyone has weaknesses of one sort or another. But a real man can assess his own weaknesses and face up to them. The good Lord created community for a reason. Sometimes a man needs a little help." He turned to level a look at Wyatt. "Sometimes a man's weakness is looking down on another man because of what he perceives as a weakness."

Now it seemed Wyatt's turn to hang his head. He gave a slight nod, and Jeremiah decided his point had been taken. He motioned Asher toward a pile of quilts that had been dumped to one side. "Ash, why don't you haul those quilts back inside. Be sure to shake 'em off good first. Wyatt and I will work on these crates over here."

To the boys' credit, they both pitched in to help when many boys their age would have wandered off and left the adults to do the chores.

Jeremiah and Wyatt hefted another crate. This was as good a time as any to broach the subject of Deliverance needing a place to stay. Jeremiah waited until the crate had been stacked into place. He dusted his hands as he said, "Wyatt, there's a woman who will be joining us soon. Her name is Deliverance. She's gonna need a bed and an oilcloth over her head. Wondered if you would object to her staying in your parents' wagon?"

Wyatt's gaze snapped to his. "She the woman the colonel was looking for?"

Caution squeezed Jeremiah's chest. He studied the boy. None of the Slade children had ever made him feel as though he were less-than because of the color of his skin, but with times being what they were, he felt the need for discretion.

Wyatt seemed to catch on to his hesitation, for he continued, "Because if she is, I'm right glad you're helping her."

A breath eased from Jeremiah's lips. They began to return some tools to the barrel they'd been pulled from. "Sometimes the less a man knows, the less trouble he can find himself in. A man like the colonel, well, he's not a man to give up easily. So for now, let's just say Deliverance is a friend of mine. And then if the colonel returns and asks you any questions, you'll be able to answer truthfully with what you know for certain."

Wyatt frowned. As they lifted another crate, he scrunched his nose. "And what if a man knows certain things without being told. What ought he to answer then?"

Jeremiah tucked away a smile. "Well, now, sometimes a man *thinks* he knows something he doesn't truly know. So, it's best in such situations to shrug off the questions and speak truthfully. You simply say you don't know."

Wyatt nodded. "Yes, sir. And of course, we are happy to have your, ah, friend stay in our wagon."

Jeremiah hadn't really expected the boy to say no. Nevertheless, he found a great burden lifted upon hearing his answer. He stretched out a hand. "Thank you kindly."

Wyatt nodded as they shook. "Of course." He hesitated for a moment and then hurried to add, "I'm sorry I wasn't so patient with Ash a bit ago. I don't know why, but sometimes I just want to box his ears."

Jeremiah couldn't help but chuckle. "I never had no siblings. But from what I've seen, it seems that siblings sometimes raise that feeling in one another. I bet Ash has felt like he wanted to tangle with you a time or two also."

"That's for sure!" Asher piped up from behind him as he hefted his ma's sewing basket into the wagon bed. One spool of thread bobbed along the ground behind him like a fishing lure trolling for bottom-feeders.

Jeremiah chuckled and hurried to fetch the spool. He set Asher to winding the thread back into place, hoping it hadn't gotten too dirty on its trip across the prairie.

It took them twenty more minutes to load everything onto the wagon and strap it down as before, and then they were rolling out.

And just like that, Jeremiah's thoughts were back on the woman who remained in hiding in the Hawthorne wagon.

Chapter 4

C hevonne Moreau huddled in the back of her wagon, trying not to listen to the sharp sounds of the battle cracking outside. They had not even reached Fort Kearny yet. The fort was meant to be the very edge of civilization, no? If they were attacked here, then what horrors might lie in the wilderness beyond?

Her heart beat so fiercely against her breastbone, she thought it would break free. And this quilt she'd instinctively clutched tight to her chest? Foolish, so foolish. It would protect her from nothing, should one of the Indians raging outside thrust open the wagon flap.

What had instigated this madness? Maybe how their uncouth wagon master, Redd Engstrom, had taken the hatchet from the body on the burial scaffold the day before? Several in their party had spoken their disagreement with the desecration of the dead Indian man, but Redd—ah, always he must scoff—declared the poor soul had no further need of his tomahawk. The weapon, he said, would serve him better than rusting away in the wind and the weather.

Whatever had instigated the attack this morning, one moment she had been sound asleep, thankful for the day of rest that Redd had proclaimed for this day while the men hunted, and the next moment she had heard screaming—wild screaming that had sent a chill straight down her spine. She had tumbled from her pallet, rushed to the back of her wagon, and pulled back the canvas to see an Indian on a swift pony galloping through the encampment with Redd fleeing before him bare-chested and holding his trousers up with one hand. That flash of a glimpse had been all she'd needed to retreat into this trembling cocoon on her bedding.

Now, as she listened to the sounds of the concluding battle outside, she closed her eyes and wished to heaven she had listened to her mother's advice and cowed to the empress's request instead of fleeing France for the freedom of the colonies. It had been a simple request—apologize for daring to kiss the empress's cousin in the gardens one moonlit eve.

But since Chevonne had been given no choice in the kiss, she'd refused to admit culpability. She'd boarded the first ship—thankful to be shed of both the empress and her lecherous cousin.

Who knew where that kiss might have ended if the empress had not been taken with a fit of insomnia and stepped onto her terrace for a breath of air—the same as what Chevonne had done moments earlier, only to find the empress's Spanish cousin, Don Tomás de Montijo, Conde de Villanueva, waiting for her. How had she been expected to know she'd caught his eye at the previous evening's soiree? She shuddered to think what might have happened had the man succeeded in finding her in her boudoir, which had been his original intention, she felt certain.

She had hoped to find freedom and work in America. However, the colonies, as it turned out, had been less friendly than she'd expected. Though Chevonne was highly educated and spoke not only French but also English, Spanish, and Latin, no one wanted a foreigner teaching their children. This had resulted in her accepting a position in the far-off territory of Oregon. A position she was likely now never to undertake.

Unless an escape she could make?

It was only a matter of time before she was discovered here in her wagon! She must try! She rose from her cowered position at the exact moment as the canvas at the back of her wagon was jerked to one side.

The Indian staring back at her was all skin and leather. And the bow in his hands was already notched with an arrow. Two tall white feathers with black tips protruded from the back of his head, and the necklace hanging about his neck appeared to be a string of the severed toes—claws, and all—of some poor fuzzy critter. A bear? Likely. She'd heard of the beasts and seen paintings, but had never seen an actual one.

She notched her chin up a degree and waited for her end. At least the glistening tip of his arrow appeared sharp enough to make a swift finish of her.

The man assessed her from head to toe and back again, and then a grin split his lips. A prominent gap revealed a missing tooth—likely knocked loose in some random battle he'd fought. The cynical thought almost made Chevonne smirk in her nervousness.

It was in that moment that she realized she stood before the man in her chemise. She'd never before been so thankful for Mother's insistence on the long, solid, white, sturdy linen garment.

Slowly, he lowered his bow, raised a hand, and flicked his fingers for her to come to him.

She remained where she stood, completely terrified of what might happen to her if she climbed down from the meager protection of her wagon. The man didn't appear to be someone who would brook disobedience, however, so she took up the dress she'd laid onto one of the crates the evening before.

"I must dress first." She unfurled the dress with a flap and held it up to herself.

Someone outside said something in a language Chevonne couldn't understand, and the man was momentarily distracted, but all too soon his gaze returned to her. His lips pressed into a thin line. He grunted. But when he flicked the canvas closed, Chevonne took it as permission to dress.

Never in her life had she flown into her petticoats and outer garments faster than she did that day. She was just tying the laces of her second boot when the canvas parted again. The nerve of the man! Thank heavens she'd made swift work of donning her garments!

She folded her arms and glared at him to make sure he understood her pique.

He only chuckled. The few words he uttered in his language sounded guttural and unfriendly, but he was smiling as he waved her toward him.

Despite the smile, she remained wary as she finally obeyed his instructions and moseyed toward him.

He took her arm and yanked her to the ground, none-too-gently. He reeked of something sharp, smoky, and acrid. She did her best not to cringe when he kept his grip on her arm and leered down at her with that gap more clearly revealed by the light of day—and the odor of his breath—as a tooth that had rotted away.

His stomach, which was only covered by the leather strap of the quiver angled across his back, was fleshy and flaccid like a man overfond of his drink. Heavens, what she wouldn't give to see Don Tomás riding to her rescue, and that was something she never thought she'd say.

Her captor tugged her toward the center of the circled wagons, where she could see most of her party on their knees in the grass, guarded by warriors dressed similarly to the one gripping her arm. As he pushed her forward and she fell to her knees beside Mrs. Hubbard, Chevonne could only be thankful that she was away from the rank warrior. From the corner of her eye, she noted that he stalked to one side and stood still, seemingly waiting for some command from another warrior who paced the ground before the kneeling captives. This other man wore a large feathered headdress and had a breastplate of beads woven on leather strands tied about his chest. He wore knee-high moccasins over leather breeches. Her mouth dried when his stern gaze settled on her. For where her previous captor's assessment had shown interest—even perhaps a repulsive desire—this man's gaze revealed naught but a cold disinterest and indifference.

Chevonne leaned closer to Mrs. Hubbard. "For what are we waiting, do you think?"

"Shhh!" The woman shook her head, her gray hair flying loosely about her shoulders. Her sharp reprimand and terrified eyes revealed her fear of drawing the Indian's attention.

The man in the headdress took one step toward them, barked two short words, and swung his hand in a gesture that looked very much like he would enjoy removing their heads from their shoulders.

"Oh, dear Lord, have mercy." Mrs. Hubbard cowered behind her arms.

Right, then.

Silence seemed the better part of wisdom.

Chevonne gave the man a sedate nod that she hoped didn't appear too fearful. She didn't want to give him the satisfaction of knowing he terrified her.

She would simply have to wait in silence and hope she would at least have a chance to write Mother a farewell missive, if it came to it. If their captors took them past the fort, perhaps one of these wild men would be so kind as to allow her to post a letter? Her shoulders slumped.

Doubtful. Very doubtful. Would they even take them near the fort after such a shamefully unjust attack?

Chevonne sighed. Again, doubtful. These were the times that made a woman wish she believed in the power of prayer.

She would pray herself up a brawny, strapping warrior who would come to her rescue, not be lecherous or dangerous—and would have all his teeth.

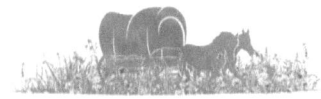

The wagon bumping along jostled Deliverance until she felt ready to come unglued, joint from joint.

How long had they been traveling now? Fifteen minutes? Twenty? Her concern for the laboring woman above her was growing with each passing minute. From what she'd been able to hear down here in the dark, there had been several moments when Tamsyn had tried to turn the baby, but there seemed to have been no progress. Several times, the woman's children had come to check on her, but Tamsyn had shooed them back out just as quickly.

Del could help. And surely they'd traveled far enough to let her escape this stuffy confinement—at least into the interior of the covered wagon bed? Besides, wouldn't Master Boone be distracted by his brother's hanging this morning?

Del closed her eyes, swallowed the dryness from her mouth. It was safer here in the dark. Goodness, she might be content to ride right here the whole way to Oregon. They could pull her out once they reached their destination, and she'd be completely fine and dandy.

Yet, there was her unwanted child to consider. And another babe— one who was presumably wanted.

For several long minutes, there had been no conversation above. She hadn't even heard Tamsyn's feet traipsing the aisle. Had the woman left to go see to her own family? That baby needed to be turned, or both it and the mother were in danger.

She worked more moisture into her mouth and called softly. "Excuse me? I can help with the baby." Hopefully, she had spoken low enough that only those in the wagon would hear.

She heard muffled shuffling above, and then, "Can you rise?" Tamsyn's voice. But not speaking to her. Asking Mrs. Hawthorne.

"Can't leave her in that tiny box forever," Mrs. Hawthorne puffed. The boards above squeaked.

Del pulled in a long, slow inhale, willing herself not to panic at the thought of stepping into the light.

More shuffling, a crack of light filtered in as the tick above must have been lifted, and when the lid of her compartment was removed and she felt the first cool waft of fresh air, she took a deep breath and forced herself upward. When she reached her feet, she realized one of her legs was sound asleep, and she took a moment to let the blood flow resume lest she fall flat when she tried to climb over the tick.

Thick oilcloth walls concealed the interior of the wagon, filling her with relief. This wasn't so bad. Maybe she would ride all the way to Oregon, huddled on some tick in a wagon bed. Again, her hand settled over her abdomen. This child would need her to exercise, or she might not have the strength to push her free when the time came. Her? She almost smiled at the thought. If good could come from the evil that had been done to her, then she hoped that good would be a girl—wanted, or not.

"You coming? Or staying?" Mrs. Hawthorne moaned as she bent over the roundness of her belly.

And Del knew she needed to move. Her leg tingled something fierce as she scrambled past the two women. It was a tight squeeze with all three of them trying to maneuver around each other in the cramped aisle of the wagon, but it only took a moment for Tamsyn to resettle the tick, and then Mrs. Hawthorne flopped back down like a hound at the end of a long hunt. Her hands turned white where they curved around her belly.

Del exchanged a concerned look with Tamsyn. She couldn't think about the danger of the open prairie behind her right now. Couldn't worry about being seen. There was a task to do, and it was best she get to it quick-like. "The babe still the wrong way?"

Tamsyn nodded, face pale. "I tried to turn it. But I was afraid of hurting it . . . or her. I don't know what to do." She wrung her hands.

Del took both of Tamsyn's hands in her own and lowered them with a slight shake of her head. Mrs. Hawthorne didn't need to know how concerned she was.

Balancing on her good leg, Del pivoted to look at Mrs. Hawthorne. She pasted on a smile, willing herself not to worry about the trail beyond the tiny cinched gap at the end of the wagon, which could lead

Boone right to her. Why was such a heavy fear suddenly upon her when she'd already made her escape?

The answer hit her square in the chest. Because she'd had a taste of freedom now, and to lose it would be the worst of tortures. She would rather cower, clinging to her freedom in a dark corner, than expose herself and lose it!

She took a breath. *Lord, You are the strength of my heart and my portion forever.*

Mrs. Hawthorne's concerned gaze brought her back to the present. "Would you object to me helping you, ma'am? My mama, she was the midwife back on the plantation I grew up on before . . . well, never mind that." She refused to dwell on the painful memory of her mother's screams as she'd been carried away on Boone's horse. "I learned a fair bit. I think I can help." At least she hoped she could.

Mrs. Hawthorne stretched out a hand and gripped her forearm with a strength that renewed Del's hopes for the woman's survival. "'Course. I'm h-happy for any . . . help. P-please, you can call me Evelyn." Behind her, Tamsyn released a loud breath that could only be interpreted as relief. "I've been praying for help. I didn't know it was you."

Evelyn took another breath as her gaze slipped over Del's cloak and dress. "Best you put on that apron there." She nudged a finger toward a garment hanging from one of the overhead stays, then rubbed her hands over the roundness of her belly. "This babe was a surprise gift from the Lord, best we get on with bringing—him . . . her? . . . them?" She chuckled, then winced. "Best we get on with bringing 'em into the world."

Del swallowed, feeling the pressure of that statement. Was the safe delivery of this child going to be all upon her? At least her leg was only tingling slightly now, and she felt confident she could move without tumbling sideways. She laid aside the blue cloak and set to rolling up her sleeves and donning the apron. The abrasions on her wrists might be a hindrance if she had to reach inside, but hopefully it wouldn't come to that.

She approached the mattress slowly and nodded to the woman's blouse. "I need you to lift your shirt." When the woman hesitated, she urged, "This ain't no time to be modest. I need to see your skin so's I can assess what this baby is doing. And Tamsyn, you got to get this wagon train stopped."

Tamsyn gaped at her. "But what if . . ."

Del shook her head. She could *not* think about Master Boone catching up with them to search the wagons once again, or she would be utterly useless. "The Lord already spared my life once today. Maybe it was just so's I could help with this baby. I'll leave the future in His hands." *Please, Lord, don't make me go back.* "Right now, she needs this jostling wagon stopped."

"I hear you." A man's voice called from the wagon bench. This was followed by a sharp whistle, and then the wagon trundled to a slow stop.

Thank goodness the jostling had ceased. Del had a brief moment of wondering if the man on the bench would be friend or foe when it came right down to it, but she supposed he sounded like he was at least thankful to have someone stepping in to help his wife.

"Your water break yet?" Del asked as Mrs. Hawthorne tucked her blouse up beneath her breasts.

She shook her head.

"Good. That's good." Del immediately realized there wasn't enough light in the wagon. But the woman couldn't be moved either. To do so would risk her waters breaking. It had already been a risk to have her stand to let Del out of her hiding place.

Del knew what she needed to do. It was finding the courage to do it that was the problem.

She closed her eyes. Drew in a fortifying breath. Repeated her verse. *Lord, You are the strength of my heart and my portion forever.*

One more breath. Then, "Listen now," she called to the man she could not see outside the cinched canvas. "I need the sides of this oil-cloth lifted as far as they can go. I need light and I need it now."

"We'll do it right away."

There was no going back now.

Ignoring her own trembling, she flapped her fingers at Tamsyn. "I need something to lift her pelvis. Something firm but soft, like folded quilts, please. And I need that jar of ointment you used on my wrists a moment ago."

Would it be slippery enough for the task? Her mouth went dry, but there was no time for doubts.

She heard approaching footsteps, and the wagon shifted slightly as several men outside worked together to roll up the sides of the canvas.

A flood of sunlight streamed in, and her gaze shifted to the flat, open prairie that stretched all around them. Several in the wagon train murmured their surprise at seeing her standing there, but she couldn't focus on them. All she could see was the unhindered view between here and the distant horizon. How exposed she was! Nothing but prairie grass and vast open space stretched in every direction.

"Del?" Tamsyn prodded.

She took a sharp breath. Forced her focus to the task at hand. To Evelyn's blue skirt. To her round, white belly. *Do not panic. Do not.* "Good, that's good." Could they hear the fear in her voice?

Tamsyn handed her a jar. Squeezed her shoulder. "This is the ointment. And there's an extra quilt here." She laid a patchwork blanket at the end of the pallet. "Will it be enough?"

Del set the jar of ointment aside for the moment. "I'll need one more, I think."

"All right." Tamsyn strode toward the tailgate. "I'll fetch another and be back as quick as I can."

Del nodded and placed her dry hands on the woman's stomach. "You feeling pains up high? Under your ribs?"

Evelyn nodded.

Sure enough, Del could feel the head high on the mound of her round belly. Thankfully, the roundness of her belly was also still close to her ribs. The babe had not yet descended into the birth canal.

For a breech birth, these circumstances were the best signs a body could hope to see. Still, Ma had always told her this was one of the most dangerous births to assist with. And if she didn't get this babe turned, it was likely both the mother and the child would die. Would the company of wagon folk blame her in that case?

She removed her hands from the woman before she could feel them trembling.

For one brief moment, she was tempted to walk away, but she had just said she would leave the future up to the good Lord, and so that was what she intended to do.

She suddenly noticed that the sides of the wagon were lined with men peering in at her. "Thank you for the light, gentlemen!" A flap of her hand shooed them on their way.

The men all lurched back as though to a man they'd been surprised to find themselves there peering in.

Del couldn't stop a grin as she took up the jar of ointment and greased her hands. "I need that quilt!"

She hadn't meant to snap, but Tamsyn was already back by her side, breathless and with a blessed armful of another blanket.

"Good. Fold it up, and that other one, too, please, about one foot by two. Yes, good. Just like that. Now, Mrs. Hawthorne, I need you to lift gently so we don't break your waters. And Tamsyn, you put the block of quilt under her backside. Good, just so. One more."

With her hands still greased, she waited impatiently for the woman to settle back down, this time with her hips higher than her shoulders. The angle would ease the downward pressure on the babe.

"Good. You done good." From the corner of her eye, she could see one man still lingering near the wagon. Since he seemed intent on pacing a trench, she assumed he was Mrs. Hawthorne's husband. Some midwives might have sent the man packing, but Del supposed if he was close enough to the woman to have created this condition, he ought to be allowed to linger near while she tried to help his child into the world.

She already had the ointment smeared all over Mrs. Hawthorne's belly. She smiled at the woman, willing herself to be calm and not panic. Ma had said that was one thing a midwife could never do. "You got a name picked out for this upside-down mite?"

Mrs. Hawthorne blew out a slow moan as a contraction came on, and Del once more drew in a calming breath. Every contraction could cause the child to kick out a foot that might break the waters, and turning this babe would be near impossible if that happened. *Lord Almighty, keep those waters from breaking and give me skill.*

Finally, Evelyn eased and shook her head. "We were still cogitating."

"Well, best you cogitate fast, ma'am, you don't mind my saying so." Del smiled as she pressed her hands against the woman's stomach, taking advantage of the lapse between contractions. "How long between your pains?" She felt down near the woman's hips for the little buttocks, then up high by her ribs to curve her other hand around the little head.

Mrs. Hawthorne shrugged one shoulder. "Ten minutes, maybe?"

Ten was more than she'd hoped for, and yet still might not be long enough. Del pushed inward on the little rump and stroked firmly downward at the hard, round head. "Tamsyn, we're gonna need warm water. Can you get someone to build a fire and put a pot on?" The little head slipped from beneath the cup of her hand, and Del felt the babe's rump bump against her left hand once more. Drat this stubborn child!

"Y-yes. I already did that when I went for the quilt. It should be ready when we need it."

After this was through, Del would need to tell the woman what a fine job she'd done. Did she even have experience with births?

She repeated her earlier motion, pushing in on the rump and sweeping down on the baby's head more firmly this time.

The large bulge of the baby's head rolled down Mrs. Hawthorne's abdomen, but at the halfway point, slipped into retreat once again. Del pressed her lips tight against the exasperation begging to be voiced. Instead, she said, "Tamsyn, I need you to squeeze in here beside me. We need this child to have no choice but to somersault. Here, put some of this ointment on your hands. Good. Now, we have to give this little one no choice. We both push in and up from the bottom, and then sweep our hands down firmly from the top. But at the same time, we have to be as gentle as we can so we don't break the waters, understand? Because if those break, we likely won't get another chance."

Tamsyn was a little wide-eyed, but she nodded.

"Right." Del nodded reassurance. "On three. One, two, three!"

Both women pushed inward and swept their hands firmly down. The babe rolled, but at the same time, Mrs. Hawthorne grunted and drew in a sharp breath as another contraction came on. The woman's belly jostled as the babe gave a sharp kick.

Mrs. Hawthorne gasped. "My waters just broke!"

Del felt her shoulders sag. They'd failed. She exchanged a concerned look with Tamsyn. Shook her head.

It would be near impossible now to turn the child—and with as small as Evelyn was, also nearly impossible to birth this child.

Still, she'd felt the babe roll a good way before that contraction hit. Maybe . . .

"Oh!" Mrs. Hawthorne's eyes grew round. "Something feels different. Better. More like normal."

Del exchanged another look with Tamsyn. Could it be?

"Did it work?" Tamsyn asked, hope touching the words.

Del didn't have an answer. She set to cleaning the ointment off her hands. "Give me a moment and I'll check."

Chapter 5

From his place outside the Acheson wagon, where he stood watch over the pot of boiling water Striker had promised Tamsyn they would take care of, Jeremiah looked toward the Hawthorne wagon as many all around him did the same.

With the sides of the canvas rolled up, they could all see Del and Tamsyn, who stood in the aisle of the wagon, but Mrs. Hawthorne remained out of sight.

At first, only Del seemed to be snapping orders and leaning over the woman, but now both of them were doing so. However, after only a moment, the two women exchanged a defeated glance.

Frowning, he squinted back in the direction they'd come from. Still empty, just as it had been when he'd checked two minutes ago.

Not long after they'd left the fort, he'd ridden ahead and found Del's pack where Striker had said he'd left it. He'd then ridden on ahead and hidden it again under a weeping willow near a little creek he'd figured they'd pass today. But they hadn't yet reached that place.

It was all likely more precaution than they needed to take, but with a woman's life on the line, they wanted to be as careful as possible. Yet, with Del out in the open as she was now, if anyone rode into sight, it might be too late to hide her. Still, he had to admire her willingness to help a complete stranger.

As for her bag, did she need it? If so, would they be camping here for the night to allow Mrs. Hawthorne to labor? Cranston had said they should leave the Hawthornes behind if something like this happened, but he'd also put Striker in charge until his return, and Striker had said they would stay put until this babe was born.

Jeremiah should ride ahead for the pack. From the defeat in the women's shoulders, it seemed like they might be here for a while.

Del said something he couldn't hear and then bent over the area where he knew Mrs. Hawthorne labored on the bed in the wagon. Suddenly, Del stood upright and threw her arms around Tamsyn's shoulders. Tamsyn drew back, asked a question that Del replied to, and then the women were hugging and bouncing in the aisle of the wagon again.

Footsteps drew to a stop beside him, and Jeremiah realized he was grinning like a cat in a creamery when he glanced over to see a similar expression on Striker's face as he looked toward the wagon also.

"Seems the Lord had a plan bigger'n any of us could have guessed." Striker's drawl was always thicker when he was happy.

Jeremiah pondered how many strings the Lord had pulled to orchestrate them helping Del escape so that Del would be here at just the time when Mrs. Hawthorne and her family needed her. He angled his smile toward the sky, blinking back tears of happiness that the fellows always made fun of him for. But today, he didn't care. He sure did love serving a God who worked in such amazing ways!

Tamsyn's brother, Edi, shuffled up beside them. "Edi hungry."

Striker chuckled. "I think them women folk are gonna have their hands tied for a while yet, Edi. What say you and I take ourselves fishing? We can have ourselves a big ol' fish fry for lunch, hopefully in celebration of the arrival of a new little'n."

"Edi like fish." The big man who was Tamsyn's twin brother grinned from ear to ear. "Sure do like fish."

"All right then." Striker clapped him on one shoulder and started toward the Platte, already pulling that fishing hook from the little folded leather flap he kept in his back pocket for times such as this.

Jeremiah shook his head as Striker strode jauntily by Edi's side. The man sure did like to fish. Knowing him, there would be enough fish for every wagon in the train come evening. He might as well throw a mess of potatoes in the coals. That was something he couldn't very well mess up.

Chevonne, still kneeling by Mrs. Hubbard, had barely had time to grow weary of the morning sun beating her shoulders when the man on the pony that she'd seen earlier trotted back into the encampment. This time, he had Redd dragging from a long leather whip behind his paint. Redd gripped the whip with both hands, doing his best to make his breeches take the worst of the friction, but his face, torso, and arms had all been rubbed raw.

The native man trotted his pony until Redd came to a skidding halt in the grass before their kneeling party.

Chevonne swallowed, looking away from the bloody scrapes oozing on the man's back. But then her gaze involuntarily returned to the beaten man. The whip appeared to have been wrapped about him with much force, for it dug into skin that was already swelling around the constriction. Redd loosed his grip on the extension of the whip and slumped against the grass, apparently thankful his ride was concluded. He moaned and rested one cheek against the prairie with his hands settled on either side of his face. His eyes fell closed, and if it weren't for the bloody abrasions all over him, he would have looked like a man asleep on his stomach.

Ahead of him, the native who had dragged him into camp swung down from his horse. This man was younger and more lithe than the Indian who had pulled her from her wagon and from the one who stood before them. He was dressed similarly to the first, right down to the claw necklace around his throat—though his necklace bore many more claws than the flaccid man's.

Chevonne's eyes widened when the warrior withdrew a tomahawk from a strap at his waist and balanced its weight in his hand with a couple of tosses. From the mustang engraved into the head of the handle, she recognized it as the one Redd had stolen from the body on the scaffolding the day before.

The young warrior glanced toward the man who seemed to be in charge—the one with the feather headdress and the cold eyes.

The chief? *Oui*. She thought yes.

He gave a sedate nod.

There was a feral spark of pleasure in the young warrior's eyes before the tomahawk flew.

Chevonne gasped and covered her mouth with one hand.

Redd screamed and surged to his knees, clutching the bloody stumps of the two severed fingers on his right hand to his chest.

The young warrior stalked toward Redd and snatched the tomahawk from where it had stuck fast into the ground without taking his gaze off the wagon master.

"P-please," Redd begged. "I'll never touch an Injun grave again!"

The young warrior yanked Redd's head back and placed the blade of the tomahawk to the front of his scalp.

Chevonne tore her gaze to the trampled brown grass before her.

The chief spoke several quiet words. And then seemed to repeat the same phrase more insistently.

From her peripheral vision, Chevonne saw the younger warrior release Redd with a fierce shove.

She loosed a sigh of relief. It appeared their wagon master would get to keep his scalp.

Anger glittered in the young warrior's eyes, and he spat on the ground in front of Redd, contempt clear in his every action. Finally, he turned and stalked back to his horse, yanking his whip with him.

The whip unfurled from around Redd's body with a sharp *zipp*, and he bellowed in protest. Blood trickled down his ribs from the sliced circumference.

The chief said a few quiet words to his men and swung a gesture above his head. All the Indians began to mount up. Chevonne sighed in relief. Clearly, this *had* been about Redd taking that tomahawk the day before, and it seemed he was the only one who would be punished for the action.

Chevonne rose and reached a hand down to help Mrs. Hubbard to her feet. Her attention snagged on Missing-Tooth, who strode to his chief's side and spoke softly with a gesture in her direction.

Chevonne's eyes widened. *Non!* He wouldn't—

After assessing her with one more cold glance, the chief gave a single nod.

Chevonne felt a swirl of dizziness as Mrs. Hubbard labored to her feet and Missing-Tooth smiled and stalked toward her.

Before Chevonne could hardly fathom what was happening, the man had her by her arm and was hauling her toward a sway-backed pony that stood munching grass only paces from her wagon.

She glanced back toward the others. "Someone, help me, if you please!"

But everyone seemed focused on Redd. They surged around him, and Mrs. Hubbard pulled the strand of scarf from around her throat to wrap around Redd's hand.

Missing-Tooth grabbed her unceremoniously by one shoulder and her derrière and tossed her, belly-first, onto his pony. Chevonne was left clinging to the beast's mane so she didn't tumble off the other side and break her neck! Missing-Tooth set off at a steady lope across the prairie, leading his horse behind. The horse's bony shoulders gouged into her stomach.

Chevonne studied the ground slipping past. It was just grass. How hard could it be? If she tumbled just right...

She shoved herself forward and landed in a gangly heap. "Oof!"

The tumble was more violent than she'd expected! When she hit the ground, her arm twisted at an odd angle. As she rolled, a rock gouged into her shoulder, and another into the small of her back. She tried to scramble to her feet, but her skirts tangled her legs. And when she looked up, the pony was pawing the air above her!

"*Non*!" Chevonne shot one arm above her head, but too late, the pony's hoof clunked into her temple. Pain shot through her head, the prairie spun like a whirligig, and then blackness overcame her.

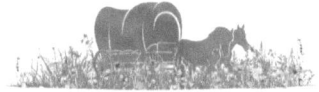

Cody Hawkeye wished Cranston had chosen one of the other scouts to remain with him and watch the hanging. He'd witnessed his fair share already and could go a whole lifetime without seeing another. Nevertheless, he plunked his buckskin-clad backside into one of the white wooden chairs the soldiers had arranged in a gallery of sorts before the gallows.

Cranston scooted into the chair beside him. "Back row? You sure you don't want to be right up close to all the action?"

Cody only grunted. He didn't appreciate the humor, considering a man was about to die. He clasped his hands before himself and held his silence, willing away the unwanted images of his uncle dangling in the breeze beneath an Oregon oak.

All around them, others from the fort began to mosey into their chairs. Noticeably absent was Boone Baxter.

Cody couldn't blame the man. He wouldn't want to be present at his own brother's hanging—not that either Colt or Creed would do anything to warrant a hanging. But neither had Uncle. Cody had only been eleven when the man had been sentenced for horse thieving, and the punishment carried out before anyone could do anything about it. The horse thief had been captured with the stolen mounts still in his possession only a week later. He, too, had been summarily dispatched. But it had been too late for Uncle.

At least this time, he knew the man sentenced to die was guilty of the charges. He'd been there himself yesterday and helped rescue the kidnapped minister's wife and the children the man had absconded with.

As though his thoughts of the man had conjured him, Brad Baxter was led by two soldiers from a building down the way with his hands tied behind his back. An elderly woman—the proprietress of the mercantile, if Cody wasn't mistaken—walked by his side. And to his surprise, the colonel walked stiffly behind.

"All rise!" A man in a white periwig had climbed onto the gallows platform. He unfurled a document as Brad's guards pulled him to a stop a few paces from the base of the gallows steps.

"Hear ye, hear ye! Be it known, Bradley Conan Baxter, that you have been sentenced to hang for crimes of murder, thieving, and kidnapping. Sentence to be carried out on this fifth day of May in the year of our Lord 1853. May God have mercy on your soul!"

The soldiers on either side of him nudged him forward, but Brad resisted.

"Boone, please. You have to do something!" Brad's boots skidded across the grass of the parade ground as the two soldiers bodily lifted him and carried him forward.

Boone didn't speak. Cody watched him walk to a chair in the front row of the gathering and sink into it. Though he sat stiffly in his uniform, he looked pale and shaken. Was it his brother's hanging he was worried about or the missing slave he'd come looking for earlier this morning? That had been the first time Cody had noticed him looking ready to come apart at the seams. He was glad they had helped her make her escape.

Brad planted his feet against the front edges of the stairs and fought every step of the way. At one point, Cody thought all three men would fall off the gallows steps, but the two soldiers prevailed and finally hauled Brad onto the gallows platform.

A man wearing a black hood over his head tromped up the stairs and slipped the noose over Brad's head.

Cody looked at the ground between his moccasins. He kept his gaze there as the sound of the trapdoor releasing and the gasp from the audience told him the deed was done. At least the hanging had been quick, as promised by the colonel when he'd been at the wagons this morning. Now Cody and Cranston could be on their way back to join the caravan, and hopefully the rest of this journey would go smoother than this first part of it had. Between that Donahue fellow and now Brad Baxter, they'd seen more than their fair share of trouble on this trip! Cody remained as he was, quietly studying a ladybug that crawled on a blade of grass until Cranston stirred beside him.

"Well, I'm glad to say we'll be able to report to the Houstons that they won't have to worry about that sorry cuss anymore."

Cody nodded, face still to the ground. "Can we go now?"

At the back of the parade ground, a shout rose up, accompanied by the sound of thundering hooves. Everyone turned to look.

A pale man with hair so blond it was nearly the color of fresh milk, hauled his lathered mount to a stop. "Indians!" He gasped.

Cody's eyes fell closed. *Stay out of it.*

"We was attacked only a few miles back. They chopped off our wagon master's fingers—and that was after they dragged him around the prairie behind a horse like a plow! Also, one of our party has been kidnapped!" As if to emphasize his point, the man pointed to where a group of wagons straggled into the clearing, where only a bit ago, Cranston's own wagon train had departed. Sitting beside the driver on the front bench of the first wagon was a man who cradled a hand wrapped in a bloody rag.

A rumble of outrage traversed the gathered soldiers.

"And what did this wagon master do to provoke this attack?" Cody suddenly realized he was on his feet and all eyes were on him.

Blast it. Hadn't he just been telling himself to stay out of it?

When the two women set to hugging and laughing and jumping in the wagon, Declan Boyle felt a smile stretch his lips. Relief swept through him, and he knew he needed to find Wren Hawthorne. She would be so thrilled to know things seemed to have taken a good turn with her ma.

He'd seen her run off toward the riverbank earlier, but had figured she wanted some time alone, or she would have stayed with her siblings and father, who were all huddled in the shade of a cottonwood not too far from the Hawthorne wagon, with Whitley acting the mother hen. Whitley was always the stronger of the two—more in control of her emotions, to his way of thinking. Wren needed more support and encouragement.

He didn't think he was the only one surprised to see the black woman in the back with Wren's ma. He'd seen a few folk exchanging glances when the sides of that oilcloth had been rolled up.

It made him smile even bigger to think of helping the woman escape from the fort. She was obviously the one the soldiers had been searching for this morning, and she'd evidently been hiding in the Hawthorne wagon, using the woman's labor as a cloak!

Now, he couldn't wait to bring Wren the news that her ma was likely going to be fine.

He turned and jogged toward the river. He'd seen the approximate area where she'd slipped through the brush, likely to sit like she was wont to do with her arms wrapped around her knees as she stared at the moving water, which often calmed her.

"Wren?!" He parted the leaves between two chokecherry bushes, didn't see her, and moved on down to the next likely spot. She'd slipped down to the water somewhere in this area. He felt certain she hadn't been much farther downstream. "Wren?"

This time, when he parted the brush, he did find her. But she wasn't alone. She stood on a flat spot on the riverbank below, wrapped in the arms of Royal Carter.

Declan froze. Not wanting to see the sight before him, and yet unable to step back and leave them be. Royal Carter was a lanky man in his twenties—older than Wren by several years. But Declan had heard Wren twittering to Whitley about how handsome he was on more than one occasion, and it seemed the man had won out over Declan in her estimation.

He felt like the biggest of fools. Here he'd been harboring feelings for her, and there she stood in another man's arms. An older man's arms.

A man who would get a quarter section on his own, but a half section if he had a wife.

Declan swallowed the bitter thought. He shouldn't paint Royal with such a harsh brush. After all, Declan was interested in Wren, and it had nothing to do with getting more land—of course, he wasn't old enough to be granted any land yet. He still had a year and a half before he would be eighteen. Still, he could imagine Royal *could* be in love with Wren simply for love's sake and not for any ulterior motives.

As for Wren's feelings for Royal . . . The man was tall and strong and had saved up to buy his own rig. He would at least have a place to start once he reached Oregon—unlike Declan. Of course, Wren would look up to a man like that.

And yet . . . There was something about Royal that set Declan's teeth on edge—something other than jealousy, though he'd have to admit to feeling plenty of that.

The couple was so engrossed with one another that they hadn't even noticed him standing here. Declan cleared his throat.

Royal released her like a man caught with his hand in the bank's register. Wren's face immediately flushed red. She hung her head and nipped at her lower lip.

"Wanted tae let you ken that your ma took a turn for the guid. Leastwise, I'm fairly certain. The midwives were a'jiggin' a moment ago." He hated that his brogue seemed to thicken whenever Wren was around. He'd been working on his English pronunciation with her and with Whitley, but from all appearances, those lessons might be over, at least the ones with Wren.

Wren's red-rimmed eyes widened. "Ma's better?! And the baby?"

Declan lifted one shoulder. "Haven't heard anythin' aboot the babe yet, but my guess is you'll soon be havin' that wee sibling ye were so happy for." He stepped back.

Royal grinned down at Wren. "A wee sibling! What do ye think o' that?" His forced accent was an obvious attempt to mock Declan.

But Declan refused to lower himself to the man's level. If Wren wanted Royal, then Declan wasn't going to stand in her way. "Anyhow, juist thought ye should ken."

Should he leave them unsupervised? Wren's pa certainly wouldn't like her gallivanting all over the country with Royal and no chaperone. But Declan wanted no part in nannying the pair o' them.

Despite that, he lingered on the embankment. And the longer he lingered, the narrower Royal's eyes grew.

Which made Declan content to stay right where he was. Yet after another couple of moments, the manners Willow had been trying to instill in him took over.

"Right. I'll see ye both back at camp then. Would ye like tae come wi' me noo, Wren?" He hated how apparent his hopefulness was in his tone.

She started toward him, but Royal snatched her hand and held her in place. His gaze remained fixed on Declan.

"We'll be right along," he said dismissively.

Now it was Declan's turn for narrowed eyes. But he didn't want to fight the man. Royal was twice his weight and had a good six inches on him.

He looked at Wren. "Ye dandy?"

Royal's jaw dropped. "Of course she's 'dandy.'"

The man took a step forward, but Wren put one palm against his chest and said something too quietly for Declan to hear.

"You got something to say to me?" Royal snapped, eyes still fixed on Declan.

Declan kept his gaze on Wren, willing her to trust him. To come with him.

But she only nodded her head. "I'll be right there, Dec. Thanks for coming to let me know. It's such a relief."

Reluctantly, after one more glower in Royal's direction, which only gained him another smirk, Declan turned and started away. He shook the trembling from his fingers and willed down the wild pounding of his heart. He'd like to go back there and give Royal a drubbin', and that was the truth of it!

Behind him, he heard Royal's derisive chuckle, but thankfully, the quiet rushing of the river kept him from hearing the man's words. Otherwise, he might have been tempted into something he'd regret.

Mebbe.

Nae.

I wouldnae likely regret it a'tall.

He kept walking.

Chapter 6

Cody swallowed. He hadn't meant to blurt his challenge, but maybe it was good that he had. These folk were coming west, where they would run into many more tribes. It was best they learn the customs of the peoples whose land they planned to traverse so they didn't get themselves—or others—killed.

He waited, seeing the uneasy way several in the newly arrived wagon train shifted and refused to meet his gaze after his question. So, he was right. Someone in the wagon train had done something to instigate the attack. Imagine that.

"What provoked the attack?" he repeated. In this area, it was likely the Sioux they'd run up against.

An older woman stepped forward. "Redd there—" She pointed to the man with the missing fingers. "—took a hatchet off a fresh Indian grave we came across."

"Hush up, woman!" The man who seemed to have dubbed himself the spokesman in place of the moaning wagon master glowered at her. "He didn't do nothing what deserved having his fingers chopped off!"

Cody stepped into the grassy aisle from the row of chairs where he'd been standing. That served to keep his back to the corpse, which he didn't imagine anyone had bothered to take down yet. "If you desecrated a Sioux graveyard, you're lucky any of you were left alive, much less all of you. The Sioux believe a burial ground is sacred. The place where fallen warriors can find their way from this world into the next."

A murmur of disapproval traversed those gathered, and Cody shot up one hand. "You might not believe that to be true, but the tribe does, and to their way of thinking, his two fingers—" He pointed to the moaning man. "—are a small payment for maybe condemning the man they mourn to wander the plains for eternity."

"Oh, falderal!" The spokesman complained. "Whoever heard of such foolishness? Who are you anyway?" His lip curled as he gave Cody a once-over. "You look exactly like those men who attacked us!"

Cody didn't move, but maintained eye contact. He didn't owe the man any explanations as to who he was. Most of these soldiers had witnessed his part in Mrs. Houston's rescue yesterday and knew he was one of Caesar's scouts.

Caesar stepped forward, with one hand resting casually on the butt of his pistol. "This here is one of the best men I know, and ought not to be confused with anyone else on account of his skin color and long black hair!"

With a sweeping glance at Caesar's height and broad shoulders, and then the position of his hand, the spokesman backed up a step, making no reply.

The fort's doctor arrived with his medical bag, and several people helped the wounded man down from the wagon's bench. When the doctor pulled the rag away to get a look, the man set to caterwauling worse than a pair of hungry barn cats.

"What about the person who was taken?" Cranston asked.

Yeah. That too. Cody supposed he should have gotten to that question by now. But it irritated him that those who came west in the name of a loving God often seemed so indifferent and callous to the ways of the people who had lived on the land before them. Sure, because of what was taught in the Bible, it might seem foolish to think someone would believe a warrior could be stuck wandering the plains.

Still . . . they believed their God had made all people, didn't they? So, couldn't they fathom that maybe God also valued different cultures? At least love people enough to have a conversation with them about what the Bible taught that was different? These were the questions he had pondered at the mission school he'd attended as a boy.

All the wagon train folk seemed interested in what the doctor was planning to do about the wagon master's fingers.

Cody frowned when he realized no one had responded about the captured member of their party. "What about the one they took?" He pressed more loudly than Cranston had.

The blond spokesman waved a hand. "Just some Frenchwoman. We didn't have no time to go after her what with Redd maybe dying. She joined our train at the last minute and has mostly kept to herself. Don't know aught about her."

Cody sighed and exchanged a look with Cranston.

Cranston wagged his head. "Would hate to think what those Sioux might be planning to do with such a woman. Could be planning to offer her as a slave to appease the family of the desecrated warrior."

Cody sighed. "Guess we aren't heading back to our wagon train right away."

"Could you live with yourself if you did?" Cranston cocked one brow at him.

Cody grunted. He spun to face the gallows and forced himself to take a look at the body hanging there. If anyone wanted assurances that Baxter had hung, he wanted to be able to say he'd seen it with his own eyes. After satisfying himself that the man was indeed dead, he turned and strode toward their horses. "Best we get a move on then."

Boone couldn't find it in himself to be worried about a party of travelers who had been foolish enough to desecrate a Sioux graveyard. He sat in the front row, with Betsy by his side, until the fort's physician finally finished patching up the man's missing fingers and saw to the lowering of Brad's body. Now, several men were carting his corpse down the gallows steps.

As he sat beside Betsy in the front row with most everyone else dispersed, she laid a hand on his shoulder.

"I'm right sorry, Boone. Right sorry. No matter what he done, he was family, and it hurts to lose him."

He glanced at her and took note of the dampness around her eyes. She'd been a good sister-in-law to him. And was the only family he had now.

Well, except for that babe.

His teeth ground together so tight his jaw ached. The ungrateful little whore. He'd fed her. Clothed her. Sheltered her. Even given her a child. And she'd repaid him by running off? Running off and taking his child!

It vexed him.

He coughed and pounded his fist to his chest. For several days, anxiety had been tightening his chest and making him constantly feel like he needed more air. What he needed was less stress and a stretch of days where he would get more than a few hours of sleep each night, yet now, he'd have to track Delilah.

How had she gotten free?

His gaze settled once more on Betsy. Could she have . . . No. Surely not.

"How'd she get free, Betsy? How did that little devil get free?"

Betsy shifted and looked over at him, then turned her gaze back to the doctor and his men, who were transferring Brad's body to the coffin someone had built from old pine boards. "Could one of your men have seen her and developed a soft spot for her, do you think?"

That thought hit him in the gut.

He'd been careful to keep his little Delilah out of sight. But there was one small window in the basement wall. Could one of the men have seen her in there? Any number of them, he supposed. She was a beauty. She'd even turned his head, after all.

He rose and pivoted to study the group of soldiers who were still taking statements from the new arrivals about the Indian attack. He would have to grill them about their involvement, and it would take time he didn't have.

He muttered a curse beneath his breath.

The crazy thing was, she'd simply vanished! When he walked into the basement this morning and seen that she was gone, such a terrible rage had filled him that he'd felt a physical pain in his chest. But then he'd taken a moment to assess. He'd felt certain he would find her hiding in one of those wagons this morning, but even though he'd trained his men well and knew they were quite thorough in their searching, they'd turned up nothing.

His fists clenched.

When he got his hands on her, she was finished! Well, maybe after she gave birth to his child.

The child would be tainted, that was true. Tainted by her blood.

But it was still his child.

After, he'd take his sweet time paying her back for all the angst she'd put him through.

To do that, he had to find her. With this business about Brad now concluded, he could devote his whole effort to the task.

If only he had hounds! Back east on the plantation where he'd grown up, they'd utilized dogs often to track runaways. But out here on the edge of nowhere, he hadn't been granted access to any.

By the time he got some, it would be too late for tracking little Delilah, but he'd send for some pups and a competent trainer anyhow. Next time, he wouldn't be caught unprepared.

"Johnson!" he snapped at the nearest soldier. "My office. I have some questions."

The baby came squalling into the world under the denim skies of early evening. A little girl with a headful of dark brown curls and pink fists balled in defiance of the prairie breeze.

"There now. Almost done." Deliverance couldn't believe how perfect the tiny girl was. Ten tiny toes, wrinkly and pink. One strawberry-colored angel kiss on the top of one chubby, round shoulder. Del wanted to drop her own kiss on that spot, but the babe's mama was waiting. Warm water waited in a nearby basin, and Tamsyn quickly washed and wrapped the little one in a tight swaddle while Del, after instructing that the sides of the canvas should be lowered, helped Evelyn into clean clothes. When Tamsyn passed the baby to her, the child was suckling miserably on her first two inadequate fingers.

Deliverance didn't think she'd ever smiled so big as she did when she looked down at that tiny, scrunched face. When she laid the little pink-cheeked infant on her mother's chest and covered her with the quilt that had been waiting for her, Evelyn pressed a kiss to the mop of still damp curls, her own brow damp with sweat.

"You're a wonder," the woman smiled tiredly at Deliverance.

She only shook her head. "You did all the work. Now I think there are a few folk chomping at the bit in excitement to see this mite." She squeezed Evelyn's hand and stepped back.

She and Tamsyn barely had time to exit the wagon before the whole passel of the Hawthorne children had piled in to view their new sister.

After she jumped to the grass, Deliverance hesitated nearby. With dusk rapidly falling, the open prairie didn't feel like such a threat, still, she wasn't certain where she should go. She really had no home here. No wagon. Not even a change of clothing. What should she do now? She'd been so concentrated on the birthing for these past several hours that she hadn't even had time to consider what might come next.

Across the center of the circled wagons, Jeremiah stood next to a fire that glowed bright in the gloaming. He lifted one hand and motioned her toward him, but before she could even take a step, Tamsyn looped her arm through Del's.

"Come to my fire and we'll get something to eat. We'll figure things out from there." She must not have seen Jeremiah's gesture.

Torn over what to do, Del glanced back at Jeremiah, and he smiled, nodded, and swung a motion to indicate she should go on with Tamsyn. He pointed to himself, and then to a fire a few down from his. An indication that he would join her there? A boy approached his side, drawing his attention.

Tamsyn was still talking. "But first, I have to express my gratitude. I honestly think that child would have died if you hadn't been here."

And her mother, too. Del simply nodded, feeling surprisingly ill-equipped to know how to respond to the appreciation.

As she walked by Tamsyn's side, her legs weary from a long day of activity she wasn't used to, she looked up to find Mr. Hawthorne in their path and looking right at her. He stepped forward, and Del hesitated. His blue eyes shimmered, red-rimmed and watery in the evening light. He sniffed and glanced from Del to the wagon where his children exclaimed in excitement over their new little sister, blinked hard a couple of times, and then returned his gaze to hers. A smile tilted his lips. He nodded. Then nodded again more firmly and held out one hand.

Surprise shot through Del, and she reached to accept his handshake before she even realized she was doing so.

He pumped her hand with gusto, clasping the back of it with his other hand. "Only the one, then?"

Del smiled, taking in the passel of twins swirling in and out of the wagon. "Only the one."

After another nod, he headed toward his wagon, thumbing at his eyes.

Deliverance smiled, and weariness hit her. She'd not slept for more than a couple of hours the night before, nor was she used to standing, bending, talking, and worrying for hours on end. With the adrenaline wearing off, she wanted nothing more than to collapse into a heap and sleep the night away. However, Evelyn's apron was soiled. She would have to find time to slip down to the river to wash it at some point later tonight, after the others were asleep.

The man named Striker waited for them at the fire Tamsyn led her to, and Del glanced in surprise between them. Was he her husband?

The man reached for two plates and set to forking something from the cast iron pan over the fire onto each.

Tamsyn stiffened and released her arm. "Mr. Moss. Thank you for watching Edi today."

There was a hitch in Striker's movements. He glanced up and narrowed a look on Tamsyn.

Ah, not her husband then. Perhaps only a man who hoped to be her beau?

The man tossed his head to sweep a shag of too-long brown hair from his eyes as though to shake off Tamsyn's cold greeting. "My pleasure." He held out two plates, one to each of them. "Edi and I went fishing and caught a whole mess of catfish."

Tamsyn took the plate gingerly, as though to ensure her fingers didn't brush his, and retreated to the other side of the flames.

"And Jeremiah cooked up those potatoes. It's not much, but it's filling." Striker's disappointed gaze followed Tamsyn's retreat, even while he still held a plate toward Deliverance.

As she accepted it, her stomach rumbled embarrassingly loudly.

Striker returned his attention to her and smiled. "Seems it's a good thing we took the initiative to make dinner. We wouldn't want our most recent heroes to go hungry, now would we, Edi?"

Across the fire, a burly man with a mop of dark brown hair sat on a large stone, staring into the glow. "Nope" was all he said.

"Thank you for the food, Mr. Moss." Tamsyn's words were clipped and rapid-fire. "I'm sure you have many things you need to be doing. I do appreciate that you took time with Edi today."

"Actually, I don't—"

"Deliverance," Tamsyn continued, cutting the man off. "This is my brother, Edison."

"Pleased to meet you." Del clasped her plate in both hands and gave a little dip of her knees, but curiosity had her glancing between Mr. Moss and Tamsyn. The man hung his head and draped his hands against his hips. He prodded the toe of his boot at the end of a log protruding from the fire pit. Tamsyn seemed intent on looking anywhere but in Mr. Moss's direction.

The tension around the fire was almost as dense as the pound cake Mama used to make.

"Evening, folks."

Jeremiah's low voice rumbled from right behind her, nearly making her drop her plate of vittles as she spun to face him with a gasp. Her piece of catfish slid dangerously close to the edge of her plate.

She reached to stop its slide at the same time Mr. Jackson's reflexes had him doing the same. His hand settled over hers, sending a zip of apprehension through her. Not fear exactly, but something close enough to it that she felt a tight coil of unease in her stomach. However, before she could protest, he was already withdrawing.

"Sorry about that." He stopped a respectful distance away and clasped his hands behind his leather duster.

Deliverance wished she could feel something other than cold horror in the presence of a handsome man such as this. And yet, after her years with Boone, panic was all she seemed able to muster. She gave her head a shake. All these thoughts proved she was naught but the fool Boone had constantly claimed her to be. Jeremiah hadn't even hinted at interest. He was a gentleman, and as such, he'd been duty-bound to help her escape from Boone. His kindness and consideration were something she hadn't experienced in quite some time, that was all.

She realized her heart was racing and drew in a slow breath to ease it. Now, who was feeling tense? She almost smirked at herself.

Heavens. She really needed to rein in her runaway thoughts.

She withdrew a step and licked the catfish grease from her thumb. For some reason, Jeremiah's gaze lingered intently on the movement. So intently that she found herself brushing at the corners of her mouth to make sure she hadn't left a crumb of corn flour there.

He cleared his throat and retreated another step, yanking his focus to the stars beginning to pierce the canopy above. "Ah." He snatched off his hat, swept one hand over his head, and resettled it again. "I think it might be best if we get you into the wagon since we won't be able to see if anyone is coming." His gesture encompassed the prairie all around them.

And just like that, her earlier fears resurrected. Here she had been thinking of the darkness as a friend, and yet it would also cloak anyone who might approach. Deliverance lost her appetite. She would have happily complied with his request except she had no place to go. "Anyplace on the ground beneath a wagon will do, but I am afraid a weariness has settled over me. I've not been used to—" She stopped herself before the word *freedom* popped from her lips and instead settled on, "—so much activity." She didn't want to seem like she was angling for sympathy.

Firelight glinted off a muscle that bulged at the back of Jeremiah's jaw. "I'm sure you are exhausted. It's been a long day. Since we stopped for such a length of time today, we'll want to get an early start, so you can eat your food here or bring your plate to the wagon and eat inside."

She recognized the hopeful note in his voice and felt renewed concern prickle along the back of her neck. She scanned the darkness of the perimeter. Was he truly worried that Boone might ride up on them in the night and see her here? Perfect. That made her even more terrified. After all, she knew Boone well enough to know he wouldn't be willing to let her escape go. He would hunt her until he found her.

Her mouth went dry. She leaned to set her plate on one of the stones near the fire, not wanting to take one of Tamsyn's plates with her. "Perhaps at a wagon would be best. At least . . . somewhere away from firelight?"

"Yes'm." Jeremiah nodded and intercepted her plate. "I'll carry this for you." He stretched out one arm. "This way, if you don't mind."

Del turned to Mr. Moss. "Thank you kindly for the fish, Mr. Moss, sir."

His expression seemed flinty, but she didn't feel like any animosity was directed at her. "Mr. Moss was my father. Just Striker will do." For some reason, his gaze flicked irritably off of Tamsyn as he said the words, but he was smiling when he turned back to Del. "Have a good evening. I hope you sleep well." He offered a sketch of a bow.

Del blinked, not sure what to think about a white man who treated her like a lady. But it was the mention of sleep that made a thought hit her as she followed Jeremiah's broad shoulders through the rapidly falling dusk!

Last night, he had slept in the aisle of the wagon. That hadn't bothered her, considering she'd been so fearful of Boone at the time and so weary from her day of escape and hiding. But . . . Would the man expect similar arrangements this evening? Where did he plan for her to sleep?

Gracious! She didn't want to seem ungrateful, but neither did she want to share a wagon with a man she wasn't married to!

She'd already been forced to do that by one man.

As long as she had her freedom, she would never be forced to do such a thing again!

Chapter 7

Tamsyn wished Jer and Del hadn't left so quickly, leaving her here with none but Edi as a buffer between her and Striker—no, not Striker. Mr. Moss. *Mr. Moss!* She plunked her plate on the tailgate of the wagon and clamped her teeth together.

The man was as stubborn and insistent as they came. But this was all her fault. If only she could bring herself to tell him the real reason why he needed to stay away. She hadn't been able to shake thoughts of Sam—the man she'd loved with all her heart and who she'd *thought* had loved her in return—since he'd come to mind when she'd seen Del's wrists. This morning, she'd been feeling vulnerable and had let Striker get too close. It was for his own good that she was keeping him at arm's length. Besides the danger that might be chasing her, the man had no understanding of the future she'd taken on when she'd sacrificed everything to be Edi's caretaker.

It was a sacrifice she had been more than happy to make, but now, she was beginning to see the costs.

Striker hadn't moved. He remained standing quietly across the fire with his head down, and she felt frozen in place as well, standing by Edi's side.

Her conscience pricked her for the stiff way she'd responded to him, and after he'd helped keep an eye on Edi all day.

She pressed the backs of her fingers together and then laced them into a tight clasp. She willed her thumbs not to fidget. "I do mean my thanks to you for keeping an eye on Edi today, Mr. Moss. It was a great relief to my mind to have him taken care of while I helped with the birthing."

His head snapped up, and his eyes narrowed slightly.

She took a breath and waited for his response.

His gaze never left hers. The glow of the fire flickered off his features, golden and bright against his cheeks, nose, and forehead, but disappearing into the dark stubble on his jaw and the shadows beneath the hat he'd pushed back on his head. He clasped his hands behind his back and rocked into his heels. "I sense a 'however' coming."

"Y-yes." She lowered her gaze to her hands. "I'm not quite sure how to say what I need to say without sounding ungrateful."

"What is once spoken can never be retracted. Sometimes words are better left unsaid."

Had his shoulders slumped slightly as he said those words? She wasn't sure what had her feeling his dejection to her very core.

"S-sometimes they need to be said." She closed her eyes. She couldn't stutter her way through this. Footsteps crunched, and her eyes flew open.

In three swift strides, he was around the fire and standing before her.

She withdrew a step but then felt foolish when she saw he'd stopped. Of course, he hadn't been advancing on her to, well . . . She willed away the heat in her face. There was no fear of him kissing her without her permission. Only the fear of how he tempted her heart. Tempted her to saddle him with a burdened future—the rest of his life—of caring for Edison. Not a moment of freedom. Not a moment of resting without half an ear listening to make sure Edison hadn't risen to wander off or find some mischief. And always the myriad of moments of wondering if Sam might catch up to them.

Striker's brow ticked when she withdrew. His hands returned to a clasp behind his back, but he continued to look down at her as he said, "Edison? Remember that pile of brush we broke up?"

"Uh-huh."

"Fetch an armful for your sister, please. You can set it there with the other wood. She can use it as kindling to restart the fire come morning."

She can use it... Tamsyn wasn't sure if those last words were spoken to her or to Edison. Disappointment clogged her throat. Either way, he was letting her know he wouldn't be by to start her fire in the morning. For the past several days, she'd emerged from her wagon to find her cook-fire already crackling steadily. Several mornings, he'd lingered and shared coffee with her. She'd been careful to maintain her distance but had been ever so thankful for the company. And of course, she now realized she'd been fooling herself. How could she think otherwise? Her allowing him to linger and chat was what had given rise to this morning's faux pas of letting him so close.

Now, as Edi rose, said "all right," and shuffled off, Tamsyn felt her palms turn clammy, and she could feel her pulse beating at the base of her throat. Having Edi here had at least been *some* buffer. Now she had no buffer at all. Yet she must find her courage. For Striker's sake.

Striker's gaze intensified. He scrubbed the side of his first finger along his jaw, resettled his hat, and clasped his hands behind his back again. His shoulders stiffened, and he seemed to be braced for impact. "Have your say, Tam, but I'll not be apologizing for this morning."

She fidgeted. She hadn't meant to, but the man made her positively antsy. "I don't have anything to say that I haven't already said in the past. This morning, I was tired, distressed, anxious." She waved away her list of excuses for why she'd allowed him to get so close earlier. "You were kind, and I thank you for that, however ... Well ..." She looked away, unable to see the hurt in his eyes. "For your own good, I'm asking you to maintain your distance, Mr. Moss."

"For my own good?"

"Yes. You know why." She swept a lame gesture to where Edi had disappeared into the darkness. Of course, she couldn't lay out the real reason, or he would be even more insistent that she needed his help and that might get him killed in the long run.

Striker's eyes narrowed. His jaw bulged. And for the first time, Tamsyn feared she may have finally gotten through to him. "You seem to think I would find life with your brother a burden. Maybe because it's how you view him yourself. That's your own affair. Not mine. I enjoyed my time with him today. He's got a good heart which simply needs redirecting from time to time. And I'm tired of being reminded what a burden he is. I assume he's tired of it too. Now, I'm going to distance myself from your fire before my words get away from me. Good evening, Miss Acheson."

With that, he turned and stalked into the night, leaving her feeling weak with the impact of his words. He didn't know her true motives—of course, he couldn't. But was he right about her treatment of and feelings toward her brother?

Were her thoughts about Edison wrong? Maybe he'd only been living up to her expectations? She'd been caring for his every need like he was a child—since he *was* a child, in point of fact—and yet, even now Edi returned and placed the armful of small sticks he'd fetched in the exact right spot.

Feeling a tremor sweep through her, she smiled at him. "Thanks, Edi."

He nodded, then glanced toward the darkness. "Striker gone?"

She sighed. Yes. She feared he was gone. Gone for good this time. Of course, they would see him daily, but there was more than one kind of way to be gone. She only nodded.

Edi sighed. "I like him. He's better than Sam."

Tamsyn jolted at that. It was the first time she'd ever heard Edi mention him. That thought also gave her pause, because he often spoke of Striker when he wasn't around.

"I'm going to sleep." Edi tromped to his hammock.

"Okay. Night." She wished those two words hadn't sounded so broken.

Edi shuffled to his bed in the hammock beneath the wagon and tumbled into it, then pulled his quilt up over his shoulders.

Tamsyn folded her arms and stared into the glowing embers of the fire. Sam was a problem she wouldn't soon be able to solve, if ever. And Striker Moss had a lot of nerve challenging her treatment of her brother when he himself had talked to Edi like he was a child a time or two. Who was he to stand in judgment when she had been living with her brother for his entire life? Who knew his dependencies better than her?

Anger began to roil. She felt a swirl of it in the pit of her stomach, and then a wave of hot tremors swept outward and all through her until she felt heat radiating from her face and hands. The nerve of the man to almost not let her join the wagon train because of Edi, but then tell her she was mistreating him!

The next time she had a few minutes alone with the man, she would not hesitate to give him a piece of her mind!

Despite her anger, as Tamsyn stood staring into the dying embers of the fire, she suddenly felt like she might have pushed away her last hope. Striker, after all, had been a great help to her these past few weeks.

She drew in a long, slow, calming breath before blowing it out between tightly pursed lips.

His response was proof she'd been right not to let him get close! Her conscience pricked her. She was judging him unfairly. But she didn't care! The man had her riled worse than a bear with cubs!

She ought to sleep, but there was no way she'd be able to sleep right now. With a grunt of irritation, she turned for the wagon. She wanted to gather some clothes to share with Deliverance and needed to take them to her wagon before crawling onto her own tick for the night.

Then, she would endeavor not to cry herself to sleep. But with as angry and tired as she felt, there were no guarantees.

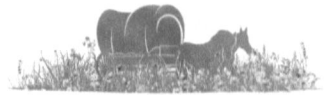

Jeremiah was relieved to reach the Slade wagon. He'd felt an itch crawling down the center of his back all day. They may have escaped Colonel Baxter once, but that didn't mean the man wouldn't turn back up.

He had set a crate on the ground, ready to act as a step for Del, and he motioned to it now, still holding her plate so she could use both hands to climb inside.

But instead of entering the wagon like he hoped she would, she plunked her hands on her hips and turned to face him. "I don't mean to be rude, but I feel there is something we should speak of right away."

Jeremiah frowned. For being such a petite package, she looked mighty intimidating standing there with her hands on her hips like that. "Go on."

She suddenly didn't seem to want to meet his gaze. She turned her attention toward the river. "Last night, well, last night was unusual. And I know I took your bed inside." She scanned the surrounding area. "But I truly am h-happy to sleep on the ground somewhere."

Ah, that was what had her concerned. His estimation of her grew because of it. "Miss you really don't—"

"Maybe under that tree there? It would offer shelter and some cover if M-Master B-Boone arrives in the n-night."

"He's not your master anymore." Jeremiah stepped forward. "Besides, what kind of a gentleman would I be if I left you to sleep under a tree?" He hoped the humor he infused into the words would set her at ease.

Her gaze once more settled against his. "I know last night you didn't—Well, that is, I just wouldn't feel comfortable—"

"Deliverance." When she waited, he pushed the food toward her and motioned toward the crate. "Set yourself down there. There's no fire here, so no one will be able to see you from a distance, and no need for too much concern. The night watch will give a shout if anyone comes moseying around."

He was thankful when she took the plate and sank to a seat.

"As to your, ah, concerns . . . This wagon belonged to a party who were killed by Brad Baxter. We came upon their train and rescued their children. I drive it by day but generally sleep beneath it most nights—the storm last night being the lone exception. The boys, well, they haven't been ready to face the memories in this place, and they sleep with the Houstons. I already spoke to them, and they say it's fine for you to sleep inside."

She poked at the fish and potatoes. He wished she'd eat something.

"I see." She lifted soulful eyes to him. "And if another storm comes?"

"Striker has a wagon he'd be happy to share with me. Last night, I was already in and changed into my dry clothes, not to mention beat off my feet. I should have thought that I was making you uncomfortable, and I apologize for that."

"No. I didn't think of it at the time. It's just . . ." Her attention drifted the perimeter of the other wagons. "I wouldn't want folk to think that—" She dropped her attention to her plate and prodded at the potatoes again, still without taking a bite.

Wouldn't want folks to think they were unwed and sharing a bed? He wouldn't want that either. "I can assure you your reputation is safe with me."

She flicked her gaze to his, then off toward the river. Was there something he was missing here?

She didn't offer anything more, other than, "Thank you for your understanding." She put the plate aside and rose. Reaching behind herself, she set to untying the strings of her apron. "If you'll forgive me, I find myself quite exhausted, but I need to mosey on down to the river to wash this apron before I sleep. I'm afraid delivering babies isn't the cleanest of work. Borrowed this from Mrs. Hawthorne and would like to give it back come morning."

Jeremiah frowned. His gaze slipped over her before he thought better of it. And then betrayed him and traveled right past all those moonlit curves to her face again. Too late, he realized he hadn't been paying much attention to the state of her apron, but it was best he not look again, considering his palms were already sweating and he likely wouldn't be able to see what concerned her in the dark anyhow. Besides, she was pulling it off over her head now anyway.

If she were anything like his ma, she'd want a quick wash in the river herself if she went down to wash that apron, and the thought of standing guard while she washed in the river made his pulse race—not because he'd be watching, mind, but simply because . . . Well, hang it, he didn't rightly know why and probably shouldn't be pondering on it anyhow!

Despite that, he couldn't very well let her go wash without a guard, now could he? And he didn't trust anyone else in the camp to do as good a job keeping watch as he himself would. Well, except maybe Striker or Cody, but Striker had his own concerns tonight, it had seemed, and Cody wasn't here.

When she turned toward the water, he sighed and reached to nudge her plate toward her again. "Will you at least eat a little before we head to the river? The day's been long, and I never saw you pause to eat."

She dropped the apron on the grass nearby, accepted the plate, and sank back onto the crate, but instead of eating, she settled it onto her lap. Her focus seemed to blur into the darkness of the distance. "You ever been scared, Mr. Jackson?"

His heart went out to her. Was that why she wasn't eating? "Reckon I have a time or two, yes'm."

"I mean, so scared you can hardly fathom how to take your next breath?" Her voice was small in the darkness.

And, oh, how he understood. "Terrified of losing a gift you didn't even know would be so precious before you got it?"

Her gaze darted to his, large and luminous in the moonlight.

"Striker's daddy, he was a mean, sorry cuss. Sold both my mama and my papa to different folk. Those days scared me. Scared me so bad that I wept the night through. But for days after Striker gave me my freedom, I had this terrible fear that eclipsed all those others. A fear that somehow my freedom would be revoked. I still get that tight-chest, choking-on-my-own-terror feeling sometimes. That what you're talking about?"

She nodded. "Think so. I didn't know I needed this so badly." She swept a gesture between them, then to encompass the whole wagon train.

Jeremiah nodded. "I know just what you mean. The devil, he hates freedom. Freedom is just the opposite of what that fallen angel wants for us because he once knew what it was, the very essence of it, and he threw it away. Now he wants all men to be as miserable as he is. Thing is, there's all sorts of things that enslave people. You and I, we might feel like we had the worst of it, and I don't make light of what we and many like us went through. But a man like Striker's daddy—well, he's enslaved too, just in a different way. Unhappy. Never satisfied. Can't find a kind thing to say or do. I feel sorry for him." He paused to snatch a blade of grass, sank to his haunches, and began to shred it. "Freedom is of the heart, you see? The body can be chained, and the mind can still be free because, when we humble ourselves to Christ's Word, we recognize that this mortal flesh is only a stepping stone, and that sooner rather than later, judgment day is coming. Jesus is the only one who truly can set us free."

She reached to trace a finger over one of the white bandages on her wrists. He clenched his teeth. Snapped off another section of the grass in his fingers.

"My flesh and my heart may fail; but God is the strength of my heart and my portion forever." She spoke the words so softly in the darkness that he almost missed them.

He nodded. "Yes. Exactly so."

He saw the flash of her white teeth in the dark. "Thank you, kindly, Mr. Jackson. I needed that reminder this evening." Her stomach rumbled, and she placed a hand over it in embarrassment. "I confess that it's been a month of Sundays since I had me a good slice of catfish. What I wouldn't give for some black-eyed peas and greens to go with it."

"Ah," Jeremiah tugged another piece of grass from its stem. "A woman after my own heart. Where you from?"

"Born in Georgia. Lived there . . . most of my life."

Though her words 'most of my life' tugged at a long-familiar ache, he was happy to see her finally lift a bite of the meat to her lips. Her eyes fell closed as she savored it. He ought to keep quiet and let her eat in peace, but there was so much he wanted to know. "You seem educated. How'd you learn to do that doctoring?"

She nibbled on a bit of potato. "First, when I was little, the master wanted me to be a companion to his little girl. She was being taught to read, and I was right there learning along with her. Sums were my favorite, though, and they came easy to me. As soon as Master McNeilly found that out, he started having me keep the books for the plantation. Evenings, whenever Mama was called out to a birthing, she'd have me come with her. If it was too late, I'd sleep in a chair or on the porch until she needed me to help. If a birthing were hard, I might be up most of the night helping Mama, and then come seven, I had to be at the plantation house to work on the books till Master came down. But do listen to me go on. You seem educated, too. How'd you learn to do that hiding-a-runaway business?" She laid a bite of catfish in her mouth and cocked a brow at him.

He chuckled. "All my education I owe to Strike. I had a way with horses and worked in the barns by day. That's how I met Striker. His daddy was teaching him to break a stallion, and that critter was as stubborn as they come. The kind that needs to be gentled into submission, not broken into it. So, I started bringing that fella carrot tops from the waste bin, or apple cores if they were available. One day, Striker arrived at the barn early and caught me at it. So, then he started to sneak that critter things too. Only he brought whole apples, and that horse was smart enough to know he liked those better than my garbage scraps. Pretty soon ol' Strike's father was bragging about what a good horseman he was, and Striker and I became fast friends." Since Del was still eating, he continued. "Striker taught me to read. Only a little at first, since his daddy would have frowned on it. But once we left and Strike gave me my freedom, he taught me a whole lot more."

"Excuse me?" Tamsyn approached, carrying a bundle of some sort in her arms.

Jeremiah rose, and Del did the same.

"Please don't let me bother you." Tamsyn smiled. She held out the bundle. "It's only . . . I figured you might be able to use a change of clothes. I have extras, and though you might have to hem this skirt to the right length, we seem about the same size, so I brought these by." She offered the bundle to Del.

Del was taken aback, and that was plain to see. She stood, jaw hanging, staring at the proffered bundle, plate clutched in both hands. The kindness had obviously left her speechless.

With a smile, Jeremiah stepped forward and took the plate from her. He was happy to see that she'd finished all the food while he'd been prattling.

Getting her hands free seemed to jolt Del into reality because she reached for the bundle. "That's right thoughtful. Thank you so very much."

"My pleasure." Tamsyn smiled. "Well, good night."

Jeremiah stepped forward. "I think this is yours." He offered the plate to her.

"Oh, yes. Thank you." She hurried away, head down.

Across the encampment, one of the Hawthorne twins started a tune on her fiddle. It was only a moment before he saw several couples twirling through the orange glow of the firelight. Hiram broke out his mouth harp, and Royal Carter sank onto a stump with his Spanish guitar.

When he turned back around, Del was smiling wistfully at the dancing couples. "They used to have dances at the fort sometimes. I would sit in the basement and listen to the music, wishing my little window faced the festivities. But the music was enough, and the good Lord always sent it just when I needed it most."

Jeremiah's fists clenched tighter and tighter with every word. Until finally he'd heard enough. He stepped close to her and offered one hand. "Care to dance, miss?" He gave a courtly bow.

She chuckled and gave him a once-over. "Do go on with you. We can't be dancing like fools over here in the dark. One of us is likely to twist an ankle but good."

He suddenly wanted very badly for her to say yes. "Come on. Ain't nothing over here to trip on but some bits of grass. And if you twist your ankle, you can claim delivering that baby's what done it."

Her laughter did his heart good. "Twisted my ankle delivering a baby?"

"Sure." He nodded gravely, trying to keep a straight face. "Happens all the time, I'm sure."

She laughed again. "And if you twist yours?" Even in the moonlight, he could see the pert quirk of one brow.

He waggled the fingers of the hand he was still holding out to her. "I'll say I was wrasslin' cougars."

With another chuckle, she turned and put the armful of material she was holding into the wagon bed, and his heart kicked into a sprint because he knew he'd convinced her.

When she approached and settled her hand into his, she gave him a cheeky grin. "Well, I'll just have to stomp on your feet as much as I can because I want to see everyone's reaction to this cougar story."

Smiling down at her, Jeremiah settled one hand gently at the small of her back and swung her into a waltz. And as he looked into those light brown eyes still crinkled with her teasing, he knew he was a goner.

A complete goner for sure.

Chapter 8

Del willed down the tympany of her pulse as she waltzed through the grass. Jeremiah didn't hold her too close. Nor did he grip her possessively.

Still, her heart pounded and her hands turned clammy. Each breath seemed harder to release until her chest felt tight, and unease dragged her feet to a stop. "Sorry. So sorry." She retreated, holding out one hand to fend him off if he followed.

Thankfully, he remained where he was, hands falling to his sides.

"If you don't mind. I think I'll just rise early to wash the apron. Weariness has caught up to me." She didn't wait for his reply—only clambered upon the crate and swung her legs over the tailgate, making her escape into the darkness beneath the wagon's oilcloth before she collapsed into a trembling heap.

Sobs shook her, but she made sure to keep them quiet.

She hated this terror that clogged her throat until she felt certain she would choke. Hated that the joy of life seemed to have been snatched from her.

"My flesh and my heart may fail; but God is the strength of my heart and my portion forever." She whispered the verse over and over, drawing deep breaths between each repetition until her pulse eased and her trembling ceased.

So tired. So very tired.

"Lord, I need Your strength now more than ever. This fear threatens to pull me under." She whispered the prayer as she crawled to the pallet. "Please keep me safe from Boone. I don't think I could survive going back there." She pulled herself onto the tick and eased her head onto the pillow. "Help Jeremiah understand that I truly do know he wouldn't harm me. Help me to take hold of these fears and rest in You."

She worried that she wouldn't be able to sleep with all this emotion coursing through her, but somewhere between her prayer for the new baby and her mother's recovery, and the ones of thanks for these good people that the Lord had brought near the fort just when she needed them, she drifted into the oblivion of rest.

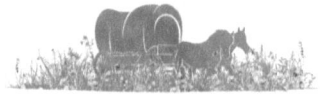

Chevonne had awoken hours ago in a strange little conical hut, with leather walls held aloft by poles that leaned against each other at the peak. During the whole long day, no one had come to see her. She wasn't bound, nor did she seem to have been molested other than the gash at her temple, which had likely stemmed from that dratted pony's hoof, and her arm ached something fierce, but she'd likely done that to herself when she dove from the trotting horse.

Not daring to draw attention to herself lest that odious man return—was this his home?—she had sat huddled on a fur on the far side away from the flap that must be the door, and hadn't dared to poke her head out of the opening. The inside of the pole building was quite cool, even though she could see through the hole at the peak that the sun was shining outside. But now she found that the curiosity that had been building inside her for quite some time could not be put off any longer.

What was it like outside these walls? Would there be a whole circle of natives simply waiting for her to attempt an escape so they could finish her?

She crawled across the furs that lined the floor and hesitated at the flap that covered the doorway. Would poking her head out get it lopped off?

She pressed one hand to her throat. Winced at the throbbing agony in her head and shoulder.

Despite its current pain, she quite liked her head exactly where it was. Perhaps she should start by putting out a finger. She held up both hands and looked at them. Not her right one—she used that one the most.

Left it was.

Taking a fortifying breath, she poked her left pinky finger through the opening. She scrunched her eyes closed and waited for the consequences.

Nothing.

Relieved, she withdrew her finger.

Working up her courage, she thrust her whole left hand out of the opening.

This time, she only scrunched one eye shut.

Again, nothing.

Bon. On y va.

Before she could lose her gumption, she tucked her injured arm against her chest and poked her head through the opening. The bright sunlight burned her vision, and all she could see were black spots for a moment, but when her eyes adjusted to the light, she was shocked to find no one in sight. Several other little hide-covered huts stretched before her, but then blessed thick bushes of some sort tempted her forward.

With a glance right and left, she surged through the opening, hoisted her skirts in her good hand, and ran as quietly as she possibly could. She had played this game many a time in the palace gardens while trying to remain hidden from the empress until the royal would throw herself down in a heap and demand that Chevonne and the other maids come out immediately.

The sun had slipped just below its zenith, so darkness would not soon be on her side. Too bad the Indian was missing a tooth instead of an eye.

She made it past the first little pole hut, hearing the soft humming of a woman inside. The next one seemed altogether empty.

Then she faced the thick wall of brush. She'd been able to travel the few feet from her prison to here without so much as a rustle due to the cleared grounds of the encampment, but there was no way she could press through here without causing all manner of rustling. And her skirts were much too voluminous for this undertaking!

No matter. She had to try. She winced her way through hoisting her skirts higher, needing to use her aching arm this time, and crammed them into as tight a wad against her chest as she could, and then pushed forward. The branches crackled and snapped like prattling little princes who were shouting for someone to notice her!

But she was into the thicket now and kept plowing forward. Perhaps they would mistake her for some wild animal if they heard her and be afraid enough to keep their distance. If only she knew how to mimic the call of something feral and ferocious.

Despite the burning in her lungs and the pain pulsing through her arm, high and near her shoulder, she didn't dare stop. She pushed forward through the thicket of brush until—blessed heavens!—the bushes thinned out. She hit the more open space under a sparse grove of trees at a full-out sprint, hindered only by an arm that insisted on as little movement as possible.

Casting a look behind herself, she could hardly fathom that her escape had been so simple. If only she'd tried it sooner! But then maybe someone would have been in a position to see her.

She ran until she was forced to stop or fall flat to breathe. By then, she was once again on the endless plains. Blast this country with the nothingness for miles in any direction. All the brush must have been close to the river with the strange name they'd been traveling along for several days now. Something like Platter or Plate or . . . Pallet? *Non.* That still wasn't quite right.

She spun to get her bearings. She could see nothing in any direction save for the thicker brush along the riverbank she'd left behind a bit ago. She would much rather have cover than be out here in the wide open by herself, but to go closer to the river would also be to go closer to the Indian encampment again.

With a sigh, she trudged onward. One foot in front of the other, in front of the other, in front of the other. Was she even heading in the right direction? The sun hung low on the horizon before her. That was the place it hung every evening as they were making camp. This must be the right way.

She had been plodding for a full ten minutes when, from behind her, she heard a shout.

Non!

Looking back, she saw several native men riding toward her from the brush.

Heart in her throat, she hefted the hem of her skirts and sprinted! *Seigneur, aidez-moi!*

There she went, praying to a God she wasn't sure she believed in.

Her lungs burned. Her legs felt on fire. A glance back revealed that the men giving chase had gained significant ground.

She faced forward and tried to renew her speed.

Ahead of her, a warrior rose from the prairie right in her path! She screamed and tried to angle around him, but he was too close! One firm hand wrapped around her wrist and yanked her to a stop.

Pain spiraled up her arm. She cried out and froze, willing him not to tug on her.

Caught! *Zut!*

Her good shoulder slumped in defeat, but at least her lungs and legs were relieved to be at a standstill. She hauled in a deep breath as she studied the man who had caught her. There was no sense in struggling, for his grip was like an iron band, and she would be no match for the strength in those broad shoulders.

Gracious! He was much better looking than a savage ought to be allowed to be! Certainly nothing like the paunchy Missing-Tooth. Why couldn't a man like this have claimed her? The thought almost made her smile despite her annoying circumstances.

His hair hung in a long, thick, dark braid across one shoulder with a few wavy wisps framing a smooth, angular face. His eyes—such a soft brown that they might have been mistaken for gray—emphasized high cheekbones that swept down to full lips.

Lips that were moving, though her blood was rushing so rapidly through her ears that she'd missed what he said. "*Pardon?*"

Those lips pressed together into a thin line of irritation as his gaze flicked to the rapidly approaching natives behind her. His grip on her arm grew firmer.

Despite her resolve not to let these men see her fear, pain made her wince, and surprisingly, the man's grip eased a little.

"I said, 'Are you the French woman taken from a wagon train yesterday?' But I can see by your accent and this foolish dress that you must be."

Improbable hope flared despite his disparaging remarks about her day dress! "*Oui. Oui!*" Could it be that this man wasn't with those chasing her? The very thought made her throw her good arm around him! "*Sauvez-moi, je vous en prie!*"

Did he need her to beg him to save her? Panic had her acting the fool! He'd obviously come for her.

When the woman threw herself into his arms, Cody figured all the trouble of getting to her might just end up being worth it. He smirked.

He and Caesar had found the place where the wagon train had been attacked the day before. Several of the wagons that had been too damaged to continue had still wafted spirals of smoke. They'd followed the trail left by the unshod horses of the attackers until the party had crossed the river. After that, the trail had gone cold. Caesar had followed the river west. Cody had headed east. But only after he'd dismounted to be better able to look for sign. He always preferred solid ground beneath his feet rather than riding anyhow.

He'd been at it for almost a full day when he'd noted the smoke from the teepee. He'd left his horse to graze, knowing the faithful bay mustang wouldn't go far, and had been heading this way, hoping he'd found the right band of Sioux.

He'd expected trouble.

Not a vision of beauty hurtling through the sea of tall grass with her red silk dress clutched above her knees—nor the hitch in his breath. The dress was a foolish frippery better suited to a royal garden party than the prairie. Her wagon master ought to have forbidden the garment, but from the little he knew of that thief, he'd probably liked the sight of her in it.

The thought made something turn cold in Cody's chest.

The seam at her shoulder was torn badly enough that part of her sleeve flopped near her elbow. Her golden and brown hair wafted behind her, tangled and twisted.

And on the horizon behind her, galloping toward them with intense ferocity, a war party of Sioux riders.

Facing down those men was about as appealing as walking barefoot over jagged lava—and with higher chances of blood and death. But if there was one thing the Sioux respected, it was courage. And right now, that was the only thing he had going for him.

Cody waited, slunk low in the tall grass, until she was close and then surged up to grab her. He couldn't risk her getting away, so he wrapped his hand firmly around her forearm.

She gasped a sound more like pain than shock. He loosened his grip but kept hold of her.

"You the French woman taken captive from that wagon train yesterday?" Even as he voiced the question, he knew it was foolish. What other woman in a dress like this would be barreling across the prairie with a pack of Sioux on her trail?

"*Pardon?*" Terror filled her expression. She tugged for release even as she tossed a glance over her shoulder. A shoulder he could now see was scratched deeply with a fresh and tender-looking wound.

Blast. She was injured and couldn't understand a word he said.

Did the woman only speak French? He spoke only a little—not enough for a decent conversation, not that they had time for one.

What was a woman like her doing way out here anyhow? Shouldn't she be in some French court somewhere?

He repeated the words even though he didn't figure it would do a bit of good.

Blathering a string of French, she threw herself against him with her good arm slipping behind his back—yet another thing he hadn't expected. She clung to him, nestled just beneath his chin like he was her last hope.

And she wasn't far from wrong. The weight of that thought hitched his breath again.

He set her firmly from him. Blast it, he needed his wits about him if he was going to save—

A new plan hit him. The riders were too close for them to make a run for it now. And even if they tried, his mustang would be carrying two and was already tired from a long day of travel. But if they thought she was his . . .

It might work.

She blinked up at him, chest still heaving for air. "Sorry. So sorry. Only I am so happy, you see, to find someone other than, well, them." She tossed a gesture toward the Sioux, who were almost on them now.

So she did speak English! Good. That would make this a whole lot easier, even though she wasn't going to like his plan. He took her by the shoulders, mindful to keep his grip gentle. "I'm going to get you out of this. But you have to trust me. Did one of them claim you?"

"Claim me?"

Hang it, there was no time for civility. "Did any of them bed you?"

Her face flamed, and she tried to pull away, drawing his attention to the blue bruise that covered half of her temple.

He held her and gave her a gentle shake. "Did they?!"

"*N-non!* A fleshy man with a missing tooth captured me, but his horse, the hoof—" She clunked the heel of her hand against her temple, then winced as though she hadn't realized she would hit herself so hard. "When a chance I found, I ran."

Relief washed through him. "Good. I think I can save you then."

Her lips parted. "How?"

"No time." He glanced past her shoulder. The men were only an arrow's flight away now, five Sioux riders leaning over their horses' necks. "Make this believable."

Her brow knit in confusion. "Make what believ—"

He drew her close and kissed her.

She stiffened, as expected, and pressed hard against him. He captured her hands against his chest with one splayed palm, holding them firmly so that she wouldn't pull back and slap him—that would ruin his whole plan. At the same time, he held her close with his other arm.

He'd meant to maintain the kiss only long enough for it to be seen. A claim. A message to the oncoming riders.

But then she melted against him, and those soft lips gave way beneath his. Even her hands relaxed, and instead of pushing him away, curled into the front of his buckskin shirt.

A soft floral scent enveloped him. Something sweet, tantalizing, and unfamiliar.

A warrior yipped.

Right. He ought to release her. Surely the approaching riders had seen his declaration, but he lingered, stroking his lips one more time over the soft fullness of hers—only so the Sioux would be certain to take note.

When he pulled back, she blinked up at him, lips parted, and breathing almost as hard as she had been when he'd grabbed her a moment ago. Though she remained where she was with her hands pressed to his chest, her expression rapidly transformed from one of rapture to horror and then to narrow-eyed outrage.

"You are no gentleman, *monsieur*." She snapped the words softly, but from the sparks igniting her gaze, he had a feeling that if there weren't warriors riding down on them, her reaction might have been more . . . volatile.

A woman with smarts. She rose a couple of notches in his estimation.

He quirked a brow. "I came to save you, didn't I?"

Her only response was a soft huff of irritation.

They were out of time. He drew her close, faced the riders, and waited.

The warriors slid to a stop in a semicircle, a cloud of fine brown dust rising around them.

A young warrior whose face was painted black from his nose upward swung down from his pony and stormed forward, fury in his eyes. He looked at the woman. Then at Cody. He jabbed a finger at her, then slapped his palm to his chest, chin high. The man had all his teeth, so he couldn't be the one she'd mentioned.

"He is the one who hatchet Master Engstrom's fingers," she whispered, chopping one hand into the palm of the other.

The one who avenged a desecration was usually the one closest to the deceased. The son of a fallen warrior? Brother maybe? It didn't matter.

What did matter was that, as Cranston had suggested, she'd likely been taken as a gift for this man—restitution for the grievance of the desecration of his relative's grave. It was the most likely scenario.

Cody took a breath and swept her behind him. He splayed his hands, palms out. He wanted no fight. He could only hope that if they thought she was his, maybe they'd let him "reclaim" her.

But the warrior again jabbed a gesture from himself to the woman and back again.

Cody shook his head. He signed clearly, slowly, each motion deliberate. With two fingers, he traced the edge of his cheek on the path a woman's braid might lie. *Woman.*

He pressed an open palm over his chest. *Mine.*

Again, he gestured *woman*, then curved his hand from his shoulder across his chest. *Wife.* The little minister at the mission school would be aghast at the deception, but Cody figured the Lord could forgive him since he was trying to save the Frenchwoman's life.

Lastly, he clasped his own wrist and then opened both palms and held them toward the warriors. *Peace.*

The young warrior's jaw clenched. He looked to the others. Two nodded solemnly. One shook his head. The last one, a paunchy fellow, only hung his head.

Defiance lit the young warrior's eyes. He stepped forward, fists clenched. He jabbed a thumb toward his own chest, then stabbed a gesture at Cody. He gestured the sign for *fight.*

So be it. Cody sure wished Cranston were here to even the odds a little. The Sioux might not have been so eager to fight since both he and Cranston had guns, and they had only bows and knives.

Cody eyed the warrior's lithe form. This young pup might be able to take him.

One bullet could end everything right now. But the others would see it as disrespectful if he pulled out his gun and shot his rival. He'd never be able to take them all before one of them got an arrow off—and they wouldn't care if they were aiming at a woman. Cody couldn't risk that.

He would simply have to fight the man on his level. If he could get the upper hand, maybe they'd have a chance. He gave a slow nod, unbuckled his holster, and tossed it aside. He did the same with the rifle scabbard on his back. Then he shucked his knife from its sheath, held it low, and slid away from the woman.

She stepped after him. "*Monsieur*, please, I beg you, do not leave me."

He pushed her good shoulder. "Stay back." He hadn't meant to bark the command so sharply, but hopefully she'd listen. He couldn't worry about her while he was trying to stay alive himself. If he didn't make it, she would likely be consigned to this man as a wife. Maybe a second wife—and one who would always remind him of his grief, loss, and humiliation. Nothing good could come for her from that.

He circled the man who'd issued the challenge, not worried about the other warriors doing something underhanded. One thing the Sioux valued was a fair fight.

The young Sioux moved first. A quick jab of his foot.

Cody didn't flinch.

Then the warrior lunged. His blade flashed a reflection of the sun.

Cody pivoted, deflecting the blow with his forearm. Cool steel grazed his skin. Pain bloomed along his bicep. But his buckskins had done their job, and the slice seemed shallow.

This kid was fast.

Cody countered, striking low, but the warrior danced back, light on his feet. Grinning a taunt.

Cody cinched down his irritation.

They circled.

Another strike—faster. Cody blocked high, shoved hard, and had the upper hand for half a breath. He advanced, thrusting, striking. The warrior back-pedaled, parrying each blow, but off balance now. The scents of earth and sweat and fear filtered to him, and as they twirled past the Frenchwoman, that tantalizing floral scent, too.

The warrior stumbled backward, and Cody leaped forward, intending to drive his knee into the man's thigh. He saw the man's grin too late.

The pup had been baiting him.

Cody barely twisted fast enough to avoid a blade in his throat. A ribbon of pain caressed the top of his shoulder. Another exploded against his cheek as his face met an elbow. His head snapped back. Stars flashed across his vision.

His shoulders hit the ground, and he used his backward momentum to flip himself into a somersault that returned him to his feet.

The warrior hadn't expected that and was off balance from the exertion of his blow.

Cody dropped low and swung a kick at the only leg still holding the man upright.

The Sioux grunted. Flailed.

Cody surged forward, slammed his shoulder into the man's chest, and drove him to the ground. The force knocked the warrior's blade free, and they slid along the grass on the man's bare shoulders until a stone embedded in the prairie brought them to an abrupt halt.

Cody was almost thrown over the man's head, but he managed to hang on and took advantage of the warrior's dazed head-shaking to press his blade to his opponent's sweaty throat.

Silence.

The young man went still, chest heaving. He lifted his chin, offering his throat, eyes glittering defiance.

Cody held the knife there for a beat longer. Then he eased back, stood, and kicked the dropped blade away.

After transferring his knife to his left hand, he leaned down and offered his right.

The warrior stared at it like it was a snake about to strike. But when Cody maintained the offer, slowly, the youngster reached out and gripped Cody's wrist.

After hauling him to his feet, Cody released the man, stalked over to stand between the Sioux and the Frenchwoman, and waited. He heard her breaths shuddering in and out, but kept his gaze on the mounted men.

One of the elders flicked a hand and pointed toward the horizon.

Relief swept through Cody. The fight was done. He thrust his knife back into its sheath as he turned to the woman. His shoulder ached and when he glanced down, blood dripped along his upper arm. He grunted. That was going to need stitching as soon as he felt it safe.

She had gathered his holster and rifle at some point during the fight, and cradled them against herself, but she clutched one of his pistols in a trembling hand.

Smart. He almost smiled as he tugged the holster from her and swung it around his hips. Next, he eased the Colt from her feral grip. "Easy, *chérie*. It's over."

At his use of the French endearment, her gaze flashed to his. Right, he probably shouldn't have called her "dear." But was that what had surprised her? Or the fact that he knew a little French?

He let her keep the rifle for now. Taking her hand, he turned and they walked away. He could feel a tremor sweep through her now and then. And she clung tightly to him as though he were her only lifeline.

At the mission school they would have said that Someone much more sovereign than Cody had a part in saving the woman. And maybe they were right. He understood their explanations about God. Even wished that he could believe them. He just wanted to be sure before he crossed that line. What he did know was that he'd been in the right place and time to help her. Cody angled a glance toward the sky. *If You had anything to do with all this, thanks.*

He figured praying couldn't hurt because if the missionaries were wrong, he was only thinking thoughts toward the sky, but if they were right, well, then it only seemed smart to acknowledge such a great spirit.

When they'd walked far enough that he felt like it would be okay to pause, he gave a sharp whistle, and only a moment later his mount trotted into sight from wherever it had been munching grass. He helped her onto the bay's back then swung up behind her, never more thankful for his tendency to ride bareback.

Now they just needed to find Cranston and then fetch her wagon.

He rotated his pulsing shoulder. And stitch him up. He grimaced. At least he was still able to use the muscle.

Blazes, this pretty little Frenchwoman had been a whole pack of trouble!

Chapter 9

Deliverance woke the next morning with another round of fear pumping through her chest. "My flesh and my heart may fail; but God is the strength of my heart and my portion forever."

She was determined to say the verse until she could truly believe it in her heart. She wanted God to be the strength of her heart. She wanted Him to be her portion. If she had that, held onto that, she could survive anything that came her way. Yes. Even returning to life with Boone.

The very thought shot an acrid, metallic prickle across her tongue.

She would not think on Boone. She turned her thoughts to the man she'd left on the grass outside the wagon the evening before.

Up until he'd asked her to dance, she had enjoyed her time with Mr. Jackson. Maybe enjoyed it too much. How long had it been since she'd teased and laughed with anyone?

He had held her gently as they danced, and the way the man looked at her, well, it was likely what had raised her fears and sent her running. She never wanted a man to look at her like that again!

She closed her eyes. She was being unfair. The man hadn't looked at her like Boone looked at her. There had been no lust in his gaze.

And yet, that very feeling was what had her fears on the rise. She hadn't run to find another man. She doubted she'd ever want to be with another man again. Not after the way Boone had—

She was being unfair again. In her mind, she knew that not all men were like Boone. And yet she'd had hopes when Boone first bought her. He'd been kind, fed her, let her ride when another might have made her walk behind. Then they'd reached the fort that dark evening, and all her hopes had been shattered with one swift swing—like boys playing baseball with a clay pot. She was the clay pot.

From that point on, she'd known that if she wanted to survive, she would have to escape. And yet whenever she wasn't with him, he'd kept her chained. But now, now, she'd done it, thanks to Betsy and the good folk of this wagon train.

But Boone wouldn't let her go. She knew that without a doubt. Would today be the day that he caught up to her?

If he did—when he did—she must never let him know that Jeremiah had been part of the reason she'd escaped. Boone would shoot him without second thought and claim he was some runaway he recognized or some other such story. He could later say he was certain he'd been right and apologize for the mistake he'd made in trying to protect the country from the insurrection escaped slaves could foist upon the land. She'd heard him bellyaching about that enough to know he believed it to his very core.

Del drew in a breath. She needed to stop fearing the past or she'd never find the strength to face the future. Yet, all she could think about was what if today was the day she was taken back? Her trembling fingers stroked across the bandages at her raw wrists. The side of her face still ached from the slap Boone had given her a few mornings ago when she hadn't fetched his coffee fast enough. What would her punishment be if he caught up to her? A tremor swept through her.

She squirmed on the tick, terribly afraid of stepping out into the daylight. And yet she needed to wash Mrs. Hawthorne's apron so that she could return it to her. She just had to work up her courage to emerge into the light.

In her mind, she knew that the flimsy walls of canvas would be no protection if Boone descended on the wagon train a second time. There would be no laboring woman to hide beneath. No crate that wouldn't be opened and searched.

And yet, still, she clung to the meager hiding place. Her legs refused to work. Her every muscle quavered, and she wondered about the possibility of riding the whole way to Oregon right here without ever stepping outside again.

Footsteps sounded outside the wagon. A knock tapped against the tailgate. "You awake in there?"

Jeremiah.

She blew out a breath. "Yes."

He hesitated as though waiting for her to say more. When she didn't, he added, "I, ah, I went down to the river and scrubbed that apron for you last night. Hung it up to dry on the side of the wagon here, and it's dry and ready to be returned."

Del closed her eyes and eased out a breath. He'd scrubbed the apron? Had she ever had a man do something like that for her? Not even back on the plantation. Of course, when an assignment was given, woe to anyone who didn't follow orders and right snappy. One of the other slaves may have wanted to help but had known it would cause trouble. At any rate, Jeremiah had taken care of the only thing that might have induced her to leave the wagon today.

He cleared his throat. "Would you like to come to the fire for some breakfast with the Morrans? You haven't met them yet, but they're a nice family. Two boys. Miz Morran, she's making flapjacks, bacon, and eggs, special like, on account of you this morning."

Her stomach betrayed her and rumbled at the mere mention. But her terror kept her glued to the tick. "Thank you, kindly. I think I'll just stay in this morning and ride a ways."

His feet rustled in the grass. There was a long pause. Then he said, "Could you move this canvas aside for a moment?"

Del squirmed at the thought of that back canvas opening even a fraction, but forced herself to rise and untie the cinch. Then reached a trembling hand to part the canvas a few inches. She stayed well back in the shadows.

Jeremiah peered in at her, morning light casting a golden swath across one brown cheek. "Morning." The word was hesitant, as though he wasn't sure how she might respond.

She laced her fingers into a tight clasp to keep them from snatching the canvas closed again. "Morning." What she could see behind him was only a sliver of a view—the side of the next wagon, golden grass, the glow of someone's campfire in the distance, a buttery sunrise beyond.

Jeremiah glanced over his shoulder, then back to her. "The scouts and I have been out. Didn't see any strangers in the area. You're safe to come out."

"Am I?" The sharp question was out before she thought better of it. She didn't want to be a burden. But she certainly didn't want to go back to being Boone's slave. "Sorry. I had a short night, and my mind is spinning this morning with all sorts of scenarios."

Jeremiah reached in a hand and held it there, waiting for her to take it. "Let me make you a deal. I will carefully scout the area every morning and will come and get you only when I know it is safe for you to come out. Here"—he waved a hand over his shoulder—"the prairie is open and there aren't many places for a man and horse to hide. We'd see them well before they were on us, giving you plenty of time to hide. Evenings, well, that's a different story, which is why I wanted to get you away from the firelight last night. I hope my caution hasn't caused you alarm."

Del sighed and took his hand, allowing him to help her down. "Your caution is appreciated, and I can assure you that my alarm is all my own and no burden of yours."

He helped her descend to the crate he'd set near as a step. "'Tis never a burden to care for someone."

She snapped him a look. Snatched her hand from his. The man may be attractive, but the very word *care* shot her through with dread!

He frowned. "I meant caring like any God-fearing folk would care for another. Naught more."

She carefully maneuvered the descent to the ground, backed up until she felt the comforting press of the wagon against her spine, and then clasped her hands. At least right here, she was mostly hidden from behind and could keep an eye on what was happening ahead and to the sides.

Jeremiah stepped close and tugged the apron from where he'd hung it over a water barrel on the side of the wagon. "You've nothing to fear from me. You know that, right?"

She focused on her clasped hands. She did not know that. Not really. "Of course. I apologize. Back home on the plantation, I used to have to pack the picnics for their hunts. One time, those hounds chased a deer straight across the blanket I was laying out. Poor beast was consumed by panic, and it was that panic that did her in. She turned and ran straight back toward the hunters. I feel like that. Don't quite know which way to turn. So for that, I apologize."

Compassion filled Jeremiah's gaze as he looked down at her with his hat in one hand and that apron gripped in the other. "You don't owe me any apologies." He swept a hand. "The Morrans' wagon is just this way. We'll pass the Hawthorne wagon, and you can return this apron, if you like?"

She gave him a nod as she took the material and fell into step behind him.

The openness made her feel exposed. After one quick glance at the vast prairie, she decided it was best to keep her gaze fixed on her feet. She didn't like this wide-open nothingness in every direction. Not even a little. But one thing did give her a measure of ease. They would certainly see riders coming long before they arrived. Long before they might recognize anyone in the party. That was, unless—

Her head snapped up.

Boone would have a spyglass. Of course he would. He had access to all the latest gadgets that the army could supply.

She froze. Her breath wouldn't come. Black spots danced in her vision. The circle of wagons began to spin around her.

"Please." The word came out breathy and broken. Dizziness took the strength from her legs. She crouched to the ground, wrapped her arms around her knees, and buried her face in the folds of her skirt.

Jeremiah stopped and looked back and was shocked to see Deliverance in a tight little ball on the ground behind him.

His heart faltered, and his gaze immediately swept the surrounding countryside. Had she seen something? Had he and the other scouts missed someone on their morning sortie?

All around, the prairie lay empty. "Deliverance?"

He returned to her side and squatted before her.

Still clutching the apron in one hand, she had her arms wrapped around her knees, and her face buried against them. She rocked a little, and he could hear words stuttering past her lips, but couldn't make them out.

Jeremiah called himself every sort of fool. He'd pushed her too hard when she hadn't wanted to come out of the wagon. He wasn't sure what her life had been like at the fort. She hadn't had the opportunity to tell him much. But when he'd been to the mercantile back in the fort, there hadn't been any sign of her. His gaze settled on those bandages at her wrists. He'd bet whatever existence she'd lived hadn't been pleasant.

Footsteps approached, and she gasped and snapped up her head, those caramel eyes wide.

"Easy." Jeremiah crooned. "This here is Declan. He's one of us. Morning, Dec."

"Mornin'. Anything I can help with?" Declan's gaze flitted from him to Del on the ground and then back again.

Jeremiah eased the apron from Del's clasp. "If you wouldn't mind, could you return this to Mrs. Hawthorne?"

Declan took the material. "Of course."

Jeremiah nodded his thanks, then turned his attention back to Deliverance. What was the best thing to do here? Indulge her fears for a few days and then try to encourage her to return to normal life once they were further from the fort? Or try to make her face those fears right away?

He reached to lay one hand at her elbow, simply wanting her to know he was here and would support her. "What did that man do to you?"

She only shook her head. But at least she wasn't scrunched into a tight ball anymore.

His thumb grazed over the nearest bandage. Chained. That was certain. He'd seen the evidence with his own eyes.

Del's gaze continued to flit from one gap in the wagon circle to another. Her wide eyes, clamped lips, and trembling told him she expected Boone to ride upon them at any moment.

"Del, look at me." He waited for her attention.

It took her a moment, but finally she dragged her focus to him.

"You want to go back to the wagon? I can take you back."

She nodded vigorously.

"All right, then. What about the, ah, necessary. You need that?"

She shook her head. "I went out while it was still dark a bit ago."

"Can you stand?" His hands felt clammy, and he sure wished his heart would quit thrashing around in his chest. He didn't want this deep concern that filled him. But it was there, nonetheless, all-consuming and terrifying. Yesterday, she'd seemed so capable. But here, cowering in this heap, he wondered how she had managed to hold things together long enough to deliver that baby.

She still hadn't responded to his question about standing. Did he just scoop her up and carry her? Maybe mentioning the baby would bring her back to herself? "Would you like to stop by the Hawthorne wagon and see that little mite you brought into the world yesterday?"

Del blew a long, slow stream of air through her lips. Shook her head. "I just . . ." Tears filled her eyes and spilled over to streak shiny tracks down her cheeks. She swiped at them angrily. "I don't want him to have this power over me."

"I know." He let his thumb stroke a soothing path from her wrist to her elbow.

"I just know what he'd do to any folk that helped me, and it terrifies me. But not more than the thought of returning to those chains in that basement." She trembled. "I'm sorry. I don't want to be a burden."

"You aren't a burden."

"I am. Look at me." She tossed a gesture to the grass around them. "Can't even stay on my own two feet!"

"I pushed you too hard, too soon. I'm sorry about that. From the way you were yesterday, I would never have known all that you were feeling."

She pressed one hand to the ground and started to stand. "Yesterday, that woman needed me to be the strong one."

Jeremiah rose with her, and when she reached her feet, she swayed. "Easy now." He took her elbow and waited until she seemed steadier. "You all right?"

She frowned. Shook her head. "Not sure I'll ever be all right again."

The words were like a knife to his heart. He had no rejoinder for that. Anything he tried to say would sound trite in this moment, anyhow. "Let's get you back to the wagon."

Her frown deepened, and she remained where she was. "You sure he ain't out there?"

Jeremiah's admiration for her rose another notch. He scanned the land all around, then looked back at her. She searched his face.

He shook his head. "Micah, Gideon, Striker, and I rode out this morning. Each of us took a different direction and went out five miles or so. Mine was to the east—back toward the fort. On my return, I rode back and forth across my section. Flat as the land is, I can't see how anyone could have been hiding. I truly wouldn't have you out here if I didn't think you were safe."

Her shoulders shifted back. Her spine straightened. Her chin lifted. A spark of gumption flashed in her eyes. "Fine then. Let's go on to meet this family you mentioned. And I'd like to see that new baby too."

Jeremiah grinned down at her. "Mrs. Morran's flapjacks will have you feeling better in no time."

He swallowed. The words were empty, but she seemed to appreciate his attempt at encouragement.

She smiled. Took a step.

Jeremiah released a breath. It was a start.

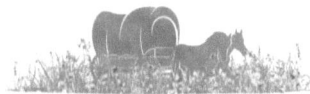

The morning after his brother's hanging, Boone woke with blood on his pillow. Not much. Just a few specks that he didn't actually even notice right away. He'd risen, dressed, shaved, and then, like any good soldier, returned to set his bedding to rights.

He frowned at the droplets. Swiped a hand at his cheek, but didn't feel anything amiss. He pivoted to the small looking glass and inspected his face, but saw no nicks or cuts from his razor, and then felt foolish because he hadn't lain in the bed again after he'd shaved.

Returning to the bed, he picked up the pillow and examined it more closely.

It was nothing. Likely, nothing.

Maybe even something left by Delilah? Sometimes her wrists bled after he released her from the cellar of an evening. That must be it. But how hadn't he noticed it earlier? He felt certain that the pillow had been clean the night before.

A shiver worked down his spine. He swallowed.

He yanked the pillow's casing off and pelted it into the corner, before drawing a calming breath and walking calmly to retrieve it. He set it at the end of the bed, retrieved a new case, and tucked the pillow inside, smoothing it neatly as he set it back upon the bedding.

Then he took the soiled case down to the laundry, made sure no one was looking, and shoved it in among the soldiers' ones. It wouldn't do for the washerwomen to know the pillowcase was his. Couldn't have rumors getting about that the commander of the fort might not be in the best of health.

Boone stroked his fingers over his throat as he left the washhouse and returned to his office above the mercantile.

All the world's a stage, and all the men and women merely players;
They have their exits and their entrances . . .

The quote from Shakespeare's *As You Like It* tormented him all morning. He couldn't settle. He paced from his desk to the window, looked out upon the fort, and then paced back to his desk again. He didn't feel sick. Only had a slight tickle at the back of his throat. And when he coughed a couple times—the same dry cough that had been plaguing him for a few days now—nothing felt different.

Bah, this was no good!

He snapped open his watch and checked the time. Five minutes until his next interrogations.

He settled behind the desk, took up his pen, drew the ink pot close, and set to writing in his account book. The details of the day before were clinical, analytical. He didn't allow any feeling to filter through over his brother's demise. ". . . saw to the hanging of outlaw Bradley Baxter. The doctor pronounced him deceased just before the noon hour, and he was summarily buried." The fact that Brad hadn't been buried in the common graveyard reserved for criminals, he left out of the book. The soldiers called that graveyard "The Devil's Acre," and Boone couldn't bring himself to abandon his brother there.

A knock on the door made him jolt. A blob of ink splattered onto the page, bringing to mind the spatters of blood on his pillowcase this morning. "Come!" he snapped as he took up the blotter and carefully blotted the extra ink. Blast. It had marred a couple of words. That was not like him.

Two soldiers entered, hats in hand. "Morning, Captain."

"Sit." Boone carefully closed the account book and put the pen and ink away in his drawer.

The soldiers exchanged a glance and then both sank into the chairs across from Boone's desk.

Boone drew a breath. Willed himself to gather his thoughts. "Tell me about yesterday morning. Which wagon did you two search?"

"Ah, I believe their name was Hawthorne, sir. There was a woman giving birth inside. But we searched it careful like and saw no sign of . . . anyone else." Gerald Johnson seemed to be the spokesman between the two.

Boone settled his gaze on Bert Hackman. "You concur with that, soldier?"

"Y-yes, sir. We searched it real g-good." Bert tried to meet his gaze, but didn't quite pull it off.

Gerald shifted in his seat.

Boone narrowed his eyes. There was something these two weren't saying. A woman giving birth . . . "You made the woman leave the wagon so you could search it thoroughly?"

"Yes, sir," Gerald said, at the same time that Bert said, "No, sir."

Boone willed every ounce of authority he possessed into his voice. "Well? Which is it?"

Bert looked to Gerald.

Gerald swallowed. "We didn't exactly make the woman, indisposed as she was, leave the wagon, sir, but we made her rise and searched the wagon thoroughly. There wasn't anyone else in there other than the midwife."

Again, Boone leveled his gaze on Bert. "You're squirming worse than a schoolboy at the end of the school day. What is it?"

Bert shook his head. "Nothing, sir. It was just as Gerald said."

"Then why do you look guiltier than the devil himself?" Boone drew on all his military training in comportment and authority. What he'd like to do would be to smack these two's heads together!

"I was only going to say that we d-didn't make her leave the wagon, sir. But like Gerald said, we made her rise and searched, and there was no one else there."

"You opened every crate?"

"Yes, sir," the two men chorused together.

Boone's gaze narrowed. He steepled his fingers and studied both soldiers. This time their gazes were steady, and Bert was no longer shifting.

Boone waved a hand. "And what about before that? Did you know that, ah, she was living here with me?" He cleared his throat, hating that he'd stuttered.

Both men shook their heads.

"No, sir. We never knew," Gerald said.

"Had no idea," Bert added.

Boone sighed. Turned his gaze to the window. These were the last two soldiers he'd needed to interview. He'd questioned all the others the day before, but these two had been out on a scouting mission.

Maybe he'd lost her. He frowned. How in blazes had she escaped?

"Thank you. You're dismissed." He fluttered his fingers at the two men.

They leapt out of their seats and practically had a collision in the doorway as they both tried to pass through it at once.

When the door closed behind them, Boone tapped his steepled fingers against his chin.

Del had been chained in the basement when he'd ridden out after Brad that morning. All but a few of the soldiers had been with him on that mission, and to a man, those who had been in town had said they'd seen nothing out of the ordinary, and none of them seemed to have known about Del.

Del couldn't have escaped those chains on her own. She simply couldn't.

That left . . . Betsy!

Boone rose and tromped down the stairs into the mercantile, but instead of finding Betsy there, he found one of his soldiers helping several folk from the wagon train that had arrived yesterday during the hanging.

Boone felt something go cold inside him. He stopped at the front counter. "John? Where's Betsy?"

John shook his head. "No one seems to have seen her, Captain. Lieutenant Dockery said I should man the store until she shows up."

Boone cursed, grabbed the nearest item, and hurled it at the wall behind the register. The jar of penny candy shattered, as did the mirror that hung there. The woman at the head of the line gasped and cowered.

Boone stilled. Rested his hands against his hips. Hung his head. "Sorry about that, folks." He raised a palm. "All is well. All is well." He motioned from John to the mess. "Clean that up. I'll send a man in to help you."

He stalked out the mercantile door and paused on the porch. In the distance, yesterday's newly arrived wagon train sprawled in the field outside the fort. A soldier walked down the street, and Boone snapped his fingers at the man without registering who he was. "Get inside and help John."

"Yes, sir." The man obeyed without question.

Boone surveyed the street. Betsy. It had been Betsy all along. How had he not seen it the day before? He cursed himself for a fool.

Now he had two women to find.

Chapter 10

When Declan arrived at the Hawthorne wagon, feeling like a fool with that apron clutched in his grip, the sight that greeted him froze him in his tracks.

Wren Hawthorne paced back and forth by the campfire, bouncing her new little sister in her arms. Her blonde hair was tied up in a scarf today, but several strands had slipped free to frame her face. She was solely concentrated on her sister, and the enchanting sight of her smiling, cooing, and making silly faces at the baby kept him frozen in place.

This was the Wren he knew. The one who was easygoing and kind and silly. The one who laughed easily and loved her family with abandon. The one who had been aghast when she found out Declan couldn't read more than a few words and had set about teaching him that very hour. And then convinced her sister to give him lessons also. Wren was the one who had captivated him from their first night on the trail when she'd approached to ask him for help getting one of her pa's cows out of the creek. He wasn't too proud to admit that he'd been smitten ever since.

"Morning, Declan."

He came to with a start.

Whitley was looking at him from where she was bent over the fire. A knowing smirk tilted her lips. She'd apparently been there this whole time? Why hadn't he even noticed? Several of Wren's other siblings stood around the fire, too. And now all of them were staring at him, including Wren.

"Ah . . . Mornin' to ye." He lifted the apron lamely. "Miss Deliverance asked that I bring this apron back to yer ma. Weel, nae her exactly. It were Mr. Jeremiah. But it were on her account."

He literally clamped his tongue between his teeth. Had anyone ever offered a more bumbling explanation of such a simple task?

He shoved the garment at the nearest child, Liberty. "Can ye gi'e this to your ma, please?"

The five-year-old accepted the apron with a sweet little curtsy and then dashed off toward the wagon with one of the apron strings trailing in the dirt behind her.

Declan winced inwardly. Maybe he should have picked one of the older children to entrust with the task. "Weel, I'd best be about rounding up th' coos."

"Would you like to see the baby?" Wren smiled at him from across the fire.

That smile could stop a man's heart.

He rubbed his chest. Grinned. "Och. I thought ye'd never ask." And if he wanted to see the baby more because it brought him closer to her older sister? Well, none of them needed to know that.

When he stopped by her side, Wren held the little bundle out for him to see. He was content to leave the baby in her arms and simply take in her little red face and headful of black hair. Someone had tied a large bow around the baby's head, and she was bundled up so tight that Declan couldn't see much more than her face and the one tiny hand pressed to her cheek.

He reached for that little hand before he thought better of it, and the baby's grip around his finger was quite strong for one just from the womb the day before. "Weel noo. What ha'e we here? The prettiest wee fairy I ever did see, that's what. An' all them black locks when your brothers an' sisters are fair. Determined to make your ain mark on the world, I see."

He felt his face heat. He was making a bigger fool of himself than Wren had been a moment ago. He lifted his gaze to see if she was laughing at him.

Though she studied him, there was no censure in her gaze. In fact, there was a warmth in her blue eyes that made the breath evaporate right out of Declan's lungs.

Wren blinked as though coming back from a distant place. "Ma says we all had hair just as black. She thinks Blythe will be blonde just like the rest of us."

Declan worked some moisture back into his mouth and returned his gaze to the baby to keep himself from staring at her sister like a fool. "Blythe, is it?"

"Blythe Evelyn."

Declan smiled. "'Tis a guid name." He squeezed the little hand gently and then tugged for the release of his finger. He really had best be on his way, or the cows would still be scattered when folk came looking to hitch them up. Mrs. Riley had helped pay his way west, and he was determined to make up for the favor by doing his part. "Best I be off."

Though he said the words, his feet seemed rooted to the ground, and his gaze remained fastened on Wren's face.

She smiled sweetly. "Have a good day. Tonight we could do some more reading, if you're of a mind."

Now his heart was definitely *not* stopped. In fact, it was racing faster than a wild mustang on the frisk. "Aye," he managed. "I'll stop by after I settle th' coos."

The baby whined, and Wren set to bouncing her. "See you then." She turned her gaze back to her baby sister.

Declan remembered to nod a farewell to Whitley and ruffle Silas's and Soren's hair before he departed. And for some reason, he had a downright lively step as he set out to round up the oxen.

Whitley couldn't help but feel sorry for poor Declan as he walked away. She gave the oats another stir and narrowed her gaze on her sister. "You shouldn't torment him by teasing him along. Just last night, you were mooning about Royal. And here this morning, you're flirting with Declan again."

Wren looked up. "I was doing no such thing! I've been teaching him to read for weeks now."

Whitley plunked her hands on her hips. "And do you think he's so dense that he hasn't learned the lessons you've taught? Or is he still coming around for another reason?"

Whitley nipped the inside of her lip. She was grown enough to recognize that the upsetting thing about Dec's visit this morning was that she'd taught him reading plenty of times, but he'd never once lit up like a candle when *she'd* suggested it.

Wren pressed her lips into a tight line. "Sure, he has the basics down and could likely learn the bigger words on his own, but it's easier with me there to help him. And he needs the practice. Also . . ." She pegged Whitley with a glare. "I wasn't mooning about Royal."

Whitley tossed her hands. "There's no winning with you. You are stringing both those men along, and you know you are. It's not seemly."

Wren smirked. "You're just jealous."

Whitley ground her teeth. She would not even deign to acknowledge that comment. Jealous indeed. Certainly not!

At least not of Royal.

She felt her face flame, but thankfully, she'd returned her attention to the oats and felt certain that none of her siblings had seen the telltale blush. Wren didn't deserve a man like Declan Boyle, and that was the truth of it!

But neither did Whitley want a man who saw her as second best. Well, maybe that wasn't exactly how he would describe it, but he'd certainly never given her a look like he'd been giving Wren this morning. Why, he hadn't even noticed she was there by the fire until she'd said something.

Why was that? She and Wren were practical mirror images of each other. So if he found Wren attractive, didn't it stand to reason that he would think her pretty, too? That blasted heat in her cheeks again! She wrangled her thoughts, unwilling to give any more space in her mind to wondering why so many men fell for Wren and not for her.

Sure, Wren was outgoing and unafraid to strike up a conversation. She also wasn't opposed to a bit of flirting if it got her something she wanted. Whitley had never felt comfortable with that. Of course, she was the oldest, if only by a few minutes, so she had to be the practical one.

There she went, giving Wren more sublets in her mind. She sighed. "Silas, bring me your plate. You too, Soren. These oats are done."

She needed to take a plate to Ma and make sure she had a glass of the fresh milk that Mr. Morran had brought by. Then she needed to make sure that Liberty and Serenity ate. Those two were forever wandering off before breaking their fast and then complaining of hunger come mid-morning. Cumberland was still asleep on the bed by Ma. He would need a trip to the necessary and then a meal for himself.

She had too much to do to worry about Wren and her irritating, sweet nectar personality that drew men to her like bees.

Deliverance still felt that prickle of fear along the back of her neck as she followed Jeremiah into the Morrans' camp, but she was determined not to give in to it.

"Morning, Mercy. This here is Deliverance." Jeremiah swung his hat from her to a pretty brown-haired woman leaning over the campfire. "Deliverance, Mercy Morran."

The woman straightened from the pan where she'd been turning bacon and wiped her hands on her apron. "It's such a pleasure to meet you. I'm so thankful you were able to join us this morning." She approached and pulled Del into a warm embrace.

Del felt her eyes widen at the unexpected hug, and Jeremiah laughed at her over the woman's shoulder.

"Oh, and here are the Houstons. I invited them over this morning, too, considering I was already going to be putting on a spread. No sense in all of us working up a sweat, of a morning!"

A blond couple approached with three children. The man had a white bandage wrapped around his head but otherwise seemed to be in good health.

What had happened to him? None of her affair, she supposed.

Mercy gestured. "This here is Parson Adam and his wife, Eden. And these three are Wyatt, Asher, and Afton. And these two here"— she tugged close two boys who had just quite literally hopped into sight like bullfrogs—"are my boys, Joel and Avram." She ruffled the youngest one's hair. "And my husband, Micah." She smiled warmly at a tall, broad man with dark hair and piercing blue eyes.

Del felt overwhelmed with all the new faces and names to remember—and again surprised when the parson's wife pulled her into a warm embrace.

"We are so pleased to meet you!" The blonde woman smiled. The two men shook her hands. The children grinned and waved before falling into line behind a stack of tin plates.

And then everyone was chatting and teasing. Mercy's husband tried to steal a piece of bacon from the pan and got a slap to the back of his hand for his thievery. The parson and his wife held hands as they stepped into the line behind the children.

Another woman—a redhead—approached with a broad-shouldered blond man by her side. She carried a tray filled with flapjacks that sent wafts of steam into the air. "Morning. Sorry, we're a bit late." She set the tray of pancakes on a stump near the plates and turned to

Del with a broad smile. She was already holding out her arms as she approached. "And you must be Deliverance. I'm Willow." She hugged Del. "And this here is my husband, Gideon."

The man nodded to her and doffed his hat. "Morning, ma'am. Pleased to meet you."

"Please do come join the line. If you don't, those rascals will have scarfed down their food and beaten you back to the line before you've even had one hot cake." Willow laughed as she pointed to the four boys who were already stacking flapjacks on their plates.

Deliverance felt overwhelmed by everything. Her fear, not only for herself, but for these who were so kind. The choices of food before her. The chatter of the children and women as they bustled about helping their families.

She would not cry. She would not collapse. She would not fall apart.

Even as she thought those things, she felt tears prick the backs of her eyes and the strength leave her legs. Thankfully, a sturdy crate was behind her. She collapsed onto it and willed herself to simply breathe. Hadn't she just willed herself to strength? Told herself not to let Boone win the day?

A hand pressed against her shoulder, and a plate of flapjacks, bacon, and eggs appeared before her face.

She glanced up to find Jeremiah smiling down at her. "You got to eat so's you'll have the strength to carry that baby." He grinned.

She blinked. Froze. Frowned at him.

"She sure is a chubby little—" Apparently noticing her frown, his brow furrowed. "Unless you changed your mind about stopping by to see her?"

The Hawthorne baby. Of course, that was the baby he meant. Again.

Del forced a smile. "Haven't changed my mind. Just not used to so much . . ." Again, she stopped herself before the word *freedom* slipped out. "Bustle," she concluded.

"The busyness can be more than a bit overwhelming," he concurred. "I'll fetch my own plate and be back shortly." He started toward the stack of empty plates near the fire.

Del turned her gaze to her plate, focusing on it for the first time. Her eyes widened. Four flapjacks. Enough eggs to tide her through a whole week. And a pile of bacon almost as high as the pancakes filled the plate. "Ah, Jeremiah?" She laughed and held the plate out to him as he returned to her, hands still empty. "Best you let me fetch my own plate and you take this one, otherwise I'll end up rolling all the way to Oregon."

He frowned. His gaze slipped over her. "You could stand to put on some weight, to my way of thinking."

Del loosed a breath and rose to her feet. He was likely to get his wish sooner rather than later with this baby on the way. She moved to the stack of plates and took one up, trying not to feel like a rifle might be aimed at her back. The fork clattered against her plate as she set it down, but thankfully, everyone was settled with plates of their own, and no one was near enough to notice. She pressed her thumb against it. Took a bracing breath.

My flesh and my heart may fail . . .

She set a piece of bacon onto her plate.

. . . but God is the strength of my heart.

She laid a flapjack beside the bacon and drizzled honey atop it. She whispered, "and my portion forever." A small scoop of eggs rounded out her plate.

She was quite proud of herself for maintaining her composure as she returned to settle on the crate.

Jeremiah had stepped over to join the group of men who congregated at one side of the wagon. They stood in a circle, and Striker had joined them. He spoke too quietly for Deliverance to hear his words, but from the tight pinch of his brow, whatever news he'd brought wasn't good.

Del's pulse hammered. Her plate settled against her lap. And the prickle returned to the back of her neck. Had he brought news about Master Boone?

She lost any semblance of appetite that she'd thought she might have.

After a moment, Jeremiah returned to her side and squatted next to her to finish eating.

She eyed him. "What is it?"

He looked up. Shook his head. "Probably nothing. Our wagon master and one of our scouts were supposed to rejoin us last night. When they didn't arrive, we assumed they were delayed slightly. But now they still haven't arrived this morning. Striker was left in charge and was asking our opinions on whether we should move forward or not."

"And?" The question came out sharper than she'd intended. The last thing she wanted, only a day out from the fort, was to tarry. Would she ever get far enough away from Boone to feel safe?

Jeremiah cast her a sideways glance. "We decided to keep going. They'll catch up to us . . . if they can."

His grim words sent a shudder down her spine.

Cody rose from the tanned hide he'd wrapped around himself the night before and scanned the prairie all around. Empty. Good. He'd been so tired last night that he feared any number of dangers could have snuck up on them and he might have slept through the whole of it.

He pondered their situation as he set about building a fire. A check of his stitches proved the little Frenchwoman hadn't lied about her ability to cast a stitch. His wound was still holding tight.

The evening before, Cody had been weary to his very core by the time they'd met up with Caesar, who'd been riding in their direction after his futile search. Running on only a couple hours of sleep because of watch duty had him practically dead on his feet by the time they'd reached the little Frenchwoman's wagon encampment—only to find that someone in her company had taken her wagon on ahead—whether with the intent of stealing it or taking it safely to the fort, they didn't know.

He'd halfway expected her to fall apart. Instead, she lifted her chin and started walking west like a woman determined to retrieve her wagon in the next five minutes. Cody swung down and walked behind her to give his horse a rest—and maybe to wake himself up a little.

Caesar rode up beside him, cast a look at his shoulder, and then trotted a few paces ahead and picked out a campsite. Cody had never been more thankful to see the sun nearly to the horizon. He practically slumped into camp behind the limping woman. He wanted only sleep, but she likely had a blister that he'd need to tend to avoid infection.

He filled his small canteen from the river, nudged her to a seat on a large boulder, and squatted before her.

Her gaze lowered to his bloody sleeve. "We should have stopped so your shoulder could be stitched, no?"

Cody's gaze lowered to her own wound, visible through the torn seam where her sleeve dangled. A blue bruise was spreading beneath the scrapes on her arm. "Seems you have an injury of your own. What's your name?"

She glanced down, then tried to lift the sleeve and tuck it beneath the material that still covered the top part of her shoulder. It immediately drooped again. She shrugged. Winced. "I tried from the pony to make an escape. It was not a nice pony." She touched her temple—also blue and painful looking.

She must be tough because she'd made not one complaint all day. "You still haven't told me your name."

Her chin lifted another notch. "As you have not told me yours, *monsieur*."

"Name's Cody Hawkeye." He pointed to Caesar, who was wandering back into camp from the direction of the river. "This here is Caesar Cranston."

Why hadn't they all introduced themselves earlier? For some reason, after he'd rescued her, they'd simply fallen into a weary silence. And once Caesar had joined them, he hadn't said much either. Caesar was never much of one for words. Cody silently chastised himself for the oversight. Mrs. Whitman from the mission school would have taken him to task for such a lack of manners. His heart panged him at the thought of his mentors and friends who had been killed in the attack on the mission station several years back.

Cody looked at the woman, as did Cranston, both waiting for her to respond.

She sighed. "My name is Chevonne Moreau."

Cody dipped his chin. "Pleased to meet you, Miss Moreau."

"Ma'am." Caesar tugged on the brim of his hat, then moved to stand beside Cody and motioned with a needle and thread toward his shirt. "Best you get that off so's I can stitch you up."

Cody reached instead for the needle. He angled his glance toward Chevonne. "Can you sew?"

She nodded. "*Oui.*"

"Good." Cody handed her the needle and rose, stripping off his buckskin shirt as he did so. "I've seen Caesar's stitching, and I don't want him coming anywhere near me." He grinned at his boss as he tossed the shirt onto the saddle Caesar must have removed from his horse.

Caesar grunted and stalked away. "I'll fetch some wood."

Chapter 11

Chevonne felt her brows nudge upward as Cody tugged his soft leather shirt over his head.

Ah, magnifique. She was weary and tired. But she wasn't dead! She felt her face heat with the wonder of the sculpted torso.

Back home in France, she and the other ladies-in-waiting had sometimes spied on the male servants when they'd gone swimming in the estate's lake. But those men had been pale and soft compared to the golden man standing before her, who had her blinking like dust had gotten into her eyes.

His gaze had followed Cranston, and heaven knew she wasn't above studying a creature of such beauty while she had a chance.

His chest and stomach could have been carved from stone.

He bent and set something beside her.

Had she even known that muscles on a man's stomach could look like a corduroyed street? Or that shoulders could be so broad and bronzed?

He straightened again and looked down at her, arms folded.

Several leather cords hung around his neck. One held a sheathed knife. Another, a few bright blue feathers. Still another, something metal that was partially obscured by the feathers. These were all cradled in a valley between two thick muscles.

Cody's brown hand rose to gather the items. He gripped them so tight that tendons stretched taut from his knuckles to his wrist. "Can you sew, or not?"

Chevonne blinked herself back to the present. What her assessment had not taken in was the blood dripping down one chiseled arm and also from the top of his shoulder.

She leapt from the boulder where she'd been sitting, feeling her face heat at her overlong scrutiny. "*Oui. Asseyez-vous, s'il vous plaît.*"

Her nervous embarrassment had her speaking the wrong language!

But he didn't seem to notice. He brushed past her and plunked onto the rock with a weary sigh. She had irritated him.

Chevonne willed herself to concentrate on the task at hand as she stepped close enough to the man to assess his wounds. The one across the top of his shoulder was deeper. She would need—

He lifted a canteen and a rag and thrust them toward her.

She swallowed and took them. That must have been what he'd set beside her a moment ago. "*Merci.*"

That French again.

He only nodded and tilted his head away to give her better access to the flesh that needed stitching.

Flesh. She swallowed again. This time for a very different reason. She could sew, yes. But she certainly had never sewn *flesh!*

Cody kept his head tilted, but angled his eyes toward her. "It's the same as any other sewing. Needle in. Needle out."

She glanced around their paltry camp. "Do you want some . . . spirits before with this needle I go to stabbing you?"

"No."

He offered nothing more, so she shored up her courage and stepped close. She wetted the rag and then dabbed away the blood to see what she was doing. The first stitch, then. She thrust the canteen into his good hand and draped the rag over his shoulder, where it would be near at hand when she needed it again.

Then she took a breath and pushed the needle through. "Sorry. So sorry." She winced.

But he made not a sound, and the only indication of any pain was the twitch in the muscle beneath her stitch.

Eh, bien. She needed to get this over with. He, after all, had received the wound while coming to save her. The least she could do was to stitch him up.

The task only took her a few minutes—the second wound only needed two stitches to the first one's nine—and when she was done, she felt certain that Maman would be proud of her neat needlework.

But now that the task was done and she had rinsed the blood from her hands with a sliver of soap that Cody had handed to her to take to the river, she felt quite weak in her knees.

Cody had donned his still-torn shirt—more's the pity—and now motioned for her to retake her seat on the rock.

She plunked herself down quite thankfully. Was this day ever going to end?

Cody squatted before the woman, looking up at her. "Thank you."

She nodded. Her mass of curls tangled about her face, and she reached with one hand to give a strand an irritated swipe behind her ear as she stared off toward the pink and gold beginning to touch the sky to the west.

Cody reached to unlace her boot.

She snatched her boots beneath the hem of her skirt and surged to her feet, retreating from him so quickly that she almost fell backwards over the boulder. "What are you doing?" Her eyes were wide with horror.

Cody raised both palms. "Easy. I need to look at your foot." He pointed to the one she'd been limping on. Hadn't that been obvious?

Her mouth fell open. "No such thing you will do!" Her tone clearly indicated her affront.

Cody frowned. Scrubbed fingers and thumb against his exhausted eyes. "I meant nothing by it, miss. Only meant to clean the wound so you won't get an infection, as you have just done for me." He willed away that soft floral scent that still lingered in his nostrils from her closeness. She was a duty, nothing more. And it was best he remember it. Except what he remembered was the softness of her lips beneath his. The way her hands had curled into the front of his shirt. The way she had looked at him just now that tempted a man to see if those lips would be just as soft a second time.

Caesar strode back into camp, hauling not only some brushwood but a large catfish, too. He tossed the fish into the grass and set to making a fire.

Cody returned his thoughts to the woman's foot. While the fish cooked, he needed to get a look at her injury. "Was your foot hurt when you ran from the Sioux?"

She frowned and lowered her gaze toward her hem, which hid those small boots he'd glimpsed. "In truth, it has been paining me for several days. The boots, they are new. And a size too large. But the store had none smaller. I thought they would be okay."

Cody stepped toward her, but she shot up one palm.

"I can clean the wound myself."

"So there is a wound?"

She sighed. Nodded.

He motioned her back toward the boulder. "Take off your own boots, but I need to see that sore."

She narrowed her eyes at him.

He stood his ground, weariness sapping his patience. "Like it or not, you are my responsibility until we can get you back to your own wagon train, and I need to see your foot to know how to treat it."

She arched a saucy brow. "A command it is then? Not a request?"

He felt his teeth mash together. "Please, Miss Moreau, will you take off your boots so I can see how to help you?"

Her shoulders seemed to lose some of their stiffness. "You'll know? How to treat it?"

He nodded. "Yes." She didn't have to believe him. She only had to listen. He swept a hand toward the boulder once more.

She huffed and sank onto it. "You are most stubborn, *monsieur*."

He grinned, but it was more a stretch of his lips than a feeling of actual levity. "I think we might be cut from the same cloth on that score, miss."

Despite the fact that she sank onto the rock and seemed like she was ready to capitulate, she hesitated, and Cody felt his eyes narrow.

She glanced toward the Platte that meandered along the north side of their camp. "I should at least wash before you see it. The—"

"I already brought water." Cody held up his canteen, then dropped into a squat before her, and this time, when he reached for her boot, she didn't resist other than to release an irritated puff of breath.

He balanced on the balls of his feet and glanced up at her as he undid the laces. "All our feet get dirty on the trail, miss. We'll get it washed up, soon as I see what we're dealing with."

Carefully, he eased her boot off over her heel and heard her sharp gasp as he did so. When he looked up, her eyes were closed, and her lower lip was tucked between her teeth. So, this tough one had been suffering for how long?

She wore the same knee-height stockings that his sister used to wear. He swept one hand up her leg to find the top, but he'd only reached her calf when she gave his shoulder such a shove that he had to scramble to maintain his balance. He ended up with both arms propped on the ground behind him, pain shooting through his newly stitched shoulder, and her towering over him with a glare that could have arrowed directly through him.

"*Tu es un homme dépravé!*"

"Depraved?" Anger boiled in his veins. All he wanted was to wrap himself in his blanket and catch some shut-eye, but he was here, trying to help her. And this was the thanks he got?

That semblance of a smile stretched his lips again as he rose to his feet. He took her elbow and leaned toward her. The smile fell from his lips. "I can assure you, miss, that if I were a depraved man, I would not have come to rescue you. Even now, I'm only trying to save your life by tending to your wound, and yet you seem to think I intend to assault you and with another man sitting right across the fire!"

Her blue eyes widened, and she leaned away from him.

Across the fire, Caesar cleared his throat pointedly.

Cody glanced over.

Caesar cocked one eyebrow and flicked a glance toward where Cody gripped the woman's arm.

Cody promptly released her and took a step back. He propped one hand against his hip, hung his head, and ran his other hand over the long braid at the back of his head. He raised his head to survey the prairie. What was it about this woman that could rile him quicker than a wolf with a fresh kill?

He lifted one hand and turned to face her, but couldn't seem to bring himself to look her in the eyes. "And yet here I am acting like the very depraved man you labeled me. Last night was my watch back at our camp. I'm running on very little sleep—and patience, it seems. I apologize. Please remove your stocking, so that I might see the wound and then get some sleep."

After one more glance at Caesar, who gave her a nod as though to indicate he was there to protect her, the woman sank back onto the boulder. "You look there." She pointed for Cody to turn his back.

Cody faced Caesar and glared at him. The old man only laughed and gave the catfish a quarter turn on the spit he'd rigged above the flames. "I've never seen you like this."

"Like what?" Cody's tone dared the man to imply anything more.

Caesar only chuckled again and focused on jabbing at the coals in the fire.

"Now, you may look. But I need the water—as I tried to tell you."

Cody spun to find the heat of her ire leveled up at him. He uncorked the canteen and squatted before her once again. She held her dirty red hem just above her ankle, and he could see that her stocking was crusted and stuck to the seeping wound at the back of her heel.

A hiss of breath escaped his lips. "Did that fool of a wagon master not recognize your injury?" He sloshed water over her stocking to loosen it. He waited for the water to do its work as he looked to assess her response.

She tucked her lower lip between her teeth and then shook her head. "The job that in Oregon I secured was late to contact me, you see. And I, at the last moment, scrambled to find a wagon train. Monsieur Engstrom alone would take me—and only if I could pay the required sum, which was double what others had been asking."

She stopped the story there as though that were all the information he needed to form a picture of the wagon master—and she'd be right. It was a picture that made another tremor of anger work through him. He sloshed more water on the stocking, then rose. "Sit tight."

He stalked to his saddlebags and withdrew the pieces of folded leather. They weren't large, but she had small feet, and they would do. He also withdrew a roll of cotton, his stick of pitch-glue, and the bar of soap that she'd only given back to him a moment ago. He returned to her and shucked his bowie from the sheath at his hip as he sank back down and set the knife, cotton, soap, and pieces of leather aside.

She had worked the stocking off of the wound now, and he could see that several blisters had broken open, and one looked red and swollen. The wound needed a good soaking and then a scrub. What he wouldn't give for a bucket. His gaze shifted to the river. Here it was shallow and sluggish with hardly any embankments, and there would be no place deep enough for her to sit to soak her foot unless they waded out a ways. If they did that, her skirts would get drenched, and that would make for a miserable night for her.

He snatched up the roll of cotton and sliced off a section. This he soaked with more water from his canteen before he swiped the bar of soap against it a couple of times. He looked up at her. "This is going to hurt."

She nodded. "Do what you must." She pressed her lips into a tight line as though preparing to handle the pain.

Cody had to admire her grit as he went to work cleaning the wound, and she made no sound other than to breathe sharply a time or two. "Done." He leaned forward to blow air against the broken skin to soothe it.

Chevonne swallowed and blinked hard to hold back her tears as the Indian warrior bent over her ankle and blew against her wound like her father used to do for her when she was but a child. It wasn't the pain that had her near tears, but the emotion of connection with this man who was naught but a stranger. When was the last time someone had taken time to think about her needs and care for her?

Life at court had been nothing but a series of moves and counter moves where everyone fought for their own gain. She had been a lady-in-waiting to the empress and once believed the woman a friend. But the empress had only elevated her for access to her father—and the renowned wine from their estate that she wished to serve at her banquets.

Then there had been the incident with the empress's cousin that had proven the woman cared not a whit about Chevonne or her reputation. And none of the other ladies of the court had come to her defense either. Nor had Father when it came right down to it. For her stubbornness in angering the empress, he'd spurned Chevonne and sent her off with nothing more than a few francs to her name.

Yet now, here on the edge of nowhere, a man who didn't even know her had come to her rescue and cared enough to pause and pay attention.

He cut another strip of the bandage and wrapped it around her ankle, split the end, and tied it in place. Still squatting before her, he washed his hands with water from the canteen and the bar of soap he'd used to scrub her wound, then dried them on a clean scrap of cotton.

He glanced up. He opened his mouth as though he'd intended to speak, but then seemed to freeze in place. His gaze fastened onto hers.

She was surprised to note that the dark color of his eyes was more gray than brown. His lashes were long enough to give any woman envy, but it was the intensity of his gaze that held her captive.

She blinked. Moisture touched her cheek.

He reached up to swipe it away with his thumb. "Sorry. I know that must have been painful."

Chevonne blinked. Came back to herself and gave her head a little shake. Right. He thought she was crying from the pain. The truth was, she welcomed the pain because it meant someone cared. How pitiful did that make her? She sniffed. Eased her spine into a straight line.

The man must never know how his simple act of kindness had affected her. He was only doing what he saw as his duty and nothing more. Besides, she'd caught a glimpse of his ferocity a moment ago, hadn't she? He was likely to be a man like her father who would turn on her when she needed him most. She would be wise to rein in her thoughts lest she make a fool of herself.

The older man by the fire took the fish off the spit. "Dinner is served," he said grandly.

Chevonne's stomach rumbled loudly, and when she looked down at the man squatting before her in embarrassment, he was grinning up at her.

"Best we give the lady here the first piece, Caesar. Sounds like her belly is about to eat her alive from the inside."

She reached for her boot, but he snatched it out of her reach. "I need this for a bit. Take the other one off, too, please, while I get you a plate."

Chevonne tamped down her irritation. But she was too weary to fight him. If he wanted her stinky boots, he could have them. She took off the second boot and watched as he strode to his horse and tugged a blue enamelware plate from a saddlebag. Back before Caesar, he held out the plate and the older man laid a slice of meat on it. This Cody brought to her. "It's not much, but we're a little low on supplies."

When she took the plate, he gave her a nod. "I'll return your boots come morning."

She was too tired to even be curious as to what he might want to do with her boots. She turned her attention to her plate.

Fish had never been her favorite food. And with her first bite, she scrunched her nose. Catfish was even worse. But she forced herself to finish all of it, knowing that her body needed it.

After she forced down the last bite, she rose to take the plate to the river, but Cody was before her once again. "I'll clean this after I use it. Catch some shut-eye. We'll rise early."

With that, he turned his back and stalked over to remove the remainder of the fish from the spit.

There was a weary droop to his shoulders as he set about eating.

Chevonne glanced around. The prairie was vast. There was no cover. No blankets. No—

"Here." Cody was back by her side. He kicked a couple of rocks from a spot near the fire, unfurled a roll of padded canvas covered by a hide blanket, and returned to his plate. "Sleep well, miss."

Was this his only bedding? She bent and scooped up the soft leather blanket from atop the padding and turned to hand it to him, but he thrust up one hand. "I'll be fine."

"You must sleep, too, *monsieur*. You must let me share."

Caesar stepped toward him and handed him a large leather poncho. "I have my bedroll, so don't worry none about me."

Cody gave the man a nod. He looked back at her and lifted the poncho. "I'll use this. Get some sleep."

Chevonne wanted to weep with weary gratitude as she sank onto the bedroll and covered herself with the hide. The scent of leather and a hint of the soap that Cody had used on her foot enveloped her. An altogether pleasant scent that had her nuzzling her nose deeper beneath the hide covering.

Above her, the stars glittered. Her mother would have said that God had sent these men to her rescue. And she *had* prayed for rescue, after all.

Merci, Père. Thank You, for sending these men to my aid.

Was there even a God up there to hear her?

The stars blinked to blackness, and when she woke the next morning, it was to find Cody squatting above her with Caesar's poncho still wrapped about his shoulders and a tin cup of coffee gripped in one hand.

She surged upright, shoving her mass of curls back from her face and giving him a sleepy squint.

He grinned. Held the cup toward her. Balanced atop it was a strip of dried meat. "Time to rise, miss. We need to be on our way. Sorry I don't have more food to offer than this strip of jerked beef this morning. At least the coffee's hot." He rose to his feet. "Oh, and I took the liberty of lining the inside of your boots with some leather. I think they'll fit better now."

Surprised, she lifted the boots and examined the insides. He'd not only lined the bottom of the shoes with a new piece of smooth leather, but put a piece at the heel. And somehow, the man had glued the leather in place. How had he done that? At the top where the piece of leather met the heel of her shoe, she could see a thin, smooth black line. Some kind of glue? What was it?

Someday, she'd have to ask him. For now, she slid the shoes on and could already feel that they fit better. Her heel no longer slipped against the back of the shoe.

When she looked up, he was watching her. "Better?"

She nodded. "*Merci beaucoup.*"

He kicked dirt onto the smoldering coals of the morning fire. "Welcome. Best eat. We need to move out."

She sighed and took a bite of the meat he'd given her. More accurately, she tried to take a bite and was foiled. She glanced down at the meat and heard him chuckle.

"Bite and pull from the edges. You'll like it once you get the hang of it. But you'll have to do it from the back of my horse. Here comes Caesar now, and he's been raring to go for at least thirty minutes."

She sighed and allowed him to help her once more onto his mount. She tried to ignore the strength of his arms as he swung up behind her and took the reins. Tried not to envision the sculpted smooth ridges of the torso she'd gawked at the day before.

She failed miserably.

This time, when she chomped on the meat with a vicious ferocity, the fibers gave way to her teeth. And true to Cody's promise, the flavor was good even if she did feel like she might be chewing on the new shoe-leather that the man had pressed into her boots.

Chapter 12

It only took Boone a few questions at the fort's livery to learn that Betsy had requested a mount the day before, sometime right after the hanging. Maybe even right after she'd spoken to comfort him about the loss of his brother.

Boone's jaw clenched. Platitudes. She'd helped Del escape and planned her own escape, but had dared to offer him platitudes?

The liveryman said she'd told him she was riding to Independence to deal with a misunderstanding over a load of supplies. He hadn't questioned her because she'd always come and gone as she pleased from the fort.

Boone stood in the livery doorway and scanned the surrounding prairie. "Which way did she go?"

The liveryman pointed. "Rode east. I figured she was headed to Independence just like she said."

Boone swept his tongue along the inside of his cheek. He tasted blood, and his heart gave a jolt, but he couldn't ponder on his suddenly failing lungs right now. If Betsy had a day's head start and truly was headed to Independence, she would beat him there, and then she'd have lawmen and plenty of friends around to protect her.

If she wasn't headed for Independence, but only riding that way until she was out of sight and then changing directions, he could probably find her trail, but that would take time away from hunting Delilah.

He wanted to curse and rail, but his military training stood him in good stead, and he remained standing calmly by the liveryman. "Thanks, Fred. Appreciate your help."

He turned and walked with purpose back to his office.

As he sank into his chair, he pondered the testimonies of all his men. To a man, they'd declared that they had thoroughly searched every wagon. To. A. Man.

He pressed fingers and thumb to his eyes wearily.

His tracker had circled the area for hours hunting for some sign of Del, but had found nothing.

Boone swiped a stack of papers off his desk. They fluttered ineffectually to the floor, doing nothing to soothe his burst of anger.

It was like she'd disappeared! She couldn't just disappear.

He folded his hands, steepled his fingers, and tapped them to his lips.

Drawing a breath, he broke down the problem. First, she hadn't simply disappeared. Betsy had helped her escape. Second, Betsy wouldn't want the girl to have to fend for herself somewhere on the open prairie.

That left two options. Either the girl had gone east and waited somewhere for Betsy to come meet her the next day and they were somewhere together, headed toward Independence, Saint Joseph, or any other number of cities.

Or Del had been hiding in one of the wagons of that train, and his men had missed her.

This time, he sent his ink pot sailing across the room, and it gave a much more satisfactory performance as it crashed against the wall, sending a spray of ink in every direction. Ink dripped down the wall, and Boone felt better as he watched the pattern expand.

Two options. He could deal with two options.

He would send his tracker east. The man knew what Betsy looked like and would also be familiar with the tracks of any horse she'd taken from the livery.

Boone would ride west and catch up to that wagon train. He was good at being covert. They wouldn't even know he was there until he was ready for them to know his wrath!

His chest felt tight. He tried to take a breath, but it felt like he was sucking for air through a damp cloth. He needed to calm his emotions, or he would end up in a heap on the floor. Why was the room spinning so? He clutched for the desk. Missed. Felt himself tipping. And then somehow, he was on the floor, blinking up at the ceiling.

"Captain?" The soldier who'd been standing post outside his office called from outside the door. "You okay in there?"

Boone opened his mouth, but with no air in his lungs, he couldn't find his voice.

The door burst open, and the soldier surged in.

Black spots now bedeviled Boone's vision.

The soldier dashed to Boone's office window and threw it open. "Get the doc! Someone fetch the doctor! The captain has collapsed!"

Blazes. Now the whole fort was going to know of his malady.

Boone gave in to the tug of the darkness.

Whitley emptied the water from the washbasin onto the ground as Papa approached with baby Blythe cradled in the crook of one arm.

"Children, gather around." He swept one hand gently over Liberty's tangled curls. Wren had just finished combing Silas's, Soren's, and Serenity's hair, but hadn't made it to Liberty yet, apparently.

Whitley flipped the wash rag over the edge of the basin and tucked it against one hip, then stretched her hand to Cumberland. "Come on. Papa wants a word with us."

She was always glad on the days when it was her turn to do the dishes because at least that was a somewhat solitary task. Normally, Mama helped with dressing and grooming the children, but she'd been uncommon tired this morning. And who could blame her after yesterday's hard labor?

Ahead, Granny Marigold sat in her rocking chair. Cumberland trotted on chubby legs to clamber up to join her. Granny wrapped her arms around him and kissed him roughly on the cheek until he was naught but a heap of giggles.

"Oh, I love you, my boy." She turned him forward and settled him onto her lap, arms wrapped firmly about him.

Whitley smiled as she hung the washbasin on its hook on the side of the wagon. She laid the damp wash rag on the box next to the basin, being sure to spread it so it would dry in today's heat.

She returned to the family gathering and tugged Serenity onto her lap. Wren settled Liberty before her and began to work on her hair as Papa snapped his fingers for Silas and Soren to quit their game of marbles and pay attention.

Whitley thought of all the work they still had to do and wished that Papa would get on with whatever it was he wanted to say.

There were still all the foodstuffs to return to the wagon, the fire to extinguish, and the team to hitch. But Papa seemed at ease and unconcerned, even with Mama still sleeping in the wagon.

Just when she felt that everyone had quieted sufficiently for Papa to begin, Jeremiah and Miss Deliverance approached.

"Well, now!" Papa beamed and stretched his hand to shake theirs. "Good to have you stop by! What can we do for you?"

Jeremiah swung his hat at baby Blythe. "We just came by to gawk at that baby, truth be told."

Miss Deliverance smiled shyly, but then she scanned the encampment with a crimp of a frown on her face.

Who was she searching for?

Maybe she was worried that someone would object to her wanting to see the baby?

Whit nudged Serenity to the grass and popped to her feet.

Certainly, no Hawthorne would begrudge the woman a look at the baby who was only alive because of her intervention!

Whitley took the baby from Papa and handed her to Del with a smile. "We are so glad you stopped by. We all owe you a heap of thanks for what you did!"

Miss Deliverance's eyes grew a little round as she accepted the baby and looked down at her. A smile replaced the concern she'd worn only a moment ago, and Whitley felt better already.

Jeremiah stepped close to her side and peered down at Blythe's downy head. "My! Ain't she the prettiest baby in all the territories!"

Miss Deliverance nodded, her gaze never leaving Blythe's.

Whitley glanced at all the other wagons. Most were already hitching their teams. Mama was usually the one to keep Papa on time. She supposed today it was up to her. "Papa, hadn't we better hitch the team?"

"In a moment, Whitley girl. I have something to say, and I'm glad these two are here to hear it."

Both Miss Deliverance and Jeremiah lifted their heads. They obviously hadn't realized they'd wandered into a Hawthorne family meeting.

Whitley grinned.

"What I want to say, children, has to do with fear."

Miss Deliverance's feet shuffled, and she returned her gaze to baby Blythe, bouncing her a little just like Mama would do.

Whitley decided the baby was in good hands and returned to gather Serenity onto her lap once more. She loved these gatherings where Papa dispensed his wisdom.

"You see . . ." Papa set about putting out the campfire as he spoke. "This mortal flesh is temporary." He waved a hand. "You all are young. Not one of you has felt your mortality yet. But yesterday, I confess that I was feeling mine to the fullest, or more to the point, your mother's.

You all saw me pacing a trench right under that tree there. And after Miss Deliverance there helped bring Blythe into the world, I knew I couldn't let a day go by without admonishing you, children, that in this world, we will have tribulation, but we are instructed in the Word to take heart because Jesus has overcome the world. What we must be clear on, what I want you all to remember, is that it doesn't mean this life will always turn out great for us. Look at Gran." He swept a hand toward his mother, who still cuddled Cumberland. "We lost Pa when I was only fifteen. Your gran, though, she carried on without Pa, but not without the Lord's help, right Ma?"

Granny nodded. "Right, indeed!"

Papa gave a firm dip of his chin. "Okay, so the lesson I want you all to hear today is this . . . Even if your ma and sweet Blythe had died yesterday, God would still be good, because this life is not our everything. Eternity with Him, the One who died to save us, that is our everything. That is how we will overcome! Because of how Jesus has already overcome! He came, lived a sinless life, and then died for our sins, and that fulfilled the law, which in turn allows us to take hold of His perfection for ourselves. But only when we confess Him as our Lord and Savior. Now." Papa clapped his hands. "That is all for today. Off to your chores. And boys . . . ?"

Silas and Soren, who were already halfway into a sprint toward the oxen, froze.

"No dawdling over bullfrogs today, aye?"

"Yes, sir." They were sprinting again before they'd hardly finished the words.

As Wren and the little girls carried Grandma's rocker to its hooks on the side of the wagon, and Granny carried Cumberland to Ma, Whitley went to fetch Blythe from Miss Deliverance. Jeremiah must have already left to get their team, though she hadn't noticed when he'd done so.

"Thank you for letting us see her," Miss Deliverance said. She handed the baby over. "Please let me know if I can help in any way."

Whitley smiled, tucking the blanket away from Blythe's face. "We're pretty self-sufficient. But we appreciate the offer."

As Miss Deliverance walked away toward the Slade wagon, Whitley turned to wrap one arm around Papa's ribs.

He consumed her in a giant bear hug, careful not to crush the baby. "You've been awfully quiet lately, Whitley girl."

Whitley relished the warmth of Papa's embrace. "Just a lot to do, I guess."

Papa put her at arm's length, his big hands on her shoulders. "Come on now, girly. It's you and me. We've never kept anything from each other."

Whitley sighed. Adjusted the blanket near Blythe's face again, just to give her fingers something to do. She couldn't tattle on her twin. But Papa had been tired lately, too. He hadn't been paying as good of attention as he ought. She let her gaze slide to where Wren was just finishing hanging the rocker.

Papa followed her glance. "Ah. So, it's Wren I need to be speaking to?"

"I didn't say anything!"

Papa smiled. "Don't worry, girly. She won't know a thing." He bent and placed a kiss on the top of her head. "For now, I must hitch the team."

Chapter 13

Chevonne's backside ached as she rode into Fort Kearny on the front of Cody's horse. Forget just backside! Every muscle ached—and that despite the fact that she had leaned more heavily on Cody than she ought several times throughout the day.

Caesar had pulled up to speak to someone when they first rode into town, and now, as Cody pulled up in front of the mercantile, his arms steadied her. Before dismounting, he leaned to one side to assess her face. "You doing okay?"

"*Oui.*" She answered in French before realizing and quickly amended, "Yes, thank you." But that was a lie. She was not all right. Not even the least. Because here, she could see the people from her former wagon train, and these two men who had been nothing but kind to her would drop her off and leave her to once again fend for herself amidst a group who seemed not to care one whit whether she lived or died.

She rolled her eyes at herself. That was a bit melodramatic, even for her. She chastised herself for being weak and needy. She would make it to Oregon! And she could make friends once she got there. These standoffish people were just a means to an end. At least someone had driven her wagon here, for she could see the blue, white, and red stripes she had painted on the tailgate—an homage to the French flag and the home country she missed with every breath. All her belongings had better be unmolested!

Behind her, Cody swung down and then reached to help her descend. She leaned toward him and pressed her palms against his shoulders, feeling his own hands circle her waist. Lithe muscles rippled beneath the fabric of his buckskin shirt as he swung her to the ground. She had intended to take a step away the moment her feet were on the ground, and yet somehow, the magnetic pull of his gaze held her in place.

One corner of his mouth quirked up. "It has been a pleasure to come to your rescue, Miss Moreau." His gaze dipped to her lips for the briefest of seconds before rebounding. His quick wink revealed he was pure rogue!

Feeling heat infuse her face as she realized she'd lingered, she took a step of escape, but too late, recognized the tingles in her leg as it gave out from under her. "Eee!"

Strong hands once again wrapped around her waist. "Perhaps you should stay here until that leg of yours wakes up. Can't say that I'll mind in the least." He settled into his heels, looking like he planned to plant himself right here in the street until he grew roots. Again, that maddening quirk of his lips.

Swallowing down a laugh that would only add fuel to his fire, Chevonne pushed him back, balancing on her good leg and willing herself to forget the warmth of the rock-hard chest that now lay out of her reach. She also willed her bum leg to come to life—*rapidement!*

Cody didn't seem the least perturbed by her shove. He looped his horse's reins around the hitching post, then turned to face her. "So, this town you are headed to in Oregon? What is it called?"

If only she knew the answer to that question. She glanced up at him, trying to decide the best way to explain. His eyes were an even darker gray in this light. Caused by the shadow of the tall building they stood before? Or perhaps those enviously long lashes?

Again, that maddening slash of those tempting lips in the smooth scape of a chiseled jawline. "A man could be crushed by your lack of trust, Miss Moreau."

Oh dear. Had she hurt his feelings? She hurried to amend. "A lack of trust, it is not, *monsieur*! I assure you that—"

He laughed down at her.

She broke off with an embarrassed sigh and gave his shoulder a slap. He'd been teasing her. It ought to be against the law for a man to have such good looks and charm to boot. Just then, her stomach rumbled loudly.

Cody's brows rose. "Guess we better make sure we feed you before we head on our way. It appears there's a grub hut just a couple doors down." He turned and thrust out an elbow for her to take.

Chevonne was pleasantly surprised by his manners and automatically settled her hand in the crook of his arm even as her nose wrinkled. "These grubs . . . You eat them here in America?"

Cody threw back his head on a laugh. "Plenty of people do, I guess, but 'grub' just means food—anything you can eat. But it's also a fat worm, yes." Once again, his sparkling gaze settled on her. "But you're a fine one to talk. Don't you eat snails in France?"

Chevonne gave a mock gasp. "*Les escargots sont très délicieux!*"

Cody grinned down at her and rebutted, "*Les larves sont très délicieuses.*"

She wrinkled her nose at him. "This is not possible."

With a twinkle still in his eyes, Cody opened his mouth, but a woman on the boardwalk ahead of them cleared her throat loudly.

Chevonne startled at the loud sound, snapping her gaze forward to take note of Mrs. Hubbard with lips pressed into a tight, thin line and a narrow look of distrust on Cody.

"Chevonne, best you step away from that man. Right now."

She felt Cody stiffen. Then he immediately straightened his arm to release her hand from the crook. He stepped to one side and gave

Mrs. Hubbard a respectful nod. "Ma'am. Sorry if we were blocking the boardwalk."

But behind the polite reply, Chevonne saw a hint of weariness. The flirty humor no longer lit his eyes. And where his lips had been tilted with tease for the last few minutes, they now pressed into a grim, tight line—as though he might be attempting to keep himself from saying something he'd regret.

Mrs. Hubbard never took her eyes off Cody as she scooted sideways, fumbling one hand through the air in search of Chevonne's. When she had Chevonne in a firm grasp, she attempted to tug her down the boardwalk.

Chevonne refused to move, so the woman gave her hand a jerk, terrified eyes still pinned on Cody. "Come on, young lady!"

Chevonne frowned. She forcefully removed her hand from Mrs. Hubbard's. She fought through the French that wanted to burst from her lips and forced the English words instead. "To my rescue, Mr. Hawkeye has come, and now to eat grubs he is taking me." As though to emphasize the point, her stomach rumbled loudly again.

Mrs. Hubbard's gasp was probably heard at the other end of town. She covered her gaping mouth with one hand and swept Cody with an aghast look, obviously horrified to think how he was corrupting Chevonne's diet.

Chevonne continued as though nothing out of the ordinary were happening, because that was the truth of the matter. "At what time do we go onward to Oregon?"

Mrs. Hubbard was still eyeballing Cody like he might lunge at her with his knife—and from the glower he had leveled on the woman, it was no wonder.

"F-first light," she stuttered.

Purposely, Chevonne reached for Cody's arm again. "This is good! Plenty of time for grubs!" After a parting wave to Mrs. Hubbard, she led him toward the diner, smiling up at him in the hope of seeing a renewal of his good humor.

But outside the eatery's door, he hesitated. He fumbled with a leather poke, pulling out a few dollars. He thrust them toward her. "Maybe you should just go in and get yourself a meal, Miss Moreau."

Chevonne would have liked to march back down the boardwalk and snatch Mrs. Hubbard's hair to give the woman a few firm shakes. Instead, she lifted her chin. "And how shall I know what grubs to eat if you are not there to guide me, *monsieur*?"

Ah! Blessed providence! There was that glint of humor in his eyes again as he looked down at her. And that quirk of those tempting lips. "It's grub."

Chevonne felt a frown settle on her brow. "Only one grub? Not a very large meal, no? My stomach is sure to go on grumbling in protest all the day!"

For the briefest of moments, that smile grew, and then his gaze trailed after Mrs. Hubbard, and his humor was replaced once more by a frown.

Chevonne cleared her throat. "This door, it will not open by itself." She gave a pointed nod, hoping he would take the hint and return to his gentlemanly conduct.

With a grim press of his lips, he did, and she took his hand as she passed by. But when he yanked his fingers from her grasp, she hung her head, appropriately chastised for her forward behavior. She halfway wondered if he would abandon her, but was thankful when he dragged himself inside and sank into a seat across from her.

A man emerged from the back room, wiping his hands on a rag that appeared to have seen cleaner days. "We got chicken and taters. And black coffee."

Chevonne quirked a brow at Cody. "Grub is right, *monsieur*."

Cody held up two fingers to the man, who gave a nod and disappeared into the back once again. Then Cody leveled her with a serious look. "You never answered my question about where you are to teach in The Territory."

She squirmed, unsure why she was so uneasy about admitting the truth. Maybe because she knew he wouldn't like it. She worked her teeth over the inside of her lower lip and then decided she'd simply best spit it out. "I am to meet a man in the Oregon City, and he will guide me to the town where I will teach." She lifted one shoulder. "This is all I know."

Cody's eyes narrowed.

She sighed. Yes. Just as she'd suspected.

"A complete stranger? A man? And you thought this was a good idea?"

She shot her chin into the air, hackles immediately rising. "Some of us require more than grubs to eat, Mr. Hawkeye. A job I needed. This one was the first to take me." She lifted one shoulder.

The man from the back appeared by their table and set steaming cups of coffee before them. Just the scent of the black brew had Chevonne closing her eyes and inhaling deeply. When she looked up, Cody's hard gaze was still on her. "Join our wagon train, and when we get to Oregon, I'll escort you to your school myself."

"What's this I hear?"

Chevonne looked up to see that Caesar had drawn up a chair and was standing by their table, but he hadn't bothered to sit yet. Instead, he stood glowering down at Cody.

Cody reached for a spoon and flipped it end over end. He didn't seem to want to meet Caesar's gaze. "You and I both know we can't leave her to those wolves."

Caesar dropped his chair beside their table with a thud and slumped into it, casting a long glare in her direction.

Chevonne wasn't sure what she'd done. She hadn't even agreed to Cody's request yet. But she had to admit to a great deal of relief at even the prospect of the offer because, well, at least she would have some friends amongst the travelers. She bounced a glance off Caesar's glare. Okay, maybe one friend. She swallowed and shot her chin into the air. "I accept your offer, Mr. Hawkeye!"

Caesar growled so loudly that it made her startle. "First Striker, and now you, too?"

Cody snapped his fingers, that telltale humor back in his gray-brown eyes. "That's right. You did let old Strike bring a single woman along on the trip, didn't you? And then there's Deliverance."

Caesar's lips pressed into a sour pooch. "If I didn't have news that needs to get back to some of our folk, I'd argue with you on this, but fine. She can come too."

Chevonne wasn't sure if she ought to be offended or relieved, but thankfulness not to be left with Redd and his company was the overwhelming emotion. "I will not be any trouble, *oui*? Of this I can most strongly assure you, *monsieur*."

Cody's gaze slipped to the tear in the shoulder of her dress, and some of the humor drained from his expression. "You'll forgive us if we doubt that very much, now, won't you, Miss Moreau?" Without giving her time to respond, he turned his gaze on his boss. "News?" Cody's manner had turned all business.

The older man nodded. "Boone Baxter has collapsed, and the doc here at the fort doesn't think he has long."

Cody's brows shot up. "That is news."

Caesar nodded.

Curiosity almost had Chevonne asking who Boone Baxter was and why this seemed of such import to them, but she decided that fading into the background might not be such a bad idea, lest Caesar change his mind about allowing her to join his wagon train.

After the meal, Cody and Caesar escorted her to her wagon and helped her inside, where she lovingly caressed one hand over the hard leather case of her harp and then fell promptly onto her tick as the two men settled onto bedrolls outside. Thankfully, her wagon did, indeed, appear unmolested.

Exhausted, she slept the night through, and when she woke the next morning and peered out from the canvas, it was to see Cody standing a ways off in a deep conversation with Redd Engstrom.

Redd didn't look any too happy, and Cody looked downright angry. He stepped toward the man and held out one hand, palm up. With a slump of his shoulders, Redd slapped a leather poke into Cody's hand. Cody gave the man a nod, and Chevonne withdrew into her wagon before he could catch her watching.

When she emerged a few moments later, this time wearing her plain blue frock, Cody was waiting nearby with that leather poke still in his hand. His gaze narrowed as it skimmed over her. "Don't you have anything normal to wear?"

Chevonne's chin shot into the air. "What about this is not normal?"

Looking off toward the horizon, he pinched the bridge of his nose and muttered something beneath his breath that she didn't quite catch. After only a moment, however, he thrust the poke at her. "This is the fee you paid to Redd. Since he didn't fulfill his end of the contract and get you safely to Oregon, I figured it was owed to you."

"All of it?" She gasped as she opened the top of the cinched leather to see that it was indeed just as full as it had been when she'd reluctantly handed all her worldly savings over to Redd. *Merci, Monsieur* Cody. *Merci beaucoup.*" She pulled the strings tight and clutched the coin purse to her chest.

With one smooth leap, Cody sprang onto his bay and then reined it around so he was looking down at her where she stood near the wagon. "You'll need to pay part of that to Caesar, but he's a fair man and won't charge you double like Redd did. And since we've already completed a good portion of the journey, he probably won't even make you pay full price. You can figure that out with him later. For now, I need to fetch your oxen. What's your brand?"

Chevonne smiled. "Oh, mine are the Clydesdales. Two pair." Her heart surged with happiness at getting to see her dear pets once more.

Cody was once again pinching the bridge of his nose. He froze there for a moment as though he might be praying, but finally lifted his head. "You been feeding them grain?"

She frowned. "No. The grass they are eating and seem to have no complaints, yes?" Had she been mistreating her poor horses without knowing it?

He grunted, gave a weary shake of his head, and rode off without another word.

When he returned, leading her horses, each one had three large sacks of grain on its back!

Chevonne gaped at him. He didn't expect those to go in her wagon, did he? There was no room! "What am I to do with these?"

Cody shook his head. "These have to go inside." Unceremoniously, he swung down from his mount and then up and into her wagon.

Chevonne gaped up at him, arms folded.

He pointed to her harp. "This is big. If we leave it, some of the grain can go here."

She gasped. "This is my harp! It cannot be left behind!" Before she even realized she was moving, she found herself in her wagon, standing between Cody and her instrument, chin raised, arms folded.

Again with the muttering. And he sure did seem very fascinated with the bridge of his nose today.

Chevonne glanced out at her horses. "The grain, they must have?"

He nodded gravely, his breath releasing in a long exhale. "I'm surprised they made it this far without any. That's why most people bring oxen. You didn't know that?"

She blinked. She would not cry. She simply wouldn't. Back in France, the stable hands had taken care of all the animals. She'd only ever seen the horses out at pasture. How was she to know that she'd been abusing her poor Clydesdales? She loved horses, but to say that she'd been sheltered from all that would be involved in taking care of them was an understatement. Her shoulders sagged. Was she even fit to take on this teaching job in Oregon? She who didn't even know that her horses needed more than grass?

"*Ne pleure pas, chérie.*" He skimmed the back of his first knuckle across the point of her chin.

She jerked away from his touch. "I am *not* crying!"

He draped his hands against his hips and tilted her a look.

She sniffed and waved a hand around the interior. "The grain, you may fit in where wedged it may be, but all things must stay." She thrust a finger in his face. "Especially my harp!"

With that, she fled lest the man see that she had indeed been reduced to tears.

Chapter 14

Sitting in the back of the trundling wagon, Del smiled as she remembered sweet baby Blythe's scrunched-up face, chubby cheeks, and tiny fist that had been pressed near her temple as she slept.

Holding the baby had been sweet, but Del knew that the Lord had taken her by the Hawthorne fire at just that moment to hear Mr. Hawthorn's word of encouragement to his children. And she loved that God loved her so well.

Now they'd been traveling for most of the day, and Del was weary of sitting in the wagon. For some of the day she had tromped back and forth in the aisle between the crates, but it was an uncomfortable way to travel, because it was only three steps in each direction and the jostling wagon made for the need of holding onto the stays overhead to keep her balance in the middle, and stooping slightly so as not to whack her head on each end.

Still, she was thankful that she hadn't been expected to walk the whole way this first day. Because of her captivity, she knew her state was weakened. She must do her best, however, to regain that strength a little at a time.

They had stopped at noon along the banks of the Platte, and Del had been so thankful for a few moments of rest from the infernal bucking. After Jeremiah had given her the all-clear, she had descended to pace near the fire for a few minutes on solid ground. There had been no time for anything more than some of the leftover flapjacks and scrambled eggs from the morning meal, and she'd been ever so thankful to the women who'd thoughtfully sent some of the leftovers with her and Jeremiah.

Now this evening, they were to reach the ranch of a man named Dan Smith and stay on the outskirts of his place.

"Whoa!" Outside, Jeremiah's voice spoke soothingly to the team of oxen. "Settle down now. We'll get you some water in just a moment."

Her pallet shifted as he presumably leapt from the bench.

Del hadn't given tonight's camp much more than a passing thought after Jeremiah had told her where it would be, but now she found her familiar fears rising to the fore again. A ranch meant other people. Strangers. Those who might talk if Boone ever passed this way, asking questions.

She closed her eyes and drew in a long, slow inhale. Weary as she was of the inside of this canvas-wrapped box, she'd best stay put at least until darkness gave her some cover.

And yet, she couldn't expect Jeremiah to cook and fetch for her. What was she going to do on that score?

As if he'd suspected that she might be thinking of him, that very man pulled back the canvas at the rear of the wagon. "You need help out of there?"

She shook her head. "Think I best stay put until dark. But don't worry none about a meal, I'll get something later."

He started to speak, but then something seemed to catch his attention. He watched for a moment and then exclaimed, "Well, praise the Lord!"

"What is it?"

Jeremiah's grin was bigger than a crescent moon when he replied. "It's Caesar and Cody, and they have a woman with them. And an extra wagon, it seems." He returned his attention to her. "You sure you're going to be all right in there until later? Mighty warm today."

Mighty warm? She smiled. "I grew up in Georgia. This weather is just approaching lovely."

He chuckled, but there was still concern in his gray eyes when he said, "All right. I'll check on you after a bit, then." After one more sweeping glance, he dropped the canvas back into place and left her in the evening gloam.

She sighed and bent to stretch her back and legs.

But Jeremiah had only been gone for a few minutes when he returned and tapped on the tailgate. "You still awake in there, Del?" There was a levity in his tone that raised her curiosity.

"Yes."

"I got news!"

She moved to the back of the wagon and eased the canvas aside to peer out at a grinning Jeremiah. "What is it?"

"Lord, forgive me, I ain't never been happy to hear of a man's demise before now, but I fully confess to being happy."

"Demise? Whose demise?"

"Well, demise might not be just the right word. But Cody and Cranston bring news that Captain Boone Baxter collapsed at his desk in his office, and the fort doctor isn't certain he's going to make it." He stood still, looking up at her with brows raised as though waiting for that news to sink in.

Del replayed his words in her mind, trying to assemble the meaning. "Collapsed? You mean he's still back at the fort?" Relief took the strength from her knees, and she sank to a seat on the top edge of the tailgate.

"That's precisely what I mean." He grinned at her.

Del's heart hammered. She couldn't fathom it. Collapsed? "They're certain?" Why this melancholy? She would have expected that a thrill of freedom might pulse in her veins! But not this sadness for a man who had treated her so ill and filled her with such terror for so many nights.

Jeremiah nodded. "Apparently, it was big news in the fort yesterday. They had to stop there to pick up Miss Moreau's wagon. The captain seems to have passed out while sitting at his desk, and the doctor was still trying to cipher what might be wrong with him. But he was coughing up blood."

Del's heart hammered. "Isn't that a sign of tuberculosis?" That was contagious, wasn't it? Her hand pressed to the base of her throat.

"Come on now." Jeremiah's voice soothed as he reached up a hand to help her out of the wagon. "Don't go borrowing trouble from tomorrow. All kinds of things can cause such a symptom. The good news for right now is, you're in the clear. Want to come out of there?"

She settled her hand into his, hardly able to comprehend that her days of terror might be over. *Oh Lord, thank You for overcoming the world so I might put my hope in You. Don't let me get my hopes settled on anything else.*

When her feet were on the ground, he released her and swung his hat toward the new arrivals. "Want to come meet Miss Moreau? I have a feeling she could use a friend."

Del pressed her lips together, feeling rather like her head was spinning. She glanced around the circle of wagons but didn't see anyone lingering or looking like they were paying her any particular attention. In the distance, she could see the house that must belong to the ranch. There was a barn too. Other than two men, who went into the barn, she didn't see any dangers there either.

"Miss Moreau?" she asked, turning her attention back to Jeremiah.

"She's a lady who's going to join our wagon train, it seems." Jeremiah started them toward a group of people who seemed to be listening to a story a tall, white man with a long white beard was telling.

As they arrived, the man concluded, "And so Cody there had mercy on the young warrior and the Sioux let him and Miss Moreau go."

Striker clapped a lithe Indian man on his shoulder. "You fought five Sioux warriors on your own?"

"Nope." The man hooked a feedbag over his horse's head and gave the beast a pat on its neck. "Only had to fight the one." He smiled.

The group laughed, and Mr. Houston stepped forward with a smile still on his face. "If you all don't mind, I'd like for us to pause to give thanks to the Almighty for bringing us all back together."

"Of course," several of the men agreed as they snatched their hats from their heads and pressed them to their chests. Women bowed their heads, children clasped their hands. A couple of the men took a knee, including Jeremiah beside her. He rested his forearms on one knee, with his hat clutched in one broad hand.

It was only when the prayer was almost over that Del realized she'd been studying all the people instead of concentrating on the minister's words.

And that was when her gaze collided with the new woman across the circle. She hung her head, looking embarrassed to be caught staring, but Del gave her a smile.

The minister said, "Thank you, Father. It's in Jesus's name we pray. Amen."

And then Del lost sight of the woman in the hubbub as parties dispersed back to their various wagons. But after a moment, only Cody, the new woman, Del, and Jeremiah remained.

Jeremiah stretched a hand to Cody. "Good to have you back. Been praying for y'all."

Cody nodded. "Thanks." He turned his gaze to Del. "This must be your stowaway . . . ?" There was no censure in the word, only a bit of tease.

Jeremiah nudged her forward. "This here is Deliverance."

"Ma'am." Cody dipped his chin as he shook her hand. Then he turned to the woman who still lingered nearby. "This is Miss Moreau. She'll be joining our caravan from here on out."

Del smiled at the woman. "Pleased to meet you."

"As I am most delighted to meet you."

The woman's hair was a unique blend of dark brown beneath with sun-bleached blonde atop. Her hair caught the rays of the setting sun to shimmer like spun gold kissed with bronze. And then her stomach rumbled rather loudly. She hung her head in embarrassment.

Cody grinned. "Miss Moreau has a very vocal stomach."

She gasped and shoved the man's shoulder.

He winced and gripped it gingerly, rotating it a couple of times.

Miss Moreau gasped. "I'm so assuredly sorry. I should have thought. Are you bleeding?"

He smiled down at her. "Wouldn't be so terrible to have you stitching on me again."

Miss Moreau blushed to her roots and looked away.

With a grin, Cody continued. "In her defense, we didn't stop for more than a bit of water and hardtack at noon because we were pressing to catch up. You all made a lot of miles today."

Jeremiah nodded. "Striker figured we'd better press hard while the going was easier here in the plains. Down the line, we'll have days where we're lucky to make five miles."

Cody nodded. "This was a good place to stop. We should be able to buy some meat from Dan."

At the mention of meat, Del's own stomach was threatening revolt if she didn't fill it with something, but the only food she had was the last flapjack from this morning's leftovers. And she'd better leave that for Jeremiah.

Foraging it would be then. Surely there had to be something edible growing in this vast prairie. Would she recognize it was the main question. She could already see dandelions. Those would do in a pinch. But she didn't enjoy the bitter taste of the cooked greens.

Del despaired. Was this how she was to feed herself all the way to Oregon? On foraging and the generosity of others?

She had exactly nothing. Not even a penny to her name. She did have the nice cloak that Betsy had given to her. Maybe she could trade that for some flour at the ranch. She turned her gaze in that direction, already feeling her pulse beating from the base of her throat at the thought of going down there to speak to anyone.

She felt someone stop beside her and came back to the present with a blink, only to realize that it was only her and Jeremiah still standing here.

"You were a ways off. You okay?"

She pressed her lips together. Folded her hands. Frowned. "I was thinking on how I'm to survive all the way to Oregon. I don't want to be a burden to any of these folk, and yet in my current state, that's exactly what I'll be. You think this ranch might trade me some flour for—"

Jeremiah touched her arm, and she stiffened on instinct.

"Easy. Sorry about that." He released her, splayed his hands, and retreated a step. "I just wanted to say that there's no need to go trading anything. I retrieved your pack, and there are some food items in there."

Yes. She'd almost forgotten about the pack that Betsy had filled for her.

"There's also food in that wagon you've been riding in. The boys have said we're welcome to it, though I haven't made much use of it because I'm generally invited to someone's fire each night. But there's no need to fret over how you're going to feed yourself. We'll eat what's there, and I'll make sure the boys are reimbursed for what we use once we get to Oregon."

Deliverance frowned. She rubbed her arm in the place where Jeremiah had touched her. Of course, he couldn't know how terrified she had been of touch these last few years. It was good that he didn't understand. She liked that he was innocent of the knowledge of all she'd faced with Boone. Would she ever be able to rest easy around folk? Would she ever be able to have a relationship with another man without flashing back to Boone every time she was touched?

Relationship? She shook the thought away. Jeremiah was handsome and kind, but he treated her with the same deference he would show to anyone in her situation. She needed to pin that thought to the forefront of her mind so that her thankfulness didn't run over into some other emotion that he likely wouldn't reciprocate and that she wouldn't welcome anyhow.

She dragged her thoughts back from the edge of that precipice. What had they been talking about?

Food.

Relief swept through her.

Yes, food was something less dangerous to think about.

To accept the Slades' supplies would certainly be the easy way out. But was it the right thing to do? She sighed, hating what Boone Baxter and his kind had done to her life. She didn't like being forced to rely on others—especially now that she'd made her escape.

Even at the thought, a shiver worked down her neck, and she turned to check the horizon.

Could it really be true? Had Boone collapsed? What would have happened to her back at the fort if she'd been chained up in that basement when that happened? Would Betsy have come for her then?

Thankfully, she'd never need to know what might have happened.

But now, she had a decision to make.

When she turned back around, Jeremiah still watched her with a soft expression. "I know it's not ideal. Sometimes we just have to make do with the blessings the Almighty gives us."

"Blessings like a man's collapse?" She bit her lip and folded her hands. She hadn't meant to blurt the bitter words.

Jeremiah stepped to one side and swept a hand for her to lead the way back to the Slades' wagon. "Sometimes those are the ways that the Lord blesses us, yes. But it is also always in favor of the person in distress. Because the Lord loves us enough to knock us on our backside sometimes." He grinned over at her as they walked.

Del couldn't help returning his smile. "Just so long as He knocks him down long enough for me to good and truly get away."

They reached the wagon, and Jeremiah set about clearing a spot for a fire. "I guess maybe that's why the Good Book says each day has enough trouble of its own."

Del gave him a nod when he pegged her with a raised-brow look. He was right, of course. But that didn't mean she had to like him reminding her of it. "Where do I find the supplies?"

Jeremiah pointed. "There's a bag of flour there. And a bucket of lard. I think I saw beans and rice. Soon as I get the fire going, I'll see if I can get us some meat from the ranch."

As Del found the ingredients for biscuits, she tried to shake off the feeling of intruding on someone else's life.

What a strange evening it had been.

Boone... collapsed.

She could hardly fathom it. He'd always seemed so strong and unbeatable. And so, despite the news of his illness, Del couldn't quite shake a feeling of impending trouble. Her mind wanted to cling to the promise of freedom. Her heart wouldn't quite let itself hope.

She was thankful when darkness fell and she had the excuse to slip back into the wagon's covering. Weariness drained her, and she fell into a fitful sleep, disturbed by dreams of Boone coughing up blood.

Boone woke with light streaming through his windows and a doctor leaning over him. He jolted to find the man so near and tried to retreat, but could only press his head into his pillow. He blinked hard a few times. His head ached as though he had just escaped one of his youthful brawls. And it felt as though someone had laid a weighty saddle atop his chest.

He frowned at the doctor. Wasn't the man supposed to make patients feel better? Boone felt anything but better. "What are you doing here?" Normally, his words came out with authority, but today he sounded like a toad dragged from beneath a pile of bullrushes.

The doctor strode to a basin of water on a nearby table and set to scrubbing his hands. He sighed. "I'm afraid I don't have good news."

Boone frowned. What was he doing here in his bed in the middle of the day? He remembered being at his desk. He remembered . . . he felt his brows lift. "I woke up this morning coughing up blood."

The doctor glanced over at him. "I wish you would've come and told me immediately."

Boone felt a sickly premonition pressing at the edges of his mind. "What do you mean by that?"

"I'm afraid you have taken to spitting blood."

Boone squinted at the man. "Do you think this is news to me?"

The doctor turned to face him. "How long has this been happening?"

Boone waved a hand and tried to sit up. He felt his irritation rise when he had to work two or three times to get his body to rock hard enough to bring him to a sitting position. He swung his legs over the side of the bed and pressed his hands to the tick to hold himself upright. "I only noticed it for the first time this morning. I'm sure it's nothing."

The doctor folded his arms and looked down at him. "I'm afraid I don't agree. This could be consumption. Or it could be a rupture internally of your lungs in some capacity or another. Perhaps lung fever."

Boone squinted at the man, wishing the light streaming through the window wasn't piercing his sight so painfully. He thrust a finger at the curtains. "Close those blamed curtains." Thankfully, his room was on the second floor, so he didn't have to worry about any of his soldiers peering in and discovering that he was lying abed like a milkmaid.

As the doctor moved to follow his command, Boone stared down at his boots on the floor at the end of the bed. Why did that suddenly seem like such a great distance? Consumption? Blazes! He knew what that was. Both his father and his uncle had been taken with a lung sickness that had wasted them away in a matter of weeks. Boone's eyes fell closed. Weeks . . . "I know what consumption is. What is this lung fever that you speak of?"

The doctor turned from the window and shook his head uncertainly. "The thing is . . . If it were lung fever, you yourself should have a fever. You were slightly warm when we first found you, but after a few moments, your body seemed to regulate itself. I'm leaning more toward consumption."

Boone wanted to curse and rail. But there would be no profit in it. Consumption.

That dreaded word that could mean anything from a disease where you coughed up a little blood here and there for years and years to a disease that took you from health to the grave in a matter of weeks.

Boone's eyes fell closed again. "I felt fine just yesterday. Even this morning, my strength felt normal." He rubbed at his chest, recalling that he had woken with a tightness like a belt had been strapped around him in the night.

The doctor shifted toward his black bag that sat near the door. He bent and picked it up. "I wish I had more answers for you. The only thing I can say is that we must wait and see. It could simply be something I haven't seen before; something you will recover from." The man couldn't seem to meet Boone's gaze when he said that. "I will spend time studying my medical texts to see if I can find any answers for you."

Medical texts.

Boone almost laughed. Just days ago, he had been hunting down his no-good brother. Yesterday, he'd watched him hang and felt only a slight tightness in his chest. And now he might be joining Brad in eternity in only a matter of weeks?

His thoughts turned to Deliverance. A hot anger boiled up from inside him. She would not escape. He must find her.

Boone reached for his boots.

The doctor stepped forward, clearing his throat. "What are you doing?"

Boone glanced up at the man as he grated his teeth and tugged on the first boot. He would not be defeated by a little dizziness, a little lack of oxygen, or a little snippet of a gal who had dared to challenge his authority. "I am tendering my resignation and going to fetch my slave."

The doctor sputtered. "B-but y-you don't have approval to resign."

Hot anger flashed through Boone, and he turned to face the man. "What are they going to do? Send word back to Washington and then wait for instructions that might put me before a firing squad?"

The doctor turned pale. "I'm n-not sure you have that long."

It was the soft way the doctor said those last words that hammered Boone's condition deep into his very core.

He was going to die.

He hated that by the time he turned in his resignation to his second in command, took what supplies he wanted from the mercantile, and made it to the livery, he barely had the strength to pull himself into the saddle that the liveryman put on his mount for him.

He nudged his horse into the field outside of the fort. Now he only had to determine which way she would have gone.

Not north. The river would have prevented her from going there. And there was nothing but Indian country to the south. Betsy would have warned her off of that. He glanced first east, then west.

Betsy had gone east. She'd made sure he'd learn that she'd headed east. Earlier, he'd pondered whether Betsy might have met up with Del out on the prairie somewhere. But now that he'd had more time to think about it, he realized that Betsy was a simple woman. She never did anything fancy, not for the store, not for his brother when he was alive, not even for holiday meals. She was a steady-as-she-goes woman who simply put one foot in front of the other and took the next step. If she'd wanted to remain with Deliverance, she would have left with her when she helped her escape. After all, Boone and his soldiers had been off hunting Brad, and she would have known that she had several hours' head start. But instead, she'd waited to make her escape.

That only left the wagon train.

Boone turned his horse west, silently cursing his men for incompetent fools.

This had better be the right direction. He didn't have time to be wrong.

That thought hit him square in the chest. What an odd thought that was. Only yesterday, he would have proclaimed himself the picture of health.

Today, he was a man facing his mortality.

Chapter 15

Deliverance had been relieved to once again be on the move the next morning when the wagon party left Dan Smith's West Ranch. They had traveled for a full week with a gentle sun on their shoulders. Del walked as much as she could, but for the first several days, she had only managed a few minutes each time. Then she would have to crawl up into the wagon, where she would collapse onto the pallet and sleep.

Jeremiah was always kind about pulling the wagon to a stop to help her inside. His big hand was warm and sturdy beneath hers and never lingered too long or made her feel uncomfortable. He always waited to start off again until he'd asked, "You all settled in there?" and she had replied that she was.

This evening, the meal had consisted of a couple of grouses that Jeremiah had bagged while he was watering the oxen, and Del had been thankful for a break from bacon or beef. She'd finished the cleanup already and had thought she might head into the wagon to relish in the luxury of reading one of the Slades' books, but the group of boys playing in the center of the wagon circle had caught her eye, so she'd leaned her shoulder into the tailgate instead to watch their shenanigans.

The boys had a "ball" of beans sewn into old flour sacking. She'd seen one of the Hawthornes' oldest twin girls present the ball to the boys a few days earlier. Whitley, she thought, because she had redder hair than her twin.

Now it seemed the children's sport was to form a circle about one boy—or girl, since little Afton, Liberty, and Serenity were among them. That child, penned in the middle, made every effort to get the ball while the rest endeavored to keep it from them.

The youngest Hawthorne boy, Cumberland, was currently the one in the middle. And it made Del smile broadly when the oldest Morran boy purposely gave the bean ball a terrible toss so that the two-year-old might have a chance at catching it.

"Aw, Joel!" One of Cumberland's older brothers called. "You got to make him earn it!"

Joel only smiled and shrugged. "It slipped." He traded places with the two-year-old and encouraged him to toss the ball to his older brother.

"Good kids."

Del jolted to hear Jeremiah standing so close just behind and to one side. She glanced over her shoulder and then turned to place her back to the tailgate with her hands clasped in front of her. "Yes. Very sweet."

Jeremiah's gaze lingered on the boys. "You doing okay today? You walked for longer than normal this afternoon."

She nodded, and when a breeze kicked up, almost sighed at the relief of it cooling her. "I'm starting to feel stronger, I think."

"Good. That's real good. I'm glad to hear it." Though his attention remained fixed on the boys and he stood several feet away, his presence seemed to envelop her. Comfort her. Make her feel safe in a way she never had.

And yet in the back of her mind, she knew how fleeting that safety was.

She studied him. He stood with his back to the fire pit, relaxed into his heels. His arms, folded over his chest, stretched the white shirt he wore today to near capacity. His blue-gray eyes crinkled at the corners over some antics of the children.

She liked the way his expression softened as he watched them. The laugh lines only made his handsome face more appealing.

Without moving, he cut his gaze toward her suddenly and caught her watching him. He angled to face her more fully then, and when she hung her head in embarrassment, then peeked up at him through her lashes, a smile slowly spread on his lips. He didn't say anything, only watched her watching him.

She forced her focus to the smoldering coals of the fire just beyond him. "How about you? How was your day?" she asked to cover her chagrin.

He didn't respond at first, but she could feel him still assessing her.

As though drawn by an irresistible force, her gaze drifted back to his.

His smile grew. "Getting better all the time." His scrutiny was direct, but soft and full of invitation.

She pressed her lips together and prodded at the grass with one toe. This was not good. She'd forgotten herself for only a moment, but look at the damage she had done. She'd been doing a good job of keeping Jeremiah at the edges of her thoughts, and now there he was right smack in the middle where he oughtn't be.

She certainly wasn't ready to move on with a man. And he deserved a woman who hadn't been defiled. Her eyes fell closed for a moment as she fought to keep from blurting her thoughts.

"The boys seem to be having a grand time tonight." She peered up at him again, willing him to understand her hesitation. She might find him attractive, but they could never have a future.

His smile faded, but he gave her a gentle nod. "Yeah." He returned his attention to the boys. "They do."

Del pointed to the interior of the wagon. "I was just about to head in for the night."

"I'll help you inside." Without hesitation, he strode to stand near the crate set out as a step and held a hand to her.

With one last glance at the children, who had now dogpiled on each other with Cumberland on top and were all wrestling like a pile of exuberant puppies, she pushed herself off the tailgate and stepped over to take Jeremiah's hand.

The same as always, he helped her into the back of the wagon like a gentleman and let her go as soon as she was steady.

"Night," he offered.

"Good night." She ought to say something more—to at least explain her hesitation, but when she turned, he was already striding away toward the campfire where she could see several of the other scouts gathered.

With a sigh, she pivoted toward the pallet and sank onto it.

Weariness washed over her. She suddenly wanted only sleep. The book could wait. She lay on her side and pulled the covers over herself, trying not to think about all that Boone Baxter and others like him had stolen from her.

Boone was riding just west of Dan Smith's ranch when a wave of dizziness hit him. He blinked hard and urged his mount onward. He was close! Smith himself had said that the wagon train had come through only the day before. Though no one remembered seeing Del, he had a gut-level feeling that he was on the right track. He couldn't stop now!

Ahead of him, the prairie wavered, and each breath felt like he was inhaling through a tiny straw with the weight of an ox on his chest.

He could hear his own wheezing, his blamed horse kept trying to turn for home, and why was it getting dark so early?

Whomp!

Agony spiked through him, jarring him from his haze.

Brown prairie grass sprang up all around him, and above it, the blue of the sky shimmered in a heat wave.

He'd fallen from his horse?

A spike of pain shot through his chest. He coughed. Tasted blood. The sky faded to black.

When he came to, an Indian—a Sioux—was leaning over him. Boone shook his head and tried to sit up, but the pain had him gasping and slumping back to the ground.

The Sioux, a young, strong warrior with a strand of bear claws around his neck, muttered something to someone Boone couldn't see.

Sioux. There was something he should remember about the Sioux, but all he could focus on was the pain. That and breathing.

His body jostled, sending shafts of agony arrowing through him.

He gave in to the tug of darkness.

When he woke again, he lay in the semi-dark of a teepee, with soft furs beneath him, a leather hide covering him, and a toothless old woman smiling down at him.

She nodded a greeting and muttered words he couldn't understand around the stem of the long pipe in her mouth. Then she leaned over him and blew a hearty stream of smoke into his face.

He coughed and sputtered. It was a vile-smelling smoke that made the inside of his nose burn. He coughed and tried to push her away.

But she only smiled, leaned out of his reach, and blew another cloud of smoke his way.

After another round of hacking coughs, he gave in to the weariness and closed his eyes.

Let the old woman smoke her vile leaf.

He wanted only to sleep.

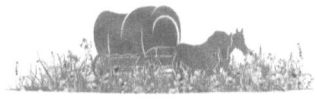

Deliverance felt weary to her very core from a restless night, but rose and fixed oats with the luxury of a few dried raisins mixed in. She had found two quart jars of the sweet treats tucked away in a crate at the side of the Slades' wagon, along with other jars of dried peaches and apples, and two quarts of berry preserves. She'd felt as though she'd come upon a treasure in the middle of a desert.

Jeremiah didn't seem perturbed over their interaction from the evening before, so she hadn't broached the subject. She sent him to ask the Slade children and the Houstons if they would like to join them for the morning meal. Somehow, she felt better about enjoying the sweet fruits if she was sharing them with the children they were likely intended for in the first place.

Jeremiah returned with not only the Houstons and the Slade children, but with Chevonne and Cody, too.

She almost burnt the oats, unaccustomed as she was to cooking these past years, but caught them just in time.

When breakfast concluded, Wyatt Slade came and handed her his empty bowl. He gave her a nod. "Thank you, ma'am. That was just the way my ma used to make it." The boy's eyes filled with a shimmer that he tried unsuccessfully to blink away.

Deliverance pulled him in for a quick embrace before she thought better of it and released him just as quickly.

He gave her a watery smile, then turned and hurried toward a group of boys who were heading out to herd the new cattle—ten extra beefs purchased from the ranch last week for butchering in the days ahead.

Cody rose. "Riding on ahead to hunt for meat. Thank you for the breakfast, ma'am."

"Yes, we'd better head out as well." Mrs. Houston gathered the other children. "It was so thoughtful of you to ask us to join you." After she hugged Del, she and the parson led the children away.

Chevonne busied herself, fetching water to help with the dishes.

When Del glanced across the fire, Jeremiah was watching her with a soft admiration in his eyes. It was a look that could make a woman feel warm clean through. It also raised a wave of apprehension about the future. She plucked at the material at the base of her throat.

He looked away. "You're strong, Del. So strong." He gave a single nod, rose, and started toward the temporary corral. "I'll fetch the team."

Deliverance released a sigh of relief as he stalked away in that broad-legged stride of his. He was a handsome man. A kind and thoughtful man. A gentle man.

No doubt, if she told him about this child she carried, he would offer marriage. But . . . She glanced around the circle of wagons. Someone was likely to raise a ruckus about it. Oh, not the nice folk she'd already met—at least she didn't think so. But what she must remember was that she needed to guard Jeremiah's reputation. It must never be surmised that he had done anything wrong.

And that meant she couldn't indulge in any more warm feelings over his—or her own—tender glances.

Del hefted the tub of dirty dishes and turned to find Chevonne hanging the pot of water on the tripod over the fire.

A sparkle of amusement lit her eyes as she gave Del a raised-brow look. "That man is very handsome, yes? He is the father of your baby?"

Del jolted so hard that a tin cup fell from the tub and clattered at her feet. She felt her eyes round as she looked at the woman. How did she know? And if she knew, then how long until everyone knew?

Chevonne plunked her hands on her slender hips. "Ah! So the answer is *non*. And he does not know?"

"How do *you* know?"

Chevonne tilted her head and cocked a brow as though to urge Del to be serious. "I did not grow up in the French court without learning to spot an unbound woman!"

"Unbound?" Despite her frustration with being called out, Del almost wanted to laugh.

"*Oui*. How do you say . . . no corsets?"

Del did smile then. She liked this unhindered woman. "We sometimes say 'expecting' or 'in the family way.'" She lowered her voice, despite no one else being around. "And yes, you are correct, and no one knows yet. Which—" She lifted one finger. "—is just the way I want to keep it." She gave Chevonne a pointed look as she set the tub of dirty dishes down by her.

Chevonne waved one hand. "Your secret is safe with me, *chérie*. This is also something we learn in the French court—how to guard the secrets!" She offered a quick wink and started loading dishes into the hot water. "So why do you not want this handsome Jeremiah to know you are upon the family trail?"

Del couldn't help a giggle as she gathered a cloth to dry with.

Chevonne pulled a face. "This I have wrongly spoken?"

Del held up a finger and thumb a fraction of an inch apart. "Only a little. It's 'in the family way.' And my reasons are . . . complicated."

"The father . . . You pine for him?" She scrubbed a dish, rinsed it, and handed it to Del.

Del shook her head, short and sharp. She shoved one now unbandaged wrist before Chevonne's face. "I was his slave."

"Oh, *chérie*!" Chevonne pulled Del into a firm hug.

Del was so touched by her concern that she couldn't even bring herself to say anything about Chevonne's wet hands, leaving splotches of dampness on her.

"This is a terrible trial you are facing, no?"

Del squeezed her hand, suddenly more than happy that Chevonne had figured out her secret. The woman's unbridled friendship warmed her clean through. She found herself fighting tears. "Oh, Chevonne, I haven't known what to do!"

The impish Frenchwoman set Del at arm's length and grinned with a pump of her brows. "I will tell you what any sensible woman would do!" She flung herself onto the stone Jeremiah had been sitting on moments earlier and lowered her voice to mimic him. "'You're a strong woman, Del. So strong.'" Then she flew to where Del had been standing, pressed one damp hand to her chest, and batted her eyes. "Oh, Jeremiah! You have no understanding of just how strong I have been. But together, we can be even stronger. Hold me! Kiss me!" She puckered her lips as though waiting for the man to lay one on her.

Del pressed her hands to her heated cheeks as she laughed at Chevonne's antics. "We ain't never gonna get these dishes done if you don't behave." She snatched the rag from Chevonne's hand and set to washing the dishes herself.

"Fine." Chevonne looked disappointed. "On my best behavior, I will be. But tell me . . ." She took up the drying towel and accepted a dish from Del. "What keeps you from trusting him?"

Del scrubbed the rag over another plate. "It's not that I don't trust him. It's that I don't want any harm to come to him."

"Ah! So the father, he lives?"

Del sighed and handed Chevonne the last dish. "Maybe. He is the colonel—the one who collapsed back at the fort."

"Oh! So this is good news, yes? His collapse?"

Del shook her head. Lifted one shoulder. "The Bible says we are not to rejoice when our enemy falls. So, I'm trying not to. And I know Boone. That man is a fighter. If he can find me, he will."

Chevonne wrapped one arm around Del's shoulders and tilted her head against hers. "You are a better woman than most—me included, yes? But know that if he catches us, I will stand with you!"

Del smiled and nodded. Squeezed her new friend in return.

"And do not worry," Chevonne continued. "No one but me will notice you are unbound for some time yet."

Del worried her lip. "You're sure?"

Chevonne nodded certainly. "Most people, they don't look beyond the surface, no?"

Del blew a frazzled breath. She hoped that was true.

Chapter 16

After cleaning up the breakfast, putting out the fire, washing the pots and pans, and repacking the wagons, the company moved off.

Del walked with the women for the morning. By noon, her legs might as well have been stones, and she felt that she might not be able to put one foot in front of the other. She rode in the back of the wagon for the rest of the day.

Jeremiah crooned hymns to his team of oxen off and on, and a picture formed in Del's mind—her standing on the porch of a log cabin, listening to Jeremiah crooning songs to the animals in the barn. She blinked herself back to reality. Gracious! Chevonne and her silliness had Del's mind wandering where it should not!

Midway through the afternoon, she fell asleep to his deep voice singing, "Swing low, sweet chariot, coming for to carry me home."

The days of May drifted together much the same, one after another. Soon, the mornings that had been cool and refreshing were nearly as hot as high noon. The low plains west of the fort, scorched by dry winds and undulating waves of heat, gave way to higher plains, broken by sloping canyons and ridges steep enough to slow their pace from the twenty miles they had been putting in each day to only ten or twelve. Though Deliverance bemoaned the slowness of the travel that prevented her from putting more distance between herself and Boone, she had to admit that she was happy to see something other than the flat plains which had been the view for weeks on end.

Each day that took her farther from Fort Kearny gave her a little more ease in her heart. Each day that Boone didn't arrive filled her with a little more belief that perhaps he really had collapsed. Hope began to take wing.

In fact, she would've been quite at ease except for her knowledge of the growing child within her. Lord forgive her, but she still hoped that she might rise one morning to find that she had lost it. And yet, just the other day, she had felt the first flutter of life moving inside her. Since she hadn't felt it for so long, she'd hoped God had maybe spared her, but her cycle never started. Then came the whisper of something deep inside that felt like the flutter of a butterfly's wings. At first, she'd been certain that it must be a figment of her imagination. But the flurry had continued, consistent, though soft.

This morning, she had woken once again to that soft fluttering and felt as though she might happily claw it from within her. She had curled in on herself and pressed her face into the tick until she felt certain that she could breathe without screaming.

Lord, I need Your help. You know I've tried to be strong. But I don't have the strength to raise that man's child. I don't have any love to give his offspring.

There is no fear in love.

Though the thought convicted her, it also made her frown. Where had that thought come from? Was that a Bible verse? She *was* afraid, she supposed. Afraid of a lifetime of living with a child who would daily remind her of the trauma she'd faced. She frowned and shook the thought away.

Oh Lord, why would You allow such evil? Why form a child in a woman who does not want it? You know the bitter memories that will arise each time I even think of this child. Please, I'm begging You to take it from me.

Silence was the only response.

Each morning before she stepped down from the wagon, she carefully adjusted her dress to cover her stomach as best she could. But this morning, Chevonne had given her one look and shaken her head. And Del realized that it was time to quit putting off the inevitable. Chevonne dragged her to the side of one wagon and fussed over her blouse, but it was no use.

The material over her stomach was beginning to stretch quite tight. If it weren't so hot, she would don the cape that Betsy had given her and use that as a cover. However, with the heat already set to sap her strength, she was going to have to find another way.

Boone woke one morning, feeling suddenly like a new man. He blinked and stretched and sat up on the pile of furs that had been his bed—what he had thought was his deathbed—these past weeks.

Each day, morning and night, the old woman had come in, mumbled unintelligible words as she lit her pipe, and then blown that vile smoke in his face. He'd given up his protests and simply let her smoke and mumble.

But today! Today, he almost felt like his old self.

He ran one hand down the stiff beard that had grown while he slept, and when the old woman came in, he gestured that he wanted a razor.

She beamed until he also asked for his horse. Then she frowned and muttered, chastising him darkly.

But no woman was going to tell him what to do.

"I want my horse," he demanded.

With a flick of her wrist, she opened the flap at the front of the teepee and snapped some words to someone outside.

It was only a few minutes before a woman arrived with a sharp blade and fresh water. Boone realized he would have to forgo the use of a mirror and pressed his lips in irritation as he strode into the sunlight outside the teepee to perform his morning ablutions.

Ah! The sun felt good on his shoulders.

When he lopped off the first hank of hair, he stared at it dumbly.

Just how long had he been convalescing here?

Blast, if Delilah made her escape because he'd fallen ill, he would never forgive himself.

He made quick work of his beard and was just finishing up when a warrior strode up with Boone's mount. The man also led a paint horse of his own.

Boone squinted at him. This was the man who had found him on the prairie.

He clapped a gesture to his chest. "Thank you for saving me."

The warrior only stared at him with cold eyes.

"Well, alrighty then." Boone strode to his horse, thankful to see that all his weapons were still with his saddle. He swung his brace of pistols around his waist and mounted up. He tipped his hat to the old woman.

She only folded her arms and glared at him.

Boone smiled. "Goodbye to you as well. I thank you for saving my life!"

The old woman said something dryly to the warrior, and the man nodded and mounted his own horse in one clean leap.

When they rode out of the Indian camp near the Platte and Boone saw where they were, he cursed. These blame Indians had carried him a day's ride east of the fort.

Boone figured the man was assigned to ride with him a ways to make sure he didn't bring back trouble. He was okay with that. He didn't plan to do anything but hunt his wayward slave!

He felt surprised when the warrior continued with him all day, and remained when they dismounted that evening, but not ungrateful.

Turned out that maybe Boone's health wasn't tiptop after all because he was exhausted clean through.

The warrior made a fire and cooked some sort of mush that wasn't half bad.

Then the man warmed a concoction and thrust it toward Boone, indicating he should drink it.

Only a few moments after he'd swallowed it, he recognized his mistake. He'd been drugged!

"Why you dirty—" He tried to stand, but didn't make it more than half way.

The warrior caught him as he fell.

When he woke the next morning, he expected to find that the man had absconded with his horse and kit, but to his surprise, the man squatted near the fire with his forearms resting against his knees and a hot drink brewing. When he held a cup out, Boone only glowered from the cup to the Indian and back again.

With a soft smile, the warrior lifted the cup, took a loud and hearty sip, and then offered it to him once more.

Boone accepted the drink and found it pleasantly bitter and nutty. He puzzled over what this man had to gain from staying with him and giving him medicines.

"Name's Boone," he offered with one hand to his chest. Then he stretched the hand to the Sioux warrior. "You are?"

"You can call me Chaytan," the man said in perfect English.

"You speak English?"

Chaytan pressed his lips together. "Several years of mission school assured that."

"Why are you here?"

The second hint of humor Boone had seen from the man ticked the corners of his lips. "Grandmother's orders. She said she didn't save your life only to have you ride off and die in the first few days."

Boone grunted. "Well, as long as you stay out of my way, you are welcome to join me."

Chaytan nodded, stood, stamped out the small fire, and then leapt onto his pony without another word.

Boone followed suit and turned his horse west.

One phrase lingered in the back of his mind as he rode. The warrior had said, "the first few days."

Did that mean he had made it through the worst of this sickness, but she wanted her grandson to keep watch for just a few more days to make sure he was truly better? Or that he was going to die for certain, but the woman had been doing her best to give him as many days as possible?

A shiver worked down his spine.

All the world's a stage . . .

His hands trembled where they gripped the reins.

"Circle up!"

Del was close enough to the front of the line to hear Caesar's call for evening camp, and she'd never been more relieved to hear it. Today, she'd walked for a full day, and while she was thankful to find her strength nearly fully returned, she was also bone-weary and wanted only sleep.

First, however, she would need to cook a meal.

As Jeremiah pulled the Slades' wagon into position in the circular formation that would pen the oxen inside for the night, she trudged in that direction. At least she didn't have to ponder long on what she ought to make. Beans and bacon? Or bacon and beans? For the past week, the men had gone out hunting each evening only to return empty-handed. The land had been stingy. And the river had proved just as stubborn about relinquishing fish.

Her lips thinned in a grimace, and for the first time in her life, she understood some of what the Children of Israel might have felt upon seeing another layer of manna on the ground.

Oh, Lord, don't let me be discontent with Your provision. I'm grateful, truly I am.

Everyone was tired. Today, the women had mostly been silent as they trudged along—even Chevonne, who normally chatted Del's ear off as she walked with her and tried to learn better English. Del had chuckled on more than one occasion about finding herself in the role of Chevonne's English tutor. Her French friend was quite proficient with English—much more proficient, Del would conjecture, than she herself would be should their roles reverse and she find herself walking the plains of France.

It was the image of a slave-born southern woman giving lessons to a high-born French woman that raised her humor.

Del loved the woman's kindness and sweet, blathering personality. There wasn't a day that went by that Chevonne didn't find a way to make her laugh. Nor one where she didn't make Del roll her eyes with proddings about how handsome Jeremiah was, and how Del would be a fool to lose him.

Tonight, however, claiming weariness beyond her years, Chevonne had already headed to her wagon. Del was determined to be fast on her heels to her own.

But as she passed the Hawthorne camp, Whitley, who bounced baby Blythe on one arm, held out her hand. "Miss Deliverance?"

Del paused. "Yes?"

Whitley smiled. "We are inviting folk to our fire tonight for food, music, and dancing. We'd be honored if you could join us! And would you please also extend the invitation to Jeremiah?"

Unease swirled at the way Whitley had grouped her and Jeremiah as though they were an inseparable pair. She resisted settling a hand to her queasy stomach, lest she draw attention to her expanding condition.

Del dreaded having to do one more thing on this day. But what else might she expect from a family of young people than unlimited energy? And, after only a moment, wonder filled her. Imagine a group of white folk including her and Jer in their shindig, not as servants, but as friends!

She blinked hard to keep tears of gratefulness from showing. "Jeremiah will have to speak for himself, of course. But I'd like that just fine. What can I bring?"

Whitley glanced toward their fire, where Del could already see that Whitley's pa was hooking a large pot above the flames. "Mama is going to make a big batch of her best beans, and Pa says he's been seeing jackrabbits all day and swears he won't come back with less than ten of them this evening. He and the boys are heading out now to see what they can find. Wren and I are mixing up a triple batch of biscuits. So whatever you might like to accompany that, would be fine."

Del smiled. "I'll come up with something. What time should we come?"

Whitley glanced around at her industrious family, sweeping a strand of that red-blonde hair behind one ear. "Give us an hour? I think that will be close. The beans, of course, won't quite be done to perfection then, but Mama has had them soaking all day, so they should be close."

Del nodded. "An hour it is!"

She crossed the remaining distance to her own encampment and was already frowning as she paused at the back of the wagon. What could she bring? She didn't have anything but bacon, and if she showed up with that, she might be sent packing before she could even join the party.

Now, there was an idea that might allow her to rest sooner than later! She grimaced to herself. If only she dared try it.

"Seems like you got a powerful lot on your mind." Jeremiah paused beside her, concern etching his brow. From the wet muzzles of the oxen he prodded, he must be returning from watering them.

Del waved a hand. "We've been invited to the Hawthorne camp tonight for a gathering—I told them you would have to speak for yourself. Anyhow, I was just pondering what I could bring besides bacon." She gave him a self-deprecating smile. "Don't want to get stoned."

He laughed. "We certainly don't want that, but I have just the thing! Get two bowls and wait for me. As soon as I give these beasts over to Dec, I'll be back." He slapped the nearest ox on its neck and gave it a friendly rub.

Del nodded, unable to deny her curiosity, but he was already walking away, so she would just have to wait to find out what he was thinking.

Inside, she gathered up the bowls, but then took advantage of the pallet to take a load off her feet for a few moments. She almost groaned as she lay back and pulled her feet up. What she wouldn't give to be able to take her boots off for a few minutes, but she didn't want Jer to have to wait for her when he returned.

She closed her eyes, intending only to relax until he returned.

Chapter 17

Jeremiah rubbed his hands in anticipation as he returned to the wagon after dropping off the oxen. He couldn't wait to show Del the patch of wild strawberries that he'd seen just a ways back along the riverbank. The fruit would be small, and likely a good portion of them had already been eaten away by prairie rabbits, but hopefully they could find enough good ones to bring a couple of bowls to the gathering.

He had expected Del to be waiting for him by the back of the wagon, but when he arrived, she was not in sight. He moved to the canvas opening. "Del?" he called without peering in. "You in there?"

When he got no answer, his heart seized in his chest. "Del?" he called more loudly.

Silence was his only greeting.

He swallowed, glancing around the encampment. Could someone have snuck into the camp and taken her without any of them noticing? He had only left her a few minutes ago! Cody had reported that Boone had collapsed. And Jeremiah would never question his word. But could the man have recovered enough to have caught up with them?

Jeremiah hated to push into the wagon if she was in there, and yet . . . He twisted his hat through his fingers.

She had to be in the wagon, right? But she would have responded if she were. "Del?"

Still no response.

She had been pushing herself more and more these past few days. What if she'd pushed too hard? Done too much? Maybe collapsed?

Enough. He was going in. "You hearing me in there, you best get yourself decent, because I'm coming in." He gave it a beat and then swung up onto the crate step and swept the canvas aside.

Relief swept through him to see Del lying on the pallet at the back of the space. But she was so still and silent. And with crates piled in the way, he couldn't see her very well. Something didn't feel right.

Before he thought better of it, he swung a leg over the tailgate and moved toward her down the aisle. When he paused beside her and saw her chest rising and falling in the gentle rhythm of deep sleep, he breathed a sigh of relief.

She must have been some exhausted to fall asleep so quickly and soundly—and with her boots on, too. He could see them peeking out from beneath her skirt. He ought to leave her alone, but if she was this exhausted, she might simply need to sleep the night through, and her boots ought to be removed. It wasn't his place, and yet, who else did she have to care for her?

He leaned to his right to reach for her nearest foot, but as his gaze skimmed past her midsection, he froze. Leaning partially over her, with one arm stretched toward her boot, he simply stared at the rounded mound of her midsection.

Dear Lord . . .

He swallowed.

How had he not noticed? He'd been trying not to study her too closely. Trying not to make her uncomfortable. And yet, in her condition, she needed better food, milk, and maybe not as much exercise as she'd put in today. She needed to be strong, but not worn down.

Horrified by all the emotions slamming into him, he straightened, swept a palm down his face, and worked his thumb and fingers into his jaw.

And then the fury hit him. Fury at the injustice that this woman he'd grown to care so much about must have experienced. He looked down at her face with her long dark lashes resting against her cheeks and her lips slightly parted as she breathed deep and steady in her sleep.

Not all children are hoped for.

His eyes fell closed as he remembered those words she'd spoken that first night.

Lord, I'm so powerless in the face of such evil. How is a man supposed to fix this?

He trembled with the knowledge of his ineptness. He'd heard some men preach that if a man did good, God would watch out for him. And, Lord forgive him, maybe he hadn't thought hard enough about that statement. After all, hadn't God watched out for *him*? Set him free? Given him a good friend in Striker Moss?

And yet, what evil had Del done to bring this travesty? Nothing. Not a single thing. She'd been a child, for pity's sake!

In this world you will have tribulation; but be of good cheer, I have overcome the world.

Tears stung Jeremiah's eyes as he remembered Hiram Hawthorne's words to his children the other day.

Lord, I know that's true, but ...

His sadness was for more than just what had happened to her in the past, he realized. It was still affecting her today. After all, he felt like he was one of her closest friends these past few weeks, and yet she hadn't shared her condition with him. Had she talked to one of the women? His heart ached for the loneliness she must be feeling.

He reached again to unlace her boots, but the moment he touched her foot, she jolted awake and surged upright on the pallet, pushing an escaped strand of her thick curly hair out of her eyes.

Jeremiah lurched back. Would she think he'd been trying something inappropriate? "Sorry. Uh, I called to you, but when I got no answer, I found you sleeping and thought I'd take off your shoes so's you'd be more comfortable."

She ducked a yawn behind one palm and tucked her feet to one side as she leaned on her other arm. "So sorry. I didn't mean to fall asleep." She squinted up at him sleepily. "Weren't we gonna go somewhere? What were the two bowls for?"

Hang it, she was cute, all sleepy and ruffled like she was. He suddenly wanted more than anything for her to trust him, confide in him, know that he would always fight for her. His chest constricted as the truth slammed into him.

He loved this woman!

The thought made him stumble a step back. He fiddled with his hat and retreated a couple more strides down the aisle. He turned to study the landscape out of the small canvas opening.

She'd walked an awful lot today and probably should rest. Especially in her condition. But ought he to mention what he'd seen? What if he did and then found out she wasn't expecting but had only put on some weight? He mentally scoffed at himself. Only on her stomach? And in a smooth round bulge?

"Jeremiah?"

His hat was practically crushed in his hands now. He turned to face her. "It was just a patch of wild strawberries that I saw earlier. But maybe you should rest. Don't want you wearing yourself too thin."

"Nonsense. Strawberries sound lovely. And I feel much refreshed after just those few minutes of sleep."

"I could fetch them, and you could rest some more. I can wake you before we need to head to the Hawthornes' camp."

She studied him with a seemingly puzzled slump to her brow. "Is something amiss? Did something happen while I was sleeping?"

Jeremiah felt his stomach roil with that familiar anger—not at her, but at the man who had treated her so inhumanely.

Something had happened all right.

A beautiful woman like her? He'd known the type of abuse she'd likely suffered. But he supposed he'd hoped that it hadn't gone that far.

He was a fool. A fool standing here with the woman he loved, looking up at him and waiting for an answer.

He gave himself a little shake, willing away the quaking that still seemed to weaken every muscle. "No. No. All's well with the camp."

She tilted her head. "You seem troubled."

He raked his fingers around the back of his neck. That was an understatement. "Just tired, I suppose."

Her lips tilted. "Maybe I should go pick the strawberries, and you should be the one to lie yourself down here for a nap."

A dry chuckle escaped.

He studied her teasing expression. Her eyes, gentle with humor. Those soft, full lips tilted up at the corners.

How did she do it? She ought to be hard and closed off, and yet she'd been so strong and resilient. Full of good humor and kindness. This woman who ought to be bitter and angry ... her beauty was much more than skin deep.

With an embarrassed press of her lips, she hung her head and fiddled with her fingers.

He'd been staring like a fool and had made her uncomfortable.

She took a breath. "Jeremiah, I—"

"I'm sorry." He immediately turned toward the opening before she could put him in his place. Because she was going to need him. And he fully intended to be there for her. And until she was ready to accept him, he needed to keep things on friendly terms.

He jumped down and turned to offer her a hand. "The strawberries aren't far, if you're really feeling up to it." He held his breath and waited.

Deliverance stared at Jeremiah. Something wasn't right. Something that he wasn't telling her. But she couldn't force the man to trust her, she supposed. And her stomach was rumbling something fierce. Just the thought of wild strawberries had her mouth watering.

She rose from the pallet and took Jeremiah's hand as she swung one leg over the gate. His fingers were warm and strong around hers and filled her with a foolish longing to be loved by a man such as this. He was kind, concerned, caring. A gentleman in the truest sense of the word. What other man would have cared enough to come remove her boots so she might sleep better?

All these thoughts flitted through her mind as she descended, even as other thoughts crowded in to taunt her with her imprudence—thoughts about not saddling the man with an unwanted child and a woman who might be too broken to ever love properly again.

There was also Boone to consider. If he ever caught up to them and found that she loved another . . . She shuddered to think what he would do.

For that reason, if none other, Jeremiah must never be allowed to get too close. And it was best that she set him straight right away, despite the longings of her heart.

She opened her mouth, but the moment her feet were on the ground, he released her and scrubbed his hand against his buckskin trousers. Like he was trying to remove the feel of her?

Somehow, that thought, which ought to be a relief, instead sent a shaft of disappointment through her.

But at least she didn't have to put him off. And maybe if they did make an escape from Boone . . .

She blew out a frazzled breath, knowing she was selfish to her very core. She might long to be loved by a man like him, but she could never be selfish enough to put him in that position.

Yet from the way he'd been looking at her a moment ago . . . Fear for him shot through her. She must hold him at bay. The sooner they reached the end of this trail and separated, the better it would be for him.

"Where do we find these strawberries?" She thrust one of the small wooden bowls at him.

He squinted down at her. "You sure you don't need more rest?"

That gentle kindness again. The man wasn't helping her resolve!

"I'm fine. Honest. The few minutes I got made a big difference." She forced a smile, trying to reassure him. The last thing she wanted to do was appear an invalid and have the caring friends in this camp swarming all over her and finding out her secret before she was ready to reveal it.

"All right." He swung the bowl toward the river. "Right this way." He canted her a smile.

Relieved to be back on familiar footing, she fell into step beside him.

The sun hung low on the horizon, and from the streaks of pink, coral, and gold filling the sky, she couldn't wait to see the beauty God planned to paint for them on His canvas this evening. The slow burble of the river gave an underlying drone for the bullfrogs and crickets that had begun to sing their evening symphony.

A few times, Jeremiah used the hatchet hanging at his side to whack back the brush so that she could pass more easily. They stepped into a small clearing surrounded by a semicircle of bushes on one side and the river on the other.

She glanced over at Jeremiah, who was sheathing his hatchet. She wanted to know more about him and yet knew she shouldn't. However, the silence was growing taut, and she wanted to ease this sudden tension that had seemed to come over him. "So, what do you plan to do in Oregon?"

He glanced over at her as he finished strapping the leather sheath onto the head of the hatchet. "Well, I figure once we get to Oregon and ol' Strike is settled with his kin, I'll head on down to California, get me a nice piece of acreage, and then maybe run a few horses that I can break and sell. Maybe a milk cow or two. Definitely some pigs because a man has to have bacon." He winked.

She chuckled. "I may never want to eat bacon again, after this trip!" It made her sad to think of him being separated from Striker. She wanted to ask why he didn't plan to stay near his friend, but she didn't want to pry, so all she asked was, "What else?"

"Have a garden. A little cabin with a creek nearby. On Sundays, after services, I'll go down to the creek and pretend to fish while I sleep the afternoon away."

Del chuckled at the picture that formed in her mind of a fish with a hook in its mouth, swimming away with Jeremiah's pole. "Good way to lose your fishing pole."

He grinned. "Maybe. What about you? What do you want to do?" His expression suddenly turned serious as those gray eyes settled directly on her.

She swallowed. Her pulse skittered as a different picture formed—one of her standing on a cabin porch waiting to welcome home a fishing-pole-less Jeremiah.

Oh boy. She needed to get her thoughts back on track. "I—Well, I don't rightly know, I guess. If I'd had a choice, I'd have run back to my mother, but I didn't want to bring... trouble on her." Trouble. That was such a benign word to describe Boone. If only she and Jeremiah could sink into the earth and find themselves on the other side of the world, where she would never have to worry about that man's retribution again. She ran her fingers around the rim of the bowl.

"But then you'd have been going back to slavery and your master would have turned you over to Boone if he showed up looking for you," he prompted, to let her know he understood.

Del nodded. Frowned. "Which, of course, is why I've stayed the course with the wagon train. But I honestly don't know what I'll do once we arrive. I know my cyphers, but I don't suppose most folk these days would trust a black woman to keep their books. And I heard some of the ladies saying that women don't get land unless they're—" She broke off with an aghast breath. She didn't want the man to think she was hinting that he ought to marry her! "Oh, look, here are the strawberries you mentioned!"

Feeling heat suffuse her face, she bent to the task, tossing the red berries into her bowl with such ferocity that one bounced right back out again. She drew a calming inhale and forced herself to slow.

Jeremiah didn't seem perturbed by the slip. He squatted and filtered through the leaves of a small bush a few feet away. "Would it be bad? Marrying? After what you been through?"

Her thoughts stuttered. Did he mean to him? Or just marrying in general? Because marrying him might not be so bad if she didn't have to worry about what Boone would do to him if he ever found them. If she didn't have to worry about what Jer might think of her if he knew she was with child.

Shame over her condition washed through her yet again. *Oh Lord, what am I gonna do?*

She willed away the tears stinging the backs of her eyes. "I don't think marrying will ever be in my future. So, I'll have to find a job I can do on my own. Maybe they'll change that law and let single women claim a piece of land too." Frivolous hope though it was, it gave her spirit a little lift to think of it.

There was a beat of silence before he said, "I know you can read. But I don't suppose Baxter ever let you read his paper?"

Del shook her head. "No." She hadn't read anything but the labels on the tins in the basement for several years before her escape. It was one of the reasons she found the few books in the Slade wagon such a delight. "Why?"

Jeremiah swallowed. Sorrow filled his eyes when he lifted them to hers. "I'm sorry to be the one to tell you, then. We"—he swung a finger between them—"can't settle in the Oregon Territory."

She stiffened. "What?"

His lips pressed into a grim line. He settled his forearms against his splayed knees and seemed to slump into himself as he stared at the nothingness across the river. "Oregon don't allow black folk to settle in The Territory."

Despair hit her so hard that she plunked herself down, wrapped her arms around her bent legs, and settled her forehead against her knees. "Why do folk hate us so much simply because our skin is a different color, Jer?" She rocked herself a little. What was she going to do now? If she couldn't settle in Oregon, why was she even heading that way?

She heard the grass rustle beside her, and when she glanced up, Jeremiah had settled into a similar position beside her, but facing her. Arms wrapped around his knees, he grasped one of his wrists with the opposite hand and shook his head. "Blamed if I know."

A sudden thought hit her. "Why are you going to Oregon? If you know you can't settle there?"

His lips lifted in a nostalgic smile. "Strike and I have been together so long that I hated to leave him right away. My heart needed time to adjust."

"But he obviously doesn't feel the same about you!" Her outrage couldn't be disguised.

Jeremiah shook his head sharply. "He thinks I'm going to settle on his land with him and his kin. I'm not sure he read far enough into the article to see that black folk aren't even allowed to stay. I think he only saw that the land was being given to white folk only. And he was disappointed. Came to me right away and said I could stay on his land. Striker is a dreamer. He hopes that once we're there, we'll be able to make things different from what they are in the South, but . . ." He lifted one shoulder. "Sure isn't a great start to that end, even if the Oregon territorial government did ban slavery."

The tears that had been threatening finally won the battle, and before she could stop them, they streaked her cheeks. She dashed at them, irritated to be giving bigoted lawmakers such power over her emotions.

Jeremiah reached to stroke her arm with the backs of his fingers. "Don't cry, Del. We'll figure out what to do."

His gentle encouragement only made her cry harder. She had no one—and now nowhere!

Jeremiah scooted closer so that they sat hip to hip, facing each other, and then he gently drew her against his chest. "It's okay. I got you." One of his large hands smoothed over her hair, sweeping it back from the moisture on her face. "I got you. We'll trust the Lord and He will guide us."

She leaned into the strength of him. His chest was warm and strong beneath her forehead, and she relished the empathetic connection with another. How long since anyone had held her this way—tender and gentle without wanting anything for themselves? Since anyone had cared even a whit what she was feeling? Sobs wracked her shoulders.

Jeremiah's hand rubbed her back. His lips pressed against her hair, and then his chin rested atop her head. And his silence gave her more comfort than any words ever could. Just the camaraderie of him lending his support filled her with comfort.

When her crying was spent, she simply settled one ear against the beat of his heart and breathed with him. "I don't want to feel all this hate in my heart, Jer."

She heard him swallow. Felt him wag his head above her. "I understand. We can't let hate fill us, or we become just like them."

She eased back from him and noticed as she did that she'd left a large damp spot on the front of his shirt. She rubbed at the spot with a chagrined wince.

He covered her hand to still it. "It's okay."

She ought to pull away. Put some distance between them. Instead, she lifted her gaze to his. Her lungs forgot to expand as she met his warm glance with one of her own.

His thumb caressed the back of her hand. He worked his top teeth over his bottom lip as he studied her. Leaving her hand pressed to the beat of his heart, he reached to sweep a strand of her hair behind her ear, and his fingers lingered to trace her jawline.

Del trembled. This was too alluring. Too needed. She felt like a woman who had been forced to run through a desert for days without water, and now she had come out the other side and was drowning. She was ill-equipped to swim in these waters and didn't have the will to try.

Despite her previous intentions to keep her distance, he had slipped right past her defenses.

She leaned into his caress, turning her face so his touch brushed against her lips. Her breaths were shallow and stilted. Her heart thrummed so hard that she could feel it tapping the inside of her sternum. Each tender stroke filled her with such a longing that she quaked with the need of it.

He turned her face toward him, and his thumb tantalized the corner of her mouth. His gaze dipped to her lips.

She swallowed. Fought for breath.

She ought to put a stop to this right now, but his caress had ignited a longing inside her to be loved for real and for true. Not because some man found her blended skin color appealing, or her face shape enchanting, or her long, silken curls enticing. And certainly not because some man needed a moment of stress relief.

Jeremiah leaned toward her.

She hesitated. Did he, too, only want her for what Boone had said was her intoxicating beauty?

"You are a wonder of a woman, Del, you know that?" Jeremiah's voice emerged husky and rough. "Ever since that first day when you sassed all those white men and told them to get on back from Mrs. Hawthorne's wagon, I knew you were a force to be reckoned with. But then I saw your tender heart for the children, and the gentle way you swayed that Hawthorne baby, all when you barely had enough strength to walk a few steps each day. And that was when I knew what a wonder you are, woman."

Deliverance closed her eyes—and lifted her mouth.

His lips swept over hers in the barest hint of a whisper-soft touch.

But the moment his skin met hers, reality rushed in to chastise her for her selfishness.

Boone, always Boone, coming between her and happiness. She took a breath and inserted her finger between their lips, nudging him to stop.

He didn't press, only eased away a fraction, stroked the back of his first finger one more time along her cheek, and then retreated to lean against his hands, which he propped behind himself. His focus remained on her, warm and soft, but a little bit hesitant, too. "Sorry. I don't mean to ... That is, I don't want you to feel forced into ... anything." He cleared his throat and looked away toward the strawberries they'd barely touched.

Sad that she had obviously hurt him, Del reached to touch his arm. "I don't feel forced. You've been kind and a perfect gentleman."

She wanted to mention that if Boone ever caught up to them, she worried what might happen. But she knew Jeremiah would see through that to her care for him. He would brush away her concerns, and then she might be tempted to allow things with him to progress further. So instead, she withdrew her hand and held her silence. It was better for him to be hurt than dead.

Still, she needed to offer an explanation. "It's only that I'm not ready for ... anything more right now." She snapped up a piece of grass and set to crimping it in her fingers, unable to look him in the eye for fear he would see the lie that she suddenly realized she'd just spoken. Because if ever she were granted the opportunity to move on, Jeremiah was exactly the man she would want to do it with.

The thought elicited a cold sweat upon her neck and a toasty fire in her belly.

He nodded and rose, dusting bits of grass from his buckskins. "I understand." He reached a hand down to help her up.

She steeled her heart not to cave at his touch and allowed him to haul her to her feet.

When she had her balance, she started to turn away, already dreading their separation, but he gently kept her hand in his own, tugging her back around to face him. Her gaze flashed to his.

He reached to touch her cheek. "Just be sure you're acting on what your heart truly wants and not out of fear for an unknown future. We may not know what the future holds, Del, but we know the One who does. He will go with us, guide us, and keep us. We only have to keep our eyes on Him, not on the waves all around us. God has not given us a spirit of fear, but of power, and of love, and of a sound mind."

She pressed her lips together. Gave a little shake of her head. "Fear has been such a constant companion these last years, I'm not sure I know how to get past it."

Jeremiah released her and stepped back. His expression was full of certainty as he gave her a nod. "Then you pray about it and the Lord will show you how to overcome."

With that, he turned from her and stooped to continue filling his bowl with strawberries.

Del followed his lead, wishing she had his faith.

Chapter 18

When they arrived at the Hawthornes' encampment, holding the two bowls brimming with the fresh fruit, Evelyn Hawthorne gasped in delight. "Strawberries! Oh my! Those look lovely." Her hands were filled with a platter piled high with golden-topped biscuits. She gave a nod toward the tailgate of their wagon. "Please set them there with the other foods and then take a load off your feet. The girls and I want to give everyone a moment of rest this evening. Welcome!"

Del turned toward the folk gathered around the fire, feeling Jeremiah do the same beside her.

One of the oldest twin girls held the baby in the crook of one arm—in the dark with the golden glow of the fire dancing off the girl's hair, she couldn't tell if it was Whitley or Wren. The girl hefted the lid off the pot of beans, obviously intent on giving them a stir, but with the baby in one arm and the lid in the other, she now looked for a place to set the lid.

Holding a baby was something Del could do. She took a step, but Declan Boyle beat her to it.

"I've been dying tae hold this bairn all day." He took baby Blythe from the girl's arms and snuggled her into the crook of one arm, looking like he was about ready to melt with love as he did so. He stared down at the baby, sweeping a finger across one chubby cheek. "Och noo, aren't ye th' prettiest thing this side o' Oregon."

The girl stirring the beans gave a chuckle as she plunked the lid back onto the pot. "Declan Boyle, your accent turns as thick as morning cream when you talk to that one." She dipped her head toward the baby in his arms.

He lifted a smile. "I suppose it does, Whit." He seemed to purposely thicken his brogue for the girl's benefit. "An' mebbe aroond ye, tae."

From the way Whitley hung her head, Del had a feeling that the girl was more than halfway smitten with the Scottish rogue.

Declan searched those gathered near the fire, jouncing the baby cradled on one arm. "And where might Wren have taken herself to, do ye think?" His accent was suddenly much less pronounced.

Whitley prodded at the ground with one toe. "She went to fetch a bucket of water from the river and … Royal is with her." She lifted her gaze as though she wanted to catch Declan's response to that information.

He froze for half a moment and then lowered his focus to baby Blythe, who was now slurping noisily on two fingers.

Beside Del, Jeremiah cleared his throat. Del followed his gaze to where both the Hawthorne parents were busy greeting and thanking folk for their donations to the gathering, and then on to the grandmother, who sat rocking the littlest boy, Cumberland.

Jer's fingers skimmed Del's elbow. "I think I'll just mosey on down to the river to fetch more water. Surely, we're gonna need more than just that one measly bucket that Royal and Wren are fetching, don't you think?" He gave her a knowing wink.

Del smiled, cupped her hands to her elbows, and buffed her skin. Jeremiah's touch may have been meant only to get her attention, but she'd felt it as surely as she would have felt a lightning bolt. "I do believe you are right! And I'd say that Whitley and the Hawthornes would benefit from Wren hurrying on back here to help with this here gathering, too. Don't you think?"

Jeremiah smiled as he took up two nearby buckets. "I'll be sure to tell her. Just like I'll tell you . . ." He jutted his chin toward an empty chair by Grandmother Hawthorne. ". . . to take a load off your feet. You've done a lot today."

As Jeremiah walked away, he watched Deliverance approach Marigold Hawthorne. The woman smiled and gestured to the stool beside her. Despite the kind way she'd been greeted, he felt reluctant to leave her side.

As soon as he'd learned about her condition, a protective spirit had risen inside him—okay, after the anger and outrage. He felt a need to stay close and make sure she lacked for nothing. But something also urged him to walk away and give her some space.

Especially since she'd made her feelings clear when she nudged him back after such a brief kiss earlier.

He sighed. That kiss may have been so brief that it could hardly even be classified as one, but thunder and tarnation! It had jolted him clean to his toes. It sure was a good thing he'd been sitting down, or he might have crashed right onto his backside, weak as his knees had gone.

As he trudged toward the river with the two buckets, he scrubbed the sardonic smile from his lips with one shoulder.

With time, hopefully, Del would come to see that she could trust him and that he would love her to the best of his ability. She needed a season to heal from the trauma of the past few years. He was more than willing to give her that.

Lord, You're gonna have to give me patience in spades, because I have a feeling I'm gonna need it. Show me how best to love and support her. How to make her feel safe and cared for. How to keep my distance while also letting her know that I do love her. Help her to conquer this fear that's only natural after what she's been through. But nothing is impossible with You, Lord, I know that. Help her to know it, too.

He shook his head with a bit of self-deprecation at his sappy prayer, smiling wryly. Only a few weeks ago, he would have unequivocally stated that his chances of even meeting a woman of interest were slim to none. And now look at him—shooting up prayers that God would give him patience with a woman he loved!

With a grunt, Jeremiah drew his attention back to the task at hand. Finding the right watering hole so that he might save Wren from that rattler Royal.

At each break in the brush along the river, he paused to listen for the conversation of the young couple, all to no avail. He was just beginning to wonder if Royal had taken Wren in the other direction—or if no conversation had been taking place at all—when he finally came to a slight break in the brush and heard Wren's voice coming from the other side.

"But Royal, why do we have to sneak off to marry? I'm old enough that Pa will let me make my own decisions. He won't stop me from marrying a man I love. But I do want my family there."

Jeremiah's brow slumped. Old enough to make her own decisions? In a pig's eye! As for Royal, that dirty rat, he was a man almost twice her age—twenty-five to her fifteen. Jeremiah would like to march through the brush and down to that riverbank and give Royal a taste of what ought to happen to men like him!

He bent and gingerly set his buckets down.

"Sssst!" The sharp attention-getting sound came from the shadows near the brush a few feet from Jeremiah. Striker emerged from the darkness that had cloaked him. He whispered, "I see that you had the same thought as me." He balled up one hand and shook a fist meaningfully.

In the background, Royal continued to cajole Wren into running away with him.

"But where are we gonna find a minister, Royal? We've got one right here with us in camp. Parson Houston can marry us, and my family can attend, too. I don't understand why we can't just do that."

"Two beatings are better than one for the likes of him," Jeremiah grumbled only loud enough for Striker to hear, cognizant that his friend would know he didn't really mean to follow through on it.

Striker's teeth flashed white in the darkness.

Jeremiah bent to retrieve the pails, thankful that Striker was here to back him up if necessary. "Stay here," he whispered, "but if he decides to take a swing at me, please do come to your only friend's rescue, yeah?"

Those white teeth again, hanging in the darkness for longer this time.

Jeremiah broke into a tuneless whistle and pushed through the narrow path in the brush, not bothering to be quiet at all. Branches crackled. Leaves grated against his clothing. He whistled loudly.

When he reached a small grassy clearing near the river, it was to find Wren seated on the crook of an oak branch that stretched low toward the water, with Royal standing much too close between her knees. They both were staring back at the brush wide-eyed, like a cougar might be upon them.

Something worse.

And Jeremiah hoped that Royal would soon understand that. He curled his fists tight around the rope bucket handles.

Wren gasped, shoved Royal's shoulder so she could squeeze past him, and dropped to her feet onto the grass below the tree, head hanging in embarrassment.

"Well, hello there, Wren," Jeremiah drawled. "If I'm not mistaken, your family needed your help a moment ago."

"Y-yes, s-sir." She nodded vigorously and practically sprinted past him.

Jeremiah hoped she wasn't going to crash into ol' Strike and get a second fright tonight. But he didn't have time to give her a warning. He was too busy glaring at Royal.

For some unfathomable reason, Royal didn't seem to want to meet his gaze! Imagine!

Without a word, Royal tried to follow in Wren's wake, but Jeremiah shot out one hand to stop him, and didn't have even one qualm when the heavy wooden bucket crashed into Royal like a pendulum. He didn't dare let go of the rope handles, or he might be tempted to do something else with his hands—something that would not benefit Royal at all.

Royal froze and glared over at him.

Jeremiah leaned in close to make sure they had good, strong communication. "You are a grown man. She is a child."

Royal huffed. "Please mind your own business, boy. I love her."

Jeremiah clamped his teeth for a moment and refused to give the man any space. How was it that one three-letter word could make his blood come so close to a boil? It was sure a good thing for Royal that he heard Striker coming through the brush behind him, or he might have been tempted to show this snippet of a man just what one "boy" could do to him with his fists.

Instead, he leaned even closer to the man's face. "If you really love her, you'll give her time to grow up before you try to cajole her into something so permanent as marriage." He stepped back and gave the man a once-over, hoping Royal could see even in the dark that he had a good six inches on him and at least twenty pounds. "I ever hear tell that you so much as touched that girl in a disrespectful way, and you'll have me to deal with, understand?"

Behind him, Striker's feet shuffled in the grass. "Goes for me too, pup."

Royal made no reply other than to press his lips into a pinched line.

But Jeremiah figured he'd made his point, so he stepped to one side, hoping he'd given Wren enough time to escape back to the encampment before this one could catch up to her.

Royal practically shot past them and through the brush.

Jeremiah sighed as he met Striker's glance. "Think it will make any difference?"

Striker waggled his head, scrubbing one hand around the back of his neck. "Only time will tell. Doesn't help that he gets twice the land if he can convince her to marry him." He swept a gesture from the buckets toward the river. "Let me help you with those."

As Jeremiah filled the buckets, he released some of his tension on a sigh and a roll of his tight shoulders. At least he'd gotten out of the conversation without killing the man.

Tamsyn Acheson walked by Edi's side toward the Hawthornes' encampment with a warm dried-apple pie in each hand. Beside her, Edi carefully carried a block of cheese.

After Striker had lit into her over her treatment of her brother a few weeks back, she and Edi had fallen into a sort of silent camaraderie that had been nice. Tamsyn had tried not to chastise him so much, and Edi really did seem to be trying to behave and do what she asked and wanted.

Tonight, for example, even though he was tired and only wanted sleep, he had agreed to come to the Hawthornes' wagon to eat. Tamsyn had given her word that he could return to his bed just as soon as he'd eaten his fill—and the bribe of her warm apple pies had helped more than a little with that.

But making them had brought Sam right back to the forefront of her mind. She clamped her teeth, irritated with herself for giving him space in her thoughts. Irritated with him for turning out to be just like her parents. He'd had her fooled. Plenty fooled. He'd seemed kind and loving until he'd opened up and revealed who he truly was.

They reached the Hawthorne encampment at the same time that Jeremiah and Striker arrived, each carrying a bucket of water. And then there was Striker . . . With his little speech the other night, he'd revealed that he was nothing like Sam Saunders. And despite wanting to give him a piece of her mind at the time, she'd realized that his words revealed a concern for her brother that ought to endear Striker to her, not have her angry with him.

So now, her pulse kicked up its heels like a spring colt just at the sight of Striker tugging the brim of his hat in her direction. She gave him a nod, but pressed her teeth together. When was her heart going to fall into line with the realization that Striker Moss deserved more than she could give him?

With a warm, hopeful smile, Striker handed his bucket off to Jeremiah and quickly reached to relieve her of her pies. "Evening, Miss Acheson. Edi." He gave her brother a friendly bump with his elbow.

Jeremiah offered a deferential tip of his head and a slight bow. "Evening, ma'am. I'll just take these buckets on over to the wash station. Edi, good to see you."

Edi gave Jeremiah a perfunctory nod, but his gaze fastened to Striker, and he was suddenly all smiles. "Howdy!"

Tamsyn sighed and folded her now-empty hands in front of herself. Edi had missed Striker's company since he hadn't been coming to their fire of an evening. But she knew Striker went out of his way to ride his big Morgan beside Edi's wagon for a portion of each day—always a portion where she herself was off walking with the ladies. She'd seen it by accident the first time, and then she'd started watching for it. Striker rode with Edi for nearly thirty minutes, almost every day, just before the nooning, but he was always out of sight by the time she could catch up to the paused wagon from where she and the ladies trailed far enough behind to avoid some of the dust raised by the hundreds of ox hooves.

Her heart was still stuttering at his nearness, and she berated herself for her weakness of fortitude where this man was concerned. "Evening, Mr. Moss." At least her voice emerged steadily. "It's been some time since we've spoken. I hope all is well with you?"

A gleam of mischief sparkled in his eyes. He lifted one of the pies to inhale dramatically. "I thought I was doing all right before this, but mmmmm, I declare that I'm doing right dandy just now."

He straightened, and his expression fell to a more serious bent as he skimmed her with a look that took her in from head to toe and back again. He made a tight sound at the back of his throat, and then hefted the pies. "I'll just take these on over to put them with the food."

Tamsyn glanced over to see Mattox, Micah's big black dog, hovering near the tailgate, nose pirouetting through the air. The dog gave an impatient bounce on his haunches, but at a snap of Micah's fingers, flopped to the ground and put his big head on his paws.

Tamsyn turned a smile on Striker. "Just mind that you put them high enough that the dog doesn't steal them."

Striker chuckled. "That dog has better manners than most of the men in this company."

Tamsyn couldn't stop the crinkling at the corners of her eyes. "Then perhaps I should give instructions that you shouldn't steal a slice before dessert is served either?"

"Whoa there!" He looked affronted. "The worker is worthy of his hire, Miss Acheson. Just look at the crowd I'll have to navigate to get these pies across to their table! That's worth at least one measly piece before dinner, don't you think?"

He winked, and Tamsyn felt warmth invade her very core. She hung her head, not willing to let him know how much she'd missed him—hardly daring to acknowledge it to herself. "Go on with you, then. Edi, go with Striker and put the cheese by the pies."

Striker froze and stared down at her as Edi started toward the food, seemingly oblivious to the fact that he was leaving Striker behind. Tamsyn wanted to call him back, but she didn't want to draw attention to herself either. They were in a group, for crying in her buckets. It wasn't like her brother had left them in some intimate enclosure. And yet for the life of her, that was exactly what this felt like. All the bustle and hustle around them seemed to fade, and all she could see was Striker staring down at her with such a softness in his eyes that the pool of warmth in her core spread to every extremity.

Tamsyn wrapped her arms around her waist, like that might act as some sort of shield. "What?"

Firelight glinted off his Adam's apple as it bobbed firmly up and down. "You said my name."

Heat flooded her face. That was what she got for thinking of him by his first name for these past few weeks. This slip might cost her the months of hard work she had put in to build a wall between herself and this man! "I-I didn't mean—that is—I don't want you to think that—well, that anything has changed."

Just like that, all the wonder and hope seemed to drain right out of the man. His shoulders sagged, and he turned his gaze toward the food table, where, from the way that Edi was looking around, he had only just now realized that Striker wasn't behind him. Striker gave a slight nod, pressed his lips together, and gestured with one of the pies toward her brother as though to say he should get going.

Tamsyn nodded to encourage him onward.

Without another word, he strode off, greeting Edi with instructions on where to set the cheese as he placed the two pies on the top of a wooden water barrel that someone had rolled near to give relief to the overflowing tailgate.

Tamsyn felt like the lowest of the low. Couldn't the man see that she only meant the best for him? Why did he have to keep pushing?

After dinner, Deliverance sat holding sweet baby Blythe in the rocking chair that Marigold had long since abandoned for her bed.

Once everyone had consumed their fill of the meal, there had been a short interlude where Whitley and Wren had played their fiddles. Royal Carter played his guitar. And Chevonne—who had arrived just before the meal and whispered to Del that her nap had been divine—had surprised everyone by bringing out a rather large harp and playing the most beautiful music Del had ever heard.

Del had wanted to close her eyes and simply revel in the tranquil notes, but she'd been too fascinated watching Cody, who had paused across the way on the edge of the gathering and propped one shoulder against one of the prairie schooners. Had Del ever seen such a soft look on the man's face before? He was normally abrupt and to the point. A stoic man who spoke little but acted when there was need for it.

Tonight, however, he seemed like a piece of wax exposed to too much heat.

Several times, he shifted as though to shore up legs that had lost their strength, and all the while, his soft gaze seemed transfixed on Chevonne, where she played the harp. When Chevonne had concluded the final notes of the song and let the gentle melody linger on the silent air, Cody hung his head and prodded one boot at a clump of grass near his feet. With a smile, Del had glanced down to adjust the baby in her arms, and when she glanced back up, the man was no longer there. Though she searched in several directions, she never did figure out where he'd gone or how he had disappeared so quickly. But one thing was certain! Chevonne was in for some ribbing about the handsome Indian scout.

Del's smile grew as she hummed to the baby in her lap. She had offered to help with the cleanup, but Mrs. Hawthorne had rejoined that the most helpful thing Del could do would be to hold the baby for her while she and her children carried out that task.

And Del couldn't deny her marvel over the smooth efficiency of Evelyn's management. With a snap of her fingers, the woman had instructed her husband to take the youngest boy off to bed. Instead, Hiram had pulled Evelyn into his arms and bent her over backwards for a lingering kiss while all of his offspring cried "Eeew!" and "Father!" with chuckles and embarrassed cringes.

When he finally pulled his wife back to her feet, a laughing Evelyn had given his chest a smack and motioned from him to Cumberland and then to the wagon once more with a saucy quirk of one brow.

Laughing, he had led his son away, but not without a backward glance and a flirtatious pump of his brows.

After that, Evelyn had the children moving like a well-managed assembly line. The two youngest twin girls, Liberty and Serenity, swept up scraps of food with long whisk brooms and pitched what Mattox didn't want into the embers of the fire. Silas and Soren fetched water from the creek and hung it over the fire, then rolled the water barrel back to the side of the wagon and were working without much success to get it back into place when Jeremiah had rescued them and hefted the barrel onto its stand on the side of the wagon. He then helped the boys get it strapped securely. After that, Evelyn sent the four youngest workers to their beds while she, Whitley, and Wren made swift work of cleaning the dishes—though most of the women had taken their own dishes back to their camps, so there hadn't been too many.

All too soon, Evelyn approached with the girls behind her. "Thank you so much for holding her. How did she do?"

Reluctantly, Del rose from the rocking chair and transferred the little one to her mother's arms. "She was silent as a lamb the whole time. She worked those first two fingers pretty hard, though." Del smiled. "I worried she might suck them clean off for a few minutes."

Evelyn chuckled. "Isn't that the sweetest thing? Always her first two fingers. Whitley sucked her first knuckle—very noisily."

"Ma!" Whitley protested from behind her.

Evelyn continued as though she hadn't heard her. "Wren just cried."

Wren batted her lashes and smiled as she held her hands up to frame her cheeks. "I just knew how to get what I wanted."

Evelyn chuckled and rolled her eyes at Del in a way the girl couldn't see. "Thank you so much for all your help."

Del felt embarrassed. "I don't feel like I did much, but I sure did enjoy sitting and rocking that little mite." She lifted a hand and turned to mosey into the dark toward the Slade wagon. Despite her weariness, she felt refreshed and rejuvenated. And she couldn't quite fathom it. She'd been so exhausted earlier, and she'd thought that holding the baby might fill her with worry over her own future, yet she found that just the opposite had happened.

Jeremiah emerged from the darkness. "You enjoy your time tonight?"

She glanced over at him. Even though she hadn't been expecting him to step out of the night, his presence didn't startle her. And for the first time in much too long, she realized that fear wasn't her primary emotion. She hadn't even thought about the darkness, or the fact that she was sitting by a fire and might be visible to anyone cloaked by it. She hadn't worried that Boone might step out of the night and resurrect past horrors.

She had simply enjoyed, smiled, relaxed.

She pressed one hand to her heart, relishing this amazing feeling. Was this what normal folk felt? Folk without a master who had the power to do whatever he wanted with them?

She drew in a long, deep breath, feeling it beneath her fingers.

"Hey, what's this now?" Jeremiah paused and turned to face her more fully.

She shook her head to allay the concern she could see in the way he leaned toward her, touched her elbow, and then scrutinized the darkness all around.

"I'm fine. All's well." She rested one hand over his, where he gripped her elbow. "I just realized that I didn't think about that . . . man, even once all evening."

Jeremiah seemed to relax. "Monster. It's okay. You can say it." Jeremiah's thumb caressed her arm.

Del felt her melancholy return as though she'd just been doused with a bucket of it. A monster who was the father of her child.

A child she suddenly wanted very much. Maybe it was those long minutes holding baby Blythe this evening that had made her realize how innocent a child was. How vulnerable. How oblivious to all danger. Blythe had simply trusted that the one holding her would handle her with care. She had snuggled in to rest against Del's breast without any concern over the color of her skin or the fact that she wasn't her mother. And Del had felt love swell in her heart for her own child, who would come into the world equally as innocent and trusting.

As she and Jeremiah continued to mosey through the darkness toward the wagon, she thought of the Hawthornes. Such a sweet family, full of love, humor, and cohesiveness. Did her child ever stand a chance of having a family like that one?

Del fisted one hand to keep herself from laying it protectively over her abdomen. For she suddenly realized that she wanted to give this child a home like that.

And her gaze slid to the man beside her as, for the first time in a very long time, she actually had hope that it could happen.

She stopped, turned, and stepped close to lay her head against Jeremiah's chest. She slid her arms behind him and settled her ear to the beat of his heart.

He froze, hesitated, cleared his throat. And then his arms wrapped around her, and his cheek lowered to rest against her own. "Well, now. This is pleasantly unexpected." His soft voice rumbled in her ear.

Embarrassed by her own forwardness, she chuckled and stepped back enough to look up into his face. "Sorry, it's just... Well, I wanted to say thank you for being so good to me since I..." She hung her head, feeling heat fill her face.

"Appeared like an angel descended straight from heaven in the floorboards of that wagon?"

She chuckled again. "I wouldn't say *angel*, no."

His teeth flashed white in the darkness. "I would. An angel that nearly stopped my heart with her beauty."

She smacked his chest. "Be serious."

He covered her hand, tucked her close once more, and rocked her gently. "I've never been more serious in my life."

She rested her forehead against his shoulder and simply breathed in the perfection of this moment. The strength of his arms around her.

The way he made her feel as though she were the most precious thing in the world.

A soft flutter of movement frolicked in her belly, and just as quickly as the feelings of awe and wonder and love had come upon her, doubt, uncertainty, and worry took their place.

She needed to tell Jeremiah about this child. He deserved to know before any of this went further. But not tonight.

She eased back from him, not willing to mar this night with talk of molestation and the consequences of it. "Best we get some sleep, I suppose."

For a long moment, he didn't move. He just looked down at her and gently gripped her arms in his hands. "You all right?"

She swallowed and looked away. "Yes. Just tired." She peeked back up at him, hoping he would believe her.

He nodded, and his hands slid up and down her arms, but somehow she could read disappointment in the tilt of his head. "You know you can tell me anything, right?"

She held her breath. Could he know? No. Not possible. She only *hoped* that he knew because that would mean that, despite knowing about her . . . unbound condition, he hadn't rejected her. She couldn't handle that rejection. Not tonight. Not after such a wonderful day. She pushed back from him. "Yes. Of course. Forgive me, but morning comes early."

He nodded. "That it does." He helped her climb inside, and she heard him sigh as he turned to unfurl his bedroll on the ground beneath.

Del frowned.

Had that been a sigh of bliss or concern?

Chapter 19

The rains started one day in early June, bringing a refreshing coolness with them. Most of the women, including Deliverance, chose to ride inside their wagons to avoid the damp. She missed the company. Cooped up here in the back of the wagon, she felt as though she might come unglued from herself. If she tried to read, with the wagon jostling as it was, she grew nauseated. And she worried about her strength waning right back into the weakened state she'd been in at the start of this journey.

Then, just as quickly as the rains had come, they were gone. The heat returned, and as Del shuffled through the undulating silver waves of it, she almost wished she were fighting nausea in the back of the wagon again. She smirked at herself as she swiped trickles of sweat from her forehead.

She drew in a full, deep breath and put one foot in front of the other. This was good. Freedom was good. Building her strength was good. Come her time, she would need that strength.

For days, the supply of wood for the cook fires had been minimal. It was during an evening meeting that Cody first told them buffalo dung made good fires.

Del wrinkled her nose.

True, they had been passing dried husks of it for weeks now, but that didn't mean she had any desire to pick it up.

All the women seemed of the same mind as they shuffled their feet and exchanged scrunched-nose glances.

It was Chevonne who gasped their feelings aloud. "Another way, there must be! Our food we cannot cook over a fire made from . . . from . . . well, from that!" She swiped a gesture at the large piece of dried dung that Cody held in one hand.

Cody only walked to the nearest campfire, which happened to be the one the scouts shared. A hare, dressed and spitted, hung roasting over the flames. Mr. Moss sat nearby, turning the handle. Cody tossed the piece of dung into the flames. Sparks shot up and showered the rabbit meat.

Chevonne gasped and made a face. Del wanted to do the same.

The Indian scout turned to face the company, propped his hands against his buckskin-clad hips, and glowered at Chevonne. "Adds spice to the meat" was all he said before turning to catch up his bay and swing aboard the beast's broad, bare back. Del was near enough to hear him mutter to Striker. "I'll take first watch tonight. I need some air."

Reluctantly, the women had set about gathering buffalo chips for their evening fires.

Now, for parts of each afternoon, the women each carried a basket that they filled with dried buffalo dung—even Chevonne had soon been forced to give in to the practice or go hungry.

This morning, as Del walked with the other women, she was surprised to note how green the grass had turned in just the few days of rain that had fallen. The oxen would be satiated, she supposed, and that was good because a few of the teams had begun to look emaciated and gaunt.

At noon, Striker Moss came to each encampment to inform the families that by this evening, they would reach the California Crossings of the Platte River. He instructed that they might plan to camp for a couple of days until they decided which crossing would be safer at this time.

Del couldn't deny relief at the thought of a day of simply lounging around. From the selection of books in the Slades' wagon, she was currently enjoying *The Three Musketeers* by Alexandre Dumas.

But more than having a day to read and sit still, she wanted a good, long soak in the river and had been trying to work up her courage to approach Mrs. Hawthorne about potentially borrowing a skirt that might have more ample room.

Chevonne had made it clear only this morning that her time of being able to hide her condition had passed. Del worried because she still hadn't worked up her courage to tell Jeremiah. But tonight she would have to find the strength. After she spoke to Mrs. Hawthorne, and had a good, long soak in the river.

Since that breath of a kiss a couple of weeks back, and the way she had hugged him that evening, he seemed to be allowing her time to process, and she appreciated that. His glances and smiles and gentlemanly conduct proved his continued interest, and she knew she wasn't being fair to him. She must find the courage to speak before he found out on his own.

He had been making sure her fire was built each night and had invited her on more than one occasion to join him and the scouts around their fire. She enjoyed listening to the men rib each other. Striker was never without a joke, and even Cody Hawkeye could give as good as he got in a quiet, dry manner that often sent the men into gales of laughter.

Jeremiah had seemed rather quiet, though, and Del felt her conscience nudging her. Despite that he still treated her as any gentleman would, she felt a barrier between them that she couldn't figure out. She had grown to rely on him. After all, he drove the wagon that had become her home. He often ate with her. And he always checked in to make sure she had no need of anything. But for the past few days, he'd seemed overly serious, solemn, and withdrawn.

Maybe he regretted the kiss and didn't want her to think he wanted more?

The thought that ought to fill her with relief brought a deep sadness instead. She tried to remind herself that she had enough concerns without needing to worry about the man's attentions, but he irritatingly encamped in her thoughts.

When the wagons circled that evening, Del shored up her courage and headed toward the Hawthorne encampment.

Bright yellow butterflies flitted through the air before her. A pair of them twirled together as though in a dance, climbing high into the sky. She put one hand to her eyes and watched them with a smile. On this June evening, there was plenty of sunlight to watch them until they disappeared from sight against the blue dome of the sky.

Del lowered her gaze and continued onward. She drew a deep breath of the loamy scents of the evening camps. Smoke from fires. Beans boiling. Bacon frying. Grass, crushed by wagon wheels and ox hooves alike.

It was a good, warm evening for a soak in the river. How far away Boone and that life seemed, and yet only a few weeks separated this freedom and pleasure from those chains. A shiver worked down her spine. She would not think of him. She was determined to put her days of living in fear behind her.

She turned her attention to the Hawthornes' camp. How eleven people were making it across the prairie with only one wagon amazed her.

Mrs. Hawthorne was shelling out instructions to her children as she held the baby on one arm and laid buffalo chips into the ring of rocks that someone had already assembled by their wagon. The family was like an efficiently oiled machine. Mrs. Hawthorne, building the fire; Whitley, mixing something at the tailgate; Wren, helping one of the little girls remove some thistles from her hair; and the twin boys "sword fighting" over the head of their youngest brother, Cumberland, with two long sticks they had somehow managed to find on the prairie. The elderly Mrs. Marigold Hawthorne sat in a rocking chair by the fire with her head tipped back and her eyes closed. Only the gentle rocking of the chair proved that she wasn't sound asleep.

Despite her busyness, when Mrs. Hawthorne glanced up and saw Del standing at the edge of their encampment, she straightened with a huge smile. "Well! Aren't you a sight for sore eyes!" She strolled over with a bouncy little jaunt, patting the baby's bottom as she came. "What can I do for you?"

Del opened her mouth, but then glanced at all of the children, who seemed suddenly fascinated with their conversation, and closed it again. She cleared her throat. "Ah, I wondered, might I have a word with you in private?"

The woman glanced back at her curious offspring and flapped a hand at them. "You all take care of dinner. Wren, you watch the fire tonight. I am going to walk for a moment with Del here and will return momentarily. Silas! Soren! Stop that! You're about to crack Cumberland in the head!"

"Yes, Ma." Both boys stopped and plopped into the grass beside their brother.

"You all listen to Grandma. I'll return shortly." Evelyn took Del's arm and turned them toward the river.

Del was relieved to be away from the bustle of the encampment as the two women walked along the shore of the river away from the activity. She needed just a moment to breathe while she decided how to broach this subject. As they walked, she laced her fingers together and twisted them tight, unlaced them, then laced them again. Her throat felt tight, her tongue dry.

Finally, Evelyn stopped and turned to face her. "I'm sorry to push, but as a mother of eight, I can imagine you understand that I am constantly short on time." She smiled. "What can I do for you?"

Del took a breath and turned to face the woman. "Y-you already know that I escaped from the captain of the fort . . ."

"Yes." That one word was soft and full of kindness.

Del scrubbed the pad of one thumb into her palm. "What you don't know is that he ... He, ah, he left me ... with child." There it was. She had finally gone and admitted it.

"Oh, darling!" Evelyn stepped forward and drew her into a hug with her free arm. Baby Blythe sucked noisily on her two fingers. Evelyn stepped back. "I'm so sorry for what you have been through. It ain't right."

Del frowned, blinked hard to hold tears at bay, and dipped her chin. After a lifetime of being around people who thought of her as less-than, it seemed strange to meet folk who didn't view her in that same way.

"How far along are you?"

"Almost five months." Her hands hurt from their tight clench. She eased them to her sides and smoothed them over the material of her skirt. "I wondered ... Well, I wondered if I could trade you some work for a skirt that would ... take into account ..." Why was she having such a hard time spitting this out?

Evelyn gripped her arm in a gentle squeeze. "Say no more. And no, you may not trade me some work."

Surprise shot through Del, and she snapped her gaze to the woman's face. Had she misjudged the woman's kindness?

Evelyn smiled. "It's just a skirt. I don't expect any payment for it. And I'm happy to give it to you. I even have one that I used to wear when I was ... smaller." She gave a self-deprecating smile. "I've kept it tucked away in a crate just in case a miracle happens and I am ever able to get back to being skinny again." She laughed.

Relief shot through Del. Tears blurred her vision. "Thank you. Thank you, kindly. You've no idea how much this means to me. No idea."

Evelyn pulled her into another one-armed embrace. "It's nothing. Truly, I'm happy to help. I wish I could do more."

Del followed Evelyn back to her camp and then was surprised to find the baby in her arms while Evelyn entered the wagon. She stared down into the sweet little face, pimpled with little dots now that she was almost two months old, and felt herself fill with wonder at how quickly the baby was growing. Fast on the heels of the wonder came despondency.

She couldn't even take care of herself! How was she to care for a child? Who in the world would give her a job keeping their books—the only job she really knew how to do other than keeping house or maybe cooking, and even that had mostly been taken care of by her mother and the other "house girls," as the master had called them with a sly smile. The thought of that smile sent a shiver down Del's spine.

She brought her thoughts back to her present predicament. Jeremiah had mentioned that he was heading to California. She knew he'd let her travel with him if she asked. Say she somehow managed to reach California without Boone catching up to her. Say she, by some miracle, was offered a job in someone's home. What if something happened that she didn't know how to take care of? What if a recipe was required for a meal, and she didn't know how to make it? What if—

"Everything all right?"

Del's racing thoughts screeched to a halt. She lifted her gaze to find Evelyn glancing between her and baby Blythe.

Del felt her pulse rise as she handed the child back to her mother and accepted the skirt. She forced a smile. "All's well. Just in awe over how quickly she's growing!"

Evelyn chuckled and gave the baby a jostle. "Isn't she, though?" There was concern in the gaze she leveled on Del. Like maybe she hadn't quite bought her story.

Del lifted the skirt. "Thanks again, ever so much."

"Of course. And like I said, if you ever need anything else . . ."

Del nodded her thanks, and as she hurried away with that precious skirt clutched in her hands, she knew that Evelyn had no idea just how much her kindness meant.

She also knew that her near future would be far from assured and that, despite her changing heart toward the innocent babe growing inside her, she had no idea how she was going to take care of him or her.

Lord? You seeing me down here? Because I confess that for the past few years I've been trying to keep my hope in You, but it's not been easy. You know that, right? Please don't let me lose faith. Thank You for these kind people. Bless Ms. Evelyn. Bless her good, Lord. And if possible, could You give me a glimpse of hope for the future? I sure could use it. I surely could.

With a sigh, she headed downriver back the way the wagon train had just come. Maybe she could find a lovely deep pool shielded by brush and would feel better after a nice long soak to wash her worries away.

Chapter 20

B oone rode, sitting straight up in his saddle, trailing Chayton's paint. Every wheezing breath filled his chest with hot coals. Each cough brought up blood. All his muscles felt sapped of strength. But he would not slump like a weakling.

He ought to have caught up with the wagon train by now, but each evening, Chaytan made him drink that concoction that knocked him out, and Boone had to admit that without the rest, he might not have made it this far.

The wagon train had been making good time. Most wagon masters didn't push their folk or their animals so hard. But this train was coming through early enough, he supposed, to have good access to un-trodden grasses and clean water. Oxen could survive well on only grass, provided there was plenty of it. But in the later months, when the land turned dry and previous wagon trains had passed through and allowed their animals to eat the grasses down to the dirt, those folk coming behind would have a harder time keeping up their animals' strength.

A pain shot through his sternum. He cursed the ineptness of his weakness. Used to be that he could ride from dawn to dusk without even needing a break. On this trip, he had been forced to pause and dismount every few miles. And each time, he had feared that he might not have the strength to pull himself back into the saddle. He had also cursed the wagon master who was pushing his people so hard. Yesterday, he had wondered if he was ever going to catch up to them!

But today... ah, blessed hope that had renewed his strength. Today, Chayton had pointed to the horizon, and relief had filled Boone's chest.

From the higher rise, where they had paused, he'd glimpsed the wagon train ahead.

Chayton pulled his horse to a stop. "From here you go alone."

Boone was fine with that. He gave the man a nod and barely noticed when he faded into the brush, for his attention had returned to the wagon train. If only this weariness didn't keep sapping his strength... But that didn't matter now. He had found them!

He would catch up to them in the next half hour.

Then he would see if he had chosen wisely back at the fort.

Jeremiah set to unhitching the team as they made camp that evening on the shore of the Platte River.

"Hello, the camp!" someone called.

Jeremiah lifted his gaze from the yoke he was unpinning from the neck of one of the oxen to see a group of black men riding into the encampment from the west. He straightened.

The men looked ragged and wary as they swung down.

Jeremiah recognized their concern. He left his oxen and strode over to meet them, stretching his hand to the man out front. "Howdy. Name's Jeremiah. Welcome." He offered them a smile.

The men shifted. Exchanged glances, and then seemed to ease some. The first man greeted him and then lowered his voice. "These folk all right?"

Jeremiah nodded. "These folk are all right."

The man loosed a breath, and his shoulders seemed to ease. "I'm John, these here are Cato, Saul, and Jack."

Jeremiah shook each man's hand in turn.

"Be all right if we make camp in that field there?" John pointed to a flat place closer to the river.

"Don't see why not. You heading east?" That was a curiosity. Why would they be heading back toward the land they had likely fled?

John nodded. "Happy to make your acquaintance. Come on by the fire whenever you have a moment." He exchanged a glance with the man named Cato. "There are things you should know before you go on ahead."

The ominous tone of his voice raised Jeremiah's curiosity and premonition. "I'll do that."

After introducing the men to Caesar Cranston, Jeremiah left them to make camp and led his oxen first to water and then to the temporary corral that Declan Boyle set up each night. After the delay from meeting the new arrivals, finding Caesar, and the introductions, he was feeling pressed for time. Before darkness fell, he and Striker needed to go ahead to assess the two points of crossing that they would need to choose between.

He handed the oxen off to Declan with a nod, and movement at the new arrivals' camp drew his attention. Cato and the one named Saul elbowed each other and pretended to be weak in the knees as they watched something across the camp.

Jeremiah had a sinking feeling as he turned to see what they were looking at. Sure enough. His fears were founded.

Del was hurrying away from the Hawthorne wagon with something clutched to her chest. She walked back along the track they had just covered.

Jeremiah narrowed his eyes. Where was she going? What did she have in her hands? A glance toward the new group of men showed that they were still watching her. Watching with much too much interest as

Del disappeared over a small rise. Though the men returned to unsaddling their mounts once she was out of sight, Jeremiah felt uneasy.

Del was likely going to bathe. He ought to stand guard just to make sure nothing untoward happened.

One of the Hawthorne twin boys passed by with a stick in his hands.

"Soren?" He took a guess.

The boy looked at him. "I'm Silas."

"Sorry about that. I need you to take a message to Mr. Moss for me. Can you do that?" He pointed. "He's right down there at that end of the encampment helping the Glovers with one of their wheels. See him?"

The boy nodded his blond head. "Yes, sir."

"Please tell him that if I don't show up in the next few minutes, he should go ahead to check the crossings with Cody. Something's come up that I need to see to."

"Yes, sir."

Jeremiah watched only long enough to assure himself that the boy was heading toward Striker, and then he turned and strode quickly in the direction that Del had gone. He would give her a word of warning and then make sure she wasn't disturbed. It was what any man worth his salt would do.

She crested a gentle rise, and he broke into a jog, wishing the land were still as flat here as it had been for weeks on end. He wanted to catch up to her before she headed for the river. But as he topped the low hill, he saw that he was too late for that. She stepped between two large bushes and turned toward the water.

But another sight had his heart hammering in his chest. For beyond where Del had just disappeared into the brush, a rider crested a rise.

The man didn't seem to have seen them yet, for he was riding tired, head down, and slightly slumped in the saddle.

Jeremiah frowned. Another member of the party that had just arrived? No. This man was approaching from the east, where those others had arrived from the west. The brim of this new man's hat covered his downturned face, and he was still too far away to be recognizable.

Who would be out here riding alone?

Del had sure picked a fine time to sneak off for a bath with strangers coming up out of the prairie like grasshoppers.

Jeremiah continued walking toward the man, intent on reaching the place where Deliverance had diverged from the path before this new rider did. He reached the bushes and realized they flanked a low gully that led down to the river. Deliverance was still nowhere in sight. And the abundance of brush here—likely the reason she'd chosen this spot—should keep it that way. Good.

He glanced back toward the rider. The man lifted his head at that moment, and Jeremiah felt everything inside him wash cold with horror. He should have hidden. He should've crawled through the grass straight to the river and found Deliverance to keep her safe. But it was too late for any of that now.

Caesar had reported that he had collapsed, yet here he was, out of uniform, but alive and very far from his post.

Boone Baxter seemed surprised to see him there and slowed his horse, giving Jeremiah a long once-over.

Be calm. Breathe. He can't know what he can't know. Just don't act nervous.

Jeremiah raised a hand in greeting. "Howdy!" he called, hopefully loud enough for Deliverance to hear him over the rushing of the river water. "I was just about to wash up, but our encampment is just ahead. I know everyone would say you are welcome."

Lies. With how much everyone loved Deliverance, hardly anyone in their company would say this man was welcome. But Jeremiah gave him a smile just the same. Then turned toward the water. That was what a man would do if he had nothing to hide, right?

"Boy! You hold up."

Dread washed in. Jeremiah froze in his tracks and lifted his hands above his shoulders. He knew that tone of voice. Had heard it too many times to count growing up. The only good thing about this was that maybe Del would hear Boone, too.

Behind him, saddle leather squeaked, and then a pistol cocked.

A shiver worked down Jeremiah's spine. He kept his back to the man and lowered his head.

His eyes fell closed. *Lord.* It was the only prayer that would come to mind. The only word that he could seem to dredge up.

What mattered now was that he stay between the man and Deliverance for as long as he possibly could. It didn't bode well that the man had come all the way from the fort. Had he been searching for their party again? Wondering if his men had not done as good a job of checking the wagons as he had instructed them to?

It didn't matter his reasoning. Jeremiah knew exactly what had brought him here.

"Turn around, boy."

Jeremiah kept his hands in plain sight and turned to face the man.

"You're him, ain't you?" The colonel coughed and used a bandanna to wipe his mouth.

He didn't look well. His eyes were red-rimmed and sagging. His beard, badly in need of a trim.

"The man who was with that party at the fort a few weeks back?"

Jeremiah broadened his stance and settled into his heels, hands still raised. "We did pass through the fort a few weeks back. Yes, sir. Something I can help you with?"

The man glanced from Jeremiah toward the river behind him and then back to Jeremiah's face. "Where are you going?"

"Been a long, hot day. Like I said, I was going to wash some of the dust off." Jeremiah offered the lie without a single qualm. He wanted to glance back and make sure that Deliverance was still out of sight. He didn't dare move, however, because he didn't want to draw attention to anyone other than himself. Had she heard and taken warning from any of this?

Hoofbeats approached from the encampment, and a glance revealed Striker on his Morgan. Relief puffed a breath from Jeremiah's lips.

Striker reined up and glanced from Jeremiah to the newcomer, and then down to the pistol the colonel held leveled at Jeremiah. His brows hitched as he dismounted. He looked back at Jeremiah. "Came out to see what was taking you so long."

Silas must have gotten distracted from delivering his message. Otherwise, why would Striker be here looking for him?

Thank You, Lord.

An idea struck, and Jeremiah hoped that Striker would not miss a beat. He lowered his head. "Yes, sir, Master, sir. I was just coming to the river to wash off some dust. I swear I wasn't going nowhere other than to take a dip in the water. I was gon' be right back. Honest, I was."

Boone had seen them back near the fort where they had rescued Mrs. Houston, but knowing the type of man Boone was, he likely hadn't paid any attention to the relationship between Striker and him. He hoped.

Someone needed to take charge of this situation, and Jeremiah wanted it to be Striker and not Boone Baxter.

Striker hesitated. A small frown touched his brow. His hands shifted against the reins. And then a light of understanding hit his eyes. "I thought I told you to meet me at the west side of the encampment?" He hesitated. Swallowed. "You know I don't tolerate slowness . . . boy."

Despite Jeremiah's relief that Striker had caught on to his plan, he swallowed. Striker's voice took him straight back to the plantation, and a memory of Striker's father dressing down his own father surged to the fore. He silently blessed his friend for the reluctance with which he had called him "boy."

He kept his head bowed and his hands raised. "I swear I meant no harm. Only washing up so I'd be clean like you like, Master, sir."

"Well, go on then, but be quick about it. We have to assess the crossing up ahead and . . . I need you there in case we . . . need someone to wade into the water."

Jeremiah nodded and started backing toward the Platte. "I'll be quick, Master. I promise. Real quick."

Jeremiah watched as Striker turned toward Boone Baxter and used the excuse of approaching the man to shift his horse into the path between the colonel's gun and Jeremiah. He stretched his hand to the man. "Aren't you the colonel from the fort?"

Only when a bush hid the two men from sight did Jeremiah turn and rush toward the river, searching for Deliverance as he went. He only hoped that Striker would be able to distract the man long enough for him to get Deliverance away from the encampment and hidden.

His heart hammered and his breath beat so rapidly against his teeth that dryness stung his throat.

Dear Lord. Dear Lord. Dear Lord.

Had a terror this severe ever gripped him?

He didn't dare call for her. That would give away their ruse for certain.

A skirt draped over a bush on the embankment caught his attention.

He stumbled to a stop. She was bathing! He'd known that, but Baxter's arrival had driven all coherent thought from his mind. He couldn't just rush out there and intrude on her privacy! And yet her life was in danger! He looked at the clothes again.

"Del?" he whispered as loudly as he dared.

No response.

"Deliverance!"

Still nothing.

He could wait right here for her to come out of the water, but would Boone's suspicions rise if he didn't arrive back in camp in a timely manner? Worse than that, what if Boone took his horse to water, glanced upstream, and somehow saw Del?

"Del, it's Jeremiah. You hearing me?"

Still no response.

Beside the skirt was Del's dress. But no petticoats.

That likely meant she still had those on, right? A man could hope. Especially when he didn't have time for propriety.

He took a quick breath and pressed through the thick underbrush—and was relieved to see Del clothed in a long white petticoat and floating on her back in a small pool of water hidden by an enclave of wild lilac. She had her eyes closed and looked for all the world as though she were sound asleep there on the water.

With her ears beneath the surface as they were, she obviously hadn't heard any of his calls. And the roundness of her stomach filled Jeremiah with that familiar fury. If he had anything to say about it, Boone would never be able to lay his hands on her again.

He strode into the water without even thinking about his boots or the fact that he was fully clothed. "Deliverance," he said quietly as he reached for her.

She surged upright, gasping in fear, eyes wide and arms flailing.

"Hush now. Hush." He touched her arm, wanting to reassure her. "It's just me. But we have to stay hidden."

When recognition dawned, a spark of anger lit her eyes, and she shoved his chest hard with both hands. "What are you doing here? You can't be here. I was washing up."

Fearing that her raised voice would be heard above the rush of water, Jeremiah pressed one finger to his lips and reached for her again to keep her from surging further into the river, where she would be away from the concealing shelter of the bushes. He latched onto her wrist and tugged her close so that he could speak softly into her ear. "He's here. We have to stay hidden and quiet."

Del fell from defiance to defeat in the space of those few words. She searched his face, lower lip trembling, then darted her scrutiny along the brushy riverbank. "Who's here?"

Though she asked the question, he could tell from the horror washing her expression that she knew exactly who he meant. When he held his silence, simply waiting for her to absorb the truth, she sagged against him, her forehead pressed against his chest. Tremors quaked through her.

He gripped her arms with both hands. Rested his chin against her shoulder. "I got you now. We're going to be all right. Striker is back there distracting him, but we have to stay hidden." He needed to think. Come up with a plan.

Something other than marching out there to shoot a colonel in the US Army in the back.

Chapter 21

S triker swallowed the bitterness his words had raised inside him. He'd never wanted to be his father, and yet how quickly the man's voice had emerged when he'd needed him to.

He hoped Jeremiah knew how much their ruse disturbed him. But it had seemed like the easiest way to extract his friend from the danger of the colonel's gun. And where was Deliverance? He certainly hoped that Jeremiah had her, because there could only be one reason this snake had turned up again.

He stretched his lips at the man—and that was all it was, a stretch of the lips—for there was no feeling of welcome in him. He hoped his revulsion didn't show in his eyes and that the man would think his smile friendly. "You've come a long way."

The colonel holstered his pistol and reached for his canteen. "Sorry to pull a gun on your boy there. I thought he might be making a run for it."

Striker's teeth clenched so hard that his jaw ached. He swung his mount toward the encampment before he offered, "Jeremiah's been trustworthy, at least up to this point." His father's voice slipping past his lips again. He wanted to spit. "Let me take you to our fire. Get you some hot coffee. There are beans and bacon, too."

The man nodded, and they'd both started forward when Silas Hawthorne jogged into sight. "There you are, Mr. Moss! I was supposed to tell you that Jeremiah—" His eyes widened as they latched onto the man riding beside Striker. He bent and propped his hands on his knees as though to catch his breath, but before he'd been in that position for even a second, he popped upright and started swinging a stick at the tall grass all around him like a jouster in a fight for his life. "I forget what he said. But I think—"

"I found Jeremiah." Striker hurried to speak before the kid could give away their ruse. "I spoke to him, so you don't have to worry."

"Oh, good." Silas flicked his gaze off the man beside Striker again. "Ma says I got to wash. So I'm meeting Soren at the river to bathe." He pointed his stick toward the path through the brush that Jeremiah had just disappeared down.

Striker gave the kid a nod. He doubted that whatever Jeremiah had said should be revealed to the colonel. But Silas was smart, and Striker wanted to tell him how proud he was of him for recognizing the danger this man presented. Instead, he said, "Well, Jeremiah is down there taking a quick dip himself. Mind that you don't disturb him because I need him to come back quickly so we can assess the crossings." Striker watched the boy. Would he get the message?

After another skimming glance at the colonel, Silas nodded. "Yes, sir."

"Go on then."

The boy hurried off, still jousting the grass.

Striker put his heels to his horse and smiled at the man beside him. "Kid's got more energy than a whole barrel of puppies."

The colonel hesitated, staring in Silas's direction. "You sure that child is going to be okay down there with your buck? He's a big one. Might do any number of things to that child."

Striker once again had to unlatch his teeth. He couldn't keep a bite of anger from his voice when he said, "Jeremiah would never hurt anyone. Silas will be fine."

The colonel looked over at him. "Never hurt anyone yet, you mean. You keep giving him such a long leash, the day will come when he proves to you who he really is."

Striker forced himself to appear thoughtful. "Maybe you're right. If he's not back in just a few minutes, I'll go looking for him, but for now, it's been a long day, and I'd like to put my feet up by the fire for a bit before we go out scouting again this evening. I'm sure you'd like to get out of that saddle, too."

The colonel sighed. Coughed. Wiped his mouth with a bandana. "Coffee and beans do sound good."

Relieved, Striker led the way. "What brings you here, Colonel?" Of course, Striker already knew the answer to that question.

The colonel spat into the grass at one side of his mount. "Hunting my runaway slave still."

"You never did find her?" Striker tried to force empathy into his tone. He tightened his hands around the reins so that he wouldn't be tempted to throttle the man riding beside him.

Chaytan lay on his stomach in the tall grass watching the colonel.

If he'd had his way, he would have let the colonel go on his own journey. The man was a warrior after all.

But Grandmother had said he needed a distraction. They all still grieved the loss of Chaska, his older brother. And then, with the incident involving Chaska's tomahawk, and Chaytan's subsequent humiliating loss of the pretty little woman who would have been his second wife—an appeasement for all he'd lost—he'd felt a fury building inside him for days now.

He ought to be fighting! Making war with those who had no respect for his people! And yet he'd been tasked with keeping one of them alive, instead.

But he wouldn't risk his life to help this one win his battle.

So now he would watch.

The colonel had a good horse. A pistol, too. These would be his payment for his degradation once the colonel died, which would be soon. In fact, Grandmother had thought he would not last this long.

So he waited.

And when the time was right, he would collect his payment.

Deliverance rested her forehead against Jeremiah's broad chest and willed herself not to panic, but she had to fight for each breath, and the world seemed to be spinning all around her.

Boone here.

She could almost feel the manacles around her wrists once more. Smell the gloomy scent of the earthen floor. Feel the loneliness of that dark basement. All of it more horrifying because of these weeks of freedom and the company of people who saw her as something more than a piece of property to be used as they willed.

Jeremiah's voice rumbled in her ear, but she couldn't make out the words. They were more like a soothing buzz.

If Boone were here, had Betsy . . . Oh! She hoped the woman was all right. But she couldn't think about what had brought Boone here. She must think about how to escape!

She pushed back from Jeremiah to eye the opposite embankment. She couldn't allow him to take a stand against Boone! Boone would obliterate him! How often had she heard Boone speak of the soldiers he'd broken? "That one will never question my authority again," he would say, with a low chuckle.

Terror clawed through Del's chest at just the thought.

Icy water sucked at her feet. The eddy that had seemed pleasant and calm only moments ago as she floated on her back, now gnawed at the skirt of her petticoat, like an entwining serpent intent on dragging her beneath the surface of the water. Suffocating. Threatening. Violent.

She would never make it!

But she had to try!

For Jeremiah.

She'd been walking each day. Growing her strength. She used to swim like a fish when she was a girl. It would come back to her! Once she reached the other side, she would run. Run like she hadn't run for a very long time.

She pivoted and took a step, but Jeremiah's broad hands wrapped about her arms and drew her shoulder blades against his chest.

"Del, you got to think calmly. *'What time I am afraid, I will trust in You.'* Take a breath and say it with me. Come on now."

"Let me go!" She thrashed for her freedom.

Jeremiah's grip didn't loosen. His voice continued to rumble. The warmth of his chest seeped into her back. The brush of his moving lips touched her cheek. Slowly, the words he spoke came into focus. The calm in his voice eased through her. "You got to stay with me, Del. I'm here. God's here. He has not forgotten us."

She took a breath. "What time . . ."

"That's right," Jeremiah urged. "Say it. Claim it." He waited for her to complete the verse.

"What time I am afraid, I will trust in You." She tipped her head back against Jeremiah's shoulder and peered upward at the blue of the sky overhead. *Lord, I'm terrified. Beyond scared. Beyond afraid.*

'You are My servant, I have chosen you and have not cast you away: Fear not, for I am with you; Be not dismayed, for I am your God. I will strengthen you, Yes, I will help you, I will uphold you with My righteous right hand.'

The words rose from deep inside her, over her, below her, all around her. They vibrated through her, warm and comforting. And she suddenly could see all the ways the Lord had been protecting her the past few months. Sending Jeremiah's wagon train at just the right moment. Betsy's taking advantage of Boone's absence on that one particular day when the birth of Blythe Hawthorne had likely saved her life. She sobbed in gratefulness and turned to press her forehead to Jeremiah's broad chest once again. She rested both palms on either side of her forehead and drew in a long, calming breath. "I don't know what to do. Tell me what to do."

Jeremiah took her by the shoulders, and when she glanced up at him, she was surprised to see moisture shimmering in his eyes. His hands rubbed up and down against her arms. His gaze remained fastened on her face. "You're strong. So strong. I'm blessed to know a woman of your strength."

She shook her head and almost chuckled her amusement. "I'm not strong. Not strong at all. It is Christ who strengthens me."

Jeremiah nodded, hands still rubbing up and down against her shoulders. "We can take heart."

"Because Jesus has overcome the world," Deliverance rejoined.

"Yes. He surely has."

Deliverance was suddenly so thankful that God had sent this man to help her in this moment. She looked up at him. "So what do we do now?"

"Mr. Jeremiah?" The young voice called from the embankment. "You out here?" One of the Hawthorne boys, she'd guess.

Jeremiah's hands squeezed her shoulders, and he had a slight smile on his face as he looked down at her. "I think the good Lord might have just sent us an angel—and that the first thing we ought to do is get out of this here water." He turned toward the embankment and then reached a hand to her, waiting for her to take it. His gray-blue gaze reassured her from above his shoulder.

Deliverance nodded and let him lead her to the low embankment where she had entered the river in the first place.

One of the Hawthorne twin boys waited for them on the river-bank, squatting beside Del's discarded dress. He squinted at them when they came into sight. "I'm Silas," he said, as though he could read the question in Del's eyes. He cut a look at Jeremiah. "Are you two supposed to be in the water together like that when she ain't dressed?"

Despite their dire circumstances, Del felt embarrassment heat her cheeks.

Jeremiah climbed from the river, grabbed Silas by one arm, and held the boy by his side as he turned their backs to her. He took several steps forward into the concealment of the brush, leaving Deliverance the privacy of the small clearing by the river. "Not every thought that pops into your head needs to be spoken, son."

Del glanced the length of her soaking-wet self with a shake of her head. At least she had kept her petticoats on. She scrambled from the river and took up her discarded dress to use as a makeshift towel.

"I know that!" Silas seemed affronted by Jeremiah's chastisement. "It's just that you two ain't married, and Pa says—"

"I'm sure I know exactly what your pa says. But saving a life must always come first. Hush now and let me get dried out a bit."

Deliverance couldn't help a smile as she listened to their conversation from the embankment. The day was hot enough that she had planned to lay her petticoats out to dry on a bush after she got out of the water, but of course, she would have to forgo that now. She wrang out the skirt of her petticoat as best she could, and then put the new skirt and blouse on over top of it, dampness and all. With the heat of this day she would soon be dry, and probably thankful for the coolness of the damp clothing until that point.

Silas was still speaking. "Mr. Striker told me to tell you to hurry up and meet him to check the crossings."

Deliverance's head snapped up. Was he going to leave her? Somehow, Jeremiah's presence had calmed her, and though she knew that the Spirit of the Lord had also helped her, she didn't want to be hiding from Boone without Jeremiah's guarding presence at her side.

And yet she recognized how selfish that was. Boone could not find Jeremiah anywhere near her! Her hands trembled when Jeremiah made no reply.

"I-I'm ready." She spoke the words as softly as she could so that they would only carry to Jeremiah and the boy in the nearby brush.

Jeremiah stepped back into the clearing, still tugging the leg of his buckskins over one boot. He was just as damp and uncomfortable as she was, she supposed. And those buckskins were going to be stiff once they dried, until he could massage the softness back into them.

"What now?" she asked.

"Marry me," he blurted.

"What?" Del pressed one hand to the base of her damp collar. She blinked a couple of times, trying to think how marrying him would help her. It wouldn't. In fact, it would only put him in even more danger. What was he thinking?

Even Silas stilled and squinted up at the man in surprise.

Jeremiah lifted one shoulder. "I know this seems abrupt and maybe like I'm making the offer only on account of needing to protect you, but—"

Deliverance shot up one palm and narrowed her eyes. "Have you gone and lost your mind?"

Jeremiah ran a hand around the back of his neck. A frown puckered his brow.

The anger surging through her made her take a step toward him. She yanked up her sleeve and thrust the scars on her wrist toward him. "You see this?" She took a breath and deliberately lowered the voice that she realized had grown too loud. "The man that done this to me is right over there in our encampment, and you standing here asking me to marry you? What do you think he'd do to you if he learned you married me?!"

A glint of steel shifted through Jeremiah's eyes. "I'm not sure, but I wish he'd give it a try!"

Terror nearly closed Del's throat. He didn't know Boone, or what he was capable of. "Well, I don't want to marry you!" She must convince him it was true!

Jeremiah shifted. Hung his head. "I only thought that as my wife, we could run together. And I'd give my life protecting you, I swear I would."

That was exactly what she was afraid of! She shook her head. Retreated a step. If she weren't hemmed in by the river, she might have fled then and there. She could never let him put himself in such danger on her account!

He stepped forward and took her fingers gently. His thumb rubbed the back of her hand. "I bungled my request." Contrition filled the gray of his eyes.

Del looked at their clasped hands, not wanting to disappoint him further.

"What I should have said was that from the moment I saw you there in the floorboards of that wagon, I knew you were the most beautiful woman I'd ever laid eyes on. But then, even at a danger to yourself and weary as you must have been that first day, you stood in the open and helped deliver that child, and I knew you were a woman any man would be proud to stand with. This protective spirit rose up inside me, and I knew I'd do anything, sacrifice anything, to keep you safe." He stepped closer and swept the backs of his fingers down her arm. "If that's not love, what else ever would be?"

Her gaze snapped to his. "You can't l-love me."

He smiled, his fingers still stroking her arm. "Why not?"

"Be-because we've only known each other a few weeks and, well, because there's too much you don't know about me." Her eyes fell closed, and she swallowed her dread down deep inside. The man might be professing his love now, but once he learned about this child she carried . . . What man would want another man's child?

A good one.

If anyone was a good one, it was Jeremiah.

"What is it?" Still, his fingers gently caressed her arm.

She shored up her courage. "Boone is here for more than just me." She forced herself to look at him. She wanted to read the emotions on his face. "I'm, well, I'm . . . carrying his child."

Jeremiah's hand did not still. He kept sweeping that gentle caress against her arm. His gaze dropped to her stomach, then rebounded to her own. But he didn't seem surprised. He swept one arm behind her shoulders and drew her close. He tucked her head beneath his chin and pressed his lips near her ear. "I know. I've known for some weeks now. And Lord, forgive me, this hatred filling my heart for a man I barely know has no place inside one who claims to love God."

She felt him tremble, and surprising relief filled her at his emotions. She hadn't known what to expect when she revealed the truth to him.

She pressed one hand to his chest and looked up at him. The honesty of his emotions gave her the courage to admit her own shortcomings. "Lord, forgive *me*, Jeremiah, because for a while . . . I hoped that maybe . . . Well, that maybe this child wouldn't make it."

He drew her once more to his chest, his big hand gentle against the back of her head. "Hush now. I've got you. I've got you. Just need to think what we do next, is all. Give me a moment."

Del shook her head. "There is no next, other than for me to keep running and hiding." She steeled her resolve with a firm inhale. "You have to let me go now."

She tried to push back from him, but he clasped her wrist, shaking his head. "I can't let you do that. Not alone."

Panic began to set in. "Jeremiah, please! I don't want anything to happen to you." She flapped a hand toward the encampment. "To any of those folk. You've all been so good to me, and it might just kill me if Boone's wrath brought harm to any of you." She gulped for a breath. "And there will be wrath. Please. He can't find me here!"

Still, he didn't release her.

"You don't know this man, Jer. You were owned by Striker's pa. Striker is a good, kind man. His father must have had *some* redeeming qualities? *Some* kindness in him? *Some* charity? That man who sold your pa and ma away from you?"

Jeremiah squinted, apparently recognizing her sarcasm. His shoulders drooped. "You're right. He only cared about those he felt were his equal."

Del shook her head and extracted her hand from Jeremiah's to clasp it before her. "Boone doesn't even care about that. Maybe he doesn't feel anyone is his equal. He cares about his reputation and his authority." She thrust a trembling finger toward the encampment. "That man finds me, he gonna kill me. You marry me, he gonna kill you. And I . . . well, I couldn't go on living if that happened." She couldn't seem to look at him. Certainly wasn't ready to marry, even if she knew the man who'd asked would be kind and gentle for all her days. He'd already proven that much.

"Your words give a man a powerful hope."

She glanced at him in surprise. He stood with those broad, blunt fingers draped over slim, wet hips, and a lopsided smile tilting his lips.

"What are you going on about?"

He reached one finger to stroke the underside of her chin. "Even after how I've bungled this, you still don't want me to die." He smiled. "Must mean you care about me at least a little bit?"

Del swatted his hand in irritation. "Do be serious, Jer! A man has arrived who could destroy everything, and you standing there like a lovestruck fool."

She couldn't bring herself to meet his gaze. She must stand strong! She couldn't let him be injured on her account. She didn't want to be so harsh, but she had to get through to him!

Jeremiah stilled and swallowed hard. "I can see your point. But I know these wagon folk. If we were married, they'd stand with us. Besides, these lands we're crossing have no formal government, so he has no standing here."

A flutter of hope filled Deliverance. Enough that it made her hesitate.

Jeremiah clasped his hands behind his back and looked down at her. "Marry me, Del. We can send Silas here for the parson."

Del glanced at the boy who had been so silent and still for the past few moments that she had forgotten he was even here.

Jeremiah continued, "He can marry us right here with Silas as our witness. Then we cross this here river and make a run for the mountains. He won't harm these folk if he never knows you were here."

His words were a temptation. Such a temptation. But she must not be selfish. Boone would never stop looking for her. "I c-can't marry you. I don't *want* to marry you." Tears filled her eyes at the lie. Wherever else would she ever find a man who had been so good to her?

Jeremiah hung his head, looking hurt by her continued rejection.

She dug her fingernails into her palm to keep herself from reaching for him.

"That man looked sick." Silas spoke up. "Real sick."

"He surely did." Jeremiah agreed.

"What do you mean?" Deliverance remembered Caesar's report that Boone had collapsed.

Silas shrugged. "He kept coughing into a bandana and wiping blood off his lips. Didn't look very steady either. Kinda pale and trembling like he was having a hard time staying on his feet."

Jeremiah's gaze returned to her. "I saw it, too."

Del shook her head. She could hardly fathom that picture of Boone. "He was never sickly. I never knew him to be sick for even one day."

Jeremiah roughed one hand over his head. "That's good. Not consumption then. That tends to come on slow."

The very word *consumption* had Del pressing one hand to her belly. Could this child have caught something from Boone? Could she have caught something from him?

Her eyes fell closed. She thanked the Lord that her first thoughts were of concern for his or her protection.

There is no fear in love.

Why did that keep coming to mind? It must be a Bible verse, right? She needed to look that up.

She was afraid. Terrified, even. Afraid of what might happen to Jeremiah. Afraid of what might happen to her. Afraid of what life would be like if she ever managed to escape Boone. Afraid of living with this child conceived against her will.

Always looking over her shoulder. Always one moment from going on the run again.

"No fear" would be wonderful.

But love?

Jeremiah's footsteps rustled through the grass.

She opened her eyes, expecting to see that he'd drawn close again, but he remained where he had been, head hanging as he prodded at something with the toe of his boot.

Could she love him? She liked him. He was kind and thoughtful and had been a blessing to her in her time of need. But not love. Right?

Wrong.

The thought bowled into her like a stampede of buffalo.

He was right. This concern inside her for his safety above her own . . . What was that if not love? Hadn't she already acknowledged that she felt safe in his presence? Each morning, she looked forward to his greeting. Each evening, to sharing a meal with him.

And yet one thing stood between them. One thing that she couldn't control. One thing that she couldn't ask of him.

She sealed her lips to keep from throwing herself and this child on his mercy.

And then Jeremiah spoke. "I don't want you to have to marry me if you don't want to, Del. I'm sorry I pressed so hard. I won't press you again." He didn't meet her gaze as he said the words—he looked out over the top of the brush around them, instead.

Deliverance felt the pain of those words in her very core. Her eyes fell closed, and she pressed one hand to her belly.

His feet shuffled. "But we got to find someplace for you to hide until I can get back to the encampment and see what's happening. If that man is as sick as he seemed, we might not have to worry none about running, and that would be good." He did pin her with a look then. "Promise me you'll stay right here. Silas will stay with you."

Silas scratched the back of his head. "But my pa—"

Jeremiah dropped a hand on Silas's shoulder even though he never took his gaze from her. "Promise me."

She drew in a steadying breath. "I promise."

He dipped his chin. "Good." He jostled Silas. "I'll talk to your pa. Just stay here with Del for me, okay?"

"Yes, sir."

With that, Jeremiah disappeared down the path leading away from the river. And if Del wasn't mistaken, his shoulders sagged as he walked away.

She tried not to feel like he'd taken her heart with him as she met the gaze of the blond Hawthorne boy.

She smiled at him. She had told Jer she would stay here. And she would, but she also needed to be able to see what was happening back at the camp. "You want to sneak through the bushes with me so's we can see what's happening back there?"

The boy's eyes sparkled. "Yes'm!"

She nodded. "Right then. This way."

She pressed through the brush along the riverbank until they came to the edge of the clearing where all the wagons were parked. Jeremiah was just crossing into the encampment. And Del felt her heart nearly come to a standstill when she spotted Boone chatting with Striker and Tamsyn in their camp. He seemed calm. Even sank onto a stump near their fire.

Despite that, she had never been more thankful for the thick concealment of early summer underbrush as she was when she settled down behind the chokecherry bush and peered from between its branches.

Chapter 22

Chaytan snaked through the underbrush in the colonel's wake.

The two men swung down from their mounts and ground-hitched them near an encampment with a fire.

Something delicious smelling boiled on the fire, and Chaytan's stomach rumbled. He was tired of the days of the same old rations he'd been forced to endure while traveling with the pampered warrior. The man wouldn't even take his own medicine! Chaytan had to mix it for him every night.

A woman bent over the fire. She had dark hair and was taller than most women. The woman of this new man, the colonel was speaking with?

Chaytan settled down to watch what was about to happen.

Striker Moss strode into Tamsyn Acheson's encampment with the colonel by his side and only one thought on his mind.

He hoped he wasn't about to get slapped.

But there was an easy way to disarm the colonel until they could all get some answers—providing Tamsyn went along with his ruse.

She leaned over her fire with a wooden spoon in one hand and wafts of smoke swirling around her. She blew on the spoon and tasted whatever was in the pot, and Striker swallowed down his apprehension as he left the colonel at the edge of her camp and continued toward her. If she was about to blow his plan to smithereens, at least he would get one kiss out of the deal.

He smiled big. "Hey, darlin'! How was your day today? Did the walkin' tire your feet out as much as it did yesterday?"

Still leaning over the pot, she stiffened and raised narrowed, questioning eyes on him. Her glance darted to the colonel, and he saw her immediate recognition of the man as all color fled from her face. Then her gaze flicked back to him.

He stepped between her and the colonel to block the man's view and give her a moment to adjust.

That moment was all it took to return a flood of angry red to her cheeks and for her eyes to narrow into tiny slits.

At least he was between her and the colonel, so hopefully the man wouldn't see her suspicious scrutiny. He continued toward her. Could she read the play-acting in his eyes?

Edi straightened from where he'd been slumped on a stump nearby. "Hi, Striker!"

"Hi, Edi. You been taking care of your sister?" He never took his eyes off of Tamsyn, willing her to understand what was happening.

"Yes."

"Glad to hear it!" He was almost to her now. She continued to lean over the pot as though his surprise entrance had frozen her in place. "And what about you? You been taking care of your brother?" Keep it light. Friendly. Just a family greeting each other at the end of a long day. He only had to fool the colonel long enough to get a cup of coffee down his gullet.

Tamsyn straightened and opened her mouth.

But he was close enough now to invade her personal space, and thankfully, that silenced whatever protest she'd been about to voice. Or maybe it was the way he'd lowered his gaze to her lips that silenced her.

Lips that were now tucked out of sight and pressed into a tight white line as her eyes shot wide and round.

Drat. Not a kiss then. Instead of kissing her like he'd planned, he pulled her into an embrace and settled his lips to the sweetly scented hair above her ear. "Easy." He spoke low. "This is all a ruse, just work with me, please. For Del." With that, he nudged her back from himself and turned toward the colonel with his arm still wrapped firmly about her shoulders. "Darlin', you remember the colonel from Fort Kearny?" He felt a tremor work through her, but she nodded, and he hadn't gotten slapped . . . yet. That was something. "Well, he's ridden a long way to catch up to us, and I told him that we would be more than happy to welcome him to our fire."

Edi giggled and blushed furiously as he eyed Striker's arm around his sister. For a moment, Striker was concerned that Edi would give them away, but he only hung his head and giggled again.

Tamsyn shot Striker a searching look, obviously uncertain what he was up to.

But to pull this off, he first had to make the colonel feel comfortable. "Please," he gestured the man toward the crate Tamsyn had set near the fire as a seat. "Let my Tamsyn get you some coffee. I'll have my boy strip and curry your horse just as soon as he returns from the river."

Tamsyn gasped, but then covered it with a wave of her hand in front of her face and a fake sneeze. "I declare, this smoke is like to do me in before we reach any part of the Oregon Territory."

Striker was relieved when the colonel didn't seem to notice anything out of the ordinary. He gave a nod and began removing his riding gloves as he sank wearily onto the crate.

Striker pressed one hand against Tamsyn's back. "The colonel is still searching for his runaway. I told him we haven't seen her, but he'd like to check all our wagons again one more time."

Tamsyn's whole body trembled beneath his fingers, but she maintained her easy stance. "Well, I hope you'll search a little more neatly this time than your men did, Colonel." She grinned and then laughed.

Striker felt proud of her gumption! A woman to ride the river with, and that was certain.

Her laugh sounded forced to Striker, but the army man didn't seem to notice. He sat hunched into his shoulders and didn't even seem to be paying much attention to their ruse. His attention had fastened to the flames below the pot.

Tamsyn pinged a glance off of Striker and then turned back, still smiling broadly at the man. "I declare it took me two weeks of travel to find where they misplaced my sugar. Pleasure to see you again, Colonel. Let me fetch a cup from the wagon. We'll have you that coffee in no time."

Striker's arm felt bare as she pivoted out of his embrace and marched smartly toward her supplies set out on the tailgate.

"I'll come help you, darlin'." Striker tried not to feel the colonel's weary, assessing gaze as he walked behind Tam. Under his breath, he urged her, "Around the wagon and stop on the other side."

Thankfully, she must have heard him because she kept walking until she'd reached the center of the far side of her wagon. She curled her fingers together in front of her and turned to face him, wringing her hands. "Striker Moss, you'd better have a good explanation for this!" Her whisper was fierce.

"Shhhh." He invaded her space again, not wanting to risk the colonel overhearing their whispers. With his lips near her ear, he said, "Those sleeping powders . . . You still have some?"

She went still as though everything had suddenly fallen into place. She nodded. "Yes. Edi's been working so hard that he's been falling right to sleep and hasn't needed them."

Striker held himself steady. He didn't allow his hands to curve about her waist as they wanted to. Nor did he allow his head to turn so that his lips could press into the soft skin beneath her ear. He did let himself draw in a breath of that sweet fragrance that was uniquely Tamsyn. What was the scent? Something he couldn't quite put his finger on.

He swallowed. Tried not to think about how nice it would be if this could be real. If only Tamsyn would quit being so independent and let him care for her and her brother.

"S-Striker?" Her breath brushed warmth against his neck.

He cleared his throat and forced himself back to the present. "Good." He felt relieved to at least have that part of his plan going his way. "Dose him heavy. I need him to be totally out, understand?"

She nodded, but she was trembling again. "What'll he do if he finds her?"

Striker sighed. He reached to cup her cheek, wanting to reassure her. "We can't let that happen because we don't want to find out."

"B-bad man!" Edi's call came from out near the fire.

The distress in his voice spiked Striker's pulse.

He surged around the wagon to see that the colonel had his back pressed to the wood, and Edi gripped in his hands. His pistol pressed firmly to Edi's head.

Lord, have mercy.

What have I done?

Del and Silas peered from beneath the bush. She felt a metallic prickle of fear coat her tongue the moment she caught sight of Boone. She laced her fingers together and pressed them to her lips, peering at her worst nightmare from between the branches.

Silas seemed to sense her terror and touched his small shoulder to hers. "Is he a bad man?" he whispered.

She nodded, unable to take her eyes from Boone seated on the crate.

Silas threw one arm along her back, gave her a quick squeeze, and then withdrew. "I'm sorry."

Del fumbled for Silas's hand and gave it a return squeeze. After that, they sat in silence side by side, and Del found comfort in the kindness and innocence of the boy.

Boone coughed and slumped forward to prop his elbows on his knees as Striker and Tamsyn walked toward the wagon. Boone did look pale. Shrunken even. Like he'd not been eating properly.

Striker and Tamsyn disappeared behind Tamsyn's wagon, but Del continued to study the man who had made her life so miserable these past few years. Her back, arms, and wrists ached something fierce just at seeing him sitting there.

He wasn't wearing blue, had no silver eagles on his shoulders, no forage cap. She wasn't sure if she'd ever seen him wear anything other than his uniform. He looked less commanding. More destitute. Older. Weaker.

And then he moved.

Deliverance gasped and covered her mouth.

As soon as Tamsyn and Striker stepped to the other side of her wagon, the colonel shot to his feet, surged to Edi's side, snatched him up by one arm, and dragged him toward the wagon!

In the space of one breath, Boone had his back pressed to the wagon and his gun pressed to Edi's head.

"Bad man!" Edi called.

Del's eyes fell closed, and she hung her head. Yes. Bad man, indeed. Her heart thumped so hard that it seemed to want to escape her chest. Her breaths beat against her teeth. A loud ringing hummed in her ears.

Beside her, Silas stiffened.

She grabbed hold of his arm to keep him from surging out of the brush to try to go to Edi's aid.

It wasn't his place.

It was hers. She couldn't just sit here and let Boone take his wrath out on these innocent folk! But her terror seemed to have grown roots that strapped her to the ground.

She couldn't move!

Lord, what do I do?

There is no fear in love. The words had been hammering into her for days now. Love always protected. Always trusted. Always hoped. Always persevered.

Her whole body trembled. She knew the right thing to do.

"Stay here," she said as she leaned forward.

Silas's hand shot out to grip hers. "We should both stay here."

Relieved to see Striker rushing from the other side of the wagon, Del froze.

She would give it one moment.

Then she would decide.

Please, Lord, don't make me go out there.

"Edi!" Tamsyn felt terror for Edi's safety, and all she could think was that she had to get to him. She surged forward, but Striker's strong forearm barricaded her advance.

"Easy." His voice was quiet. Calm. Too quiet and calm.

"We have to help him!" Her heart tamped erratically against her breastbone.

"Easy." Was all Striker said again in that irritatingly unfazed voice.

He pressed her into a retreat, and Tamsyn wanted to cling to the protective strength of that arm and never let go. Instead, she withdrew a step, allowing him to take the lead.

She clutched the material at her collar and tried to breathe normally. "It's okay, Edi. Just stand still."

"Colonel?" Striker drawled. "Care to explain what you hope to accomplish here?"

The man swayed slightly and blinked hard. Sweat beaded his brow. But his pistol didn't waver. "I came for my slave, and I'm not leaving until one of you brings her to me!"

Why had she left Edi with that man? They'd known what a danger he was just by the evidence on Deliverance's body! But he'd seemed so tired and ... broken a moment ago. Who could have thought he'd had this in mind?

She could have. She *should* have. It was her job to protect Edi. But Striker had discombobulated her with his unexpected pretense, and with him invading her space and leaning in like he planned to kiss her, she'd barely been able to breathe, much less think clearly.

This was all her fault. Just like it had been with Samuel! Yet another reason why she could never let that man get too close to her again!

What Striker had planned might cost Edi his life!

In the distance, across the encampment, Tamsyn saw Jeremiah heading this way. But Jer saw what was happening at their camp and froze in his tracks.

"I saw that boy of yours heading this way. Get him over here." The colonel spoke without wavering or even glancing in Jeremiah's direction.

Tamsyn's eyes slid closed. He must have waited to make his move until he'd seen Jeremiah approaching. *Lord, protect him. Protect Edi. Protect us all.*

"And you make sure to tell him to drop his weapon. You do the same." The colonel jutted his chin at Striker's pistol in the holster on his hip.

Striker gave Jeremiah a nod and reached slowly to unlatch the buckle on his holster. "What can you think to gain by this? Look around you. You're surrounded by armed men."

The colonel flicked a glance toward Jeremiah. "You drop that weapon, boy, and then you go fetch my slave. I got nothing to lose. I just need to see Delilah one more time."

Several people from the wagon train had noticed the commotion going on at her camp now and had started to gather around.

Tamsyn pressed her palms together, fearing what Edi's reaction might be. He'd never been good in large crowds. He was already rocking forward and back with his hands clasped tightly before him.

"Bad man," he kept repeating.

The colonel must have noticed the gathering crowd, too, because in one swift move, he thrust his gun into the air, gave a warning shot, and then had the gun back to Edi's head again before anyone could blink. "Back off! Everyone, just back off. Get me Delilah, and no one has to get hurt. You shoot me, and you know I'm going to get one shot off before I expire. This innocent boy here deserves your protection, not your harm!"

Tamsyn wanted to rail at the colonel's contradictory actions and words. He was a fine one to talk!

What was the right thing to do here? The man had her brother at gunpoint. What if she just mentioned that Deliverance was here? Would he back off and let Edi go? They didn't actually have to go get her. They could just mention her, and maybe that would relax him a little?

Immediate shame flooded through her. And yet, Edi's life was at stake.

Could she still pull off Striker's plan? She took a step forward. "Please, may I just get you a cup of coffee?"

The colonel scoffed. "You two think your little charade there had me fooled? I know what's in store for me if I drink even one drop of a healer's coffee!"

She frowned. How had he known she was adept at healing?

The man smirked at her. "I wasn't born yesterday. You got clusters of herbs drying all over your wagon, and weren't you the one who stitched up the parson after my brother kidnapped his wife? Were helping with the delivery of a child, too, on the morning we searched the wagon train."

"Fine, you outsmarted us there. But what about if I come over there and you trade me for my brother?"

Striker's boots ground into the dirt. "Tamsyn, no."

She took a step forward. Then another, skirting around Striker's arm when he shot it out to block her way again.

"Tam." There was despair in Striker's tone that she couldn't think about right now.

She kept moving forward. "Please. Just let my brother go and take me instead."

The colonel's hand shook. "I don't want you. I want Delilah."

Tamsyn shook her head. "We don't know anyone named Delilah. We already tried to tell you." Her voice trembled, and she could only hope that he would attribute it to the high tension of this situation.

The colonel's hesitation gave her hope.

"I know what girl you are looking for." The voice spoke out of the crowd.

Tamsyn drew in a sharp, silent breath and turned to see who had spoken.

Chapter 23

Jeremiah's eyes slipped closed for a brief moment as Royal Carter shouldered his way to the front of the crowd. This was a mess. And all of them helpless with the colonel holding Edi and Tamsyn putting herself right in the danger too. His heart hammered.

If Tamsyn had remained where she had been, Striker might have had an angle on the man with the extra pistol he carried holstered at the small of his back, but now she stood between him and the colonel.

He himself stood off to one side, but he'd put down his only weapon as instructed a few minutes ago. It would take him a second to dive for it, roll to his knees, and fire. And he'd never practiced such a move. Would he be able to get the shot off before the colonel shot Edi? Even if he was able to, the colonel might pull the trigger before expiring, just out of spite.

And now Royal was set to reveal Del's presence.

Jeremiah glowered at the man. If he dove for his gun, it might not be the colonel he was aiming at when he regained his feet!

"Royal, hush!" Whitley Hawthorne snapped. She glowered at Royal as she tucked a strand of her red-blonde hair behind one ear.

"I, too, think ye should put a cork in it." Declan moved to stand beside Whitley, folding his arms as he glowered at Royal.

But Royal didn't seem to pay them any mind. He smiled at the colonel. "You and I are men of reason, Colonel." He gestured at Edi and Tamsyn. "These are not the people you want, but I know where the girl you want is hiding. Right back there along the river. I can take you to her."

Jeremiah felt his jaw turn rock hard. He might have known they'd have at least one traitor in their midst. But allowing the colonel to go find Del would happen only over his dead body. He reassessed the distance between him and his Colt on the ground.

From across the way, Jer saw the man named Cato hang his head and give it a little shake. He'd told those men these were good folk. Now, Royal was putting his words in a false light.

Gideon Riley, standing just behind Royal and to one side, flinched, and his gun appeared in his hand. Before Jeremiah could hardly fathom what was happening, Gideon had knocked Royal's hat to the ground and thumped the point of this pistol into the back of the young man's head. "You'll not move or say another word if you know what's good for you, Royal Carter."

Across the way, Cato lifted his head. His brows nudged up.

Royal's hands rose to shoulder height, and he pressed his lips into a tight grim line. After a moment, he opened his mouth, but Gid rapped the point of the pistol more firmly against his scalp, and the younger man's mouth snapped right back shut again.

"That's what I thought," Gid said.

In a flash of movement, the colonel shoved Edi to one side and snatched Tamsyn into his grip. He wrapped one thick arm across the front of her shoulders and pressed his gun to her temple. "Someone better get me Delilah, and they better do it right now."

Striker moved to help Edi rise from the ground. But Jer wasn't fooled by the gesture. Strike was looking for a better angle on the colonel.

A rustling sound came from behind Jer.

"Ain't no need for anyone to fetch me. I'm right here." Del's voice trembled when she spoke.

Jeremiah spun to face her. How had she—

She shook her head at him and kept walking.

"Del, no." He sidestepped and snatched her hand as she tried to move past. He tugged her, keeping his voice low. "Get behind me. Please, Del. You got to think of that baby now. Just get behind me."

Relief filled him when she did step behind him, and he felt her forehead come to rest against his back and her trembling hands grip his sides. "Lord, please. We need Your protection now . . ."

She continued her whispered prayers as Jeremiah lifted his chin and met the colonel's gaze above Tamsyn's shoulder. "You want *Deliverance*?" He emphasized each syllable of her name, sickened by the colonel's continued use of *Delilah*. "Colonel, you're gonna have to go through me first." He swallowed.

The man would easily be able to do that. After all, Jer was weaponless, and the colonel had an almost fully loaded six-shooter.

"And me." Striker stepped purposefully between the colonel and Jeremiah.

"And me." Micah Morran moved to stand by Striker's side.

Gideon Riley gave Royal Carter a shove and another thump with his pistol. "Royal and I would also like to add our voices to the mix."

"Wait a minute now!" Royal tried to meld back into the crowd, but Gideon kept him where he was with the cocking of his pistol. Royal flinched and froze.

And then the whole crowd surged forward! All of them chorusing various challenges as they moved to stand between Jeremiah and Deliverance and Colonel Boone Baxter.

Deliverance could hardly believe what she was seeing as she peered out from behind Jeremiah's shoulder to see the whole encampment standing in her defense. She had shored up her love for these people and come out to do the right thing, and look what they had done for her!

Her legs lost their strength, and she sank to the ground, covering her face in gratefulness. "Thank You, Jesus. Oh, thank You."

Jeremiah sank down beside her. "I've got you, now. I've got you." His strong arms came around her shoulders.

She leaned against him with such deep gratitude filling her. If he hadn't been brave enough to be the first one to take a stand, what might have happened?

Chaytan smiled as he watched the commotion from his prone position on the hill. It seemed that the colonel had met his match with this group.

Chaytan liked to see them standing together in defense of a woman who would not find herself in a good position if the sick man got hold of her.

Of course, Grandmother was hardly ever mistaken. The colonel didn't have much longer to live. So if he did get the girl, she wouldn't have to suffer long.

But it looked like this group knew how to handle a bully. He liked that.

And it was time that he ride for home, anyhow. He rolled, intending to head for his horse. But as he did, a vision in a mended red dress caught his eye.

His breath stilled. Was it truly her?

Yes! There was the husband who had fought for her, standing by her side.

Chayton rolled back to his stomach.

This battle had just grown very interesting!

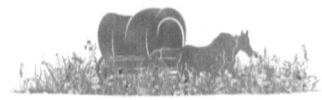

A thought suddenly shot through Del. "Tamsyn!"

Just like Jeremiah had stood for her, she now must stand for Tamsyn! She surged to her feet. Jeremiah rose with her, and she cowered behind him and worked to draw a breath of courage. Tried to see around him and through the crowd to where Boone held Tamsyn.

Maybe one of the men could help get her free? Because every muscle quaked with weakness at the thought of walking out there to face that man.

But then another thought slammed into Del's soul. She was suddenly washed through with sadness for the colonel. Suddenly able to see that he was half a breath from an eternity separated from God. An eternity of agony that no soul loved by God should ever have to face, and yet God loved the man enough to give him the choice.

There is no fear in love.

Lord, please don't ask this of me.

But she knew He already had.

She trembled with the battle. Clenched her fists. Thrust out one arm to raise the cuff of her sleeve enough to see the marks that she would always live with. A picture formed of her soul rent by scars of disobedience, fear, retribution, hatred.

She unclenched her fists. Opened her palms. Turned them toward the heavens, and took her first breath of freedom.

"Boone!" She raised her voice above the raucous crowd, and everyone fell silent.

In front of her, Jeremiah jolted around to face her. He was already shaking his head, but she couldn't let him stop her now. Not when the Lord had asked her to speak. She brushed him to one side.

She couldn't see Boone for so many standing between them, but she could still talk to him. "You put down your gun and let Tamsyn go, and I'll come talk to you."

Jeremiah stiffened. "Del, don't be fooled."

"You got to give up your gun and let Mr. Moss search you over, but then I'll talk to you. Whatever you got to say, I'll hear you out."

The colonel chuckled. "You think you have any authority here? You got none. I'm. The. One. In. Charge!" Each word grew louder and more enraged as he spewed his hatred for his powerlessness.

"No." Del shook her head, unsure where the courage she felt now had been hiding all these years. "You ain't never been in power. You been a slave to your own hatred ever since I've known you, Boone."

"A slave!?" He chuckled and then fell into a hacking cough. "You get over here and I'll remind you just who the slave is, girl."

Jeremiah's hands bunched into fists. His muscles rippled and tendons popped out near his wrists.

Del reached for the nearest one and soothed her fingers over it. The crowd of these wonderful people still stood between her and Boone. "You let Tamsyn go, give up your guns, and that knife you carry in your boot. Then I'll talk to you."

Boone laughed, but it turned into another fit of hacking that sounded like it might turn him inside out.

Ahead, Del saw Striker surge forward. The sound of running boots met a cry from Boone and a squeak from Tamsyn. Del scrunched her eyes shut. Had she just gotten Tamsyn killed?

Jeremiah's hand jerked from hers!

And then all the men rushed forward as one.

A loud thunk.

Boone bellowed.

Scuffling feet and grunting men.

Then an arm wrapped around Del's shoulders. "They have him, *chérie*. Look. You see?" Chevonne gave her a gentle squeeze. "No more trouble he will make for you."

Del looked through the crowd that had now parted. Several of the men who had stood between Del and Boone now panted by his side. Micah Morran gripped one of Boone's arms while Parson Houston gripped his other. Cody and Striker flanked them, and Jeremiah was just rising from removing the blade in the man's boot. Del searched for Tamsyn and was relieved to see her standing safely with her arms wrapped around her brother. She gave Del a nod and mouthed her thanks.

Del returned the nod, pressed a hand to the base of her throat in relief, and then focused on Boone once more—and almost lost the strength in her legs.

Chevonne held her up. "I will walk with you, *chérie*. This you must do, yes?"

Del nodded and clasped her trembling hands into a tight clench before her. *Lord, You asking me to do this, then You got to give me the words!*

She took the first step.

The crowd stepped back further to allow her through.

Boone, standing between Micah and the parson, looked like he hardly had the strength to remain on his feet. But the scrape of his gaze was just as condescending as ever. The curl of his lip, just as demeaning.

Cody stomped up with a crate and thumped it down by Boone's side. "Sit."

The two men on either side of Boone pushed him onto the crate, and Cody lashed Boone's wrists together in his lap with a leather cord. Next, he stripped the man's boots from his feet. Then the three men stepped away, leaving Boone to rest against the side of Tamsyn's wagon.

Defeated, bound, and weak with death, the man still sneered at her.

Del shot her chin into the air. "Everyone, please, give us a minute."

With a murmured release of tension, those gathered dispersed— all except Jeremiah, Cody, and Chevonne. Del didn't mind that they stayed, however. She was thankful that Chevonne wanted to lend her strength, and she felt certain that Cody lingered because he didn't want Chevonne getting anywhere near Boone.

And Jeremiah, sweet Jeremiah, still standing with fists clenched tight and trembling with a suppressed rage, ready to come to her rescue if Boone tried anything.

Boone scoffed at her. "I see that seed I planted is still growing well."

Chevonne's arm tightened around Del. "*Tu es un diable!*"

Cody shifted a glance toward Del's stomach and blinked a couple of times.

Well, it wouldn't be long before her news traveled through the camp now. Del curled one hand around her stomach. "What was it you wanted to say, Boone?"

He tilted his head against the wagon and peered at her through those slitted blue eyes. "You were the one who asked to speak to me, if I recall."

Yes. She had. She swallowed. "The Lord wants you to know you can be free."

He laughed. Coughed. Seared her with a glance. Blood trickled from the corner of his mouth. "Look…at you." He seemed to be fighting for the breath to say what he wanted. "A little mouthy…now… that you are…free and I'm…" He lifted his bound wrists with a shrug of one shoulder.

Del shook her head, taking courage from the strength of Chevonne's arm around her. She drew a step closer to him, wanting him to see the sincerity in her eyes.

"Del, please." Jeremiah's voice trembled. "That's far enough."

She stilled, recognizing the wisdom in his warning. Despite wanting to reach Boone, she must be wise. "Not trying to be mouthy. Just felt a burden to tell you that God loves you and He died to set you free from your sins. Sins like this." She curled her hands around her belly.

He leered. "Got to admit, Delilah girl, that those kinds of sins are the best ones." His leer turned into a sneer. "Surprised you haven't done away with it by now."

Tears pained her eyes. "I'd be lying if I said I didn't pray for that very thing. But the Lord has been showing me some things. One is that good, so much good, Boone, can come from evil if we'll but let God's light of transformation shine on it. You see, I was thinking this child would only ever be a horrible reminder of what you done to me—but God, well, He has a plan for this baby, though I don't know what that is, yet. I am going to enjoy every moment of watching that plan unfold. Because I love this baby, despite my best attempts not to. And there is no fear in love."

This time, there was no laugh, only a glower. He shifted his sock feet closer to the crate. "Heard enough church . . . Don't need any more from you."

Del sighed. "Okay. If that's your choice."

He grunted and leaned forward.

Both Jeremiah and Cody surged a step forward, ready to come to her aid if he tried something.

Boone only scoffed and pegged her with a look. "Why would you of . . . all people—" He paused to cough—so hard that he bent double over his knees. When he weakly raised himself up and leaned against the wagon, fresh blood touched the corner of his mouth. "Why would you try to get me into heaven?"

Del smiled sadly. "Because despite my chains, I always been free. In here"—she tapped her chest—"where it really matters. And despite your ability to walk wherever you wanted and command men to do your bidding, you always been a slave. A slave to your own wants and desires and to getting your own way. God wants better for you than that. And because I love Jesus, He's given me the strength to want better for you, too."

Beside Del, Chevonne shifted.

Cody hung his head and seemed interested in the blades of grass he swept with his feet.

"Well . . ." Boone drew a deep breath.

Del held hers. She might not trust this man. Might not dare get any closer to him. But she suddenly longed for him to find the freedom she'd had all along.

He hung his head.

She tucked her lower lip between her teeth as she studied him. Was he praying?

With a sudden lunge, he dove toward her!

"*Non!*" Chevonne gave Del a shove toward Jeremiah as she stepped in to take the brunt of Boone's charge!

"Chevonne!" Cody barked.

By the time Del crashed into Jeremiah's chest and spun to see what had happened, Boone had his bound wrists looped over Chevonne and had one of his hands twisted around her throat.

"I'm walking out of here," he growled.

Jeremiah's hands curved firmly over Del's shoulders.

"Not with her, you aren't." Cody's bow had appeared in his hands with an arrow nocked and pointed in Boone's direction. But as Del assessed the angle, she realized it was no good because Chevonne shielded Boone.

"Just watch me," the colonel growled. He cursed Del from behind Chevonne. "You're nothing but a filthy slave, and that's all you'll ever be."

Chevonne stood wide-eyed, chin raised, and chest heaving as she fought to breathe past Boone's clamped hand.

Del clenched her teeth, one hand to her chest. What had she done?! She reached out one hand. "Don't hurt her. Take me, instead. Please, I'll come. Just don't hurt her!"

Jeremiah's grip tightened.

Boone smiled. "See, I knew I could elicit your ... cooperation." He kept his grip on Chevonne's neck. "Soon as you get over here, and those men put down their weapons, I'll let her breathe."

Cody lowered his bow and then tossed it to the ground in disgust.

Del felt Jeremiah's firm grip tremble on her shoulders.

"You got to let me go, Jer. Got to let me be free."

With a shuddering breath, he flexed his fingers open, but his palms still rested against her. "God's asking too much of me, Del." The words were practically a groan.

She nodded. Reached to stroke her fingers through his one last time. "Like Jesus, we got to empty ourselves. Then we find fulfillment and wholeness."

With that, she took the first step. And then another. In only seven steps, she stood trembling at Boone's side. She touched his hand where it clawed around Chevonne's throat. "I'm here. Let her go. I'm right here."

She could feel him shaking with the effort to keep his grip on Chevonne. His skin was wrinkled and dry around eyes that had seemed much younger the last time she'd seen him.

She trembled with the terror quaking through her. *Jesus, I need Your strength now.*

Boone loosed his grip on Chevonne's throat.

Chevonne plunged her head backward. *Crack!*

Boone grunted loudly. His head shot back. His hands instinctively rose.

Chevonne ducked from between his lax arms and shoved him toward the crate. His ankles caught on the lip of it, and he lost his balance, crashing back against the wagon.

Chevonne grabbed Del's arm and dragged her forward. "Run!"

In her peripheral vision, Del saw Cody dive once more for his bow and Jeremiah bend toward his gun. They seemed to be moving so slowly! Even as she ran at Chevonne's heels with her eyes forward, all her attention was attuned to the man behind her. At any moment, he was going to have his hands around her neck, and this time, he wouldn't let up his grip for any reason. She knew him, and he wouldn't be content to go to his grave until he'd sent her there ahead of him.

"Get back here, you—"

Whump! Whump! Whump! The sounds came from the wagon behind her. One right after the other.

Boone cried out.

Del spun to see what had happened.

Three arrows protruded from his chest!

He crashed downward, first onto the crate, which splintered beneath him, and then forward, where he landed in an unmoving heap.

Frozen, Del stared down at him.

"Get down!" Cody yelled.

Del dove for cover beside Chevonne, who was already cowering behind a grass-covered mound. Del felt pebbles grind into her knees a moment before Jeremiah's weight crushed her to the grass as he shielded her and Chevonne with his body.

They all lay there frozen for a moment. And then in the distance, Del heard a series of sharp, high-pitched yips. Her blood washed cold.

On top of everything, were they also under an Indian attack?

She lifted her head to peer through the grass. An Indian man, all skin and leather, thrust a bow above his head in a triumphant victory.

Beside her, Chevonne also lifted her head. "*Incroyable!*" she murmured, pushing herself up further for a better look.

Del tried to snatch her back behind their slim cover, but Chevonne brushed her off.

Del sat up too, glancing from her friend to the Indian and back again. "You know this Indian?"

Cody stopped by them with his bow once again firmly in his grip. He hauled Chevonne to her feet. "He was about to be her husband."

Jeremiah scrambled to his feet and reached a hand down for Del.

"I would have made his life most miserable!" Chevonne lifted her chin and dusted her hands.

Cody laughed. "I have no doubt about that."

Chevonne froze. "Wait. Why is he here? Does he want me back?" Her eyes widened a little as she stepped closer to Cody's side.

A glint of amusement lit Cody's brown eyes. "He'll definitely want payment for coming to our rescue. What do you think, Jer? Shall we give her to him?"

Chevonne shoved Cody's shoulder hard. A string of French spilled from her lips.

But Cody didn't seem perturbed by whatever she'd said. Chuckling, he raised a wave to the man in the distance.

The Indian gave him a jaunty gesture, but then pointed to Boone's horse, where it remained ground-hitched with Striker's.

Cody made a clicking sound in his cheek. "It seems that he, too, realizes what trouble you would be, and would rather have the colonel's horse."

"Only because you convinced him that I was your wife!"

Cody glanced over at her with a devilish gleam in his eyes. "That's right. It did take some convincing, didn't it? Maybe we need to prove it to him again?"

Chevonne hit him harder this time. More muttering in French followed. Her arms crossed tight, and her hands fisted into little white-knuckled balls.

Cody shook his head with a laugh. He looked over at Del. "There anything in Boone's saddlebags that you might want?"

Del shook her head. "There's nothing that I want of that man."

The words slammed into her as she curled her hands around the gentle roundness of her belly. Except the one thing she already had.

She turned her gaze on Boone's lifeless body. "Oh Lord, I failed to convince him of his need of You." She breathed the words without realizing she'd spoken them aloud.

Cody and Chevonne moved off, their bickering fading into the distance, but beside her, she heard Jeremiah's feet shift. "Only thing we're responsible for is the obedience. Can't make others' decisions for them. You did all you could. And more than most would have done."

Del turned into Jeremiah's chest and wrapped her arms around him, letting him envelop her in the strength of his arms. "I was so terrified what he might do to you." She hesitated after blurting the words. Would he even still want to marry her after the way she'd rejected him by the river? She clamped her lips closed, not wanting him to think she was presuming anything. But then she realized she had one more thing to say and took a breath. "I know what I said, Jer. I know the Bible does say that all things work together for good to those who love God and are called according to His purpose. I know I'm supposed to believe it. And the Lord has brought me such a long way in my thinking about this baby. And I do look forward to seeing what God will do.

But I worry, Jer. I worry so much about how I'm ever going to love that man's child."

Jeremiah folded her to himself, wrapping her in the warmth of his embrace. "I just watched you do the hardest, bravest, least-selfish thing that I think I've ever seen anyone do. I know you are gonna love that child fiercely with the help of the Lord, because God is the strength of our heart and our portion forever.'"

Del closed her eyes. Listened to the reassuring beat of his heart. And took comfort from his words.

God had given her an unnatural love for Boone here in his last minutes. If He'd done that, He could help her love an innocent child!

She blew out a breath of relief and sagged against Jeremiah.

If God could help her with that, maybe He could help her fix this relationship with Jeremiah that she might have bungled, too?

She certainly hoped so!

That evening, Jeremiah led Del to the fire that the men who were traveling east had built near their tent.

The man named John stood and stretched out a hand. "That was some doings this afternoon."

Jeremiah shook his hand, settling his other to the small of Del's back. He almost hadn't brought her with him, and from the way Cato and Saul shifted and grinned, never taking their eyes off her, he wished that he'd listened to himself. But she was here now, so he swept a gesture to her. "This here is Deliverance. Deliverance, meet John, Cato, Saul, and Jack."

She dipped a curtsy. "Pleased to meet you all."

John swung a gesture to a large boulder they'd rolled near. "Please have a seat on our best chair." He grinned.

Jeremiah sank onto it, not even sorry that it was a small boulder, when Del sat down next to him and ended up pressed to his side.

John squatted near the fire, assessing Del's midsection. "I see that you are expecting a little one. Congratulations!"

Del hung her head in embarrassment.

She opened her mouth, but Jeremiah swept a hand around her waist before she could set them straight. "Thank you. We are."

Presumptuous? Maybe. But he was determined to convince her to have him. Now that Boone was out of the way, he hoped he'd have a little more leverage. Her words from earlier had given him hope. Had she only rejected his proposal out of fear of what Boone would do to him? He wasn't sure, but he planned to have that conversation with her just as soon as he felt she was ready to face it again. He didn't want to rush her.

Del glanced over at him, and he couldn't quite tell if the look on her face was wonder or irritation.

John shifted. "So you two heading to Oregon Territory?"

Jeremiah felt a tightness cinch his chest. "Figure we'll probably end up in California."

"You know about the, ah, exclusion law, then?"

Jeremiah sighed. "We do. We got friends headed that way. Figured after they get settled, we'd move south." He glanced at Deliverance again. Would she want to go with him?

Her head was down as she fiddled with her fingers, and he couldn't read her expression.

"Thing of it is," John continued, "there are some folks living peaceably there. You just got to find yourself some land far enough away from the settlements. You go far enough to the north, and there are lands occupied by our folk. Course you got to worry each time the local lawman changes, whether he's gonna be a friendly man or not." He plucked a piece of grass and irritatedly tossed bits of it into the fire. "That's what happened to us. We worked our land and had it producing good crops for the first year in a long time. Then a new sheriff came along, and it was either move along or take a public lashing every six months."

Del gasped softly. Jeremiah could almost see the weight of the world settling back on her shoulders.

He smoothed his hand up and down her back, wanting to relieve her of this burden. "That's why I'm leaning toward California."

"Or . . ." John let the word hang in the air for a moment as he snatched another blade of grass. "You folk could come with us."

Del's head snapped up.

Jeremiah felt his stomach knot. He was committed to this wagon train all the way to Oregon and couldn't shirk his duty as a scout. Would she leave him and travel back east with these men now that she was free? The thought ground his teeth together.

"We plan," John continued, "to start a community of our own a little east and south of here. Figure I'll call it John's Landing." He grinned. Arched a hand through the air. "All reasonable folk welcome."

Across the fire, Saul chuckled. "Cato's Landing, Saul's Landing, and Jack's Landing have all also been proposed and soundly rejected! But…" He grinned and offered a bold wink in Del's direction. "I think Deliverance's Landing has a nice ring to it!"

Del chuckled and hung her head in embarrassment.

Jeremiah wanted to stomp over there and kick the fellow.

"What do you think, John?" Saul prodded. "Would you let her name the town after herself?"

John grinned and hung his head to fiddle with his blade of grass. "Don't suppose her husband will much appreciate your flirtin', Saul."

"Oh, we aren't married." Deliverance piped up.

Jeremiah felt her words like a sucker punch to his gut. Now it was his turn to hang his head even as he noticed the way all four men across the fire perked up. He guessed she had put him in his place, now hadn't she.

She looked over at him. "But he did ask me."

Wonderful. This just kept getting better and better. Now she was letting them know she'd rejected him!

He glanced at her, unable, he felt sure, to keep the irritation from his expression.

She smiled. "And the answer is yes . . ." She tucked her lower lip between her teeth. "If he still wants me."

Jeremiah surged to his feet, drawing her with him. He turned her to face him and drew her into his arms, not even caring that four strangers were watching. He cupped his hands to her face. "Do you mean it?"

She pressed her lips together. Nodded. "I was scared, Jer. So scared of what he might do to you."

He leaned to rest his forehead against hers. "Ah, Del. You make me the happiest man in all the territories."

She giggled, eased back, and smiled up at him. "Does that mean you forgive me for telling you to stop acting like a lovestruck fool?"

He grinned. "I do, indeed." He slid his hand down her forearm until his fingers slipped between hers. "If you'll forgive us, fellas . . ." He led her away. And he knew just exactly where he was taking her.

"Aw, Jeremiah!" Saul's voice called from behind them. "You can't rob us of the best part! This was near as good as a theater show!"

Jeremiah laughed and waved his hand over his shoulder. "You'll have our answer in the morning, gentlemen." And he knew what it would be.

He led her toward the clearing by the river where he'd found her bathing earlier.

They passed Cody, Chevonne, and the Indian who had shot Boone, exchanging Boone's horse and some conversation, but Jeremiah didn't stop.

They passed Tamsyn and Striker in a bit of a heated conversation, but Jeremiah led Del on.

He skirted around Caesar Cranston, Micah Morran, Parson Houston, and Gideon Riley, who were rather forcefully loading Royal Carter onto his wagon and pointing for him to drive on out of camp.

"But I'll have no guard come nights!" Royal complained.

"Don't worry," Caesar growled. "Not even outlaws enjoy eating snake."

Jeremiah smiled as he heard a sharp slap to a horse's rump and the jangle of harness and squeak of wagon wheels as Royal's wagon lurched into motion.

Only once they were in the concealment of the purple lilacs, did he turn and pull Del once again into his arms. "Tell me you mean it, Del. Say it again."

She chuckled and settled her hands against his sides, but her attention lay fixed on the direction from which they'd come. "They're driving Royal out of the camp?"

"He'll be fine." Jeremiah tamped down his impatience, marveling at her concern for a man who would have turned her over to Boone. This woman was a wonder!

"You sure?" A furrow trenched her brow.

"What I am sure of is that Royal Carter is the last subject I want to be talking about right now."

With a smile, she turned and peeked up at him. "Wasn't sure you'd want anything to do with me after the way I spoke to you."

"Oh, I want something to do with you, all right." His gaze lowered to her mouth, and he couldn't stop himself from stealing a kiss. He meant to only graze her lightly to emphasize his point, but the moment their lips connected, she released a soft moan and rose on her tiptoes to press her mouth fully to his.

Mer.ci.ful. Heavens!

He wrapped her in tight and gave in to the kiss. They could talk later. Much later.

Del felt undone and complete. Broken apart, yet made whole. She trembled as she leaned against Jeremiah, unable to meld herself close enough to satisfy. His hands were in her hair, on her shoulders, against her back. His lips pummeled hers into a most satisfying submission. His breath warmed her lips, her cheek, the line of her jaw, and then her lips once again.

Del could barely breathe when he pulled away and rested his forehead against hers. He wagged his head. "I think it's probably time for us to get back to talking." Even as he said it, he leaned in for one more lingering kiss.

She smiled against Jeremiah's lips and stilled him with the touch of one finger. "I think you're right."

She needed to breathe. Such a thrill swept through her that tears brimmed to blur her vision.

He blinked. Frowned. "What's this?" He swept his thumbs beneath her eyes.

"Happiness." She smiled sheepishly.

His brows arched. "I'm gonna have to work on the way I make you happy, I guess." He winked.

She laughed and settled her ear against the rapid tattoo of his heart. "You make me happy just fine, Jeremiah Jackson." Beyond Jeremiah's shoulder, the sun was setting, and far in the distance, she could see the faint blue outline of some low mountains. "You think the parson will marry us this evening?"

Jeremiah chuckled. His arms tightened about her, but then he set her away from himself with a shake of his head. "No. Not tonight. Not tomorrow night. Nor the next one, either." He cupped one palm against her cheek. "You gonna have this baby first and take time to get good and rested up. And then we'll see if you still want an old rascal like me."

Del felt a flush of concern. She frowned up at him as she retreated a step. "You think you might not want this baby?"

He shook his head and drew her back into his arms. "I want that baby so much that it's a physical ache inside, sweet Deliverance. And we are going to love that child like it's our very own. Not because we are forced to by expectations or morals, but because the Lord is gonna fill us with so much love for that baby that we aren't gonna know what to do with it—just you wait and see if that's not true."

"Then why don't we just marry now? That would be easier, wouldn't it?"

He touched her cheek again. "You need time to heal. Time to come to grips with all that's happened. What you been through? That's not a light thing. The Lord is gonna help you overcome it, though, and we're gonna be just fine. I don't want to rush you into anything you might regret—even if you don't feel like I'm rushing you. We're gonna take these next months to get to know each other. To build a friendship. To learn what it means to love." He grinned and pumped his brows. "To practice kissing."

She laughed and settled her forehead against his chest.

He smoothed his hands over her back. "So that when we do get married, neither one of us have any doubts or hesitations."

She relaxed against him, realizing he was right in all that he'd said. They really had only known each other for a couple of months—and turbulent, stressful months at that.

She could still hardly fathom that she'd never have to worry about Boone again. She needed time to come to grips with that. Time to figure out who she even was now that she didn't have someone lording it over her and demanding everything from her.

"You're a wise man." She nodded, meaning it.

He chuckled. "I'm sure the day will come when I'll need to remind you of those words."

She smiled, studying the pink and gold sunset in the distance. "I'll simply be glad you are there to remind me."

He bent and brushed his lips over her cheek. "So will I, sweet Del. So will I."

Epilogue

Two and a half months later – South Pass, Rocky Mountains

Del wrapped her arms around her middle and tried not to gasp as another contraction gripped her.

It was too soon!

Lord, please, help me. I need this baby to thrive. I won't be able to live with my guilt if something happens! I want this child. I want to love him or her with Jeremiah by my side all my days!

She didn't miss the irony over the fact that she now desperately wanted a child she once would have been happy to lose.

This morning, she'd hoped that she was mistaken about her pains. Maybe the baby was just pressing a foot or elbow into the wrong area?

At noon, she'd transitioned into the wagon and tried to ride without alerting Jeremiah to her pain, but the jostling over the broken ruts of the first climb into the Rocky Mountains had about jarred her teeth out of her head.

When she'd first seen these mountains, my, how her heart had threatened to fail her! Rocky ridges thrusting straight up out of the plains like a great wall determined to hinder their progress. But, oh, the beauty! And then, as they'd climbed into the foothills with each day's travel growing more and more difficult, she'd cried out to God that it was too much, too hard, too horrendous.

Hadn't they already withstood enough?

When Mr. Glover, exhausted after helping his sick wife through the night, had fallen asleep and tumbled from his wagon bench to be crushed beneath the wheels of his wagon, Del had cried, even though she'd hardly known the man. She'd taken her turn with the other women of the train to nurse his wife back to health, but the woman hadn't recovered—maybe due to a broken heart. And it had about killed Del to drive away from the Glovers' lonely abandoned wagon after burying the woman, only days down the trail from her husband.

When Chevonne had been forced to abandon her harp at the last of the three crossings of the Sweetwater because too much rain had made the river treacherously deep and even that much extra weight might have drowned her horses, Del had cried with her while she played her last song on the instrument.

They had all gathered around to listen to the mournful tune. And then, as though in defiance of what the trip was costing her, Chevonne had broken into a lively piece with happy notes that evoked twittering birds in spring trees.

When they'd reached the other side, Del had looked back to see the instrument in its case, perched high on the top of a pile of abandoned crates, barrels, tools, and even the Houstons' wood stove as though Chevonne hadn't been able to bear the thought of the instrument getting wet on the soggy riverbank.

Caesar had called the pile of items "leav'erights." As in, "best leav'eright here so's your team will live."

All this, they had endured.

And now she had gone into labor early.

The wagon wheels jounced in and out of a rut so deep that Del was almost tossed off the pallet. Combined with a contraction, the pain felt like it was tearing her apart from the middle. A moan escaped her clamped teeth.

"Del?!" The wagon stopped. Jeremiah thrust his head through the opening of the front cinch of canvas.

Del was in too much pain to care that he might notice, and that she would be the cause of yet another delay for the wagon train. She knew by now that, Caesar's rule that anyone who caused a delay would be left behind notwithstanding, he didn't mean it. And she also knew that the group wouldn't leave her behind, despite the fact that they were only a couple of months from their destination now.

She curled around her belly and finally allowed a long, slow moan. It felt good, considering she'd been withholding the expressions of pain all day.

Jeremiah's eyes shot wide. "You in labor? You can't be! It's too soon!"

Del shook her head. "Don't think this baby knows that!"

He disappeared, and a sharp whistle pierced the air only seconds later.

The truth was, she wasn't exactly sure of the timing. Because of her lack of proper meals, her cycles had been off and on for months before she realized she'd missed two. Had she missed another without noticing? Maybe. If she was right about the timing, this birth was at least a month early. But if she'd missed an extra cycle, this baby might be right on time.

Lord, please.

She desperately wanted the baby to be fine.

Calls drifted back, and Del imagined other wagons must have stopped. The wagon shifted, and the front bench squawked. Jeremiah jumping to the ground, no doubt.

A few moments of muffled conversation must be Jer passing the word along before the wagon jostled and his head poked through the opening again. "We're on a steep incline here, Del, with mountain on one side and a drop-off on the other. We got to get ahead a little ways to where we can pull off."

"Keep driving," she assured. "I'll be fine." She clamped her lips to keep from adding, "maybe."

She would be fine, right?

It was her first baby. Laboring often took hours. She was feeling no pressure or need to push yet, and heaven knew she'd be happy to be even five minutes closer to the end of this seemingly endless journey.

"Okay, you just keep talking to me." The wagon shifted, and the familiar squeak of the rolling wheels commenced again. "How you doing back there?"

Del almost laughed. What had it been, five seconds? "I'm fine, Jer. I'll tell you if I'm not."

"Come on, get up!" He urged the team, and she heard the reins smack against the oxens' rumps. "Sent word to Tamsyn. She'll get to you soon as she can!"

Del couldn't answer because another contraction squeezed her. She blew a long slow exhale between pursed lips. Oh my, this one was a doozy!

"Caesar said it's just thirty minutes ahead, Del. Just thirty minutes and we'll be to a clearing just across the ridge line."

Del breathed through the pain, huff, huff, huffing like Mama used to teach the ladies on the plantation to do to help them through the pain. Thirty minutes! With pains this strong, would she even make it through the next thirty minutes?

"You holding it together back there? You want I should sing to you? I can sing. Well, not sure I can sing very good right this moment, but I'm willing to give it a try. Did you need water? I should have thought to get you some before we got moving again."

Jer's chatter was suddenly dancing on the last of her patience. Del growled audibly, hoping that might shut him up.

His laugh drifted back through the canvas. "Message received, beautiful Del! We're gonna have ourselves a baby! I'm hushing now. Honest, I am!"

Del smiled and relaxed as, for the moment, her pains eased.

The wagon train did find the clearing that Caesar had mentioned and none too soon. Tamsyn had arrived just in time to catch the baby, and now, as Deliverance sat, tucked carefully into her pallet and leaning against the sidewall of the wagon, she stared in awe at the rounded, pudgy, tawny cheeks of her daughter—tiny but already suckling strongly, which had relieved Del greatly.

Tamsyn approached, drying her hands on a towel. "She's gonna despise all those curls one day, but she's the most beautiful baby I think I've ever seen."

Del smiled and stroked one finger over the softness of the baby's chin. "I think you might be right about that." She grinned. "Even if I do say so myself."

"I got something to show you, and then I think I'd better let in a man who's about to pace a trench deep enough that there won't be enough rope in all the world to haul our wagons out."

Del chuckled and lifted her head. "I can't wait to show him our girl."

Tamsyn smiled. "First, look at this." She swept the canvas at the end of the wagon open to reveal the most glorious sunset that Del had ever seen. Pinks, and golds, and oranges, and swirls of blues from navy to turquoise filled the dome above the purple ridges of the jagged Rocky Mountain range before them. In the distance, a large lake reflected the colors of the sky and the surrounding mountains.

Del drew in a breath of amazement at the beauty before her. "God is so amazingly generous with His gifts to us."

Tamsyn smiled. "I knew you'd like that. I thought it was a wonderful blessing, too. Now, let me fetch Jeremiah for you."

"Tamsyn," Del stopped her with a word.

She turned back.

"Don't be too hard on Striker. He couldn't have known. He was trying to help." For the past several weeks, she'd noticed that the two had hardly spoken to each other and that a tension seemed to hang in the air whenever they were together. She longed to see them find ease with one another if nothing more.

Tamsyn sighed and pegged her with a look. "I think Chevonne might be rubbing off on you."

Del chuckled. "Well, now, maybe she is. Will you think about it?"

Tamsyn nodded. "But only because I'm so happy and relieved to have that little mite in the world and doing so well." She pointed at the baby.

Del glanced down, twirling one of the thick dark curls on the baby's head around her first finger. "You and me, both."

"I'll fetch Jer." Tamsyn made a swift exit, and this time, Del let her go.

Only a few seconds later, Jeremiah crawled over the back tailgate, eyes red with emotion. He came toward her silently, as though afraid to speak and startle the baby. Tears still glistened on his cheeks.

"Aw, Jer." Del reached a hand to him. "I'm fine. We're fine."

He bobbed his head. "I know," he whispered. "I just been having a conversation with the Lord, and telling Him how grateful I am." He sniffed and fell to his knees by the pallet, gaze transfixed on the baby.

Del rubbed his shoulder as she angled their daughter for him to see.

"Oh, my land." Jeremiah covered his mouth with one hand. "Del, I'm gonna need more than one shotgun to keep the boys away from that one! Maybe twelve! One for each corner of every room in the house!"

Del chuckled, her chest surging with a swell of love for this family that the Lord had blessed her with. "I love her so much, Jer. I don't know how I ever worried if I would."

He sniffed. Looked up at her. "Well, we both know you had cause for that battle. Don't go belittling yourself. Besides, I don't want to talk about him. Look at her!" He reached to tuck one broad finger into the palm of the baby's hand. "Look at those long fingers! And already little fingernails, too. Land, the Lord is amazing, isn't He?"

Del smiled, but her gaze wasn't on the baby in her arms. It was on the face of the man the Lord had blessed her with. "He is."

Jeremiah was still taken with the baby, and Del could hardly blame him. "What're we gonna call her?" He worked his thumb over her tiny fingers, dashing more tears from his eyes with his shoulders.

Del smiled. "I know exactly what we are gonna call her, and it's partly because of Chevonne."

Jeremiah stilled and squinted up at her. "What has that girl done now?"

Del chuckled. "Do you know that it's partly because of her that I found a place for you in my heart?"

Jeremiah pretended to be affronted. "Posh. I didn't need that girl's help. I got charm all my own."

Del laughed. "If you say so."

He squeezed his lips into an expression of disbelief, giving his head a little shake of dismay.

Del giggled over his antics and leaned down to press her lips to his. "Fine. You've got charm all your own. But this name"—Del held up a finger as she pressed ahead—"is also because of what the Lord has done for us, and more specifically for me, through these last months."

Jeremiah pressed a tender kiss to the baby's forehead and then lifted his gaze to Del's, elbows planted on the tick. He rested his chin against his clasped hands. "What is it?"

"Amour."

"Amour Deliverance." He said without missing a beat.

She tucked her lower lip between her teeth. "You think?"

He nodded. "It's perfect. Love and deliverance. What better gifts could we thank God for on this broken range than those?"

Del swept a hand over Jeremiah's hair, relishing the fact that she had the freedom—and choice—to do so. "What better gifts, indeed?"

She leaned forward to surrender her lips, and Jeremiah seemed more than happy to oblige.

Dear Reader,

I hope you enjoyed reading this story as much as I enjoyed bringing Jeremiah and Deliverance's romance to life. Every book I write is a journey of discovery, and this one, especially, led me down some unexpected and sobering paths.

As I researched the Oregon Territory, I was shocked and saddened to learn that, in its early days, Black people were not legally permitted to settle there. The exclusion law passed by the Oregon Territorial Legislature on September 21, 1849, stated:

> "Be it enacted by the Legislative Assembly of the Territory of Oregon, That it shall not be lawful for any negro or mulatto to enter into, or reside within the limits of this Territory; provided, that nothing in this Act contained shall affect persons of the negro or mulatto race who may then be actually resident therein."

This replaced an even harsher "lash law" from 1844, where any Black person who refused to leave the territory could be publicly whipped with up to thirty-nine lashes every six months until they departed. And this exclusion law applied to the entire Oregon Territory.

Reading those laws broke my heart. But history is full of people who showed courage in the face of prejudice and injustice. One such man was named George Bush. He settled in the Oregon Territory despite these exclusion laws. His property lay north of the Columbia River in what would later become Washington State. When the Washington Territory formed, it sadly carried over many of the exclusion laws. George Bush was such a kind and helpful man, however, that his white neighbors, who admired and respected him, came to his defense. Several of those neighbors served in the Washington Territorial Legislature, and they voted unanimously to let him keep his property.

Friendship and decency triumphed over prejudice that day! And I like to believe that Jeremiah and Deliverance would have found the same kindness.

As a romance writer, I'm grateful for the freedom fiction gives me—to imagine a better world and to give my characters the love and hope that real people were too often denied. I can't change history, but I can write stories that honor those who lived through it.

Thank you for reading, for caring, and for remembering with me.

With love and gratitude,
Lynnette Bonner

Please Review!

If you enjoyed this story, would you take a few minutes to leave your thoughts in a review on your favorite retailer's website? It would mean so much to me, and helps spread the word about the series.

You can quickly link through from my website here: https://www.pacificlightsbookstore.com/collections/the-oregon-promise-series/

Coming soon...

IN THE
Vale of Dreams

OREGON PROMISE - BOOK 5

You may read an excerpt on the next page...

Excerpt

The noonday sun beat down with a ferocity as Tamsyn Acheson sat in her encampment on the shore of the Snake River and tried not to feel her loneliness.

They'd reached the banks of this last boundary between them and the Oregon Territory and were in line to cross. Several other wagon trains were also encamped along the riverbank here. High winds and ferocious rain had delayed the trains ahead of them, but today the weather had cleared. Two or three days at most, Caesar had said, and they would be on their way.

One more river crossing—well, four, since this particular Three Island Crossing, involved fording sections of the Snake from one island to another and then to the land on the other side. After that, she would be in the Oregon Territory, and they could stop whenever they wanted.

She looked at the fast-flowing water, shooting through the channel just a hefty stone's throw from her fire, and shivered. The fordings were definitely not her favorites. And the recent storms made her even more tense.

Caesar demanded she drive the wagon for the fordings, not Edi. A command she agreed with. But it didn't mean she liked it. Striker had been there on his horse by her for the first couple of crossings. But this time . . .

No. She ground her teeth. His distance was all her own fault, and there would be no repairing the damage she'd done—not even with Deliverance encouraging her at every blade of grass to speak to him. She knew better than to torture herself with hope.

She tried not to worry about where Edi had stomped off to a bit ago. Tried to ignore the sense of foreboding that had hounded her since she'd woken this day. It stemmed from their three days of inactivity after months of grueling travel—surely that was all. A mere chafing at the lack of headway, this disquiet.

And yet yesterday she'd heard rumors of folk from the other wagon trains falling sick.

She rubbed at the tension between her brows and wished she could stop dwelling on that news. It had been a passing comment from one of the women from a neighboring train as they'd collected water from the river. The woman had heard that members of the party ahead of theirs had begun to fall ill.

It was Tamsyn's worst fear. A sweeping illness that she wouldn't know how to tend.

She hadn't meant to become the camp healer. In fact, it was the absolute last thing she'd wanted. She already had Sam's death on her conscience. And Evelyn Hawthorne's baby—and maybe Evelyn herself—would have died if it hadn't been for Deliverance's help. She didn't need any more anxiety. But when people asked for help, what kind of person would she be to say no?

Still, the news yesterday had struck terror to her very core. And now Edi had stalked off.

He was probably playing ball with the Morran and Hawthorne boys. She hoped.

She'd been in the middle of making lunch and hadn't been able to leave the half-cooked fish over the fire for fear it would burn if she took too long to find him or would gather flies if she took it off.

She'd decided to let her brother go, knowing that if he wandered too far, others in the camp would also watch out for him. Sometimes giving an irritated Edi his space was the best solution.

But that didn't stop her worrying.

They simply needed to make it to Oregon and get settled. That was all. The drudgery of the trail was wearing everyone down. Weariness was what had Edi—and her—feeling their emotions so starkly.

Certainly, for her, it was weariness—bone deep and strength-sapping. And it was compounded by the guilt that convicted her each time she thought of Striker Moss.

Against her will, her focus settled across the encampment on the man who sat with his friends. She immediately forced her gaze back to the fish roasting over her own fire and gave the spit handle a sharp crank.

Along with the guilt, loneliness and sorrow filled her each time she thought of him. She despaired of these weary emotions tangled into frazzled knots. And yet...

She shifted irritably.

The round of wood beneath her was hard but not too cold, and it was smooth and steady—in all honesty, the best seat she'd had for months now. The flames before her crackled warmly, taking the chill off the evening air. The sky arched above her, clear, deep blue, and resonant with the melody of twilight birdsong.

It was a good day. However, she felt such isolation and exhaustion. Both were her fault.

The one for keeping everyone at arm's length. And the other for, well, keeping everyone at arm's length. Caring for Edi all on her own ought not be so taxing. She'd done it all her life.

She massaged the fingers of one hand into the tight muscles of the opposite shoulder.

Perhaps she would apply for Edi's claim right over there across the river. She and Edi could settle in and maybe...

She angled on her stump to peer at the land past the water. Twisted her lips. Here, the plain was flat for several miles, but on the other side of the river, the ground quickly mounded into large steeps with nothing but sagebrush for greenery.

With how dry it was, it would likely take a lot of hard work to grow even a small garden over there.

Perhaps she'd travel a little farther.

Hopefully, the terrain wherever she settled would be greener and more fertile.

Had all the books and pamphlets she'd read about the verdant land in the Oregon valleys been nothing but deception to get people to risk the trip? Once here, they would likely not want to repeat the trip in reverse, after all.

Across the encampment, laughter rose from the cookfire the scouts shared.

A glance revealed Jeremiah Jackson standing by the fire with his baby daughter. Cody Hawkeye leaned over to present the baby with a miniature bow and arrow set, and Jeremiah laughingly took exception to the gift.

Even Striker smiled.

Once more, Tamsyn tore her gaze back to her own space and the orange flickering flames. Her heart panged, and her doldrums rushed in with full force. She turned the fish again, then laced her fingers tight.

She'd said such harsh words to him all those months ago. She'd been so angry. *Been?* She shifted. Yes. Maybe *been*. Though some of the frustration still lingered. Looking back now, she realized she had mostly been filled with terror—and memories of Sam.

Her terror had spilled into barbed anger directed at Striker. He'd brought the colonel who'd been hunting for Deliverance right into her and Edi's encampment, risking her brother's life.

Yet, more than terrified and angry with Striker, she'd been furious with herself for leaving Edi in the company of the colonel, a man she knew to be dangerous, no matter that the colonel had looked like he could barely remain on his feet.

Even now, nausea churned in her stomach as she remembered the helpless feeling that had washed over her. She'd come all this way for

Edi, only for Edi. To give him a better life—one not lived under the scrutiny of folk who thought of him as inferior because of his simple mind. And there he'd been, innocent and terrified, with the colonel's gun pointed at his head.

She shut her eyes.

All. Her. Fault.

And Striker's.

He'd been the one to bring that dangerous man to her fire, after all.

However, nothing but regret filled her as she recalled the sharp words she'd railed. The demands she'd made . . .

"Tamsyn? You all right?" Striker's words had been soft, filled with sincere regret as he approached her after the incident.

She had backed away from him, unable to pull her gaze from the colonel, who lay slumped against the side of her wagon with three arrows protruding from his chest. A true healer would have gone to the man to see if she could help, but she hadn't been able to move her feet.

Echoes of the victory shouts from the Sioux warrior who had shot him and saved them all still reverberated through the air.

The cold, stomach-churning feel of the colonel's gun to her temple and the press of his forearm across her throat lingered. She'd gone to her brother's rescue, of course, she had! How could she have done anything else? And yet, she'd nearly paid out her love for her brother with her life.

Striker shifted to block her view of the dead body. "Please, Tam, sit. I need to look at your neck."

Her hand trembled as she lifted it to the sting she only noticed after his words. Her neck was damp. Sticky. Was it sweat?

She held her hand out and found blood glistening on her fingertips.

She blinked slowly, too stunned to do anything but follow Striker's lead.

He pressed a hand to her back and directed her to her tailgate, then wrapped his hands around her waist and lifted her to sit on it. Warmth radiated from him when he stepped onto a crate so he might be close enough to examine her neck, but she couldn't stop shivering. His hip pressed against the outside of her knee as he tilted her head to get a better look at the cut.

How had she gotten cut? From the colonel's fingernails, maybe?

This trembling threatened to vibrate her right off her seat. She shifted. Willed herself to feel and know and see that she was unharmed. Edi was fine. Striker was fine. All was fine.

Striker's fingers were gentle as they swept strands of her hair to one side. She felt the tug when a few strands stuck in the blood, but he worked carefully to remove them without causing her more pain. His breath wafted, warm and full of life, against her cheek and neck.

He moved away for a moment, and she simply remained where he left her, too shaken to do aught else.

He returned with a rag and a bowl of water. He dipped the rag in the water and used it to dab away the blood. His tender ministrations cooled her hot skin and soothed her ragged breathing.

She felt a tremor work through him, and that was when she realized she had wrapped her hands around his ribs as he leaned close. She loosed him. Fisted her hands into her lap.

He eased back and peered into her eyes. "It's only a scratch, thank God. I'm so sorry. I never should have brought him to your fire. I simply thought—"

"Did you? Think?" Every muscle once again quaked.

The words weren't fair. She knew it the moment they left her lips. He'd hoped for her to dose the colonel's coffee with Edi's sleeping powders, save Deliverance, and avoid a confrontation altogether.

He blinked and stepped off the crate. Worked the damp rag between his hands. With one hip slacked, he hung his head.

She hopped down to join him. "I don't think you did."

Why couldn't she stop talking?

A muscle bunched in his stubbled jaw. He dropped the rag into the bowl of water he'd set by her. Nodded. "I deserve your anger."

"Yes. You do. Walk away, Mr. Moss. Walk away and don't come back. Leave my brother alone. Leave me alone. We don't need the likes of you in our lives!"

Now, as she sat by her fire, Tamsyn dropped her eyes closed, remorseful over her sharp words as she remembered the agony in his gaze. The way he'd tucked one side of his lower lip between his teeth and gripped the back of his neck. The way he'd nodded, turned, and trudged away.

Tamsyn's hands clenched so tight she felt the tension all the way to her shoulders. He didn't know she'd once put her own happiness above Edi and that she'd promised herself she would never do so again. He couldn't know she'd almost cost her brother his life. He couldn't know she already carried the heavy burden of having lost one life due to her foolish actions, and almost having lost Evelyn and Blythe, too. She hadn't been able to explain any of it.

He'd done as she asked. He'd quit seeking Edi out each noon for a chat, which had been his pattern up to that point.

Edi hadn't understood.

After two weeks, Edi had shored up his courage, and Tamsyn had watched from a distance when the wagons had stopped for a brief nooning as her brother swung off his wagon seat and hesitantly approached Striker. He had smiled and pulled Edi into a manly, back-slapping hug. They'd shared a conversation with a lot of head shaking and frowns from Striker.

From her position several wagons back, Tamsyn hadn't been able to read her brother's expression.

At the end of the conversation, Striker had jutted his chin back toward the wagon Edi shared with her, turned, and walked away, leaving Edi with his head hanging.

When her brother had returned, he'd been in a sour mood. Nothing Tamsyn offered had improved his outlook—not even the offer to make his favorite cherry pie when they camped later that evening.

That last jar of cherry preserves still languished in a crate packed with straw because each evening for the past month, Edi had wordlessly slumped to the fire, barely nibbled at the food she'd prepared, and then fallen into his bedroll with hardly a word.

Just before lunch, his sour mood had spilled over into action. "I don't want to talk to you!" he'd snapped before stomping away from her.

She'd called to him. Asked him to come back. But he'd ignored her.

Something must be done. Edi's mood had grown increasingly more foul with Striker's absence. The man simply had a way with her brother. The fact was, she needed his help.

Besides, she'd been putting off her apology and explanation for far too long already.

She glanced across the camp to where Striker sat whittling what looked like a new hatchet handle.

She'd missed him, truly she had. Missed his humor and his gentle teasing. Missed his persistent pursuit. Missed the dream of wondering what life might be like if she let him past her barriers. But always reality had rushed in. The distance between them might have made her heart ache—certainly Edi's—but that didn't mean it wasn't better for Striker.

Now that the idea was born, however, it consumed her. She could fix this. Fix it for Edi, if not for herself. One simple apology for words misspoken in a moment of stress would soothe all of this. One explanation for why she'd instinctively responded that way even though she thoroughly regretted it.

It was time for Striker to learn about Sam Saunders.

Tamsyn sighed.

All the others had dispersed, leaving Striker alone by his fire. She wouldn't find a better moment than now to speak to him. She pressed her hands to her knees and rose.

Lord, give me the words to fix this heap of anguish I've brought on us all.

ABOUT THE AUTHOR

Born and raised in Malawi, Africa. Lynnette Bonner spent the first years of her life reveling in warm equatorial sunshine and the late evening duets of cicadas and hyenas. The year she turned eight she was off to Rift Valley Academy, a boarding school in Kenya where she spent many joy-filled years, and graduated in 1990.

That fall, she traded to a new duet—one of traffic and rain—when she moved to Kirkland, Washington to attend Northwest University. It was there that she met her husband and a few years later they moved to the small town of Pierce, Idaho.

During the time they lived in Idaho, while studying the history of their little town, Lynnette was inspired to begin the Shepherd's Heart Series with Rocky Mountain Oasis.

Marty and Lynnette have four children, and currently live in Washington where Marty pastors a church.